THE ORDER OF THE WHITE GUARD
WHITE GUARD
BOOK ONE: LITO'S CHILDREN

by Wendy and Bryan Schardein

a BlackWyrm book
Louisville, Kentucky

THE ORDER OF THE WHITE GUARD
BOOK ONE: LITO'S CHILDREN

A BlackWyrm Book
BlackWyrm Publishing
10307 Chimney Ridge Ct, Louisville, KY 40299

Printed in the United States of America.

ISBN: 978-1-61318-144-7
LCCN: 2013934062

Cover Design by Wendy Schardein

Second edition: March 2013

Thanks to Jessica Bratcher for editing this book and for her help and support throughout the project.

The cover art is a photomanipulation using stock images from Deviant Art. Thanks to the following artists for the use of their stock:

- Werewolf by stiks-1969.deviantart.com
- Vampire by mithgariel-stock.deviantart.com (http://mithgariel-stock.deviantart.com/gallery/?q=nobleman#/d168pl0)
- Sword by fantasystock.deviantart.com (http://fantasystock.deviantart.com/art/King-Arthur-s-Excalibur-Sword-146656069)
- Background by ashensorrow.deviantart.com (http://ashensorrow.deviantart.com/art/Premade-Background-187-140009873)
- Crucifix and Chain by Wendy Schardein (whisper292.deviantart.com)

Prelude

It's better to be good than evil, but one achieves goodness at a terrific cost. — Stephen King

Logan Blevins sat on the stone floor with his arm encased in a manacle. The cuff and attached chain hung from a ring bolted to the wall of a claustrophobic room once used as a dungeon. No prisoners were kept there these days; everyone chained there was carried out shortly thereafter, either mutilated or dead.

He'd been in the room as a child, sneaking into a forbidden place. He had stood in that exact spot, his head no higher than it was now, gaping in horror at the shackles and dark spots on the stone and using a too-vivid imagination to envision the tortures and suffering inflicted there.

Only the manacles and two wall sconces occupied the dungeon. Wooden stairs led to a hatch that opened to the floor above. A torch burned in one of the sconces, and the meager heat it put out did nothing to warm Logan. He was dressed as comfortably as possible in woolen breeches and a heavy tunic that was open at the neck, but the clothes weren't enough to protect him from the winter chill that seeped in through the stone.

Twelve shadowy figures crowded into the room and converged around him in a half circle. They were naked, and someone murmured a complaint about the cold floor. The atmosphere was charged with anticipation, not just over the event at hand but also the Full Moon that reigned over the night above.

Logan considered himself an authority on the Moon. It was hard not to be, growing up in the House of Blevins, and Logan had studied her obsessively. He had read Ptolemy, Euclid, and the writings of the Church, and he was sure he knew as much as the scholars did. Still, in spite of everything he read, he had always felt he was missing something. The scholars had knowledge and theory, but they didn't really understand the

Moon. When he'd asked his family members, who were privy to secrets and mysteries not written in any books, they had waved him away or diverted him with platitudes. On the rare occasion when they had tried to explain, what they said hadn't made any sense.

Logan's brother Aidan knelt before him and looked him in the eye. Aidan closely resembled Logan, with dark, curly hair and deep brown eyes, but Aidan had a badly broken nose and a cold glare. Eye contact was crucial in their culture, and a glance or stare could have significant implications. Though it was a necessary part of the rite, Aidan's gaze made Logan squeamish, and it was hard to meet his eyes.

"Logan Peter Blevins," he said, "upon having reached the age of twenty years, thou hast requested admittance to the House of Blevins. By what right dost thou so petition?"

Logan drew a quivering breath and tried to remember the formal response. There really wasn't much to recall, but under the circumstances, nerves were to be expected. "I, uh, it is my birthright as third son of the House of Blevins and brother of Aidan and Ian."

"Hast thou employed a sponsor to speak for thee?"

"Yea, I have brought Amanda Blevins, who is a member in good standing."

Aidan turned and addressed a female who stood outside the circle. "Amanda Blevins, step forward. Wilt thou speak for Logan?"

Two of the others separated, and Amanda stepped through and knelt next to Aidan. Her lustrous curls cascaded over her shoulder, obscuring one breast. Logan swallowed hard at the sight of her curves and smooth skin. Nudity was commonplace in the House of Blevins, but Logan was barely out of his teens. She was stunning, and even being chained to a wall didn't keep him from wanting her.

"Yea, I shall," she said. "He is my cousin, known to me these six years. He shall make a fine addition to the House of Blevins."

She winked at Logan and backed out of the circle.

"Petition and affirmation having been made," said Aidan, "I call for a vote." He called the name of a male on Logan's far left.

Don Williamson knelt before Logan, who turned his head to the side. Don touched his nose to Logan's throat, sniffed, and backed away to look him in the eye. He said, "Yea," patted Logan on the shoulder and returned to his place.

Everyone in the lower and middle ranks assented, some of them offering an encouraging smile or a pat on the shoulder, but Logan hadn't worried about those votes. His only concern was Aidan. They had never gotten along, and sometimes it seemed Aidan went out of his way to make life difficult for Logan. Oddly, when Ian had asked to formally initiate Logan into the House of Blevins, Aidan had agreed. It should have been Aidan's place as the highest-ranking member of the family. It had made Logan wonder: would Aidan vote no? It would take a majority vote to admit him, but any dissent was a dishonor. A "no" from one of the others would be bad enough, but opposition from his own brother—and head of the house, no less—would be devastating.

Aidan moved forward and paused long enough to make Logan wonder if he was going to sniff his throat at all. He finally did so, backed away, and said, "Yea." He returned to his place and said, "One vote remains. If that vote is yea, thy initiation shall commence forthwith. Now is the time to object."

"I have no objection," Logan said shakily.

"Ian Blevins," Aidan said.

Ian went down on all fours and crept toward Logan. His eyes were pools of solid, inky black. Ian was the tallest and the most muscular of Logan's brothers, imposing not only by his stature but also by his brooding demeanor and menacing glare, but he was gentler than he appeared. While Aidan was distant and harsh, Ian was Logan's best friend. Before now, Logan had never feared him. Ian would never harm him. But accidents did happen, didn't they? Weren't they always saying that? Ian was so young. What if he did it wrong and accidentally killed him?

The time to scare himself was over. A power poured from Ian, and it felt like a million fire ants crawling over Logan's body. He turned his head, and Ian nuzzled his throat. He sniffed but didn't back away.

"Yea," he whispered.

Logan closed his eyes tightly and clenched his fists.

In the instant it took Logan to shut his eyes, Ian changed. With a snap of bones, his face elongated and his teeth became fangs that tore into Logan's throat. Not-quite-human wails and howls went up all over the room.

Nothing Ian had told him beforehand, no nightmare he'd had, not even the memory of Ian's injuries after he was brought across, could have prepared him for the assault. There was no pain at first, but when it washed over him, it was overwhelming. Blood and bile covered his tunic as he vomited, and he would have collapsed to the floor if the chain had been lower. As it was, he just hung there, retching and clinging to his ravaged throat with his free hand.

Along with the pain, Logan had the strangest sensation that Ian could see into his mind and that he understood intimately what Logan thought and felt. Likewise, he could feel Ian's worry that he might have injured Logan too badly.

The hatch slammed shut and the torch blew out, and one of the females screamed. Logan's gags punctuated less mundane noises, unnatural moans, pops and cracks, and sounds of battle as the hatch opened and the room flooded with light.

Battle? That couldn't be right, not here. He was probably delirious with shock and the chasm that was once his throat. His head began to spin, and he slipped from consciousness.

* * *

Too many of them were crammed into too tight a space. They had descended into cellars like this a hundred times, and though they were cautious, one could only prepare so much for the unexpected.

A bone-chilling crash and sudden blindness accompanied a sharp pain in Erica's shoulder, eliciting a startled scream. When the light returned a few seconds later, she felt stupid as she realized the crash had just been the hatch slamming shut behind them. Someone had thrown it open, but when Erica saw the chaos that had ensued, she wished it were still closed. The number of individuals in the room had nearly doubled, and they barely had space to move, much less fight. The enemy who had stabbed her had removed the dagger and was going for another thrust. She called it several colorful names as she parried the knife with her shortsword and swung back across, laying a deep gouge in its throat. As she reset for another strike, the dagger connected with her arm.

Unbelievable! This fiend had actually stabbed her—twice!

"Damn you!" she cried as she swung again. This time the blade went to the bone, and her opponent fell. And still moved. "Oh, for the love of God, will you just die?" Erica yelled. She abandoned finesse and descended on her enemy, hacking away until it finally stopped moving.

Farther into the room, Gerard was pulling a crossbow bolt from his side. A crossbow in this confined space? How? Then again, combatants from both sides were dropping quickly, leaving more room to shoot, if not to melee. A red mist of blood filled the air, and soon it would be difficult to discern friend from enemy.

Erica tried to step over the body of the creature she had just killed, only to trip over another and tumble to the floor. Someone yanked her up by the hair, and she jabbed her blade at her attacker. The movement was awkward, but she managed to get it in the throat.

It shouldn't have been this hard! This was their vocation, their lot in life, to stop the atrocities these monsters perpetrated, and they rarely had this much trouble.

Erica heard a pitiful gasp and turned to see one of her companions fall. Just beyond her, another lay on the floor beneath a tiny female who sat atop him, furiously slashing at his chest.

Gerard shouted, "Fall back!"

Erica's complement started making their way toward the stairs. Most of them didn't make it. A sudden sharp pain in her chest made Erica wonder if any of them would get out.

Part I

Rise and Fall

1

Along Comes a Woman

I expect Woman will be the last thing civilized by Man. — George
Meredith

1445
Rome

It was just past midday. Two hundred people moved about the
Colosseum, many of them gathering on the arena floor among
several rings of stone to watch the duels taking place there. The
Colosseum had been falling down for nearly a century, but The
Order of the White Guard still used it. The fighters were a
different sort from the gladiators who had fought there in ancient
times. Barring unforeseen accidents, no one would die today, but
that didn't mean they weren't out for blood.

The largest number of spectators crowded around the center
ring to watch a match between two of the White Guard's most
experienced swordsmen. Sunlight glinted off the steel of a
rapier as it shot toward Gerard Blevins's shoulder. Gerard was
tall, with dark, curly hair and cold, dark eyes, and he was in
the habit of using his menacing stare to intimidate his
opponents. With a threatening glare and deft turn of his wrist,
the cold-eyed Welshman tapped Richard Brentwood's blade and
knocked it inches to the side. Then, extending his blade over
the top of Richard's, he made a small, hard circle and threw
the opposing sword wide. Richard, a stocky blond from the
neighboring House of O'Shea, dodged nimbly out of range
before the counterthrust could transfix him. Gerard followed
up with several rapid thrusts, alternating high and low, and
waited for an opening in Richard's guard while keeping him on
the defensive.

Gerard forced Richard backward with his next series of attacks, bringing his rear foot inches closer to his lead foot with each step. With a final lunge, Gerard extended farther than Richard anticipated and buried his rapier in Richard's torso. The official declared Gerard the winner.

He removed his blade and saluted, and Richard returned the gesture with a groan of pain. Gerard saluted the official and left the circle as Richard's companions came in to tend to him.

Peter O'Neill and Domhnall Corbin Williamson—Don—waited nearby for Gerard.

"Well done," said Peter, a boisterous ginger-haired Irishman. He threw a towel to his friend.

Gerard plucked the towel from the air and tossed his rapier to Don in much the same manner as Peter had chucked the towel. Don caught it by the blade, cursed, and then flipped it to catch the grip.

"Oi, Gerard, next time aim higher and cut my whole bloody arm off," Don grumbled.

"It's just a rapier, Don. 'Haps you'd rather take the scabbard to avoid injury."

"Again," Peter said, "well done."

While Peter was pure Irish, Don was darker, the son of an Irish mother and a Welsh father, and small in stature, only about 'a" tall. Size notwithstanding, he exuded as much presence as his redheaded friend, and together they .with a commanded a lot of attention.

Don cleaned the blade as Gerard wiped sweat from his face with the towel. "I had forgotten how fast he was," he said.

"Not that it made a—" Don began.

When Don didn't finish the sentence, Gerard lowered the towel to see a female standing before him. With so many ambient scents and sounds, he hadn't noticed her approach; now her heady aroma filled his nostrils and produced gooseflesh on his arms, and it was all he could do not to gawk at her. She was tiny, the top of her head barely coming even with his shoulder. Her eyes were emerald green, her hair was flaming red, and her face was cute like a pixie's. Her nose was freckled, and her lips were full and pink. She wore a gold bodice over a chemise the same color as her eyes, and several petticoats billowed out from underneath. Someone who couldn't detect her nature could have easily mistaken for her fey, but Gerard had seen her before and knew she was anything but delicate.

Don and Peter watched with amusement.

"You executed that hidden step admirably," she said, "but Richard should have seen it."

Gerard fixed her with an threatening glare. The pixie took no note of it.

"He'll not make the mistake again," she continued.

"You say that with confidence."

"Indeed, I do."

"And who are you to make such guarantees?"

"Oh, the swordmaster of his pack," she replied smugly.

Gerard couldn't help returning her teasing smile. "And here I mistook you for a lost fairy."

She turned and posed. "Alas, no wings, but I'm never lost. Wings would be a nice touch, though."

"Impressive that such a diminutive female is the swordmistress of the House of O'Shea."

"Sword*master*, assistant midwife, Alpha Bitch—the usual."

"Weighty duties for such slender shoulders."

"Slender, but sturdy."

"Best be careful when in battle, so as not to trip over all those petticoats."

"They come off, I assure you."

Don made a choking sound, and Peter turned away, biting his lip to keep from laughing.

"So. Of what service may I be to the swordmistress and assistant midwife of the O'Sheas?" said Gerard.

Disregarding his deliberate omission of her status as Alpha Bitch, she said, "Oh, none, really. I wanted but to congratulate you on your win."

"I thank you. Now, please you excuse me; my friends and I have another engagement."

"Surely," she said. She started to leave but stopped and turned back. "By the by, if your opponents are of any competence at all, you ought to mind the tip of your sword and lead foot. You move them slightly before you lunge, giving away your intent."

With that, she turned her back and walked away before he could retort.

Don and Peter chortled, leaning on each other as if to keep from falling.

"Shut up," said Gerard. He moved on, and they followed.

"You've made quite the impression on that one," Don said. "When's the last time anyone save Peter gave you fencing advice?"

"To say nothing of the remark about the petticoats," Peter added.

"I don't envy her Alpha if she's his bitch," Gerard said. "That female is in dire need of a short leash."

"Erica O'Shaughnessy is nobody's bitch," said Peter. "Gossip says the only reason she's not Alpha Wolf is 'cause she's a female. Sean O'Shea's a weak Alpha, and he lets her run the house."

"I have heard of that one," Gerard grunted. "She does indeed need a leash."

Peter raised an eyebrow, a mischievous glint in his green eyes. "'Haps she needs taming, no?"

"*Our* Alpha Bitch would slap your face for that," said Don.

"Let's make sure she doesn't find out I said it, then."

"I've more important things to do than tame an outspoken female," said Gerard. "Let her run the House of O'Shea."

"Uh huh. It has also been long since a female has gotten you irritated. Especially one so lovely."

"She didn't irritate you?"

"She didn't bait us," said Don. "She baited you."

"Masterfully," Peter threw in.

Don raised a finger and opened his mouth as if to speak but thought better of it.

"Think no more on her," Gerard said.

"You neither, eh?" said Don.

"I'm trying, but you're not making it easy."

"Well, where's the fun in that?"

Peter stopped and smiled at a beautiful blonde waving at him from a nearby bench. "I'll find you later, lads," he said absently as he headed toward the maiden.

"Methinks you've lost your Beta," Don said. "Peter can still afford to divide his attentions. I can *ill* afford to divide mine."

"So what you're saying is if I wish to become a high-ranking Alpha in The Order of the White Guard, I should polish my tongue? Or should I do so if I intend to follow Peter instead?"

"You are not helping."

* * *

Though Peter and Don might have suggested otherwise, Gerard intended to forget about Erica O'Shaughnessy. There was too much to do without worrying about a female's attentions. It was induction time in The Order of the White Guard, and there were tournaments in which to participate, contests to judge, and postulants to evaluate before they were inducted into the militant order, which had been established to combat the Cartha, a faction of vampires that had cut a swath through Europe and parts of Asia.

The White Guard was sponsored by the Holy See, although only a select few knew the true nature of the order, which was comprised mostly of garou—werewolves. The House of Bianco, the White Guard's ruling house, owned the Colosseum outright. They had obtained the arena cheaply after an earthquake had destroyed half of it. They used it as their residence, but every fifth year they repaired the arena floor and opened it up for tournaments as part of the White Guard's induction celebration. Garou, some from as far away as Scandinavia and the Orient, made the pilgrimage regularly.

One would have thought such a gathering would present an opportunity for vampires to launch a monumental attack, either in Rome or in the packs' lairs, but in the nearly two and a half centuries since the White Guard's inception, no such attack had ever occurred. Lairs were breached at other times, but even that was rare. Powerful wards had been set up to protect their homes, although Gerard didn't know when they had been erected or by whom.

Gerard was highly ranked in the White Guard and therefore had extra responsibilities during his stay in Rome. As busy as he was, however, he caught himself watching for Erica. The Colosseum wasn't that large, and she was easy to spot. If they made eye contact she smiled at him; sometimes he only glared at her, but he found himself nodding hello more often. It irked him that a female could so easily distract him.

In the White Guard, distractions would get you killed.

* * *

When the two-week celebration concluded, seven packs started north through Italy together, the Houses of Blevins and O'Shea among them. It was a long trip—over 1,200 miles for the House of Blevins—and it was common for packs from similar areas to gravitate toward one another during their travels.

The first night on the road, Gerard was relaxing by the campfire with Peter and Don after setting up their tent when Erica approached and smiled at him but then turned to Peter.

"I've heard good things about you, Peter O'Neill," she said.

"Of course, you have," Peter quipped.

"And modesty wasn't one of those things. I had hoped to watch you fence in Rome, but I missed you. Would you care to spar with me?"

"Far be it from me to deny a lady." He noted the shortsword on her belt, ducked inside the tent, and retrieved a similar weapon.

Erica turned and headed for a clearing in the field near camp.

"Are ye coming?" Peter asked his friends. Don and Gerard got up and followed him to the clearing.

Erica and Peter faced each other and saluted. With her sword extended just above waist level, Erica stood her ground, sizing Peter up. Peter shrugged and attacked, apparently deciding to give her something upon which to base her evaluation.

He demonstrated great economy of motion, stepping past his blade rather than drawing it back. He planted his left foot and arced the sword around and over as he stepped with his right foot. The attack was fast and quite strong, and though he hadn't put all of his muscle into that first strike, he was clearly using his strength as an advantage.

Erica's block was incredibly quick but used a much greater amount of arm and upper body movement than Peter's efficient, solid strike. Moving that much, that fast, would sacrifice much of the driving, penetrating power of the short blade. Gerard wondered if she would stop Peter's stroke at all or just clash blades and then be hit with the recoil of her own weapon. Her sword did rebound, but the block was effective and stopped Peter's downward stroke. Moreover, the rebound put the blade in position for a horizontal slash, which nearly caught Peter across the midsection. It seemed that while her sword may have traveled farther than Peter's, there was some efficiency in her actions. But how did such a light blow stop his sword?

In avoiding Erica's strike, Peter spread his arms wide. From there, he aimed his next strike at Erica's left side. She blocked with another of those fast, broad strokes, but Peter struck quickly at the left side of her neck, then crossed over and down to cut at her right thigh, giving her no time for a counterattack as she fought to keep up with the assault. But she did keep up.

With the exchange, Gerard began to discern the essence of Erica's fencing style. Rather than try in vain to meet strength with strength, she augmented the speed of her blade by using her hips, torso, and wrist in addition to her sword arm, almost as though she were wielding a whip. There would be almost no follow-through on strikes like that, but she would have a great deal of percussive force at the focus of her strike and a lot of rebound energy after the swords met. She used that force to accelerate her draw for the next lash. She would never power her way through an opponent's defenses the way a fighter with more strength might, but missing one of those lightning-quick return strokes would leave the opponent sliced to the bone.

Gerard acquired a great amount of respect for the tiny swordswoman's abilities in that first few moments. She might be an irritating, outspoken pain in the arse, but by God, she could fight.

"You're very good," Peter said.

"You needn't sound so surprised. I did mention that I was swordmaster, no?"

"You did. My apologies."

"It doesn't help that you're shite with a shortsword," said Don.

"That hurts, brother. It really does."

"You'll live."

Erica's blade bit into Peter's arm. "'Haps not," she said.

"Ooh, first blood to the lady!" Don exclaimed.

"Oi, this is serious now," said Peter.

"Are you *ever* serious?" Erica asked.

"Sometimes, but when it happens, I sit down till the feeling passes."

He rushed forward, swinging the sword up from a seemingly relaxed resting position at his side, as if he were scooping something from the ground while running. Erica had to leap backward to avoid being slashed from hip to opposite shoulder. Continuing his forward motion, Peter closed the distance and bent his knees low, allowing the momentum of his first swing to bring the sword back around for a vicious cut, the deep flexion of his knees bringing the angle of the attack below Erica's arms, which were extended in guard position.

Reacting with equal speed, Erica pulled her arms up and back, avoiding Peter's attack. Unfortunately for her, it was exactly what Peter intended. Using the spring from his bent legs, he leapt forward, thrusting straight out with his blade and stopping it resting lightly against Erica's chest, just below her breastbone and angled slightly up.

"Oh, good," she said, "you've stopped coddling me."

The match continued for several minutes, as did the banter. After a while, they started to draw a crowd, and Peter and Erica talked with the onlookers as they fenced.

Erica didn't say a word to Gerard. He didn't say anything to her, either, but that was different. He clapped Don on the shoulder. "Let me know how this turns out," he said. "I'm going to bed."

"Weakling," Don muttered.

Gerard walked back to the tent and lay on his bedroll. He closed his eyes and tried to drift off, but his mind kept wandering back to the pixie-cute redhead who was socializing with his friends while ignoring him altogether. It stung, not because she paid him no attention, but because he let it bother him. He was a high-ranking White Guard Alpha with more control over his emotions than most, and he was pouting like a jilted lover.

When he woke the next morning, Gerard noticed Don's bed was empty. Thinking his friend was already up, he stepped outside. His sister Rhea sat alone, sipping tea. She looked a lot like Gerard, icy glare and all, and she even rivaled his height, but her long hair weighed the curls down, so it was straighter.

"Morning," she said.

"Morning. Where's Don? Do you know?"

"He spent the night elsewhere," she said with a smile. "Some pretty little redhead he met after you went to bed."

Gerard's heart sank. He should have known Erica would end up with either Don or Peter. Neither was shy when they were attracted to a female, and it wasn't like Gerard had displayed any interest.

If Rhea noticed a change in his scent, she didn't say anything. She stood up and stretched. "Ugh, 'tis gonna be a long day," she groaned. "I was up half the night gossiping with Erica O'Shaughnessy. She really is a dear, Gerard. I can't figure why you dislike her so."

"What makes you think I dislike her?" he asked defensively.

"She does."

"I don't dislike her. I just...you know, this really is none of your concern."

"Oh, I see," Rhea said knowingly. "Never mind."

Over the next few weeks, it was more of the same. Erica spent time with Gerard's friends and didn't speak to him. Don launched into a full-scale romance with Grace Monaghan, also of the House of O'Shea, and Gerard hardly saw him. Don said he and Grace were trying to make the most of the time they had together and hinted that Gerard and Erica should do the same, but neither took his advice. At some point, it became a battle of wills with both refusing to say the first word.

By the time the party boarded a ship for Dublin, the caravan had dwindled to their two packs, and Erica still ignored him. They split up outside Dublin, the O'Sheas going south and the House of Blevins heading north. Don and Grace shared a long, tearful farewell, but Gerard was so tired and ready to be home, he barely bothered saying goodbye at all. He did find himself exchanging a long gaze with Erica before she and her pack disappeared over the hill. Having her ignore him was preferable to watching her leave. Part of him wanted to go after her, but he didn't. They would meet again when the time was right. Until then, it was better to push Erica to the back of his mind.

Distractions would get you killed.

2

Refugee

Your feet will bring you where your heart is. — Irish Proverb

Male and female stereotypes were rarely the same for preternaturals as they were for humans. Garou females were not regarded as inferior, servants, property, or any other chauvinistic expressions used in medieval times. Females retained their femininity, but they were as strong and intelligent as the males and were usually treated as such. There was little chivalry with medieval garou. The only real concession they made to typical male and female roles was the tradition that a female could not be Alpha or Beta Wolf.

Erica's mother had died in battle when Erica was two, so she had been raised by her father. In anticipation of a life in the White Guard, he started teaching her how to fence when she was six. Erica had never known how to be anything but strong, and she had never known how to fail when she wanted something.

There was very little she did want, really, except for Gerard Blevins.

The first time she had ever seen him was during the trip to Rome for her induction. She watched a fencing match in which he participated, and she became so enamored of him that she went back to her room and cried herself to sleep. When she awoke the next day, she made a solemn vow never to cry over him again. Her attraction to Gerard was no more than a crush, and she was too old—at twenty-two—to get that worked up over a male. Instead, she admired him from a distance through the years.

When she saw him at the recent induction, she realized her feelings were not superficial. What had changed to cause this epiphany she couldn't say, but she knew then that she would live and die for him and she didn't want to wait another five years to get started.

She surmised that the fastest way to get his attention was to make him angry, but that doing so would not be an easy task. Gerard Blevins was practical, and he suppressed his emotions in the interest of doing his job. Erica, however, could be infuriating when she wanted. Thus, after his match with Richard, she approached Gerard and insulted him. She didn't really anger him, but she did get his attention.

The trip back to Ireland was a big delightful game. She made friends with Gerard's friends and pretended to ignore him entirely, and he pretended to ignore her too. She hoped he would approach her, but apparently he was just as stubborn as she was.

Erica was outgoing and liked most everybody, but she absolutely adored Don Williamson. When he wasn't acting like a fool, he was the kind of person one could talk to. He understood Gerard's reticence; he was going through the same thing with Grace Monaghan, Erica's packmate.

"The timing is off," Don said. "We'll separate soon, and it's not like we can stop in for a visit."

"You and Grace haven't let it stop you," she said.

"Grace doesn't have the control the rest of us have. She was just unable to resist my magnificence, and I didn't have the heart to deny her any longer."

"You know I'm gonna tell her you said that, right?"

"Oi, don't do that; she'll kill me."

"Admit it, Don. You love her."

"Till the day I die. Look, Grace and I know it's gonna be harder when we have to leave, but that's the way it is. Gerard knows that, too, and I think he's being pragmatic. I do know that you ignoring him is driving him mad."

"Better that than chase him. He may be frustrated, but at least he's interested."

Erica had no doubt she and Gerard would be together. She saw how he watched her. Males like that weren't that distracted by just any female. Gerard was hers; it was just a matter of time. It wouldn't happen for a number of years, of course. It was unlikely that she would run into him before the next induction, but garou didn't age and could expect to live for hundreds of years, so time didn't pass the same as it did for mortals. In her mind, the next journey to Rome was just around the corner.

She could be patient, but miracles happened all the time. If God wanted to align the stars so she could start her life with Gerard sooner, that was fine. Unfortunately, Erica wasn't a cynic. It never occurred to her that a cataclysm would bring them together.

* * *

The House of O'Shea lived in a converted inn in County Cork, not far from Carbery, which was governed by the MacCarthy Raegh dynasty. The MacCarthys Raegh provided all manner of assistance to the house, which was one of the few White Guard packs without a contingent of human monks taking care of them. The story went that some years back, Donal Glas MacCarthy, Third Prince of Carbery, became suspicious of the House of O'Shea's activities and had two of its members arrested. The garou were young and hadn't held up to interrogation as well as one would have hoped, and they told Donal about the White Guard. Luck was on their side, though. The prince had a guest in his castle who happened to know about the White Guard. Donal had thought he could use the House of O'Shea in conflicts with his rivals, so he began to offer assistance. Sean O'Shea had agreed to help the prince, with the strict stipulation that it would never take precedence over the White Guard's interests or conflict with their obligations to the Church. The relationship had proven beneficial for both sides, and the pack hadn't had trouble from the MacCarthys Raegh or anyone else in eighty years.

When Erica awoke to shouts one chilly October night two years after their return from Rome, she thought the ruckus had something to do with their human benefactors, so she didn't bother to get her silver sword. She grabbed her steel practice sword and made her way to the main hall, where a full-scale battle was underway—and the garou weren't fighting humans. Most of the O'Sheas were in nightshirts or undergarments, having been wrenched from their beds. Their numbers were relatively even, but the vampires had the advantage by virtue of surprise, the O'Sheas' various stages of undress, and the big blond vampire who was perched on the mantle, gleefully watching the melee.

Ardis.

Ardis Cmineralo was the bane of the White Guard. He and his covens had fought every single pack in the militant order. He was an original member of the Cartha, possibly *the* original member. The Cartha had been eradicated for the most part, but Ardis still brought vampires across in droves. He had many followers, and if he gave an order, his underlings obeyed with no regard for their own lives. There were pockets of vampires here and there throughout Ireland, but Ardis's coven was the largest and most fluid. He traveled the world and didn't stay in one place long, and when the White Guard encountered him, it was on his terms. They never found him; he found them—"paying them a visit," he liked to say. They had killed hundreds of his minions, but he always made more.

Ardis sat with a small vampire who appeared to be no more than a child. Erica had seen that one before, too; she was the only constant in Ardis's coven. They talked and laughed, cheering his vampires on as if they were watching some macabre sporting event.

Across the room, a burly vampire tore Richard Brentwood's head off with its bare hands. Nearby, a vampire with a broadsword decapitated Sean O'Shea and turned its blade on Maria Maldonado, who was facing the opposite direction. Erica charged the vampire and threw it to the ground. Its sword still connected with Maria's shoulder, but the injury was minimal and she was well enough to turn and plant her blade in its head.

The garou's numbers dwindled, but so did the vampires'. After a while, Ardis said, "Let's go, my children." The vampires vanished, and Ardis leapt from the mantle and reached into the fireplace, where coals were still burning from earlier in the evening. He picked up a log and threw it at a tapestry, which exploded. He must have used some sort of vampiric magic, causing flames to spread quickly and unnaturally heavy smoke to fill the room, impeding the garou's senses of sight and smell. Painful screams erupted across the room.

Erica sheathed her sword, thrust her hands out, and moved in as straight a line as she could. The room wasn't that big; a wall shouldn't be far away. As she moved, she called out to her packmates, and after a moment, she felt a hand on her arm. She grabbed the hand and continued onward. "I've got one," said the voice next to her, and she recognized her companion as Grace Monaghan.

"It is me: Maria," said the third garou.

Erica led her friends through the room, calling out to the others as she went, but she didn't find anyone else. She bumped into a chair, which she picked up and tossed out of the way. It smashed against a wall, and Erica turned toward the sound. In a moment, her hand touched the outer wall. The heat was almost unbearable, but she began feeling her way, hoping she would find a door instead of flames. Timbers began to fall behind her. Panic threatened to take over, but she pushed it back and continued to work her way around the perimeter of the room.

It was with great relief that she came across the door and yanked it open. She recognized her mistake too late, and air rushed in and intensified the blaze. She tugged on Grace's hand and pulled her and Maria out the door. They collapsed on the ground, gasping for air. Erica heard someone shouting inside, and she forced herself to her feet and stumbled through the door.

"Erica, no!" Grace called from behind her.

The influx of air may have intensified the fire, but it also cleared some of the smoke, and she could see well enough to find Finn O'Shaughnessy, her father, who was pinned under a heavy beam. She went to him and tried to lift it.

"Get out of here," he said. "You can't lift the beam alone, and the ceiling is about to go."

"I won't leave you."

Before Finn had the chance to argue, the ceiling caved in.

* * *

Though Gerard loved the trips to Rome, he was glad to be home, handling the day-to-day matters and working in conjunction with the monks who took care of the pack. The monks provided food, clothing, and guidance; worked as teachers, blacksmiths, farmers, and housekeepers; and acted as messengers between the House of Blevins, the House of Bianco, and other packs. There were no squires; the garou took care of their own supplies and horses and assisted each other with related tasks. They bred and trained their own horses as well, conditioning them from birth not to fear the garou in either human or wolf form.

After their return from Rome, the garou went on the occasional mission, but most of the next couple of years were quiet. Ireland was a volatile land, and the House of Blevins kept a close eye on the mortals. They couldn't afford to have their work complicated by Ireland's warring human clans.

During peacetime, Gerard had to worry about conflicts within the house as much as he did those outside it. When life was busy, the garou were always on edge, waiting for word that they could go and fight. When there were no vampires, boredom set in, and a bored garou was a dangerous one. It was rare and had never happened in the House of Blevins, but it was not unheard of to have garou kill each other during a particularly long dry spell. Thus, during the quiet periods, Gerard made sure they kept themselves occupied. They trained harder, and Gerard and his "Beta Wolf o' the Month" organized physical competitions to keep them sharp and diffuse hostilities. As it was, fights still broke out once in a while.

No matter how busy he was, Gerard thought about Erica every day. He knew how these things worked. He had seen many couples know the moment they met that they were meant for each other. Rhea had become engaged to her husband Owen the day after they had met, and their own parents had been childhood sweethearts. Even Don and Grace, who probably wouldn't see each other any sooner than Gerard and Erica, corresponded as regularly as they could, and Don was planning to ask her to come home with him after the next induction. When the time was right, the little red-haired pixie would sashay back into Gerard's life and would never leave. Until then, he had things to do, and he didn't have time to sit around pining for her.

When she showed up at his door, it wasn't in a manner he would have expected or wanted.

The House of Blevins lived in Ballybrook Monastery in County Derry on a plateau overlooking the River Foyle. October was magical in County Derry, with crisp mornings, warm afternoons, and trees dotting the countryside with a hundred different shades of gold, red, and brown. The sun was low in the sky, and the Harvest Moon cast a shadow on the hillside. She was waning now but was no less enchanting than at the peak of her glory. The garou felt a bit wilder in October, and many of them spent more time in wolf form than human. Even Gerard, who was one of the most levelheaded garou in the pack, was freer of spirit.

Brother Herschel, one of the monks who managed the monastery, came to Gerard's room, where he sat at his desk writing in the journal he had kept since was twenty-five years old, and savoring the scents of falling leaves, woodsmoke, and the perfumed soap one of the females had used in her bath.

"My apologies, Gerard," the monk said.

"No worries, Brother Herschel. What's on your mind?"

"There has been a battle. The House of O'Shea and a coven in County Cork. Most of them were slain."

Gerard was following Brother Herschel through the halls in an instant, trying to ignore the horrible sinking sensation in his chest. "Where is the messenger who brought the news?" he asked.

"There was no messenger. The surviving garou just arrived. I've taken them to the infirmary."

"How many are here?"

"Only three, of eleven."

"Good Lord! Were the three injured?"

"Aye, but they are healed; the battle was a fortnight ago. They are tired but otherwise of good health."

"I'll speak with them briefly and then let them rest. What about Grace?"

"She made it as well."

Gerard sighed with relief. "Find Don. He'll want to know as soon as possible."

"He and Peter are out hunting," Brother Herschel responded, "but I'll tell him as soon as he returns."

Gerard silently thanked God when he picked up Erica's scent and heard her voice. There was no smugness this time, only a soft, soothing tone as she reassured a weeping packmate.

"There was no pain, Maria," she said softly. "You know he didn't suffer. He'd not want you to grieve so."

Maria launched into a frantic rant in Spanish as Gerard entered the room. Except for her tears and the general wear and tear from their travels, the three females looked well. Maria, who lay on a cot with her head in Erica's lap, had the appearance of a Roman goddess, with thick, flowing brown hair and dark eyes. The other one was Grace, who had red hair and green eyes like Erica, but she had more of a natural beauty than Erica's pixie cuteness. Mary Quinn sat on the cot next to Grace. The gorgeous blonde was the House of Blevins's Omega Wolf and surgeon. She didn't say a word—she rarely did—but she still outshone everyone in the room.

"Maria lost her husband," Erica said to Gerard. "Spaniards are an emotional lot, and in our flight there was no time to mourn."

"What happened?" he asked.

"'Twas Ardis's coven attacked us. You'd think he'd brought across all of Ireland by now, wouldn't you?"

"An ambush?" he asked. Ardis was notorious for setting up elaborate traps for the White Guard, and Gerard himself had been victim to such attacks several times. He had come to expect to be waylaid every time he entered a lair, and it had repeatedly saved his life. Sean O'Shea had apparently held no such expectations.

"They attacked us in our own home while we slept," she said.

Gerard's mouth dropped open. "How were they able to breach your lair?"

"I've no idea. But Ardis is powerful, so who really knows what he can do? The vampires were better prepared, and they were stronger and faster."

"And how did ye survive?"

"They were not faster than we were."

3

She Just Wants to Be

*Woman's influence is powerful, especially when she wants
something.* — Josh Billings

Gerard sent Peter, Aeron Davies, and Adam Quinn to County
Cork with a message for the MacCarthys Raegh, informing them of
the House of O'Shea's defeat and offering to investigate. Dermod
an Duna MacCarthy Raegh, who was currently ruling the region,
already knew; his soldiers had buried the bodies and razed the inn.
They had salvaged some records and a few other items, which he
gave to Peter to pass along to Erica. They had also saved the
horses and Dermod was prepared to send them along, but on
Erica's instructions Peter took three and left the rest in Dermod's
possession. Dermod accepted the offer of an investigation, but true
to form, Ardis's coven had vacated the area.

Erica, Maria, and Grace spent most of their time until the next
Full Moon in mourning. They sat in the chapel for hours, reciting
prayers, meditating on the rosary, or just sitting in silent
contemplation. Erica didn't know what Grace and Maria did in the
privacy of their rooms, but Erica read. She was ashamed to admit
it, but mourning was boring. She could grieve just as effectively
while doing other things as she could kneeling at the altar. Her
packmates had been full of life and spirit, and it was a dishonor to
remember them with such sadness. It was better to celebrate their
lives and the good works they did. She missed Finn most of all, of
course, but he had taught her to be strong, and he wouldn't want
to see her spending weeks moaning and wailing over him.

Over the next several months, Erica renewed her friendships
with Don, Peter, and Rhea, but otherwise, she had trouble
adjusting. She wasn't used to being low in the hierarchy. For the

most part, the House of Blevins was more a family than a military unit, and formal speech and displays of submission were usually required only during ceremonies or official functions. A few garou, however, demanded it on a regular basis, asserting their authority simply because they could.

Erica met Adam Quinn in the common room one morning at breakfast time. She was going in as he was coming out. "Good morning, Adam," she said amicably as she tried to pass him, but he blocked her way.

"That's not how it works," he said. "You stand aside for me, not the other way around."

"The doorway's big enough for us both to go through at the same time," she pointed out.

"Don't talk back to me!" he said indignantly. "Remember your place."

With herculean effort, she averted her eyes, stepped aside, and let him pass. Such treatment was going to get old very fast. Erica was used to being treated with respect—not because of her station but because of her abilities and experience, and simply because that was the way the garou of the House of O'Shea treated each other. Being bullied just because she was new and lower in the hierarchy was irksome.

In order to climb in the structure, a garou could offer a formal petition or blatantly defy an order given by the garou of the next highest rank. After the challenge was made, the two garou were deemed of equal rank and conflicts were forbidden until the resulting contest—usually a fencing match but sometimes a hand-to-hand fight—which was held on the next New Moon. Such events were very common, and few New Moons went by without one or more matches. Erica had planned on making a formal petition, but she decided that defying an order would be more fun.

Adam was blond and handsome, a competent fighter, and gifted in the areas of investigation and reconnaissance. He was also arrogant, lazy, and abusive, and he was a slob. Erica entered the common room, where he sat at the table gnawing on a turkey leg. She went to the tap and drew a mug of ale, and he said, "Gmm bmm mmn nmm."

She turned to see him holding his mug up. A morsel of turkey clung to his cheek as if he were saving it for later.

"What say?" she asked.

"Get me another while you're at it."

She set her own mug on the table and took his to the keg, but Adam took hers before she had the chance to fill it. Erica said nothing, just glared at him.

"What?"

"Didst thou not want thine own mug?"

Adam waved a dismissive hand. "One mug's as good as any other."

"Aye, but that was *my* mug you took."

"Nae, you gave it. Don't you remember? Take that one."

Erica left Adam's used mug on the table, got a clean one, and filled it. She put her hands on the table and leaned forward until their noses nearly touched. Glaring him boldly in the eye, she said, "So, my lord, wouldst thou like me to drink it for thee as well?"

Adam choked on his ale.

Erica continued. "It must be a delight for you to have others under you besides your sister, no? Or do you enjoy having your sister under you?"

"Any more talk like that, and I'll—"

"You'll what! I am not Omega, and I grow weary of your bullying. I am older, cleverer, and a greater fighter than you will ever be, and I'm not taking orders from you anymore. I'm challenging you for your position."

"You've not been here long enough for this," he said.

"There is no tradition that dictates how long a garou must be with the pack before a challenge, and you know it. The only requirement is that the duel be done on the New Moon. In faith, Adam, you don't believe a female could defeat you, do you?"

"But all that bluster about being a superior fighter—"

"If you believe it bluster, I don't see the problem."

He wiped his mouth on his sleeve—the turkey stayed where it was—and said, "Right, then. I'll tell Gerard it's a go. Do you have a longsword?"

"Nae, but I can borrow one."

"Can you even lift a longsword?"

"If you have a claymore I might borrow, I shall use that."

With that, Adam smiled. "Longswords, then."

Erica got up, but before she left, she plucked the piece of turkey from Adam's cheek and dropped it into his mug.

* * *

Ballybrook had once been a grand castle owned by the O'Neill dynasty, and Peter had donated it to the Catholic Church and the White Guard in particular. It had been a warrior's castle and was more a fortress than a palace. The outer wall was massive and had once been surrounded by a moat. The area between the outer and inner walls contained stables, livestock, a vegetable garden, and other features to sustain the monastery.

A path led from the gate to the main road, which crossed the river in one direction and led to the town of Derry in the other. Downhill to the west lay a series of caves and a vast forest that was home to much wildlife. Such an environment was perfect for the garou, who were forced to surrender to their animal forms on the Full Moon and who chose to hunt or fish in wolf form during other times as well.

The keep was as imposing as the outer structure, complete with five-foot-thick walls and few windows. It was constructed in a square with towers in each of the four corners. Staircases outside each of the towers accessed the second and third floors, which served as dormitory areas for the garou and the monks. The first floor held the guest quarters, offices, and common areas. It was comfortable, with large rooms and lots of fireplaces, although most of the lavish appointments that had once graced the castle had been removed.

The keep surrounded a sizable courtyard that was as austere as the rest of the castle. Except for a grotto near the chapel, the area was free of ornamentation. A few benches and weapon racks stood around the perimeter. The courtyard was the training ground and the site for duels, and they used it in almost any weather. If conditions were too bad outside, they worked out in one of the unused tower rooms on the third floor.

Adam was warming up when Erica walked into the courtyard. Most of the other garou had come out to watch the match, but Gerard was absent.

Peter stood between Erica and Adam in a large circle marked off in the stones. The Beta Wolf was of average height with rather nondescript facial features, red hair, and vivid green eyes. Sometimes he kept a beard, but he was usually clean-shaven. He wasn't particularly good looking, but he was magnetic and women found him appealing. He usually had a lover, most often a human who lived in Derry. Peter rarely angered and could be downright silly when he wanted to, but that didn't mean he would shrink away from a pissing match or a fistfight. At nearly 300 years of age, he was the oldest member of the pack, and the only one not born into a garou family. He was a noble, but he refused to talk about his past or the circumstances under which he had donated the castle to the White Guard. He had no love for the nobility, especially the O'Neills, and when they were mentioned, he usually growled.

Peter turned to Erica and spoke formally. "Erica O'Shaughnessy, hast thou challenged Adam Quinn for his rank?"

"I have."

"And Adam, hast thou accepted?"

"I have."

"I call a duel, then, with longswords. The duel begins when I step out of the circle and ends when one of ye hath scored three solid strikes against the other, one of ye is felled with shoulders to the ground, or one of ye yields. If thy blade passes through thy opponent, I will likewise declare thee the victor. Swords at the ready, and begin."

Peter exited the circle. Erica and Adam saluted him, then turned and saluted each other.

"Let us get this over with," Adam said as he bore down on Erica with a smug grin, retracting his sword and preparing for a downward slash.

As the blade came down, Erica ducked to the right and stepped out with her left foot. Turning completely around, she sliced him deeply across the ribs as his sword missed her shoulder.

"Damn, you're quick!" he said, turning to face her again. Since the direct approach hadn't worked, he advanced more slowly, waving the sword back and forth in front of himself in order to get a feel for what she would do next.

Erica stood her ground, waiting for his advance. Adam's arms and legs were longer than hers, and he knew how to use the advantage. Instead of a rash charge, he came in with a quick feint toward her eyes that suddenly dipped toward her exposed thigh. Erica parried his thrust to the side while stepping in and making two quick ones of her own: the first to his thigh and the second to his midsection. Adam barely had time to yelp before Peter declared Erica the winner.

Adam was not amused. "Who do you think you are?" he demanded.

"She thinks she is your superior," Peter responded, "and you'll do well to mind that when addressing her."

Erica saluted, but Adam refused to reciprocate. He stormed out of the courtyard, followed by his parents.

"Methinks I made an enemy," she said to Peter.

"Pay him no mind," Peter said. "His ego has ever outweighed his ability, and he doesn't know the meaning of the word honor."

Mary Quinn approached. The Omega Wolf was blonde and beautiful like her mother, but where Abigail was haughty, Mary had a sweet face and an easy smile. Like most of the females in the White Guard, she usually wore trousers instead of dresses, but she tended to dress in more revealing clothing after having spent several years being treated like a whore. In Erica's experience, if someone was told something enough, they started to believe it. "My brother is an ass," she said, surprising Erica. Mary rarely spoke at all, let alone used a term of disrespect. "The only reason he's not Omega is 'cause I am. You were brilliant. You might even defeat Peter."

Erica figured Peter would rebuke Mary for the insult. He did react, but not as Erica had expected. He smiled at Mary and tugged playfully on her hair. Erica followed Mary's lead and gave Peter a sly grin. "How far up in the hierarchy are you?"

"There'll be no challenging the Beta Wolf," Don said, "but I'm for the taking."

"He means you'll be permitted to challenge him in due course if you so choose," Peter said.

"No, I don't," said Don.

"Not gonna happen," Mary retorted. Don threw an arm around Mary and kissed her cheek just before Abigail called from the infirmary door and demanded that Mary go in and stitch Adam's wounds.

"I didn't think I hurt him bad enough for stitches," Erica said as Mary went inside at a dead run.

"You didn't," said Peter. "They make Mary care for Adam if he so much as stubs his toe."

"Why?"

"Don't expect to understand many of the things the Quinns do," Don said.

"Especially when it comes to Mary," Peter threw in.

* * *

It would be unseemly to advance too quickly, and Erica tried to stay where she was in the structure for a while, but it was like a moth flying to a flame. She just couldn't help it. Three months after she dueled Adam, she fought Aeron Davies. Aeron was a tall brunette with deep blue eyes and a Welsh accent. She was a good fighter, but she was an easy victory and much more amicable than Adam.

Abigail Quinn, however, would not be so easy an egg to crack. Abigail doted on Adam, and the fact that Erica had put marks on her baby had enraged her. Erica didn't understand her animosity. Duels for rank were an integral part of pack life, and Adam wasn't helpless. He had gotten over the loss to Erica and had recently traded rank with Grace, who had decided to follow Erica's initiative and start making challenges. Abigail didn't give Grace a sideways glance, but she had a nasty habit of turning up her nose when she and Erica met in the hallway. Most times, she refused to speak to Erica at all, and then only when addressed formally. Erica waited as long as she could stand it before she confronted her, but it was difficult because Abigail tended to get under her skin. Erica didn't like to be ignored.

She didn't trust Abigail to acknowledge the challenge, so Erica made sure to approach her in the presence of others. Abigail was in the common room, mending a shirt by the fire. Peter and Don sat at the table with a chessboard between them, arguing because Peter adamantly refused to concede the match even though Don had him down to his king and one pawn. Grace sat next to Don, watching the game.

"Good e'en, Abigail," Erica said as she sat next to her.

Abigail didn't reply.

"Good e'en, Abigail," Erica said again with a bit more force.

Abigail gave a heavy sigh and said, "Good e'en."

"How goes it this night?"

"Adam has torn another shirt. You know lads."

"Is Adam not fifty-some years old?"

"When did a lad's age preclude a mother's love?"

"Then again, I would think a lad's *mental* age holds more sway for the garou."

"Are you saying Adam is a child?"

"Nae. *You're* saying it."

"You will address me properly. Besides, I said no such thing. I merely sit here mending a shirt for my son. It could as easily be Peter's. Or Gerard's."

"Aye, but if it were, would you be calling them lads?"

"She would if it were Peter's," said Don.

Abigail fairly growled with exasperation. "Do you want something, or did you just come here to ask for a beating?"

Erica stood up. "I came to ask for a beating. Abigail, I stand here to challenge your rank."

"I refuse," Abigail said condescendingly. "Your packmates' bodies have scant been laid to rest, and you already wish to rule another house."

"My packmates have been gone near two years," Erica reminded her, "and I need not make excuses to you for my actions."

"Indeed, you do. I'm your superior, and you will address me properly!"

"So you tell me all too often, and I'm disputing your superiority. I'm done averting my eyes and addressing you formally when even the Alpha and Beta Wolves don't require it. You must accept; you are too low in the hierarchy to refuse. Unless you wish to petition the Alpha for immunity."

Abigail dropped her sewing. "What? And be subscribed a coward? How dare you accuse me!"

"So you accept, then?"

"If I did—and I've not yet done so, mind you—I would be allowed to decide terms and weapons. I'm of higher rank."

"I do know how these things work."

"You'll turn everyone against you, you know. Life can be very unpleasant for a bitch who alienates her packmates. Just ask my daughter."

"Why ask her? It seems you have more experience in that arena."

Don and Peter studiously looked away, their shoulders shaking with suppressed laughter. Abigail gaped at Erica in astonishment.

"The challenge, Abigail?"

Abigail stood up and glared at Erica, who glared back. If this catty prima donna thought Erica was going to lose a staredown, she was sadly mistaken.

After only a few seconds, Abigail broke her gaze. "I concede."

"What was that?"

"You can have my position."

"But what of my beating?"

"Let my husband deal with you. He'll not be as easy a victory as Adam, I assure you."

"Let me confirm, if you will. You want not to be subscribed a coward, but you would rather concede than actually duel me. Is that accurate?"

Peter and Don gave up and broke into laughter, and Grace sat by, trying to look innocent.

"Oh, shut up!" Abigail said as she picked up her sewing and stormed from the room.

* * *

Erica didn't even have to approach Connor Quinn. He called her out the next day. Connor was as good looking as the rest of his family, with reddish-blond hair and hazel eyes. He had a warm, open smile, but one rarely saw it because he usually had a scowl on his face.

"I think it time to bring you down, little woman," he said as he smacked the back of her head.

"What meanest thou?" Erica asked innocently in the formal Middle English he demanded of her.

"You know what I mean. You're impertinent, full of conceit, and it is time someone reminded you of your place."

Erica surveyed the common room, where several garou of higher rank sat, including Gerard and Peter. "Shouldn't one of them be doing it, then?" she asked.

"I have as much right as they."

"Then you'll accept a formal challenge from me?"

Connor rolled his eyes. "Damn it, woman, why do you think I'm here? Indeed, I'll accept, and I shall hurt you."

"If anyone can do so, 'twill surely be you."

On the next New Moon, it took her all of thirty seconds to leave him bleeding on the ground.

* * *

Shortly after Erica defeated Connor, Mary approached her with two large buckets. She waited silently until Erica acknowledged her, then said, "I'm going to the river to get water. Wilt thou come? I thought thou might like some fresh air."

"Aye, I'd love it," Erica replied. "But pray, don't use the formal language with me. 'Tis not necessary."

"I thank you."

The two females went out the back gate and down the hill to the river, chatting mostly about the weather. Erica enjoyed the trip. Mary was the quiet type. She didn't speak much, and then only when she was spoken to unless Peter and Don were close by. In the nearly two years since she had joined the House of Blevins, Erica hadn't had an opportunity to get to know the Omega Wolf.

Mary filled the buckets and started plodding back up the hill toward the monastery.

"Mary, why are you carrying water like this?" Erica asked. "Why not use the well outside the kitchen?"

"I do it today as punishment."

"For what?"

"Who knows? Some imagined slight against Adam, I'm sure. Or 'haps she's taking her resentment of you out on me."

"Forgive me, Mary. I had no wish to make your life harder."

"No need. If not for that, she'd find something else. Besides, she likes river water for her bath. I'm sorry if I'm being too bold, but Peter said if I was worried, I needed to tell you myself and that you wouldn't mind. Most everyone likes you. Some think you are too willful, but they admire your courage and your fighting ability. But there are those who believe you are a threat, or at the very least, rude, with your swift advancement."

"I must do what my heart tells me. I can serve the House of Blevins well, but not from such a low rank."

"I believe you, but mind, I have no influence. Be careful, Erica. I don't think any of them would try openly to harm you—except in a duel, of course—but there are other ways to hurt you. Just 'cause you outrank them doesn't mean they're helpless against you."

"Is that a threat?"

"Oh, no, no!" Mary replied quickly, instinctively raising an arm to ward off an expected blow. Water sloshed out of the bucket and spilled on her clothes, and she groaned in frustration. "If it's not one thing, it's another. I mean you no harm, be assured. I only warn you 'cause I'd not put it past certain others."

"Mary, you're speaking against your own family."

"They'd do the same to me. We don't rightly get along. I'm fond of you, Erica, and I am happy you're doing so well. But I pray you will be careful in trying to take so many positions so rapidly. I wouldn't want you taking mine."

* * *

Later that evening, Rhea and Erica sat in the common room, nursing cups of wine. Rhea Masters looked a lot like Gerard, icy glare and all, and until Erica had gotten to know her during their all-night gab session on the way back from Rome, she had thought Rhea might be a bitch in more ways than one. Now they were great friends, and Erica understood that cold eyes were a Blevins family trait and not indicative of personality.

"I know it's not right, but I still can't help laughing about your duel with Connor," Rhea said with a chuckle. "I believe his pride was injured more sorely than anything."

Erica laughed in response.

"You'll be challenging me before long, then?"

Erica eyed Rhea closely and studied her scent to determine what she was getting at. They were friends, but Rhea was still Alpha Bitch. "I may hold off for a time," Erica said.

"Why so?"

"Some believe my ambitions are inappropriate."

"I see. But I would recommend that you reconsider stopping."

"Why is that?"

"Connor could make his first challenge at any time."

"I don't fear Connor Quinn."

"Had Connor chosen to duel you without weapons, he would likely have defeated you. He's very good at unarmed combat. The Quinns aren't so high in rank, but there are enough of them to hold some weight. They have been with us for many years and are strong in battle, and Adam is a pretty fair investigator. If it comes to them against you, I can't be certain how Gerard will choose. 'Tis very rare, but he has been known to make rash decisions just to quiet the Quinns' ravings."

"Why are you doing this?" Erica asked.

"I shan't insult you by asking if you're capable of being a good Alpha Bitch. I saw you with your pack on the way from Rome, and I've heard the gossip."

"Not all the gossip is true, mind you. Sean O'Shea was not so weak as everyone wishes to believe. He simply had a quiet way."

"Gerard won't be so quiet," Rhea warned.

"I'd have it no other way."

"I've helped run the House of Blevins for half a century, and I think it time to take a rest. Besides, Gerard needs a mate at his side, not a sister."

Erica raised an eyebrow. "A mate, eh?"

"Don't you be coy with me, Erica O'Shaughnessy. Challenge Owen, dear. Do it tonight."

* * *

Owen Masters was a huge, oafish-looking male, more like an ogre than a garou, but he was a gentle giant. He was highly intelligent, and his English accent was proper and polite. Garou were generally soft-spoken, their overly sensitive hearing causing them to regulate their tone of voice as much as possible, but Owen's speech was even milder than most. When he regarded Rhea, his eyes glowed with unabashed adoration.

Owen wielded a massive broadsword, but he gave Erica the option of using her shortsword. He believed using the weapons they were each accustomed to would even the playing field. While he could have easily overpowered her, he was no match for her speed and agility, weapons notwithstanding. Just two years after joining the House of Blevins, Erica was one match away from Rhea.

4

Accidents Will Happen

A true friend stabs you in the front. — Oscar Wilde

"I'm going to town to run some errands," Rhea said to Erica one afternoon a few weeks after the duel with Owen. "Care to go with me?"

They went to the stable, saddled their horses, and left for Derry.

"Did you know that Peter and Aeron are together?" Rhea asked her as they rode.

"Oh, is that what it is? Their scents suggested something was going on, but they're very quiet. 'Tis no surprise, really. Peter is always involved in one love affair or another."

"This is the first one he's had with a packmate in a long time, though."

"Well, is it serious?"

"You're closer to him than I," Rhea pointed out. "What do you think?"

"I think if it were serious, I'd already know about it."

"What of Don and Grace? Do you think he'll ever ask her for her hand? I'm starting to wonder."

"Of course he will. I know they've discussed it. He and I talk a lot about timing. He's waiting for the right time, I think. Very well, since we're gossiping anyway, what other juicy tidbits have you got for me?"

"Brother Finnius is keeping a mistress in Derry."

Erica's mouth dropped open. "Not truly!"

"Truly."

"That's outrageous!"

"The monks do that occasionally."

"I understand that, but what does she see in him?"

"I couldn't say. Maybe it's really big."

"A lass must get that far before discovering how big it is."

Rhea laughed. "We're gonna burn in hell for talking about Brother Finnius like this. You know that, right?"

Derry was a tidy little burg surrounding St. Columba monastery and inhabited mostly by merchants and fishermen. The squalor of bigger cities had not yet overrun the town. There were few nobles, if any. Most everyone had food and a warm bed, and if not, they could turn to the monastery for assistance. When the Ballybrook monks grew old and passed away, St. Columba monastery often provided replacements.

Erica and Rhea nodded hello to the sentries as they rode through the gate. "What are we doing today?" Erica asked as they entered the city.

"We're stopping at the monastery to pass along some documents from our monks to theirs," Rhea replied. "I also need to get some supplies, and I want to introduce you to the merchants and acclimate you to a few of the duties you'll handle when you become Alpha Bitch."

"'When'?" Erica remarked.

"You're still playing coy," Rhea reminded her.

"'Tis a habit. I can't help it. Rhea, I appreciate your help, but with all due respect, I was a White Guard Alpha Bitch for a number of years."

"Of course you were, dear, but that doesn't mean you have naught to learn. The Houses of Blevins and O'Shea are very different. You will have responsibilities here that you didn't have in County Cork, and I'm sure there were tasks you performed there that won't be necessary here."

"I never thought of it that way. I bow to your superiority."

"Rhea is wise," the Alpha Bitch said smugly. "Now for my next pearl of wisdom: You should call Don out so he'll stop whining."

"Is he whining?"

"Oh, little things like 'The suspense is unbearable' or 'What is she waiting for?' If you're still apprehensive about your quick advance, don't be. You've come too far to stop now. Even those against your rise watch with rapt attention. They may despise you, but they wouldn't miss a duel for all the world. I'm also finding the suspense unbearable, by the way."

"So you're saying I'm entertaining?"

"Oh, definitely. Now, if you're drawing it out in order to annoy Don, that's another matter entirely."

Erica laughed. "Haps it's a little bit of both. It's timing again. I'll do it when the time is right."

* * *

Erica decided the time was right when she sat at the bottom of the hill at the riverside one sunny spring afternoon, braiding Grace's waist-length hair and watching Don practice with his longbow. It seemed to her that he didn't need to practice; he rarely missed his mark. Then again, he wasn't really practicing as much as showing off for Grace. Peter sat with them, critiquing Don's marksmanship.

"Oi, that was pathetic!" Peter said when an arrow hit half an inch from the bull's-eye.

Don held out the bow. "If you think you can do better, go on, then."

Peter got up and took the bow. "Stand aside, little man." He held his hand out. "Arrow?" Don handed him an arrow, and he aimed and shot. The arrow hit the target, but it missed the bull's-eye altogether. "Not a word," he said.

"Wouldn't dream of it. Novice."

Peter dropped the bow and tackled Don, and they wrestled.

Grace chuckled. "They're so cute when they do that."

After a few minutes, Peter sat back down next to the females and Don went back to practicing. Don was not classically handsome, but he was attractive in an understated way. His light brown hair was too coarse and curly to control, so he usually kept it cut very short. He had a mustache but no beard. His grayish eyes were unremarkable until they caught your eye, and then they bored right into your soul. He was short and slight of build, not much bigger than most of the females—in fact, his longbow was taller than he was—but he was rock solid and much stronger than he appeared, even for a garou. Not only was he a master archer, he was exceptional at hand-to-hand combat, especially for one with so small a stature, and he was one of the best swordsmen in the house. Much of the time, Don was a clown, the most likely to make a sarcastic comment or play a practical joke, and he was noted for his creative insults. He had the most volatile temper in the pack, but he was a good listener and a devoted friend. One always knew where one stood with Don; he didn't hold back his feelings, good or bad.

Don and Peter were practically inseparable, and when they were together, they were more entertaining—or annoying—than a multitude of court jesters. Their humor was irreverent and their tongues were sharp, but when they were in their element, even their harshest barbs were often tolerated because they were simply too funny to cause offense. A large amount of their humor was directed at each other or Gerard, who often rounded out the trio, but few were exempt from their needling. Although Gerard was just as amused by them as everyone else, he never laughed. He never even cracked a smile. They also spent a lot of time with Mary, and she was the only one who wasn't subject to their wit. They taunted her when they were sparring with her but at no other time. Usually, they were fiercely protective of Mary, and they had even been known to attack garou who mistreated her.

Peter and Don were more than just partners in crime, though. They were closer than brothers and shared a deep and abiding attachment that was more profound than most anything Erica had ever seen. Erica believed that if it came to a choice between the White Guard and their friendship, they would choose their friendship.

"Huzzah!" she called as Don destroyed Peter's arrow with his next shot. "Yea, thou art a master with the bow, but how art thou with the sword?"

He stopped, turned, and rewarded her with a grin. "And so it happens."

"She doesn't have the control the rest of us have," said Grace. "She was unable to resist your magnificence any longer."

"Good, now he'll shut up about it," Peter said as Don scowled at Grace.

"Will you accept my challenge?" Erica asked.

Don sighed heavily and gazed sadly at her as if he were already mourning her passing. "I don't want to hurt you, Erica," he said with mock sympathy.

"Nor I you, my friend. Will you?"

"Hurt you? Almost assuredly."

"Will you accept my challenge, fool?"

"Oh, why not? A slap fight is probably out of the question, no?"

"You may wish to use a more formidable weapon."

"Very well, then. I shall be more than happy to pierce you with my longsword."

"Careful," said Peter. "Your definition of 'long' may differ from Erica's."

"Should we tell them we're not amused?" Grace asked Erica.

"Nae, 'twould just encourage them."

* * *

"Care for a pint, my lord?" Don asked, sticking his head in the doorway of Gerard's office.

"Surely," Gerard replied. He got up from his desk.

There was no point in admonishing Don not to call him "my lord." Don had addressed him formally for decades, strictly poking fun. In fact, when they were younger and spent a lot of time fighting for rank, Gerard had done it himself when Don had outranked him. These days Don was calling Peter "my lord" as well, mostly because it drove the Beta Wolf up the wall.

As they walked through the corridor toward the common room, Don said, "I'm glad we can drink together before I lose my rank."

"What are you on about?"

"'Twould be inappropriate for the Alpha Wolf to keep company with garou too low in the ranks."

Gerard stopped and glared at his friend. "I repeat: what are you on about?"

"Erica and I duel tomorrow at noon."

Gerard bristled. "She is the most infuriating female I have ever met!"

"So you keep saying."

"Has she no sense of propriety at all? It is not done this way! Ascendance to Alpha in a house this size should take some twenty years, at the least."

"And yet I don't see you undertaking to stop her," Don said as he started moving toward the common room again. "The rest of us trade rank every few months. I don't see why everyone's making such a fuss over Erica doing it. Besides, Rhea wants to quit. She's been grooming Erica for the office and encouraging her to make challenges for a while now."

"I'll not be controlled as easily as Sean O'Shea."

Don handed Gerard a mug and drew some ale from a tap near the long table. "Erica didn't control Sean. I have it that he was not so weak. 'Haps he simply recognized Erica's gifts and decided the best way to serve the House of O'Shea was to let her have her head."

"I have my own head, thank you."

"And another would do you no harm. Erica will do you more good than ill, Gerard. The garou of the House of O'Shea loved her, and to this day Grace believes she can do no wrong. Think on three females, injured and grieving over tragedy, traveling alone across Ireland on foot. 'Twould be an arduous journey for anyone, and human males are not as accepting of a woman's strength as the garou."

"Did something happen to them on their way here?"

"They've not said as much, but little things they've let slip led me to believe there were incidents. Grace says they wouldn't have survived if not for Erica. Her ascendance may be unorthodox, but it's well deserved. Instead of wasting your energy fighting her, you may be better served to consider how best to use her, 'cause I assure you, brother, she will be Alpha Bitch."

"I do have some say in that," Gerard reminded him.

"Aye, that's my point. Don't let your resentment blind you to the fact that you'll be doing the House of Blevins a disservice by interfering with her advance. Or, if I may be so bold, any other feelings you may still be trying to ignore."

"Nae," Gerard said frostily. "You may not be so bold."

"Forgive me, my lord," Don said humbly. He even averted his eyes.

"Damn it, Don! You know I hate it when you do that! It could be taken out of my hands, you know."

"Not gonna happen. Four garou remain that she has yet to duel, and the only two who could defeat her are ineligible."

"You can defeat her."

"Don't be so sure."

"Don, I forbid you to throw that duel!"

"Have you forgotten who you're talking to? When have you ever known me to give over a match? I'd never make it easy for her—that wouldn't be any fun—but I'd not like to make a wager on it. Times I think you and Peter and I have been at this so long, we can predict the outcome of most duels without them having to take place, but this is not one of them. I've sparred with her, and I've watched her practice, and she has a fair chance of defeating me."

Gerard pondered the potential implications of the duel and what it would mean to the house if Erica won. He knew exactly what it would mean: more fighting.

* * *

Erica faced Don the next day at noon. It was gloomy and damp, but the garou were not prone to allowing bad weather to interfere with their activities. Everyone was present, even Gerard, who normally didn't attend matches for rank. Peter started the duel and stepped out of the circle.

Despite Don's joke about his "longsword," he and Erica used rapiers. They swished their swords in salute and assumed a fighting stance.

"So you've a mind to take my rank from—" Don began. Erica whipped her rapier in a sweeping horizontal arc. She caught Don off guard, and though he was quick enough to leap backward, his last-second defense was insufficient, and a thin line of blood seeped through the front of his shirt.

"Oi, bad form!" he cried.

"I distinctly remember Peter beginning the match. 'Haps you should be paying more attention to the duel than the cheek."

"Point taken."

"Actually, she got that point," Peter whispered.

Don glared at Peter. "You're not helping. Very well, I'll take this seriously."

"Aye, we all believe that," said Peter.

"Shut up, brother, or I'm fighting you next."

The two combatants circled, each making an occasional feint or probing lunge to test the other's defenses. Don made a quick hop toward Erica and beat her blade down strongly with his own. He continued his advance and made two rapid thrusts, the first low and the second high. Erica easily deflected both strikes and wondered why Don was attacking so bluntly with almost no finesse. It was as though she were battling a beginner who thought he could bull his way past her guard and score with nothing but brute force.

"Ye gods, Don, are we fencing, or did you have something more primitive in mind?"

Don smiled in response, and with a sharp *thwack*, he knocked her sword out of position before stepping in and crashing into her with his shoulder. Too late, she realized the strikes with the sword were the feint and the true danger was Don's own body. Don may have been small, but so was she, and he had far more mass and muscle than she did. Unable to keep her footing, she landed heavily on her backside, bracing herself with her hands to keep from falling completely prone at his feet. With cool precision, Don took a step back and whipped his blade across Erica's chest just above her breasts, returning the shallow wound she'd given him earlier.

"I thought we said no slap fighting," she said.

"I didn't slap you."

"That was beneath you, Don."

"You wanted me to be serious; that was serious. You may thank our distinguished Alpha for that particular technique. He taught it to me himself, the painful way, back when we were trading the Beta rank with Peter every other month." He helped her to her feet. "And what have we learnt from this little activity?"

"That you don't fight fair?"

"'Tis not a fencing match, little sister; 'tis a fight for rank, and the rules aren't the same. Don't focus so wholly on the sword, lest you forget there are other weapons."

"Ooh, that'll leave a mark," Peter said.

"It already did," said Don, nodding to the cut on Erica's chest.

"You're right," Erica said. "Thank you, Don. Lesson learnt."

They resumed their game of cat and mouse with the testing blows coming faster and the series growing more complex. They orbited each other, coming together in a blur of motion and the ring of steel on steel, then separating again to consider, breathe, insult each other, and prepare to engage again.

Erica had sparred with Don many times, but she had never seen him fight like this. She couldn't tell whether he was suddenly possessed of a demon, if he'd been struck by genius, or if he'd simply been toying with her before. More likely, he had never been motivated to do his best until now. While she hadn't thought the duel would be as easy as her previous trials, she'd thought she knew what to expect. It was disconcerting to discover she'd been wrong. For all of Don's jests and frivolity, he was more than just good with a blade; he was a master.

In her other matches, her speed and agility had compensated for the size difference, but Don equaled her in all three aspects, and he was stronger. He launched another series of attacks, initially starting out at the centerline and alternating apparently at random between high, low, and middle, but consistently moving out to Erica's right side. Even when his strikes moved beyond her vital organs, they were still directed toward her sword arm and she had to respond. She discerned his intent, but even so, his rapid onslaught left her no time to take advantage, and she barely had enough time to return her guard to her center before the final lunge of the series threatened to skewer her. As good as Don was, however, Erica was a master in her own right. When his initiative played out or he paused to catch his breath, she'd be ready to go on the offensive and give as good as she had gotten.

It was the longest duel Erica had ever fought. Sweat flew and they panted heavily as the match wore on, neither of them able to make any definitive inroads into the other's defenses. When their stamina waned, each was able to score light wounds before launching into another long volley.

Erica employed Gerard's strategy of surreptitiously moving her rear foot in closer as she drove Don back. He noticed what she was doing and tried to step out of the way, but it was too late to save the match. Erica buried her blade deeply into his right side.

"Bloody hell," he grumbled. "I should have caught that sooner."

"Especially since it was another tactic borrowed from our Alpha," she remarked.

Erica removed the blade from Don's side and saluted, but he didn't reciprocate. He gave her an uncertain expression, sort of confused, then his eyes widened as he dropped to his knees, his sword clattering to the ground as he used his hand to support himself.

"Don? Are you hurt, or are you making fun?" Peter asked.

Don didn't answer. The color drained from his face, and he convulsed into a fetal position and vomited explosively. Seconds later, he lapsed into unconsciousness. Grace screamed and Mary rushed to his side.

"Peter," she said, her meek voice taking on an air of command, "turn him on his side, lest he choke."

Peter did as Mary instructed, and she used Don's sword to cut his shirt off and examine the wound, which was barely bleeding. She checked his pulse and lifted one of his eyelids to examine his pupils, then cursed. "We must get him inside," she said. "Straightaway!"

"What is it?" Gerard asked.

"I think he's bleeding inside. Pick him up and carry him to the infirmary. Haste is more urgent than comfort, and he'll not wake anyway."

She turned to Grace, who stood nearby, sobbing and chewing nervously on her long braid. "Go get Brother Marcus and bid him come to the infirmary. I have to do surgery, and I'll need a human to help me."

Grace ran into the keep, and Peter picked Don up and carried him inside. Mary and Erica followed.

"Surgery?" Erica said. "Mary, what did I do?"

"I must cut him open to tell, but I think you severed a major blood vessel, and that's not something that'll heal itself."

"Dear Lord, I've killed him!"

"Don't you be panicking on me, Erica O'Shaughnessy! I don't want two patients on my table."

Peter laid Don on one of the two operating tables. The garou and a handful of monks crowded in the door, and Mary said, "Send them out. Peter, find Grace a task or errand so she has something to do other than sit and fret. Grace, stop chewing on your braid. It'll only put hair in your stomach, and I'll have to cut you open to get it out. Peter, you find something else to do, too. You don't need to be in here."

"Mary—"

She put a hand on Peter's shoulder. "I'll take care of him, love," she said soothingly.

Somebody murmured something about taking orders from the Omega. It was no surprise; they did it every time Mary took charge in a medical situation. Except, of course, when they were the ones needing treatment.

"*Out!*" Gerard commanded, and they started to move away. Peter reluctantly left, too, herding them down the hall, chiding them for their comments, and reminding them that even Gerard deferred to Mary in such circumstances. He told Grace to follow him to the stables.

Erica stayed put.

"Erica," Gerard said.

"I'll not leave until I know he'll live." Her voice made it a statement; her eyes made it a plea.

"Let her stay, Gerard. She can help," Mary said as she finished undressing Don. "Erica, bring that tray under the table there to me. Have you done surgery before?"

"I've helped."

"Can you help me without becoming ill yourself?"

"Aye, I'll be all right."

"We'll use silver, so Brother Marcus will help with the wet work. You monitor Don's heartbeat and pour water into the wound to clear out the blood when I call for it. If his insides look like I think they will, we'll need quite a lot of it. Gerard, go get me a pail of water."

Brother Marcus passed Gerard on the way in. Mary cut into Don's abdomen. The blade of the knife she used was silver so they didn't have to fight Don's body, which was already trying to heal itself and close off the outer wound. The silver would slow the healing process long enough for Mary to locate and repair the severed artery. The drawback was that it made the operation more dangerous for Don. Though they didn't have to worry about infection, the fact remained that silver was toxic to garou.

Erica monitored Don's pulse as Mary cut through layers of skin and pulled apart fibers of muscle. Brother Marcus assisted by holding the wound open.

"Gerard," Mary said when he returned with the water, "you've prepared needles before, no?"

"Aye."

"Fix me a needle and cat gut. Erica, give me some water and clear away some of this blood. I can't see what I'm doing."

Erica took a cup and dipped it into the bucket, then slowly poured the water into the wound. With some of the blood cleared away, Mary was able to locate the artery and pinch it closed.

"'Tis a good clean cut," Brother Marcus said as Mary tied the artery off.

"He should be fine," Mary confirmed with relief. She squeezed her eyes shut to hold back tears.

"Was there a doubt?" Gerard asked apprehensively.

"Indeed, there was," she said bluntly. "He's lost quite a lot of blood. If he were human, he would already be dead. As it was, another minute or two would have killed him."

"Dear God," Gerard murmured.

"I'd say the errant reminder that we're not wholly immortal is a good thing, no? Keeps us alert. He will be weak for a while. The silver will cause his wound to heal more slowly, and he'll be in some pain. And his whole midsection will be a lovely shade of purple for a few days. A little more water, Erica."

Erica complied, and Mary sewed the two sections of the artery together. She couldn't repair it perfectly, but she only needed to tack it long enough for Don's body to heal itself. She finished stitching and untied the catgut to let the blood flow again. When she was certain the sutures would hold, she closed the incision.

After finishing, Mary went up a narrow spiral staircase to her room to change as Erica cleaned Don up and, with Gerard's help, moved him from the operating table to a cot. Mary returned after a few minutes and mixed a cup of foul-smelling liquid.

"If he wakes and I'm not in here, give him this. It will relieve his pain and help him sleep." She kissed Don's forehead and left the room.

"You should rest," Gerard told Erica. "I'll abide here with him."

Erica shook her head. "Not till he wakes."

"He'll be all right, Erica."

"Would you leave if you were in my position?"

"Nae, I wouldn't," he admitted.

Erica settled down in a chair near the bed. Gerard sat on the next cot. Mary brought Grace and Peter in a few minutes later, and they took up the vigil with them, Grace sitting on Don's cot and holding his hand and Peter next to Gerard. Mary went to work cleaning the infirmary. Grace no longer cried, but her cheeks were wet and her eyes were bloodshot and puffy.

"Did you two actually do anything out in the stable other than sit and fret?" Gerard asked them.

"No," said Peter.

"I found them sitting on the floor, holding hands and just waiting," said Mary.

"You didn't expect us to do any different, did you?"

"Nae, love, I didn't."

"He knew you would win," Gerard said to Erica.

"Not me. I didn't know we were so evenly matched. On my soul, I didn't mean to hurt him so badly."

"Of course you didn't," Grace said. "He could as easily have hurt you. We know where and where not to strike, but the smallest mistake could be lethal, and he was moving when you transfixed him. I'm surprised it doesn't happen more. The life of a garou in the White Guard is one of painful lessons."

"And what was today's lesson?"

"That mishaps occur, even for the most skillful," said Peter.

After a while, Don's breathing changed, and he started to toss his head and groan a bit, indicating that he had risen out of unconsciousness into a more normal, if fitful, sleep. Mary checked his pulse, then kissed him and sat on the third cot. The other garou and the monks stuck their heads in from time to time, checking on his condition.

Four hours after they had moved him from the operating table, Don opened his eyes. He blinked and peered around for a few seconds, getting his bearings and recognizing his surroundings, and his eyes settled on Grace. He smiled at her for a long moment and then looked over at Erica.

"I wish you could have seen your face," he said with a chuckle.

Erica raised an eyebrow and tried hard to keep from smiling. "I will remind you, Domhnall Williamson, that I now outrank you, and I'll not tolerate such disrespect."

"What wilt thou do, milady? Bust me to Omega Wolf?"

"Don't tempt me, underling."

Don started to laugh again but winced in pain. "Damn it, woman, what did you do to me?"

"She let out your hot air," Peter said. "Who knew you needed it?"

"I severed a blood vessel," Erica said, ignoring Peter.

"Here," said Grace, retrieving the cup from the table. "Drink this."

Don struggled to sit up, but Peter had to help. Grace held the cup for him. He took a sip and grimaced. "Ugh! You're going to poison me now too? Finish what she began in the courtyard?"

"It's pain medicine, you fool," said Grace.

"It tastes like lamp oil."

"If it tasted good, it wouldn't work as well," Mary said.

Don swallowed the medicine and then lay back down. "Is she Alpha Bitch yet?" he asked Peter.

"Let's see, what time of day is it?"

"What?" Erica said. "Do you think I would leave you lying here to go off and challenge someone else?"

"She nearly challenged *me* when we brought you in," Gerard said.

"Don, please forgive me," she asked somberly.

"There's nothing to forgive, little sister," Don said. "Do you think you're the first garou to nearly kill a packmate? I've been on that table before, as has everyone else in this house. You should see Peter and me when we fight for rank. Now, all of you go rest. I'm tired."

He closed his eyes, and Mary went upstairs to her room. Erica got up to join Gerard at the door. Peter grudgingly got up as well, but Grace stayed at Don's side.

"Call if he needs anything," Peter said before leaving.

5

Controversy

The moment politics become dull, democracy is in danger. —
Quintin Hogg, Lord Hailsham

Don was out of bed in a few days, and he was back to full
strength in another week. He complained that he had never been
laid up for so long, but it was mostly just to tease Erica. He was
restless, though, and he was anxious to get on the road. They
would leave for inductions in a few months, and he was looking
forward to a break in the monotony.

Gerard agreed wholeheartedly. It had been a long dry spell,
and waiting for the next mission wore on him, especially when
politics were so volatile. Gerard was a fighter, not a politician, and
though leadership was in his blood, he liked it better when he
didn't have to babysit disgruntled garou.

He wasn't surprised they were disgruntled. He and Don
weren't the only ones who got bored between missions. The
meekest of them was still a warrior. If there was no outlet for their
aggression, they turned on each other. It had been nearly three
years since Ardis's coven had attacked the House of O'Shea, and in
that time the House of Blevins had not received the first report of
vampire activity. Gerard wished they would stick their heads out
of the ground so the garou could have someone to fight besides
each other.

When Erica had come to Ballybrook, Gerard had intended to
initiate a relationship with her, but he had waited too long. He
didn't know what it was. Gerard wasn't shy, and he'd never been
reluctant to approach a female he was interested in, but every time
he had tried to approach Erica, something had caused him to
demur. Once she had started her advance through the ranks, he

had decided to distance himself so he could remain objective. He chided himself that it was just another excuse, but he knew there would be controversy, and he couldn't maintain impartiality if he was sleeping with her. It was hard enough to stay neutral as it was, and to say there was controversy was an understatement.

"The time has come for you to do something," Connor said as he sat at Gerard's desk a few weeks after Erica injured Don. This was the fourth such visit from the Quinns since the duel. "You have remained silent too long on this matter, Gerard. This female must not be permitted to come in and take over. She's been with the House of Blevins but three years, and she's already opposing the Alpha Bitch."

"She's not yet called Rhea out," Gerard reminded him.

"But she will. She's had her eye on Rhea's position since she came."

"Rhea doesn't mind. Indeed, she's in favor of it."

"My family and I'll not acknowledge her as Alpha Bitch."

"If she becomes Alpha Bitch, you will acknowledge her."

"I'll not have this!" Connor cried.

Gerard flinched, his ears smarting at Connor's loud voice. He was at a loss. Except for Mary, the Quinns had always been difficult, demanding this and that when they thought they were within their rights. They often got tired of whining and moved on, but sometimes Gerard gave them what they wanted just to shut them up. Connor was in the middle of the pack, but Abigail and Adam were low in the hierarchy—even lower now after losing matches for rank—but they were still an asset to the House of Blevins. Even Adam, who was their weakest fighter, was more than competent. Thus, Gerard put up with a certain amount of grandstanding. It didn't appear, however, that they were going to move on this time. He hadn't seen Connor this worked up since he had demanded Mary's demotion to Omega.

"If Erica petitions to duel Rhea," Gerard said, "there will be a moot, and you may voice your objections then."

"It'll be up to you to judge, not me. I'm only trying to make you understand that she's not good for the house."

"Tell me during the moot."

"But Gerard—"

"I grow weary of this, Connor," Gerard said. "I should not need to remind you that you are too low in the order to make such demands or that, having defeated you in a duel in due course set out by the traditions, Erica is your superior and you owe her all duty and respect. You shall be heard in the moot, but until then, you have no influence over anything she does."

"But you do—"

Gerard stood and glared Connor in the eye. "Connor Quinn, am I to take this as formal notification of your challenge for Alpha status?"

Connor opened his mouth to speak but thought better of it, closed it again, and lowered his gaze.

Gerard continued. "Despite your exhaustive protestations, Erica has broken no traditions and she has attained her rank honestly. The Order of the White Guard honors and respects talent, and that, she has. This conversation is finished. You are dismissed, and this matter is closed until there is a moot."

Connor got up and left, cowed.

Erica stepped into the doorway a moment later. "Thank you for that," she said softly.

* * *

Erica petitioned to duel Rhea on the next New Moon. When garou requested a challenge to the Alpha or Beta Wolves, the Alpha held a moot where the garou could give their input and opinions. There had been many such inquiries over the years, usually involving Peter, Don, and Owen jockeying for the Beta Wolf rank, and they were fairly painless. Nobody really had any objections. All three males were worthy, and much of the time, they were just asserting themselves because they were bored. It happened so often that Gerard had started to dispense with the formalities. He would convene the meeting, ask if anyone dissented—almost no one ever did—and adjourn.

This moot would be different, though. Not only did everyone have strong feelings on the subject, the garou typically had trouble following formal protocol. Gerard gave them leave to speak their minds at most any time, so to speak in turn and in formal voice was difficult to adjust to. But more, it was as if the mere idea of an official meeting compelled them to act out. Even he had trouble remembering to use formal voice. Beta moots were easy because the garou didn't have a real reason to misbehave, but there was no chance this one would go smoothly. And he already knew without a doubt who would behave and who wouldn't.

On the way to the common room for the moot, Don said, "Hey, Gerard, are you gonna gag Connor during this meeting?"

Gerard shook his head. "Not gonna happen, brother."

"Might as well go ahead and demote me now, then."

"I give him five minutes," said Peter.

"Do you two ever think of making my life easier?"

Don and Peter responded with exaggerated laughter.

The garou gathered around the long table in the common room with Gerard at the head. Rhea and Erica sat across from each other at his left and right, and the rest of the pack was seated according to rank. Mary sat at the other end with quill in hand, ready to take notes. When the proceedings concluded, she would record the minutes in the pack's log.

Gerard stood and began. "Erica O'Shaughnessy appeals this day for leave to duel Rhea Masters for her position as Alpha Bitch. As said office carries with it certain privileges and duties, consideration must be given to a candidate's merits above and beyond her prowess in combat. Thus, the Alpha Wolf calls for the opinions of all garou in the House of Blevins in regard to the matter. We shall use thy recommendations in our decision to approve or reject the request. Erica has proven herself in battle, but her worthiness to take the rank of Alpha Bitch has not yet been determined. Erica O'Shaughnessy, having defeated all eligible garou, thou hast earned the right to speak first on thine own behalf. By what right dost thou now petition to challenge the Alpha Bitch?"

Erica stood. She met each garou's eyes before she spoke, her voice firm and confident but not forceful. "I was a member of the House of O'Shea for seventy-nine years, and I've been a soldier in The Order of the White Guard for seventy-seven. Thirty years ago, I ascended to Alpha Bitch and remained so until most of the pack was killed and I came here. During that time, I served the best I could and fulfilled the roles of administrator, assistant midwife, and swordmaster."

"*She* served," Adam said.

Gerard raised an eyebrow, turned to Adam, and said, "Adam Quinn, if thou would care to enter thy petition to assume the rank of Omega Wolf, that hearing may convene immediately following this one."

Adam slouched in his seat.

When Erica sat down, Gerard stood. "Petition having been made and credentials having been presented, we open the floor for commentary and recommendation. Each of thee shall speak in turn, according to rank from lowest to highest, or with our permission. Speak quietly in formal voice. Outbursts will not be tolerated. A simple yea or nae will not suffice; thou must give cause. Adam Quinn, what sayest thou?"

"I dissent," Adam said and then sat down.

Gerard merely stared at him.

"My lord," Adam added.

Gerard continued to stare.

"What?"

"Thou hast naught to add?"

"My father will speak for us."

"Your father will speak in his turn. Stand up and give cause for thy dissent."

Adam gave his father an expression of sheer panic. Connor shrugged, and Adam stood back up and said, "She oversteps her bounds. She's been with the House of Blevins too short a time to be Alpha." He waited for Gerard to ask for more, and when he didn't, Adam sat down quickly.

"Maria Maldonado."

Maria stood. "I am sorry, Erica, but I must dissent. You move too fast; you forget your friends for more powerful ones. Grace and I need you, and you have no time for us anymore."

"Formal voice," Abigail singsonged.

Maria glared at her and said, "I dissent, my lord."

"Abigail Quinn?"

She didn't even bother getting up. "I dissent."

"Stand and give thy reasons, Abigail."

"My husband shall speak—"

Gerard slammed his fist on the table, and Abigail, Grace, and Mary jumped. "Nae, he shall not. Was it not thee who but a moment ago rebuked someone for a breach in protocol? How convenient for you to forget now that each member of the House of Blevins is responsible for the pack. There shall be no blind allegiance to anyone that supersedes the authority of Alpha or the well-being of the house as a whole. Now, stand and state the reasons for thy dissent."

Abigail stood and said, "Taking into consideration her acts of these past months, I am fearful of going into battle with her. We have been enemies, have we not? How might I be sure I can trust her with my life? She could allow me to die just to be rid of me."

"And that will be different if she *doesn't* become Alpha?" Don retorted.

"Tempt me, Don," Gerard dared him.

"Sorry," Don muttered.

Peter held five fingers up and mouthed, *five minutes.*

Gerard ignored him. "Abigail, sit down. Aeron Davies."

The Welshwoman stood. "I assent, my lord. I love Rhea, and she does a grand job, but I know she's tired and wants to spend more time with her Owen. Erica shall be a fine successor."

"Grace Monaghan."

Grace stood up, playing absently with her long braid. "Erica was Alpha Bitch of the House of O'Shea for many years," she said, "and she did indeed serve. She was honorable and forthright, and she did not assert her authority unjustly. When most of our house was slain, she brought us here quickly and without further injury. There is no reason to believe she would do any less here. I assent, my lord."

"Connor Quinn."

Connor stood and said, "You well know my vote."

"'Tis not a vote, Connor. Thou hast asserted thy opinions in an unofficial capacity for months. Now is the appropriate time and venue for them to be heard. Give unto me thy recommendation, and in the proper manner for an assembly such as this."

"Has it occurred to anyone that this female is responsible for the fall of the House of O'Shea? She dominated her Alpha so; he could not function. If she had submitted as she should, Sean O'Shea would have been a stronger Alpha, and they would not have all died in the ambush and subsequent fire. Ye keep saying she has proven herself in battle, but I have yet to see such matter. All we have are the results of a few duels and the word of two low-ranking garou."

Grace raised a hand. Gerard acknowledged her, and she stood. "We did not all die," she said. "Erica was only able to get two of us out and sustained grave injuries while trying to rescue another. Even after that, she managed to lead us here safely. Sean was not a weak Alpha, and Erica did not dominate him or the rest of us. Such speculation from anyone at this table not from the House of O'Shea is naught but gossip." She looked over at Connor and crossed her arms. "'Twould be interesting to hear the Quinns' thoughts on our present Alpha Bitch, for she's no more submissive than Erica. Furthermore, our rank says nothing of our integrity or our voice, and Maria's and my comments are just as valid as

Connor's. Erica has exterminated dozens of vampires, and if thou doubtest my word, pray feel free to peruse any records which have been salvaged from the lair in County Cork."

"For all we know, she could be working for the vampires!" Connor exclaimed.

"Are you daft?" Don cried.

"Hast thou evidence of such an alliance?" Gerard asked.

"Is eight dead garou not enough? She showed no grief for them. Oh, she sat in the chapel for a fortnight or so, but then she was up and about, socializing and carrying on as though nothing had happened. She tried to kill Don, a fact that everyone discounts 'cause she shed a few tears. She cares naught for us; she cares only about her own ambitions. If she is allowed to rise to Alpha Bitch, she will take over here as she took over the House of O'Shea. Once she ruins the House of Blevins, she'll move on to other packs and destroy them."

"Tread carefully, Connor," Peter said. "Thou art impugning the Alpha's ability to assert his authority."

"At the least, Gerard—my lord—she is bad luck, a curse for any house in which she lives. We should not take the chance that she will bring Ardis and his coven down on us."

Peter rolled his eyes.

Through clenched teeth, Gerard said, "If that is all, you may take your seat. Grace, you may sit down as well. Owen Masters."

Owen stood. "I assent, my lord. Erica's rapid advance is unseemly and may have caused some small offense, but she did so within the pack's traditions. Her deeds here and with the House of O'Shea are a testament to her ability to lead. For this reason, and because she has done naught truly outside the traditions, her request should not be denied."

Abigail said something under her breath about Owen's marriage to the current Alpha Bitch. Owen chose to ignore her, but Peter said, "Abigail, shut up."

Abigail turned to Gerard, who said nothing. As Beta Wolf, Peter was permitted to speak at any time. He had every right to call her down.

Owen sat down, and Gerard nodded to Don. "Domhnall Williamson."

Don stood up, but instead of talking to Gerard, he turned to Connor. "Connor, how did you come to be so stupid? Do you hear yourself?"

"Don," Peter said sharply.

Don turned to Gerard, eyes blazing. "If Connor had bothered getting to know Erica, he would know that she did mourn and still does to this day. She lost her father, for God's sake! As for the House of Blevins, she has shown nothing but concern. She did not try to kill me, and Connor knows that. What happened was merely a mishap. And she did more than shed a few tears; she assisted with surgery and never left my side till I was out of danger, something Connor never bothered to do the half a dozen times *he's* put me in the infirmary. She brought Grace and Maria near three hundred miles—"

"Thou makest it sound as though Grace and Maria were helpless," Adam said. "They're far from it."

"Were you there? No. Have you even thought to ask what condition they were in when they left? I'm betting that's a no, too. Questioning her intentions is bad enough, but to stand there and suggest that she's in league with vampires is beyond idiocy. If anyone breaches protocol, it is Connor and his family, who have used this moot as a vehicle to demonstrate their disrespect for their superiors and the Alpha's authority."

Peter was unable to suppress a snort of mirth. Gerard shot him a dark look and turned back to Don.

"Dost thou assent?" Gerard asked.

"Of course, I assent!" he replied, fairly shouting. Several garou winced and instinctively covered their ears. He sat down, his face red, his eyes black, and his human scent mixed with his lupine.

"Go take some time and cool thy anger," Gerard told him quietly.

"Bloody right." Don got up abruptly, knocking his chair over behind him and growling as he walked out of the room. The outside door slammed shortly thereafter.

"*Somebody* can't control his temper," Abigail whispered to her husband.

Grace narrowed her eyes hatefully at Abigail. "I've had just about enough of—" She stopped herself but couldn't suppress a low growl.

Gerard stared Abigail in the eye until she looked away. When she did, he said, "Abigail, thou art dismissed. Go to thy quarters and confine thyself there till morning."

Abigail recoiled as if he had slapped her, but she got up and left the room. When she was gone, Gerard said, "Need I remind all of thee again that this is a formal proceeding? I'll tolerate no further disruptions. I recognize this is a grave issue, but ye all know thy places, and as of now, ye shall mind them or take Mary's place at the end of the table. Peter O'Neill, Beta Wolf."

Peter stood. "I've made little comment regarding Erica's advance through the ranks, and I've tried to remain as neutral as I could. I've no knowledge about her capability as an administrator and thus cannot give an opinion, but no one can deny her fighting skills. Had she not proven herself in combat, she would not have been swordmaster of the House of O'Shea, and everyone at this table should know that. It is unfortunate that she hasn't had the opportunity to fight alongside us, but I've no doubt of her ability to lead others in a battle. I assent, my lord."

"Rhea Masters, Alpha Bitch, what sayeth thou?"

"I recognize Erica O'Shaughnessy's right to challenge me for the position of Alpha Bitch and assent, my lord."

Gerard glared at her, prodding her for more, and Rhea sighed and stood up. "I despise moots," she said. "In such matters, it is difficult to remain detached. We are too emotional a lot to argue objectively. I love Erica, and she is my dear friend, but even so, as Alpha Bitch, I've spent several months evaluating her capabilities. She is indeed a good administrator and a fast learner. I have faith that she'll be as good an Alpha as I or better. I assent, my lord."

Gerard regarded Erica. Her eyes and scent betrayed none of her emotions. There was a lot of anger in the room, even with Don and Abigail gone, but none of it was Erica's. She hadn't let any of the insults the Quinns had thrown at her get under her skin. She simply waited silently for his response. While she was definitely high-spirited, she didn't anger easily, and that was a plus.

Still, there were four dissenters out of ten. It wasn't a vote, and majority did not rule the House of Blevins. He did. But he had to keep the peace. Which decision would cause the most animosity? Most of the arguments were the result of emotion, not reason. The three highest-ranking garou were firmly on Erica's side, but emotion played a large part in their recommendations as well. Even Peter, whose case was the most objective, had made no secret about his fondness for her. It seemed the garou either loved her or hated her.

Abigail had made a valid point. With so much hostility, would they be able to rely on each other when they went into battle? But as Don had pointed out just as eloquently, would her rank make a difference either way?

And what about Gerard? There was no question that he had strong feelings for Erica, but he had worked too hard to keep his emotions out of play to let them influence his decision now. He did believe she wouldn't have been able to advance so quickly without superior abilities. Luck and charisma only carried one so far. But the Alpha Bitch rank in a White Guard pack carried a lot of administrative responsibilities, and Connor was right in stating that all he had to go on was the word of her packmates and a few of Rhea's observations.

Alpha and Beta ranks required longer waiting periods between challenges, and if he denied her petition, Erica could not make another request for six months. In that time, maybe the garou would be able to come to a consensus about her worthiness.

"On merit alone," he said, "I believe Erica is well deserving. However, to be an effective leader, one must have the support and trust of those she leads. Four dissenters of ten is too large a number to ignore, but I also cannot discount the fact that the higher-ranking garou are among her supporters. I'll take the matter under advisement and give my decision before the next New Moon. As for Don and Abigail, each will be reduced one rank."

He got up and left the room before anyone had a chance to argue.

6

Time to Ride

Women speak two languages—one of which is verbal. — William
Shakespeare

After the moot, Grace went to Abigail's room and found her on
her bed, crying.

"May I come in?" Grace asked softly. She didn't wait for Abigail
to reply; she just walked in and stood before her.

"Things were tense during the moot," she said. "I thought I
should come see you."

Abigail stood up. "We all said things that we—"

Grace's fist lashed out and caught Abigail squarely in the jaw.

"—regret," Abigail mumbled. Her eyes rolled back into her
head, and she collapsed onto the bed, unconscious.

* * *

Connor burst into Gerard's office and told him what Grace had
done. "I demand that you punish her immediately!" he cried.

"Truly, Connor? You're demanding? Again?"

Connor averted his eyes and lowered his voice. "My apologies,
Gerard, but you're always saying we don't condone violence
against subordinates."

"Nae, I say we don't condone violence against the *Omega*, who
is not allowed to defend herself, and even that hasn't stopped you.
The garou fight all the time, you among them. The only reason
you're here is 'cause Grace didn't give Abigail the chance to defend
herself. I won't punish her, but if it'll shut you up, I'll talk to her."

Gerard called Grace to his office the next morning.

"Grace, was it absolutely necessary to knock her out?"

"I'm sorry," she said, "I didn't mean to knock her out. I was trying to break her jaw in the hope that Mary would have to sew it shut and we wouldn't have to listen to her yammering for a fortnight or so, but my aim was off." She thought for a moment and said, "Hmm, maybe I should have tried to break Connor's jaw instead."

Gerard couldn't help chuckling. "Connor wants me to demote you."

"And yet when he picks a fight, nobody says a word. Truly, Gerard, if Abigail could take a punch, or if she had hit me, we wouldn't be having this conversation. Nae, I take that back; we would still be here. If it were anybody but Abigail, we wouldn't be here."

"The Quinns are a tight family, Grace. You can't do something like this and not expect Connor to retaliate."

"If Abigail is so cowardly that she needs Connor to fight her battles, I understand perfectly," she said, raising her voice so if Abigail was in the building, she could hear.

"Has anyone told you, you spend too much time with Don?"

"I'm sorry, my lord," she said. She wasn't, though, and Gerard knew it.

In truth, neither was Gerard. Abigail had opened her mouth one time too many. The moot had been an exercise in frustration, and Gerard was surprised there hadn't been more scuffles. Don and Connor had a really brutal fistfight a couple of times a year, and he had been expecting the two of them to go at it all morning.

Brother Herschel knocked on the door. "A messenger has arrived from Dublin, Gerard," he said.

"Whose messenger?"

"He said he represented the Talbots."

Gerard groaned. "The great hall, then. Show them to the guest suite for now and get Peter, Rhea, and Erica."

When Brother Herschel left, Grace said, "Haps they'll have a mission for us."

"We can only hope."

The lavishly decorated great hall was one of the few rooms in Ballybrook that bore any evidence that wealthy nobles had once lived there. It boasted tiled floors, high ceilings, and a dais at one end. Three large chairs—thrones, really—stood on the platform. A massive fireplace was built into one wall, and four chandeliers and dozens of sconces provided light. It was also one of the few rooms in the castle with windows. The columns were inlaid with gold and pearl mosaics of chariot races from Roman times and other epic battles, and elaborate tapestries depicting similar images hung on the walls. A red carpet ran from the double doors to the dais. The doors were kept closed most of the time, and a musty smell hung in the air. The space would be an excellent place for indoor training, but the garou disliked the garish room and preferred to train outside in the snow rather than use it. Peter hated the great hall more than anyone, and he would not go in unless Gerard gave him a direct order.

Today, unfortunately, they both had to be there. Peter mused about conceding his rank to Owen so he didn't have to sit there.

"Don't even think about it," Gerard said.

"Owen wouldn't mind. We could even forego the moot."

"You are in jest, no?"

"I guess. Well, partly, anyway. But just so you know, when I'm Alpha, the great hall is getting torn down."

"I don't need to worry, then, 'cause you'll never be Alpha."

"I might consent to it for five minutes just so I can get rid of the great hall."

"Come now, brother, you could never bring yourself to do it."

"You keep telling yourself that."

Whether they liked it or not, there was no other room suitable to receive a herald from a noble. If they saw the messenger in a more humble place, he would tell his master, who might take it as an insult. This particular herald was from Malahide, home of Sir John Talbot, an individual few people dared insult. The man was big and intimidating, and mothers all over Europe frightened their children into good behavior with threats of The Talbot.

Gerard sat on the center throne, flanked by Rhea and Peter. Fortunately, looking unhappy to be sitting there wasn't against any rules of etiquette. Erica showed the messenger and his guards into the room.

"May I present the herald for Lady Margaret Talbot of Malahide in County Dublin," Erica said. She gave a little bow and stepped aside, and the messenger moved forward.

"Greetings, Brother Gerard Blevins. I present thee a letter from my mistress, Lady Margaret Talbot, wife of Sir John Talbot, Lord Furnival, Marshal of France, Earl of Shrewsbury, Wexford and Watford, and Lord Lieutenant of Ireland." He handed an envelope to Erica, who brought it to Gerard.

Gerard broke the seal, opened the letter, and read feminine and highly embellished script:

> *My Dear Brother Gerard Blevins:*
> *Upon advice from my brother Richard Talbot, the Exalted Archbishop of Dublin, I write to thee with an appeal for assistance.*
>
> *In recent weeks on my land has been an illness affecting the blood. First, only serfs and commoners were in bed with the sickness, which weakens or kills even the sturdiest among our servants, but verily it has now begun to affect the nobility. In mine own family has been more than two in bed with pale complexion and weakness. My beloved cousin is not expected to live out the week.*
>
> *My physicians have proved unsuccessful in finding a cure. But my brother Richard Talbot, the Exalted Archbishop of Dublin, informs me that thy order is familiar with such a disease and that thou might use thy skills to rid my land of this affliction. Thou shalt be well compensated for thine efforts.*
>
> *I remain yours,*
> *Lady Marguerite Beauchamp Talbot*

"Take word back to thy mistress that we shall come to Dublin within the week," Gerard told the messenger. "Erica, have Brother Herschel see to our guests' needs before they return."

The messenger nodded and followed Erica from the room, with his two guards clanking along behind him.

When Erica closed the door, Peter said, "Finally!"

Rhea had to laugh. "Just think of Lord Furnival's face when he finds out Lady Margaret is calling on the Church for help."

"Thankfully he's off to war, so he won't be around while we're there, and we won't be there for the temper tantrum. I've met the man, and many of the rumors are true. He's not to be trifled with. Even as garou, I'd rather not clash with him. It would have been nice if they'd sent for us a month ago. It's almost time to leave for inductions."

"Hopefully we'll be back home in time to make it," said Rhea. "It'd be a shame to miss such a trip after sitting at home doing naught for three years."

"To say nothing of the fact that this will put us in Malahide a week before the Full Moon," said Gerard.

"We'll have to get away for a few days," Peter said.

"I'll work it out. Tell the garou we shall leave at first light." Erica returned from showing the messenger out, and he said, "Erica, my decision will have to wait till we get back."

"Understood." She smiled at him.

"What?"

"Just you. In this room. Looking uncomfortable."

Gerard had to bite his lip to keep from smiling back at her.

* * *

If a report of vampire activity was close to home, Gerard would send two or three garou to investigate. They would take care of the matter if the coven was small enough, or they would send for the rest of the pack. At nearly five days' ride, all the back and forth was impractical, so all of the garou would go to Dublin.

The garou spent the rest of the day preparing for travel. They reshod horses, checked weapons, honed blades, and packed provisions. Everyone moved with a sense of purpose, and arguments were set aside. Plans for battle reminded them that when fighting a vampire, there was no time to squabble over politics. In all likelihood, this would be a coven of just a few vampires and there would be little or no bloodshed, but the garou hoped it would be a chance to get their hands dirty.

For the most part, Gerard was as exhilarated as the rest of the garou, but he couldn't help having concerns. Connor's words hung heavily in his mind; he had said outright that the Quinns wouldn't follow Erica if so charged, and Gerard didn't trust them to have her back. He knew beyond doubt that he could trust Erica, but there was still too much potential for something to go badly wrong.

As if thinking about Erica had summoned her, she came into the stable where Gerard was working with his horse. She didn't say anything, just waited for him to acknowledge her. When he did, she said, "You don't like me."

"'Tis not my lot to like you. 'Tis mine to lead this house and determine if you can do the same."

"I'll take that as a no, then."

Gerard offered his trademark icy stare.

Erica pouted and moved closer. "You've avoided me for three years, Gerard. Do you not even like me a little? There's naught I can do about the Quinns, but I had hoped you and I could mend our rift before we go to Dublin. I need you to trust that I'll pull my weight in battle. Connor's remarks about me bringing down the House of O'Shea—"

"No one believes such things, Erica, not even Connor. He merely made the most outrageous accusations he could think of, and no one put stock in his words."

"What of you, then? I know you agree with him about my attitude, if nothing else. But I can help you, Gerard, if you will let me. You need not like me, but it would make things easier if we could get along. That is, unless you intend to reduce me to Omega for my insolence."

"I do not intend to demote you. If I did, I'd have already done so. That doesn't mean you may come to me after the moot to try and sway my decision."

"Your decision's already been made, my lord. I meant what I said about making peace before we leave for Dublin."

"Don't call me 'my lord.'"

"Don calls you 'my lord.'"

"That's different. I may not like the way you attained your status, but you did come by it fairly and within the traditions. My advisors know you better than I. They trust you wholeheartedly, and I trust them. But I am grateful to you for giving me leave to dislike you."

With that, Erica smiled. Gerard felt heat climb up through his neck and face. Her scent changed, and warmth poured from her body. "You *do* like me," she said softly.

"You can go now, Erica." As hard as he tried to keep his voice cold and impersonal, he was barely able to speak above a whisper.

"Want to go with me?"

"Nae, I do not."

She held his gaze for a moment, stood on her tiptoes, and placed a soft kiss on his lips. He responded, reaching up to caress her cheek as she moved in closer and opened her mouth to his.

"Aye, I do," he admitted when he pulled back, "but there are matters more urgent than this."

"Having you say it is enough for now."

Erica turned and left the stable. Gerard would have given up the struggle and followed her without hesitation if they hadn't been leaving for battle the next day.

Distractions would get you killed.

7

Looking for Clues

A long series of sterile weeks lay behind us, and here at last there was a fitting object for those remarkable powers which, like all special gifts, become irksome to their owner when they are not in use. — Blaise Pascal

When they arrived at Malahide Castle north of Dublin, Lady Talbot put the garou up in the plush suites of the guest wing with a view of Dublin Bay. They only saw her once; their dealings were exclusively with Richard, Archbishop of Dublin.

The garou barely noticed the majestic vistas, marble flooring, brocade upholstery, and overstuffed featherbeds. The extravagant decor was just so much background. They were warriors, and with the sole exception of Peter, commoners all. If they hadn't been so busy, the splendor of Malahide Castle would have made them as uneasy as Ballybrook's great hall did. As it was, they ignored it and began to investigate.

According to the archbishop, otherwise healthy people were dying overnight or becoming bedridden with some strange form of anemia. "The commoners are sure it is vampires," he said. "Vampires. Can ye imagine? Vampires in Dublin! Peasants and sailors are a superstitious lot. Such tales are not for the sophisticates of the city but for the backward workers and farmers who paint ancient symbols on their barns."

"How did you know to contact us?" Gerard asked.

"'Twas the Archbishop of Cork advised me to send for you. Some cohorts of yours were of assistance to them upon a time with similar matters."

The garou hedged around questions the archbishop asked about the nature of the investigation, but he didn't ask many. It was pretty obvious they were soldiers and not physicians or monks. Though he adamantly denied the existence of vampires, he gave the impression that he might be afraid of any answers they did give. He was stuffy, imperious, and too wealthy for a man of God, but for all that, he did appear faithful. The existence of such supernatural creatures, and the fact The Order of the White Guard counted itself among them, would shake his faith more than he could bear.

Once in a while, the garou were given enough information to go in, eliminate the threat, and leave, but the hard truth was that vampires rarely came to them, so reconnaissance was necessary. The garou may have been good fighters, but that didn't always mean they were good investigators. Thus, Gerard tried to pair the less skillful with those who were better at it or have them focus on more conventional tracking.

The garou's enhanced senses and hunting experience made them all excellent trackers, even in human form. Unfortunately, vampires had no discernable scent, making them difficult to track. There were some trails leading through the meadows west of town, but they were marked with scents and led in a circle. The scents themselves were suspicious, not those one might find outside of town, but if vampires had made the tracks, they had done so in such a manner as to throw the garou off the real trail. Also, although the garou had never seen it, there had been rumors that vampires could fly, meaning they might be able to leave no trail whatsoever.

While others talked to villagers and merchants or went to the docks to speak to sailors, Peter interviewed the aristocrats. As a noble himself, Peter spoke their language, but he would rather have done most anything other than associate with the gentry. He had abandoned that way of life long ago, and it grated on him to have to act as if he cared for anything those overdressed, over-perfumed dandies had to say. The English nobles were even worse than the Irish. At least the Irish chiefs cared more about a fight and a good ale than whether their shoes matched their doublets. All of them were petty and selfish at best, and at worst, they would kill their own mothers to suit their ends.

Peter had been to dozens of castles, and most were essentially the same: oversized, ostentatious, and crowded, and they all smelled like chamber pots. This one was no different, and it was easy to find his way around.

One of Malahide Castle's three ballrooms was busy, even in the middle of the day, and a handful of courtiers milled around. Sporting his White Guard dress uniform, Peter fit in nicely with the other military types and those who just wanted to *look* like knights. His crisp white shirt was tucked into black pants, which were in turn tucked into his boots. His brocade doublet was maroon with gold and black trim and black laces. His boots, gloves, and sword belt were all black leather. His shirt and doublet were usually open at the neck to show a silver crucifix and the scar it produced, but for this occasion, he had tied the laces tighter so as not to arouse too many questions about the scar.

He strolled through the room, sipping a cup of excellent wine a servant had handed him when he entered and eavesdropping on conversations until he heard something he could use.

Four ladies stood in a huddle near large double doors that opened onto a tiled balcony, letting in a fresh breeze. Two were young and pretty, one was rather plain and frumpy, and the fourth was elderly. All were overdressed for midafternoon. He overheard one of them say, "Lady Anne Beardsley alone has lost two serfs to the disease."

Peter approached the group. "Ladies," he said.

The one who had spoken of Lady Beardsley's serfs turned and gave Peter a winning, fake smile. "Good day, sir knight," she said with overt politeness.

Though he would have loved to see her reaction, he didn't bother to tell her he hadn't been a knight in well over 200 years.

"I've not seen you before. Are you new to Dublin?"

"Aye, milady. I am here as a guest of Lady Margaret and the archbishop. You are...?"

"Countess Elizabeth Main," she said, holding her hand out to him. The other ladies smiled knowingly and wandered off.

Peter took her hand and kissed it, glad she was one of the pretty ones—so he was shallow; he had to have *some* faults. "'Tis a pleasure, Countess. I'm Sir Peter O'Neill." He cringed inwardly when he called himself "Sir," but it was better than his real title.

"O'Neill!" she cried, loudly enough for her voice to carry across the room.

Peter briefly mused about choking the life out of her but decided it would probably be frowned upon here after afternoon tea.

"Would that be the Belfast O'Neills or the Tyrone?" she asked him.

"Well, we all came from Tyrone originally, now, didn't we?"

The countess tittered. "How are you enjoying Malahide, Sir Peter?"

"'Tis lovely, but what is all this I hear about a blood disease?"

"Oh, it's just dreadful! Lady Anne has lost serfs, and others have lost servants. It has been so inconvenient for them."

"I can imagine. Was it just the servants?"

"Oh, a few sailors and merchants, but that doesn't matter."

"Well, is it all over town?"

"I don't know about Dublin, mind you, but in Malahide, all the cases I've heard about are between here and Beard."

"On the west side? I rode through there on the way in."

"You would think the peasants would take better care of themselves, wouldn't you? They're so dirty!" The countess leaned in close and lowered her voice. "I'm not one to repeat gossip, but I heard that a relative of Lady Margaret's passed to the illness."

Peter feigned outrage. "Oh, Lord!"

"I don't like to speak ill of the dead, but rumor has it that he had a mistress in Beard and contracted the disease from her."

"That's scandalous."

"Oh, pshaw. All lords take their serfs into their beds. Present company excluded, I'm sure."

"'Tis not proper to speak of such things."

"Oh, me, I've done it again, haven't I?" she said sheepishly. "I speak my mind far too often. It is unseemly."

"No offense taken, milady."

"Oh, but this blood disease is such an unpleasant subject. Let us talk about happier things. Do you see the lady over by the fireplace? The one with the gown the color of something that came out of her nose. I'm not one to repeat gossip, but I heard she..."

* * *

Beard was a village on the westernmost edge of the district, actually closer to Swords Castle than Malahide. Swords was the archbishop's residence, and the Church didn't claim proprietorship of surrounding land. Thus, responsibility for the people of Beard fell to Malahide.

Beard was one of the poorest, dirtiest places Don had ever seen. The district seemed to be made of mud, and the shacks looked as if they were in danger of sinking into the mire with the next big rainstorm or falling over with a brisk wind. The stench was overwhelming.

"How can they live like this?" Grace said with pity.

"Makes you thankful for what you've got, no?" said Don. "I'd love to have a word with the landowner, but it would probably just make things worse."

They approached a man who was tinkering with a rickety cart. He eyed them suspiciously, and fear practically burst into his scent. "What you want?" he asked unceremoniously.

"We were sent by the Church," said Grace. "To learn about the plague that has afflicted the area."

"God can't help us."

"Maybe we can," said Don.

"Nae," he insisted. "Go 'way."

Everyone they talked to gave them more of the same.

"They're stubborn," Grace said as they plodded down the muddy street.

"They're scared," said Don.

"Aye, of us."

"Well, you *are* scary."

Grace punched him on the arm.

"See? This is what I'm on about. I'm terrified of you."

A boy came running up the street, feet flying and mud sloshing all around him. He didn't even slow down when he reached Don and Grace, and he tried to push his way between them. Don grabbed him.

"Whoa, slow down, little man. What's the rush?"

"Sun's setting."

"Not for a while. You've got time to get home."

"I don't wanna be out when it gets dark. Please let me go."

"Go on, then. Just be careful."

The boy took off again, slipped in the mud and fell, but he scrambled to his feet and kept going.

Don and Grace walked through the streets for a while, but all they got were leery stares and wary eyes watching them pass. The closer it got to nightfall, the fewer people were outside. By full dark, the streets were deserted and silent. Even inside the homes, there was very little talking. It was as if the villagers were hiding, which, Don supposed, they were.

The only voices they heard were those of Rhea and Owen, who were in the next district a half mile away.

"Should we go meet them and ask if they've turned anything up?" Grace asked.

"Aye, but let's make one more pass through Beard first."

Grace nodded. "These people are afraid of more than just a blood disease."

"Keep those pretty green eyes open," said Don. "Haps we can catch ourselves a vampire."

* * *

The garou gathered around a dining table in the guest quarters the next day to report on their investigations.

"One of the courtiers mentioned that the blood disease is most prevalent between here and Beard, a village on the west side," Peter said. "They've lost a dozen men and women in that area, one or two sailors, a merchant, and the one noble."

"Grace and I spoke with quite a few people in that district, and they didn't take kindly to outsiders," said Don. "No one told us anything. They wouldn't even speak of the illness."

"They were as afraid of us as they were of whatever was making them ill," said Grace.

"The only thing we got while we were there was muddy."

"Wanna trade?" said Peter.

"I think I'd rather slosh through the mud, thank you. Now that I think about it, there was the one lad who was unusually afraid of the dark."

Grace nodded. "This wasn't your normal fear of the night; 'twas much more severe, near to the point of terror."

"We'll go back and try again," said Don. "If we can convince them we can help, they may be more forthcoming."

"Offer to pay them for information," Gerard suggested. "A coin might go a long way toward getting them to talk."

Once Don and Grace persuaded the residents of Beard to open up—and started paying them—everyone had something to contribute. They were all firmly convinced that the affliction was the work of vampires, or demons at the very least. The interviews suggested that the creatures were not actually living in town. They came in from farther west, struck quickly, and then got back out, which was why the majority of the attacks were concentrated in Beard. Not all the victims perished; more than half ended up in bed and recovered in a few days, but they had no memory of any sort of assault. The number of victims was low enough that the garou estimated it to be a small coven, possibly even a solitary vampire.

"I've never heard of a vampire that did not kill its victims," said Grace.

"'Tis actually fairly common," said Aeron. "If a vampire wishes to stay in one place for a while, it finds it easier to avoid notice if it doesn't kill its victims."

"Aye," Gerard said, "but we've never seen a vampire that only kills *some* of its victims."

"'Haps we did," Connor replied, "and investigations only turned up one half or the other."

"Or think on this," said Maria, "he tried to control himself and not kill, but he was no good at it, and he had accidents."

"It is possible," Connor said, "especially if it's young."

Owen said, "It is evident that we shall not locate its lair on the word of the townspeople."

"Nae," Rhea agreed. "They don't know where their attackers go when they leave."

"They may have left altogether," Owen speculated. "We have received no word of new attacks since we came."

"We've not been here long enough to assume such," said Gerard. "Could be they are hiding themselves or hunting in another part of town."

"Which would mean they know we're here," said Don.

"We patrol then," Peter said, and the others agreed.

The garou set up a staggered patrol with pairs covering different areas and watching for signs. Although they focused mostly on Beard and the road to Malahide, they made sure to maintain a presence in other areas of town as well, to listen for word that the vampires were attacking elsewhere. Three nights later, they had still seen no evidence of vampire activity and the gossip was mostly about how cases of the disease had dropped off.

"'Haps they've indeed moved on," Rhea offered.

"It has been longer than I would have thought for a sole vampire or small coven to hide," Gerard said. "Unless they're planning something."

"It doesn't feel like Ardis," said Erica, "and I've never seen other vampires set up a trap."

"How does Ardis feel, exactly?" Connor sneered.

"Ardis doesn't strike and leave as these vampires have done. He sets up housekeeping, feeds, and brings a dozen vampires across, and he doesn't try to hide."

"He actually tries to draw us out," Peter told her. "He calls Gerard, Don, and me his friends, and he all but dotes on Gerard. Once he even tried to hug him."

Erica couldn't help laughing at the thought of the big vampire trying to hug Gerard.

"'Tis not funny," Gerard said.

"It's hilarious," said Peter.

Don said, "We've seen him kill other garou in our pack and tell his followers to let the three of us be."

"Why does he do that?" Erica asked.

"We haven't a clue."

Unfortunately, we're running out of time," Gerard said. "The Full Moon is in three days, and I do not want to be in Lord Furnival's castle then."

"Surely it's happened before," said Erica. "What have you done in the past when the Full Moon came during a mission? It was rare in the House of O'Shea, but if we had to, we made an excuse and left town for a few days."

"Aye, with us, too, but they usually don't like it," said Don.

"There's no alternative, unless luck is on our side and we can complete the mission in the next two days," Gerard said.

"A thought," said Adam. "What if they *have* been hiding, waiting us out? We'll not be helpless on the Full Moon, but we'll not have weapons, and we won't be patrolling. It would be a convenient time to attack."

"It is a problem," Owen agreed, "but there is naught we can do about the town while we are in the woods in wolf form."

"The best we can do is guard ourselves against an attack," Gerard said. "Stay close, within howling distance at all times, and just pray that the vampires don't wreak havoc while we're gone."

* * *

Gerard made up an excuse about pressing business to attend to nearby and assured the archbishop they would return in a few days. When the Full Moon approached, the garou retreated into the wilderness and surrendered to their wolf forms.

Garou had three forms: human, wolf, and *faol mòr*. *Faol mòr* form was a monstrous half-human, half-wolf form and was extremely rare. Garou typically shifted to their wolf form, which was similar to that of a conventional wolf, only much larger. Owen was the biggest garou in the pack, both in human and wolf form. He was six feet four inches tall and heavily muscled in human form. As a wolf, he could stand face to face with Don and look him in the eye. The garou's senses were also stronger than those of a typical wolf, with their hearing being the strongest. They could hear and distinguish one another's howls from as far as twenty miles away. The most significant difference was their eyes, which turned solid, inky black. The eyes were normally the first to shift, and a garou fighting a shift was easy to spot, if for no other reason than the change in eye color.

Garou could shift to wolf form at will, but they were forced into that form on the Full Moon. They could also lose control and shift when extremely angry or under stress. They kept their minds, even when they lost control of the shift, although they tended to think differently. Their thoughts and ideas were simpler, more primal. They cast off most of the inhibitions of human society, and their instincts and actions were more visceral.

It was during their time in the forest near Malahide that Gerard and Erica first made love, so caught up in their wildness and the freedom of the wolf form that they cared little for anything as mundane as politics or the war against vampires. Those things would still be there when they returned to their human forms, but for that night, all that existed was the Moon, the two of them, and their desire. When they returned to Malahide, they didn't speak of it, but their relationship had taken a turn and there was less tension.

That is, until Erica went to Gerard and asked to be paired with Abigail on patrol.

* * *

"You know," Gerard said, "I think sometimes you do things like this just to get on my nerves."

"Sometimes I do," Erica admitted. "But not this time."

"Why would you put yourself—and Abigail, for that matter—in that situation?"

"I can think of no other way to convince her I'm not a threat to her."

"What if she's the threat to *you?*"

"We'd know then, wouldn't we?" She flashed her pixie grin at him, and he realized it was true: she did use that grin to manipulate him. Well, not this time.

"Nae, Erica," he said, "'tis not gonna happen."

"Will you at least agree to think on it? It doesn't have to be tonight, and it doesn't have to be *every* night. Just give me one."

"You've been patrolling with Mary. Would you have me pair her with Connor?"

"Put her with one of the other pairs for the night. Connor can patrol with Adam and Aeron."

She gave him a pleading expression, and Gerard half expected her to say, "*Pleeeease,*" like a child asking for a treat.

Well, *maybe* this time.

"I'll think on it," he said, "but not tonight."

"Thank you."

"Don't thank me yet. I've not agreed."

"But you will."

"So I was correct: you *are* doing this to get on my nerves."

8

Blood and Fire

Evil is easy and has infinite forms. — Blaise Pascal

There was nothing to indicate that vampires had attacked during the Full Moon. In fact, they waited another fortnight to finally come out of hiding. Gerard and Peter found one sitting in a pub on the second night of the New Moon, talking to a prostitute. They sat near the fireplace in an effort to mask their scents and watched silently as the vampire talked the woman into leaving with it and exited the pub. Gerard and Peter went outside and split up to flank the creature.

Gerard stepped in front of the vampire as it turned a corner. It stopped and eyed the silver sword in his hand.

"I heard about you," it said. "I didn't believe the tales were true, but here you stand in front of me. Who would have thought?" It grabbed the female and pulled her in front of itself, thereby blocking any attack Gerard had.

"My, wasn't that courageous!" said Gerard. "Do you think I'll not put my blade through her to get to you?"

The woman screamed and tried to wriggle free.

"You won't kill a mortal," the vampire said.

Gerard shrugged. There was no point in denying it; the creature was right. "You're a mite chatty, aren't you? Let the lady go, and we shall settle this between ourselves."

The vampire laughed. "Lady! Are you daft? She's just a common whore that no one'll miss. Besides, you wield silver. That's hardly a fair fight."

While Gerard had the vampire distracted, Peter moved swiftly up behind it and slammed his silver dagger into the hollow at the base of its skull. It fell dead, and the woman wailed and ran away. Peter retrieved his dagger, wiped the blood on the vampire's tunic, and stood back as Gerard drew his sword and decapitated the vampire.

"So much for a good fight," Peter said gloomily.

* * *

Rhea couldn't believe her luck. A vampire was actually stalking her! It seemed to have no fear of the large, silver sword at her side. Or maybe it just couldn't sense the silver from its distance. Even so, surely it could tell she was garou from her scent. It couldn't think it could defeat her. It was either very young or very stupid. Or both.

When they had first spotted the vampire, Owen had ducked into a doorway until the creature passed, then trailed behind it. It also didn't seem to know or care that he was following.

Rhea sat on a bale of hay and fiddled with the laces of her boots. The vampire rushed, knocking her to the ground and pinning her arms beneath her. Rhea brought her knee up and kicked the vampire in the testicles. It grunted and rolled to the ground. As Rhea reached for her dagger, it snarled, "You have bigger problems than me, werewolf."

Before it could say anything else, Owen's blade came down, taking off part of its head.

"Have you ever seen so foolish a creature?" he said as he helped Rhea up.

"Not in many years," she replied, "and that worries me."

Owen nodded. "If it seems too easy, something is likely afoot."

"Precisely. The Cartha's vampires were feral and didn't have enough sense to know or care that they were stalking someone who could kill them."

"But they normally did not speak."

"It said we had bigger problems. Do you think it was sacrificed to give us a message?"

Owen used his shirttail to wipe a spot of blood from Rhea's cheek. "If so, it was indeed foolish. Such a message only leaves more questions."

"It called me 'werewolf.'"

"It is not unheard of these days."

"Nae, but I've not heard any vampires use it before save Ardis and his covens."

Owen groaned. "Lovely."

* * *

After much beseeching from Erica, Gerard finally agreed to pair her with Abigail for one night. He waited for the New Moon in the hopes of reducing any chance of a conflict. Abigail was one of the least aggressive garou in the pack, but there was still no point in courting disaster.

Erica had thought the trip to County Dublin might be an opportunity to prove herself to the Quinns, but it had just been a source of new ammunition to use against her. Now it was her fault they couldn't find any vampires. She wondered if the Quinns had a real reason for hating her so. Maybe she was impertinent, but she certainly wasn't the only one. Erica thought if she could get some time alone with Abigail, she might be able to win her over. So far, all Abigail had done was ignore her.

They patrolled the district for an hour, and neither spoke a word. Abigail was alert and had more on her mind than picking on Erica. It didn't relieve all the tension, but it helped.

Beard was the worst place Erica had ever been. Cows and chickens roamed the streets but avoided the garou. An undernourished dog wandered up and sniffed at them, then slinked away with its tail tucked between its legs. A few shacks had small gardens of sickly crops behind them, but mostly there was mud. The odor was terrible. The salt and fish smell that was pervasive so close to the sea was accompanied by those of feces, mold, and garbage. The air was choked with smoke. Erica couldn't imagine living like this. The life of a White Guard garou could be hard, but they wouldn't starve if they missed a day of work and they rarely lacked decent shelter. Erica thanked God that she had been born into better conditions than those she walked through and prayed that these poor people had some joy in their lives.

Abigail's scent was laced with sadness; perhaps she was thinking the same thing. Maybe their sympathy for the less fortunate would be the common ground on which they could start.

Erica had little time to consider the notion. As they passed a rickety barn, they heard a muffled cry. Abigail took the front door, and Erica went around the side of the building, where she found a second, larger entrance, probably for wagons and other implements.

The scents inside indicated a recently dead human, hay, manure, and lamp oil. It was very quiet; the only sound was

Abigail's breathing. Erica drew her sword and pushed the door inward. A few pieces of farm equipment hung on the walls, and the floor was piled with hay, upon which lay the body of a young woman. A lantern sat on the floor a few feet away from the haystack, and another hung on a hook by the opposite door, where Abigail stood smirking at her.

Something leapt onto Erica's back, grabbed her by the hair, and flung her across the barn. She crashed into the wall, and her head hit something hard. Colors and images swam before her eyes as she staggered. A bright flash and the smell of blood helped clear her head, and she saw the opposite wall ablaze and a vampire tossing the second lantern onto the pile of hay.

Fire again. Wonderful.

She didn't see Abigail, and Erica assumed she had left the barn, but Abigail's painful cry drew her attention. She peered through the flames to see Abigail impaled on something that appeared to be nothing more or less than an instrument of torture. Six vertical wooden slats were connected by two horizontal ones, attached to a steel bar and hung on the wall by several rings. Six metal spikes protruded from each of the wooden slats. Four of them jutted out from Abigail's trembling body. The vampire's aim had been poor; otherwise it might have killed her instantly. As it was, the implement only pierced her left side. She hung a few inches off the floor, trying desperately to put her toes down and take the weight off the spikes. Erica got a piece of wood and placed it under Abigail's feet, and the pinned garou sighed with relief.

The vampire had somehow bent two of the spikes so Abigail could not be pulled off easily. Erica was strong, incredibly so by human standards, but the strength and speed the vampire must have used to bend the steel astounded her.

"He moved so fast I couldn't even see him," said Abigail. "How do they move so fast?"

Fueled by hay and rotten wood, the fire spread rapidly through the barn. The flames would consume the building in minutes, and they would be roasted alive. Abigail screamed as her tunic caught fire. Erica took her own tunic off and smothered the flames.

"Gerard, I need you!" Erica shouted.

"Get yourself out!" Abigail cried.

"I can't make this painless, but I think I can bend these spikes back."

"Erica, go!"

Erica ignored Abigail's urging, wiped sweat from her brow, and using her tunic as a cushion, she grabbed hold of the first spike. It had penetrated Abigail's pelvis, breaking it, but it was bent far enough up for Erica to get a good grip. She growled with the effort as she fought to straighten it. "Bloody fire," she grumbled. "I hate fire!"

Her arms and legs began to ache as her wolf form threatened to take over. If she shifted and couldn't use her hands, Abigail would die.

"Not now," she said with a wolfen snarl.

The second bent spike was just below Abigail's breast. The point was curled tightly only a couple of inches from the end, and it was impossible to get a grip, even with the tunic. How the vampire had been able to do it without leverage was beyond her. The fiend's handiwork was a harsh reminder that there were still things about them that the White Guard didn't know or understand. Erica wrestled with the spike in vain until she felt a searing pain and looked down to see her leg on fire.

"Bloody hell!" she shouted as she slapped at the flames with the tunic. By the time the fire was out, Abigail's clothes were burning again. She couldn't keep fighting the fire; she had to get Abigail off the spikes.

Abigail's scent carried pain but also abject grief and no small amount of fear, and she began to cry. "Go," she said miserably. "Please just get out."

"Why are garou always telling me to leave them in burning buildings? I'm not leaving you here, so hush. The second one is too near the end; I can't bend it. My God, how did it do this?"

"Erica, I'm so sorry. Forgive me."

"Whatever you did, consider us even," she said regretfully, and then she grabbed Abigail around the waist and pulled straight toward herself. Abigail shrieked as the spike caught on her rib, and Erica pulled even harder. Abigail finally came off the apparatus, and they tumbled to the floor.

* * *

Gerard and Peter heard Erica's call and hurried through the village. The smell of smoke was so widespread that they didn't suspect it was the cause of Erica's distress until they saw the burning barn. A vampire was running in their direction. Peter drew his sword and stepped in the creature's path. It halted before him, hissing and baring its fangs. Peter nodded at Gerard, who left him with the vampire and continued down the street toward the fire.

Inside the barn, Abigail screamed. Gerard darted for the door, but she and Erica crashed through. They collided, and all three of them fell to the ground. Gerard recovered and knelt over the two females, who lay in each other's arms, singed and covered in blood. Abigail was unconscious, but Erica, who was naked from the waist up, peered up at him groggily, coughed, and said, "Oh, good. You're here." Then she passed out cold.

* * *

Erica awoke to the sound of angry voices. She lay on the muddy ground, fully dressed and no longer entwined with Abigail. Her legs stung, and she opened her eyes to see Grace applying a field dressing to her burns.

"This is what I'm on about," said Connor, who stood a few feet away with Gerard, Peter, and Don. "Do you see now? She got them caught in that barn, and my wife was near killed!"

"Connor, if you spent as much energy training as you do finding fault with Erica, you'd be a better fighter," Peter said.

"Gerard, you don't truly believe what he's saying," said Don.

"Nae, but I do want to hear from them what happened."

"I demand satisfaction!" Connor shouted. "She must not be allowed to duel—"

Connor's speech broke off abruptly. Abigail lay at his feet, yanking insistently on his pant leg. "Connor, my love," she said, "would you please just shut up?"

* * *

"'Twas my doing," Abigail said when they were back at the castle and on the mend. She lay in a soft featherbed, propped up against a mountain of pillows. Most of her upper body was heavily bandaged. She had suffered a broken shoulder, rib, and pelvis; serious burns; and four holes back to front. She was pale and weak but on her way to a full recovery. Erica, whose legs were also bandaged, sat on the bed next to her, and the rest of the garou sat in chairs around the apartment.

"I entered the barn and saw the vampire on a beam above Erica," Abigail said. "I didn't warn her, thinking it was my chance to be rid of her. And then she saved me. Why did you do that after all I had done? You could have been rid of *me*."

"I didn't want to be rid of you, Abigail. I wanted to get you out of that barn."

"But you could have died trying to get me off that harrow."

"And if I hadn't, you would surely have been killed."

Abigail took Erica's hand, squeezed it, and looked over at Gerard. "I assent, my lord," she said with a smile.

9

Master of Insanity

I don't suffer from insanity. I enjoy every minute of it. — Unknown

Ardis Cmineralo. Hated and feared by preternaturals the world over. Even the old ones left him alone rather than deal with his erratic behavior. He was six and a half feet tall, with a powerful build, golden hair, blue eyes and a melodic voice. His accent defied description, but his words were eloquent, powerful, and insightful. He was ancient—more than 2,000 years old, according to him— and he had long ago gotten over his allergy to sunlight and the lavender eyeshine that all but the oldest vampires possessed. Though Pippa Tryggvason could remember when he was quite handsome, he wasn't much to look at these days. Pippa supposed madness could do that to a vampire.

Oh, and he was surely mad. He said insanity ran in his family, that it was his heritage. His mother would sit in a chair by the window for weeks at a time, sucking her thumb or rocking back and forth and humming lullabies, then come out of it and act perfectly normal for a month or two before drifting back into her own world. She had once been lovely, he said, but her beauty had faded in proportion to her mind. Her eyes were wild, and she had bald patches where she had yanked her hair out. Ardis's father was shallow, and he finally got tired of living with her and killed her. Ardis tried to kill him after that, and when it didn't work, he attempted several times to kill himself.

The pain of having to live with what his father had done to his mother proved too much for Ardis, and he began teetering on the brink of madness. That was centuries ago, and Ardis had long since dropped off the edge and gone tumbling into the abyss. The amazing part was that he knew he was crazy and didn't seem to mind. At times, Pippa thought he might actually nurture that part of himself.

She wondered what the other side of Ardis's story was. Whenever more than one person was involved, there were always other versions of a tale. The account would be quite different if told from Ardis's father's point of view. Pippa was too wise to believe he had killed her because he was tired of living with her. She knew how vampires loved. They felt every emotion with their whole hearts, and Pippa didn't believe that Ardis's father hadn't cared for his wife. More likely, he had killed her as an act of mercy, but poor Ardis would never see that.

Ardis never spoke about when he was brought across, and for a long time, Pippa had assumed it was sometime after the split with his family; but then Ardis had mentioned that his parents had been together for hundreds of years, and she realized that "father" referred to the vampire who had brought him across. Ardis's appearance suggested that he had become a vampire sometime in his mid-twenties, but he refused to give her any details. He talked about his coven as if they were blood relatives. To hear him, one might think he was actually born a vampire.

Ah, well. It didn't matter to Pippa how he was brought across, how he felt about his sire, or if he sat in the window sucking his thumb, as long as he didn't hurt himself or her, and she doubted that would happen. For everyone else, all bets were off. Ardis had killed his entire coven one night when one of them had insulted her. Even his closest followers gave him a wide berth when he was irritable. Others avoided him altogether. Pippa had no need to fear him. For all his lunacy, Ardis worshiped her.

Ardis had found her when she was twelve years old, freezing, starving on the steppes of Norway after her family had been killed by a rival tribe. Ardis and his coven were in the area cleaning up the spoils when he saw her wandering around, clutching a doll. He walked up to her, took her hand, and, in a Norse accent so perfect he could have been from her own village, said, "My dear, you are the loveliest creature I've ever laid eyes on."

He took her with him when he left and somehow hid his nature from her for several months. One night about a year after they met, he bit her.

She never had time to make a choice. He forced her into vampirism before she even understood what was happening, and it was weeks before she finally got the gist of what he had done to her. She didn't hate Ardis, but she figured many vampires hated their sires. Most of Ardis's followers hated him, but they feared him more. He forced them into a life of darkness and death without ever giving them a choice. Some did choose vampirism willingly, but Pippa couldn't imagine anyone wanting to go through such a change. Still, whether she'd had a choice or not, the things she had seen and done since Ardis brought her across made any violation she might have felt at the time seem inconsequential. After all, she'd be long dead by now. She had recently turned 600.

Ardis taught her, showed her the world, loved her, and took care of her. He showered her with gifts and affection, sometimes treating her like his child and other times like his lover, but always with the utmost kindness and respect. Some nights he sat and gazed at her for hours with such adoration that it made her uncomfortable.

Perhaps that was why he had no love for anyone else. He gave Pippa so much, there was nothing left for others. She regretted that she couldn't give Ardis as much as he gave her, but tonight, as she wandered through the streets of Malahide, she discovered something special she could do for him.

They had been in France for several years, enjoying the war. Ardis was fascinated with wars, and he loved to be present when one was going on. He didn't just watch, though. Oh no. He liked to help one side or the other—or both—just for the sake of livening things up. Sometimes Pippa thought the war might not have lasted so long if not for Ardis's intervention. He made up stories for generals, captured women or children and turned them over to the other side as hostages, brought across key players or whispered to their minds and convinced them they were spies for the enemy. He was very creative. Pippa had never had much interest in war before, but Ardis certainly made this one exciting. It had been going on for decades, and there was no end in sight.

They had followed a messenger from Calais to Dublin a few weeks ago. Ardis had brought the messenger across, and they had planned to go back to France, but they'd heard of a small coven causing trouble north of Dublin and decided to see what they were up to.

They observed the vampires in Malahide for a while and even socialized with them. They were very young, not one of them over twenty-five years old, and Ardis gave them loads of advice.

And then the White Guard showed up.

Ardis was overjoyed. His old friend Gerard had come! If there was anyone in the world that Ardis loved besides Pippa, it was Gerard Blevins. He was actually fond of a few of the garou. He called them his friends and refused to allow them to be killed—as if the younger vampires could do it anyway—but he had special affection for Gerard. In Pippa's view, he was just a typical White Guard garou, but Ardis apparently saw something she didn't.

He followed Gerard around from a safe distance for several nights as he and the other garou patrolled Malahide. He had no desire to fight Gerard's pack at this time; he just wanted to watch them search for the other coven. Ardis could be like that. Pippa never knew if he was going to attack or just sit back and watch. He didn't make Gerard's job easy; that wouldn't be sporting and hardly fair to Malahide's vampires, who had no chance of surviving against the garou. Ardis explained the White Guard to the youngsters and admonished them to lie low for a while, but they didn't believe him. Werewolves? Using silver and hunting vampires? It was more likely a delusion created in Ardis's tortured mind. A reminder that a few short years ago they had been mortal and didn't believe in vampires did little to convince them. Ardis had killed one of them for his disrespect and threatened to find their sires and turn them over his knee for not training them properly. Now, as Ardis had predicted, their impetuosity had gotten them all killed.

Pippa also enjoyed following the White Guard. Not being as powerful as Ardis, she couldn't follow as closely, but she still got a good show. The Alpha Bitch from the pack in the south, Elizabeth or something, had made her way to the House of Blevins along with a few others and had made quite a name for herself. She had offended some of her new packmates, but Pippa thought they ought to have been proud to have such a mighty female leading them.

It amused Pippa to see how in love she—Edna?—and Gerard were. Their desire was like a big pink cloud swirling around them, yet they stubbornly pushed it away in the interest of their mission and politics. Their love had to wait because of the vampires they hunted and too much concern over—Erica? Why couldn't she remember that girl's name?—over her rise through the hierarchy.

They needed to be honest with each other and get on with it so they could be happy like she and Ardis were. They could be together and still rule their pack. All they had to do was look at

Don. He and his female had gotten it right. They did everything together, and their love made them stronger. Why couldn't Gerard and—Enid?—not see that love would strengthen them, too?

Pippa's interest in—Elizabeth? Maybe it *was* Elizabeth—had caused her to be in the right place at the right time. She had been following Elizabeth and her companion and musing about her love for Gerard when they had stumbled upon one of the young vampires.

Though they had tried many times, Pippa and Ardis had never been able to ascertain the location of the House of Blevins's lair. Getting the information by reading their minds had proven impossible. Garou were normally immune to many of the mind control tactics vampires used, but the old ones could often see into their minds. Even so, the White Guard garou protected the location of their homes ferociously, and none of them, even Ardis, had ever made one of them disclose it. They had found the House of O'Shea not through the garou but through a herald for the MacCarthys Raegh whom Ardis had brought across.

And then that female got impaled on a spike harrow in a burning barn.

Pippa had seen garou in pain before, and they were hard to break. They were the hardiest of all the preternatural creatures, even the ones who *weren't* in the White Guard. They were scrappers, natural fighters who healed so fast that one could almost watch their wounds disappear. The White Guard werewolves were even tougher. They lived with pain all the time, wearing silver crosses under their shirts and wielding silver weapons. Pippa didn't understand this at all. Preternaturals were allergic to silver; just touching it was like burning oneself with acid. Maybe *they* were the ones who were mad. Ardis said it helped them learn to endure pain in case of injury or torture, and over time, the constant exposure to silver would lessen their allergy. Pippa supposed it did make sense in a twisted, masochistic sort of way, because pain barely affected them.

But the female on the harrow was not just in pain; she also had intense fear and guilt, and her mind went all to pieces. It was a thing of beauty. Vivid images of a castle flashed through her head, as well as the words "Ballybrook" and "Adam." Pippa knew Adam. His mind was easy to get into, and she had always found him to be weak of will and lazy, the kind who would rather get away with something than take responsibility. She thought it might be fun to rip his beating heart out of his chest, but alas, she'd never gotten the chance to do so. Ah, well. Maybe someday soon, because now she knew where to find him.

She made her way through Malahide to the apartment where she and Ardis were staying. Ardis sat naked at a table, sketching a castle on parchment with a piece of charcoal. The castle was jagged and distorted, like a castle in Hell might look. A chicken stood in the corner, pecking at some grain soaked in blood.

"Ardis," she said, "why is there a chicken in our room?"

"I thought a pet would be nice," he replied.

Pippa didn't think a chicken would make a very good pet, but it wasn't worth arguing over. Ardis would kill it when he got tired of it, which could be any minute now.

"Lovely castle," she said, resting a hand on his shoulder.

"Thank you, my love. I'm afraid my hand isn't as steady as it once was. It does give my artwork a certain flair, though, don't you think?" His voice was clear and rational, as if his fanatical thoughts went through some sort of filter between his brain and his mouth.

"I have news," she told him.

"Did the White Guard find our friends?"

"Yes, and killed them all."

"It's not like they weren't warned. No use for a stupid vampire, say I. Just keep quiet for a few weeks, I said. Till the next Full Moon. Why don't the young ever listen?"

"They're young. They believe they are invincible."

Ardis chuckled, his fangs showing. Pippa couldn't remember the last time his fangs had retracted. "They were wrong."

"Did you know Don had found love?" she asked.

"I figured that's what it was. He hides it well when he's patrolling, but I knew something was different. His scent and his aura—he's just so happy. Is it the female he was with? The ginger?"

"Yes, that's the one."

"Pretty girl. I'm so glad for him! Lot of red hair in Ireland. Have you noticed that?"

"Gerard and that redhead from the other pack are in love as well, although they haven't yet done anything about it."

"Well, they should just get on with it so they can be happy like us."

"That's exactly what I thought. But that is not my news."

"Oh? What is it?"

"I learned the location of Gerard's lair."

"Where?" he asked eagerly, standing up and grabbing Pippa by the shoulders. The chicken startled and hopped around the room, clucking furiously.

"A castle in the north," said Pippa. "One of the women let it slip."

"Now, how did that happen?" Ardis asked, his eyes wild with curiosity. Pippa told him about the spike harrow and the fire.

Ardis whooped and lifted her up, swinging her around until she was dizzy. When he stopped spinning, he continued to hold her as if she were a toddler. "Ha! What a scandal! Do you think she knows what trouble she's in? Must have been quite a trauma for her to give away such secrets."

"I think she was afraid she was going to die without giving her confession. I got the idea that she had done something terrible."

"Well, I'm sure God will forgive her. Do you think the White Guard will?"

"Men aren't as forgiving as their God."

"What was her name?"

"Abigail."

"That's what we'll call the chicken! You know, we may just have to pay them a visit sometime. Do think Gerard would like that? He always gets so worked up when I'm around."

"I'm sure he'd love to see you, my darling."

"It's settled, then. But not too soon, of course. Such a secret will be fun to keep for a while, don't you think?" He gazed out at the sea. "France calls. We've been gone too long, and we're missing all the excitement. The House of Blevins won't go anywhere. We can spend awhile in France and then come back for a visit."

"It might be a good idea to leave someone here. You know, to keep an eye on them."

Ardis's eyes gleamed with admiration. "Excellent idea! After all, you never know what you don't know. You know?"

Pippa giggled.

Ardis fairly giggled as well. "Gerard Blevins. The little wolf. My friend."

10

One on One

An Irishman is never at his best except when fighting. — Irish
Proverb

The garou patrolled for ten nights, and when they found no
evidence of further activity, they made arrangements to leave.
Lady Margaret offered them a large sack of gold, but Gerard told
her they weren't in the practice of accepting money for their
services and suggested she donate it to the Church and designate
it for the White Guard's use. When preparations were complete,
the garou left Malahide. They stayed in the forest until the Full
Moon passed, and then they went home for Erica's challenge to
Rhea, which Gerard approved after the incident with Abigail. It
was also time to make plans for the trip to Rome, and Gerard had
to decide what to do about Abigail.

Unlike the rise to Alpha or Beta rank, there were no
formalities surrounding a demotion to Omega. That didn't mean
no one had an opinion. The arguments were even more heated
than they had been during Erica's advancement. Though most of
the confrontations were verbal, the controversy finally led to
blows.

Don and Peter sat in the common room playing chess while
Grace and Mary watched. Connor and Adam walked in and drew
tankards of ale while discussing the possibility of Abigail's
demotion.

"We're gonna have to accept it," Adam said.

"I can't accept it. What good would demoting Abigail to Omega
do? It wouldn't do anybody any good."

Don grunted.

"What?" Connor barked.

"It would do Mary plenty of good," said Don.

"What would you have Gerard do?" Peter asked Connor.

Connor started to shout but thought better of it and spoke more softly. "She should be punished, aye. She knows she should be punished, and she'll freely accept anything Gerard hands out. But a demotion to Omega is so harsh."

"Harsh?" said Don. "Are you daft?"

"It's all right, Don," Mary said quietly. "Don't worry about it."

"Too late," Peter murmured.

"Why are you here?" Connor asked Mary. "Don't you have things to do?"

Mary started to get up, but Peter placed a hand on her arm. "Stay here, love."

"Your memory is failing, Connor," said Don. "You seem to have forgotten that you demanded that Mary be reduced to Omega after she accidentally injured Adam while they were fighting a vampire. Abigail *intentionally* tried to kill Erica. As far as I'm concerned, that's harsh."

"As far as you're concerned," Connor jeered. "It's none of your concern."

"How do you figure?" said Peter. "Seems to me it concerns the whole house."

"Well, it 'seems to me' that Don doesn't care much about the whole house, only the ones he's fucking. Which is it, Don? Are you only concerned about protecting your females, or do you just want Abigail where she can't defend herself? If she's made Omega, you can do whatever you want to her."

"Connor, that was beneath even you," said Peter.

"Breathe, Don," said Grace. "He's just trying to pick a fight."

"Are you challenging his rank?" Peter asked Connor.

"I'm not challenging anyone," Connor replied. "I was simply having a conversation with my son, and Don chose to interrupt with snide remarks."

"You knew what you were doing when you walked in the room," said Don. "But I'm betting a duel wasn't what you had in mind. If you *have* a mind in that pea-sized brain of yours, you'll walk out of here and quit stinking up the room. But if you want to go now, you arse-faced heap of diseased pig shite, just say the word and we'll see how well you can eat without any teeth. Then you'd better hope Gerard makes Abigail Omega, 'cause she wouldn't let you touch her otherwise."

Connor's scent flared with renewed anger. He threw his mug at Don and dove over the table at him, scattering the chessboard and pieces. He bore Don to the floor and leapt on top of him, but before he could throw a punch, Don slapped his ears with his palms. Connor yowled and raised up, grabbing his ears, which gushed with blood.

With the fingers of both hands interlaced, Don delivered a powerful hammer blow to Connor's chest, knocking him away. He threw the mug back at Connor and started to scramble after him, but Connor got hold of a chair, which he flung wildly, smashing it into Don's face.

The other garou stood back as Connor and Don struggled to their feet, both a bit stunned from the blows they had taken.

"Peter, you need to stop this," said Grace.

"Nae, I don't think I do." He took a seat on the table, and Mary sat down next to him. Grace rolled her eyes and joined them. Adam stood by as well, making no effort to end the fight.

Connor swung a fist at Don in an attempt to land a haymaker. Don blocked the punch with one hand and threw an upper cut under Connor's jaw with the other, knocking his head back. Before Connor could stagger backward, Don grabbed his shoulders and pulled him forward to knee him in the gut.

When Connor doubled over, he caught Don's legs and hauled up, dumping Don on his backside. The chessboard was within reach, and he grabbed it and prepared to hit Don with it.

Don threw up his hands and shouted, "Not the chessboard!"

Connor paused, tossed the board aside, and reached for the nearest object, which happened to be another chair, and he dropped it on Don's abdomen.

"Connor," said Peter, "you should probably leave *some* of the furniture intact."

When Connor glanced up at Peter, Don kicked his feet out from under him. Connor hit the floor, and Don jumped on top of him and started hitting him.

The others continued to watch as Don and Connor rolled on the floor and pounded on each other until Gerard and Owen burst into the room and dragged them apart. They had to restrain them heavily as they struggled to break free and go at each other again.

"This ends now!" Gerard roared as he wrestled Don to the floor and pinned his shoulders.

Don raised his hands in supplication.

"Are you done?" Gerard asked him. When Don didn't answer right away, he shouted. *"Are you done?"*

"Aye, I'm done! I'm done!"

"Connor?"

"I'm done," Connor replied from his position on the floor beneath Owen.

Gerard and Owen let them up, and Gerard turned on his Beta Wolf, who still sat on the table, placidly watching the altercation.

"What the devil are you doing?" he demanded.

"Letting them cool some of their ire," Peter replied. "It's been coming for a long time, don't you think?"

"Well, you can go to the infirmary and make sure they don't start again while Mary stitches them up."

Don glared Connor hatefully in the eye, spat a mouthful of blood on his boots, and left the room.

"Thank you for coming to my defense again, love," Mary said as she followed Don to the infirmary, "but do you really think it does any good?"

"Sure, it does."

"Oh? Now that it's over, what do you have to show for it other than two black eyes and ten or twenty stitches?"

"I think I may have a couple of broken ribs as well."

"Don!"

"What?"

"My point is that after all that, nothing has changed. I'm still Omega, and Abigail is still in danger of taking my place. You're lucky Gerard didn't demote you and Connor. I ask you again: what good did it do?"

"Well, for one thing, it was pretty damn fun. Don't you agree, Connor?" he called over his shoulder.

"Aye, it was a good time," Connor replied. "But did you have to box my ears?"

"Oi, you hit me with a chair. Twice!"

"Well, next time, don't throw me so close to one."

"I didn't throw you. You fell when I hit you."

"Lovely," Mary grumbled. "Don, I'm used to being Omega. It'll kill Abigail."

"Only if Connor kills her."

"Are you daft?" Connor retorted. "I would never hurt my wife."

"Nae, just your daughter. You know, if she gets promoted and can defend herself, you might want to think twice before you try to slap her around, 'cause she's a better fighter than you. It would warm my heart to watch her leave you bleeding on the floor. Or your wife."

Connor made a move toward Don, and Peter stepped between them. "Once is enough for the day. Don, shut up and stop baiting him!"

* * *

Gerard would have thought Mary and Erica would be in favor of Abigail's demotion, but Mary was ambivalent. She wanted to be promoted, but she worried about what would happen to Abigail if Gerard demoted her. Although she swore she had no love for her mother, she still didn't want any harm to come to her, and she didn't trust several of the others not to mistreat her, Don and Connor included.

Erica begged Gerard not to make Abigail Omega Wolf.

"She didn't know what she was doing," she said as they sat across from each other in his office.

"She tried to kill you," Gerard pointed out. "She knew what she was doing; she admits so herself. If Don and Peter had their way, she would be put to death outright. Busting her to Omega is better than killing her."

"You know good and well they wouldn't actually have her killed."

"That's not the point."

"She didn't have to admit what she did. She could have let Connor blame me, but she didn't. Please, Gerard. Don't make her Omega."

"Mary is your friend. I would think you'd wish to see her promoted."

Erica's face reddened. "Don't you play that game with me, Gerard Blevins! Of course, I wish to see her promoted, but not at the cost of what little dignity Abigail has left. She spends most of her time in the chapel these days; do you know? She's begged me for forgiveness, and she begs God's as well. If we can forgive her, why can't you?"

Gerard demoted Abigail to Omega despite Erica's protests.

"I can't just let your actions go without consequences," he told her. "I don't believe I need to point out that had Erica died, you would have perished in that barn as well. We must be able to rely on each other, even if we don't get along. Any betrayal cannot be condoned or tolerated."

"No, no," Abigail said tearfully, her scent fraught with fear. "I understand, and I do deserve it. I'm so sorry, Gerard."

"Tell Erica."

"I have, and I will again."

* * *

Connor stood outside Gerard's office with tears in his eyes. Abigail's demotion hurt him as much as it hurt her, but despite what he had said to Don, even he had to admit she deserved it. He would never let her know that, though. It would crush her.

He was partly to blame. Erica had gotten on his bad side at an induction decades ago, and he had never liked her. He wasn't a forgiving sort, so when she had joined the House of Blevins, he had refused to even give her the chance to redeem herself. If not for his stubbornness and endless criticism of Erica, Abigail would never have tried to hurt her. He had to believe that. He could live with being petty and vindictive, but his wife couldn't be so terrible without his influence.

Connor went to find Erica. She was in her room, crying. He stopped in the doorway and said, "You heard?"

"I did."

"Thank you for defending her, Erica. I don't know that we'll ever be friends, but I may have been wrong about you."

"It's a start," she said. "'Haps we'll be friends yet."

* * *

Rhea wanted to concede her rank, but Gerard said no. He told her that Erica didn't want Rhea to hand her the position and that such an act would dishonor her. She was to defend the office to the best of her ability. Rhea's forte wasn't the longsword or shortsword, but something a little different. She fought Florentine-style, using rapier and main gauche, a discipline known to most of the garou in the White Guard but one many eschewed in favor of a single blade because of the added difficulty coordinating the two in combat.

Erica had seen Rhea spar with the two weapons and felt she had a good understanding of Rhea's capability. Erica didn't normally use the two-handed style, but she was no stranger to it and was confident that her skill with the rapier alone would be sufficient to win the match. As she stood face to face with Rhea while Peter reminded them of the rules, she pondered how best to prevail without hurting her friend's pride too much.

When Peter stepped out of the circle, Erica began a series of probing attacks to measure the quality of Rhea's defense. She kept her body turned to the side, attacking and defending mostly with the rapier, only using the dagger as a last defense or if the fighting became too close for her to use the longer blade. She was surprised to find how difficult it was to score on the Alpha Bitch. While most fencers turned to the side, Rhea turned to the front. It would seem that the stance would leave her center more open to attack, but she actively defended with both rapier and dagger and left no openings.

Rhea engaged Erica's rapier with her own and began a circular parry, but the movement lacked a master fencer's finesse and the spiral was larger than necessary. Erica was about to show her why she should keep her actions minimal when she felt Rhea's main gauche slice across her midsection. She leapt back with a mild oath, cursing the luck that Rhea had chosen just that moment to attack with the secondary blade when Erica's vision had been obscured by the longer blades. She guessed she wouldn't have to worry about embarrassing Rhea after all. As the match continued, she consciously devoted more attention to her opponent's dagger.

For a few moments, the two females fenced solely with the rapiers. Seeing an opening, Erica tried to follow Rhea's lead and strike with the main gauche. Rhea countered with a broad sweep to the outside with her rapier. If they had been fencing with rapiers alone, she would be completely open for a riposte by Erica. Instead, Rhea continued the sweeping motion and intercepted the long blade with her dagger, throwing it out in the same direction. As Erica was bringing her weapons back to bear on Rhea, she caught sight of her opponent's rapier crossing under her arm and coming straight at Erica's midsection. Although Erica was able to leap backward to prevent being run through and losing the match, the blade still scored.

She had to stop underestimating her opponents! It seemed that the less threatening the garou appeared, the more dangerous he or she was. Mary must be a right holy terror. Erica had always thought Florentine style just meant fencing while using a dagger in the off hand. This was a hell of a time to discover she still had a lot to learn.

Erica stepped back and pointed her weapons at the ground. Rhea stood on guard and watched Erica expectantly. She looked the Alpha Bitch in the eye and said, "I'm sorry."

Rhea smiled and nodded her acceptance. "I was beginning to think I had misjudged you."

Resuming her stance, Erica prepared to continue the match with newfound respect for her opponent's abilities. Initially, she remained on the defensive as she worked to comprehend the level of coordination Rhea possessed and to get a feel for how she could make her weapons act in unison as Rhea did. As she started to understand how using the two weapons together altered the tactics and strategies of the match, she began to look for openings to take the offensive. While she didn't have Rhea's level of mastery with the two weapons, she was a quick study and had some impressive skills of her own.

In deliberately considering the possibilities present in the interplay of the two weapons, Erica had a moment of inspiration. She made a powerful thrust directly at the forte of Rhea's rapier using the crossguard of the dagger to maintain contact as she forced it directly in the path of Rhea's main gauche. Briefly engaging both weapons with the dagger, Erica angled her rapier across the front of her body and thrust it directly at Rhea's shoulder as she continued her lunge. Rhea, caught off guard by the unorthodox tactic, was still trying to disengage her blades when Erica's rapier passed cleanly through her shoulder.

"Very nice!" Peter said appreciatively. "That's the match."

Erica removed her blade and stepped back, instinctively saying a silent prayer that Rhea didn't drop to the ground with internal bleeding, and saluted. "Thank you," she said meaningfully to her friend.

Rhea returned the salute and nodded. "You're welcome," she said softly.

* * *

Gerard stood off to the side, looking on as Erica saluted Peter and handed her weapons to Don. She turned to Gerard and walked to him slowly, then turned her head and bared her throat.

Several of the garou's scents changed, and over Erica's shoulder, Gerard could see expressions of surprise and approval. Even those who had been offended by her rise through the ranks were impressed.

Gerard didn't know what to think. While her audacity had annoyed him, he had never really thought she would try to dominate him. The gesture was unnecessary, but he understood Erica's desire to make it. She submitted to him in full view of the others to show that she would not try to usurp his authority and would defer to him as she should.

The veins in Erica's delicate throat throbbed, and Gerard wanted nothing more than to kiss it. He decided to do just that later in the day. He had waited too long. For now, though, he nuzzled her, sniffed, and said, "Aye."

Erica drew back, flashed her pixie grin, and then turned and joined the others, and Gerard went to Rhea.

"Come inside," he said pointedly.

Rhea followed him to his office, and he shut the door. "Tell me you didn't throw that match," he said.

"I didn't throw the match."

"Then why did she thank you?"

"She thanked me for teaching her the dangers of underestimating her opponents and her packmates."

"Is that why she apologized midway through?"

"Of course. Really, Gerard, did you not see anything that happened out there? I'm sorry, big brother, but you have a new Alpha Bitch."

"You're not sorry," he accused.

"Nae, and neither are you. Now, I'm going back outside to celebrate. You stay in here if you want and do whatever it is you do. I wouldn't know; I'm just a normal member of the rank and file now."

Gerard kissed his sister on the forehead. "You're not helping."

"Not anymore."

* * *

Later that evening, Gerard lost track of Erica and followed her scent to find her in his room, sitting on his bed.

"Did you know Don was planning to ask Grace for her hand this evening?" she asked.

"Of course I did."

She got up and came to him. His heart thrummed as she placed a trembling hand on his chest. He took her hand and kissed it.

"Are we ready to do this, then?" she asked.

"I don't know. Do you think you can behave long enough that I can be more than just your Alpha?"

"I make no promises."

He bent and kissed her. "I've wanted to do that for so long," he said. "I've waited too long to tell you how much I love you."

Erica half giggled and half sobbed. "I forgive you. Just don't wait so long to tell me again."

"Not gonna happen," he said as he bent to kiss her again.

11

The Mighty Quinn

The greatest test of courage on earth is to bear defeat without losing heart. — Robert G. Ingersoll

Mary began making challenges immediately and with more tenacity than Erica ever had. She took Adam on the first New Moon after her promotion and hurt him badly, slashing his throat and coming dangerously close to decapitating him. She dueled Maria two months later and fought Aeron two months after that. After she defeated Aeron, Grace conceded her rank.

As one might have expected, Connor went to Gerard to complain.

"We're not gonna do this again, Connor," Gerard said.

Before Connor could respond, Mary burst into the room. "You know, my beloved *athair*, I think it very amusing that you didn't say a word until I was in position to take your rank."

"You're not helping, Mary," said Gerard.

"Let me have this one, Gerard. Please."

Gerard nodded, and she turned back to Connor. "I'm done listening to you bluster about anything that doesn't go your way. As Alpha, Gerard has to be diplomatic and try to keep everyone happy, but since I'm no longer Omega, I don't have to hold my tongue anymore. You made my life hell for years, and you're not gonna do it now that I can defend myself. I'm not using formal voice with you, and I'll no longer cower when I pass you in the hallway. I'll fight you on the next New Moon, I'll hand you your arse, and after that, you're gonna learn to mind your own fucking business."

She stormed out of the room.

"Gerard—" Connor began.

"Don't," he said. "She was within her rights to say it. Challenges for rank are frequently harsh, and you know it."

"Lovely." Connor got up and left the office, grumbling about being insulted by his own daughter.

* * *

The higher-ranking garou chose the weapons when challenged, but they were strongly encouraged to choose something that would even up the match. For instance, if Owen chose to fight hand to hand with one of the women, the Alpha might recommend swords instead. Connor wanted to fight Mary hand to hand, but Gerard stepped in and instructed him to use swords.

Peter thought Mary could beat Connor on her own, but he gave her some extra instruction just to be sure.

"You know I'm not gonna mind *my* own business, don't you?" he said as they sparred. "Watch your lead foot."

Mary adjusted her footing and said, "I thought you were supposed to stay neutral so you could call the matches."

"Aye, but I can't remain neutral with this one. I'm gonna ask Gerard to call the match."

"But why?" she asked as she parried a thrust.

"I waffle between rejoicing 'cause you're doing so well and worrying that you're advancing so rapidly out of some need to retaliate against those who abused you for so long."

"Well, can you blame me?"

"Nae, and that's why I can't remain neutral."

"I love you, Peter O'Neill," she said as she connected with his side and sliced a hefty gash.

"I love you, too, little sister, but this was my favorite shirt."

"You'll live."

"So will you, if you keep an eye on your footing. Connor is good at judging his opponent's next action by watching the position of their feet. Don't let yours give away your intent."

Mary lost the match with Connor, but footing wasn't her problem. As far as she had come since leaving the Omega rank, she still found Connor intimidating. He knew it, and he used it to his advantage. He advanced on her boldly, and it unsettled her so badly that all she could do was back away. He made three quick strikes before she could even gather her thoughts.

The loss was humiliating, especially after the insults she had thrown at him. He twisted the knife when he found her in the infirmary afterward and backhanded her across the face so hard that it cut her cheek.

"If you talk to me that way again, you'll wish you were never born," he warned her.

"Connor," she said as he started to leave the room. He turned back, and she said, "Next New Moon."

He laughed at her. "Fine, but you really should give up before you're hurt badly. Accept it, little one. You're not advancing any further in this pack."

This time, Mary went to Don for help.

"I've been afraid of him for so long," she said, "I don't know how be anything else."

"Fight dirty," Don replied. "Play to his weaknesses. He's got plenty of them."

"But I can't play to his weaknesses if I can't even get started. He stood across from me in that circle and stared me in the eye, and I crumbled. Then I let him come into the infirmary and hit me because that's what I was used to."

"Aye, and when Peter heard about it, Gerard had to hold him back from kicking Connor's head in."

Mary's jaw dropped. "I didn't know that."

"It's hard to get him angry, but Connor hitting you will do it every time. I truly think he might have killed him if Gerard had let him. Gerard told Peter this was your fight, though, and now that you can defend yourself, he—we—had to let you."

"He's right. Now if I can just find the courage. When I confronted him in Gerard's office, I'd never done anything like that before, and I don't know if I can do it again."

"He said we had to let you defend yourself, but he didn't say we couldn't help you."

"All right, what do I do?"

Don considered her problem then said, "What's the best way to get over fear of the dark?"

Mary shrugged.

"Be the scariest thing in it," he said. "When you engage a vampire, are you afraid?"

"Nae."

"Never?" he said with surprise.

Mary shook her head. "Never."

"That's remarkable, love. Even I get scared sometimes."

"I never have."

"Why?"

The question gave her pause. She didn't know why she wasn't afraid of vampires; she just wasn't. "'Cause I'm more dangerous than it is?" she guessed.

Don chuckled. "You're so cute, saying it like that, but aye, that's the answer I wanted. You are the scariest thing in the dark. You're a gentle soul; I've always said that. But even so, you're still a killer."

Mary chuckled. "That doesn't make any sense."

"It's still true, though. Listen, when you fight a vampire, it wants nothing more than to kill you, but that doesn't frighten you. Connor doesn't want to kill you. He does want to hurt you, scare you, and put you in your place, but the only way he can do that is if you let him. I said once that you were a better fighter than him, and I meant it. But I can tell you that till your ears bleed, and it won't make a difference if you don't believe it. When you defeat Connor, you'll do it in the first few seconds of the match—when you start believing you're scarier than he is."

"That's easy to say, but not so easy to do."

"Nae, you've had too many years under his thumb. I remember him beating on you even before you were Omega. And feeling responsible."

"What? Don, don't ever think you were to blame for anything Connor did to me. You never did anything but protect me."

"I might not have had to protect you so much if we had made different choices. But the reasons don't matter. What matters is that you're stronger now than you were then. You're starting to stand up for yourself for the first time in your life, but you still haven't had time enough to see all the tripe Connor's been spouting at you for the shite it is. Deep down you still believe it, at least enough to be afraid it might be true. I can see the changes in you clear enough to know that in time, you'll come to know your true worth, but that's going to take more time than we have.

"There's a way we *could* do it, with Peter's help. It's the way some armies train raw recruits in short spans. We could push you and work you and scream at you and then push you more until you break; then we could take the broken pieces and put you back together again, and you'd be someone who could take Connor without a second thought."

"Oi, sounds like a good time," Mary said sarcastically.

"Sure, it would be. But you wouldn't be our Mary afterwards, and Peter and I could never again be who we are now. And I, for one, really like me."

He thought for a moment, and when he spoke again, he was talking more to himself than Mary. "However, we might be able to borrow a trick or two from that ... oh, ho, ho, that might actually work. Sometimes I'm so bloody clever I amaze myself." He looked up at Mary, grinning broadly. "You should be frightened now, by the way."

"Love, I've been frightened ever since you started talking about pushing me till I break."

"Your fighting ability isn't the problem; we know that. The problem is that your head is getting in the way of your sword. What we have to do is make it so your sword works without your head!" He beamed triumphantly in his eureka moment.

"Um, what?"

"It's this," Don explained. "When you walk, or breathe, or throw out a hand to steady yourself when you trip, or flinch away from a loud noise, you're not *thinking* of those actions. Your body does them on its own without you having to tell it to do so consciously, which is a good thing, because otherwise you'd suffocate when you fell asleep. If we teach you a couple of techniques designed to counter some of Connor's favorite attacks and then have you practice them a few tens of thousands of times over the next few weeks, you'll practically be able to do them in your sleep. Once you actually engage him, your natural instincts and training should take over enough that you won't have the opportunity to be afraid. We just have to get you to the point that the fight's not over by the time you engage. If we can do that—and we can—you can take the time you need to realize who you really are without Connor pushing you down at every turn."

"I still don't understand."

"But do you trust me?"

"Of course I do."

"You'll come to understand. You may not like Peter and me very much for a while, though."

* * *

"Again!" Peter commanded.

Mary groaned and assumed the crossed guard, a defensive stance where she held the hilt of her sword high with her gripping hands crossed beside her head and the tip of her blade pointing downward at an angle. As Don stepped in and slashed down diagonally at Mary's left side, she stepped quickly to the right and extended her arms forward to block Don's sword with her own. As soon as the blades clashed together, she leapt forward with her left foot and propelled the tip of her sword at Don's thigh.

Don leapt back, anticipating the counter, and exclaimed, "Oi! You almost clipped me again!"

"Don, she's supposed to," Peter said pedantically. "She has to practice like it's a real duel. It's up to you, who already know what she's going to do, to get out of the way."

"I don't know what *you're* complaining for anyway," Mary chimed in. "My arms feel like they're about to fall off my shoulders, and my hand went numb almost an hour ago."

They had been practicing all afternoon, and it was the third day in a row. Peter and Don had brought her to a meadow near the entrance to a cave where Don said he and Gerard had played as children. The meadow was far enough away from the monastery to make it unlikely that anyone from her family would happen by and see her training. Connor would expect them to help her, but there was no point in giving him the advantage of knowing exactly what they were up to. That was all well and good, but Mary was starting to assume the stance in her sleep.

"We've been practicing this same technique over and over again," she said. "What do I do if Connor recognizes it and knows a counter?"

"That's unlikely," said Peter. "I learned this particular tactic from the swordmaster of a pack in the German Territories. I've never seen it done anywhere else. Plus, don't forget I've taught Connor everything he knows. If he knew it, I'd have seen him use it by now."

"Well, what if he doesn't attack like this?" Mary asked uncertainly.

"Don't think I don't realize you're asking all these questions just so you can sneak in a breather," Peter chided. "Again!"

Mary growled at him and assumed the stance. After they repeated the attack and counter another dozen times, she said, "But what if he doesn't?"

Peter buried his head in his hands and laughed.

"It's one of his favorite attacks," Don said, "especially when he's feeling confident and wants to put his opponent on the defensive quickly."

"Besides," Peter added, "this is only the first counter. We're gonna teach you two others that will work against other tactics he's likely to use. Connor's not very imaginative. In truth, if skill at arms were the only consideration, we wouldn't need to do this at all. If you can score on us, you can score on him. But because of your current mindset, we need to ingrain a few techniques so firmly that you'll respond to the attacks instinctively. Once your initial freeze is broken, I have all faith that your skill and the training you've already received will be enough to carry you through."

"But don't expect these counters will work on Connor if you wind up dueling him a third time," Don warned. "He's an ass, but he's not stupid."

"Again," Peter said once more.

"I hate you two," she groaned.

* * *

Everything felt surreal as Mary stood in the circle while Gerard announced the match and reminded everyone of the protocols. Connor was standing across the circle, smirking and fixing her with an intimidating glare, so sure this match would end exactly as the last one had. Was it only a month ago? It seemed like years, and everything in between was blurred together. She'd never worked so hard in her life. Nearly every day for the last four weeks, she had trained with Peter and Don whenever they could get away from their regular duties. She had practiced the techniques they had taught her thousands of times over. Even with accelerated healing and recuperation, she'd needed every fourth day or so just to recover.

She refused to look away from Connor's eyes, but the longer she went without breaking the stare, the more terrified she grew. Peter and Don said this time would be different, but it all seemed so uncertain now. *You're a better fighter. If you can score on us, you can score on him. You are the scariest thing in the dark. You're stronger now than you were then.* Their words swam in her head like the vague memory of a dream. Maybe that was all this was: a dream, a naïve fantasy that was about to be brutally demolished with the first swing of Connor's sword. What if Connor didn't use any of the attacks Peter and Don thought he would? And if he did, would she be any less paralyzed this time than before in the face of her father? Even if she wasn't, would she be able to counter correctly, and in time? Or would Connor just read her moves, beat her down anyway, and then laugh at her? And then find her later and thrash her within an inch of her life?

She had worked so hard, but here she was, just as uncertain, just as full of doubt, just as scared as before. And just as furious with herself for feeling this way. She didn't want to believe it, couldn't stand to voice it in her own head, but maybe Peter and Don were wrong and Connor was right. Maybe this was as good as she would ever be and as far as she would ever go in the pack. She knew they hadn't lied to her, but they cared so much for her, and sometimes that caused people to see things in others that weren't really there.

Gerard was just finishing up, saying something about how they were family and not to get carried away, and it amazed her to realize he'd only been talking for a few seconds. She didn't think she or Connor had heard anything he'd said as they had stared into each other's eyes.

As soon as Gerard stepped out of the circle, Connor strode forward eagerly. "I'm gonna beat you worse than last time, lassie. Beat you until you learn your place." He practically spat the words at her, but there was no anger, just perverse enthusiasm.

Mary couldn't move. It took all her energy to hold her sword out in front of her and keep from stepping back. She knew that if she took that one step, she wouldn't stop. She would turn and run out of the circle, and she didn't think she'd ever be able to step in again. It was irrational, she knew, but that didn't stop it from being real. And if it happened, Gerard might as well demote her back to Omega, because she would never be more than that.

Connor's sword bashed hers aside, and he thrust straight for her midsection. The movement was completely unfamiliar; she didn't think it was one of the attacks they had practiced. If it was, she couldn't remember. They all flew from her mind. She couldn't think, and she couldn't move. He was going to run her through and the match would be over.

Someone was lifting her sword. She reached out with her left hand and grabbed the blade. She needed that sword; they couldn't take it away. The world was spinning.

No, wait. *She* was turning. She was stepping back and around with her left foot and pushing her sword out crosswise, like it was a staff. Connor's blade continued on its path, but she was no longer in its way; she was standing to his side. She turned her torso and pushed his blade down, then reversed direction and struck her father between the eyes with the pommel of her sword.

Connor's head stopped, but his feet kept going. His sword flew from his grasp, and he landed flat on his back at her feet. His eyes glazed over as he looked up at her in utter confusion.

She suddenly realized that the tip of her sword was pointed at his throat. She didn't even know how it got there. But it didn't matter, because now she understood. Don and Peter were right. She was the scariest thing in the dark, and she had already beaten Connor. A sense of calm washed over her like a wave on a beach.

Gerard stepped tentatively into the ring, but Mary just held up her hand, not taking her eyes from Connor's. Still holding his gaze, she walked over to Connor's sword, picked it up, and threw it to him. It hit his chest with a thump.

"Want to try again?" she asked.

Two minutes later, Gerard stopped the match. Mary had her father's rank and his blood on her sword, and he had never even touched her. The look of confusion hadn't left his face, and now she thought it might just have a hint of fear as well.

She nearly collapsed into Peter's arms when he and Don ran up to congratulate her. Abigail and Adam collected Connor and started leading him off to the infirmary. They didn't say a word or even look at her. Somebody else would have to tend to his wounds. She wouldn't.

12

2 Become 1

Two souls with but a single thought. Two hearts that beat as one.
— Friedrich Halm

With most of the tensions of the past few years laid to rest, there was more peace in the House of Blevins than there had been in a long time. Vampire activity picked up, and the garou went on three missions in the next year, which was an incredible amount of activity for so small an area, especially after such a long dry spell. Ireland was isolated from the rest of Europe, and people didn't just pass through. If a vampire was there, it had come there intentionally. Although no one knew why, the island was a mecca for preternaturals. Tales of spirits and fey had always run rampant, but the ghosts didn't or couldn't hurt anybody and the fairies kept to themselves. There were a few conventional garou in Ireland, but they likewise didn't draw undue attention. The vampires caused more trouble.

If activity was on the upswing again, the White Guard might send a second pack, but for now, the House of Blevins handled the burden. What kept Gerard awake at night was the notion that if they were this busy with reported activity, how much was going *unreported*?

Though he hated to admit it, Gerard had been concerned that Don and Peter might mistreat Abigail in retaliation for her abuse of Mary in the past, but they behaved themselves. Abigail, though her pride was severely damaged, had a relatively easy time as Omega. She had expected poor treatment as well, and their kindness surprised her.

"The rank of Omega is necessary to take the brunt of the garou's frustrations," she said.

"Bullying you 'cause you can't defend yourself is not necessary," Don told her, "and truly, it's not very satisfying. I'd rather take my frustrations out on your husband."

As busy as the garou were, the women still managed to find time to plan a wedding, and Don and Grace married in August. Although it was a foregone conclusion that Gerard and Erica would marry as well, they waited until after the excitement had died down from Don and Grace's nuptials to announce their engagement.

Because garou's lives were so long, commitments that in mortal terms would be for a lifetime, such as marriages, were made for a century at a time. After all, for garou, "till death" could be a *very* long time. Since a garou marriage wasn't really considered permanent, it was not sanctioned by the Church, so the Alpha Wolf normally officiated at the wedding. If the Alpha married, the Beta Wolf or an Alpha from another pack presided. When a White Guard Alpha married, however, the ruling house had to be notified, and the Aleph—the Alpha Wolf of the White Guard's ruling house—came to perform the ceremony. Gerard officiated at Don and Grace's wedding, but when he proposed to Erica, they had to send word to the House of Bianco and wait for them to arrive. Erica found such procedures annoying.

"I don't see why the order has to make such a fuss," she said to the other females as they sat watching her in her partially finished wedding dress while Abigail made measurements. "Wouldn't it be easier on all parties if we just had Peter do the ceremony and then sent word to Rome?"

"You knew what you were getting into when you decided you wanted to be Alpha," said Grace. "You say all the time that White Guard packs do things differently from conventional ones."

"When Alphas marry, the union is more likely to affect the White Guard as a whole," said Rhea, "especially when one is highly ranked like Gerard."

"And don't forget they love to keep their records," Mary remarked.

"Besides," Aeron said, "it's not as though you're waiting for anything but the ceremony. You lead as a pair, and you're already sleeping in his bed. If the House of Bianco wants to have their formalities, let them."

"You have a point," said Erica. "I'm just moaning and complaining."

"You'll be moaning and complaining even more if you don't stand still," said Abigail, "lest my hand slip and I stick you with a pin."

"The wait does give Abigail more time to work on your dress," said Grace.

"And her dress will still be no lovelier than yours, dear," the Omega promised.

* * *

Franco and Teresa Bianco, the Alpha Pair of the White Guard's ruling house, arrived with several of their packmates six months after Gerard sent word to Rome. They were a matched set, both gorgeous, with olive skin, dark hair, and brown eyes. Franco looked pompous and superior, but he was actually very open and friendly. Teresa was the opposite with warm, soft features and a haughty, self-important attitude, at least as far as Erica was concerned.

Teresa seemed to have brought everything she owned, and Erica wondered just how long the Alephey planned to stay. She found out soon enough that House of Bianco didn't intend to stay long, because Teresa didn't even unpack. Franco announced that the wedding would take place the next day. The edict didn't cause much of a problem; they had been prepared for several weeks, a fact Erica went out of her way to tell Teresa.

Because her father was dead, Erica wanted to walk down the aisle alone, but Franco insisted that she have an escort to present her to Gerard. She asked Don.

"A hundred years is a long time," he said as they stood at the door of the chapel. "This is your last chance to walk away."

"Not gonna happen."

"Well, if you're sure."

"Domhnall Williamson, you had best behave during my wedding!"

He kissed her cheek. "I promise. Just this once, though."

A few of the monks played a lilting melody as Don walked Erica down the aisle. Tears welled in her eyes when she saw Gerard. Normally stoic and expressionless, he was the image of emotion, all the love clear on his handsome face. This was it, the fulfillment of everything she had hoped for since she had first seen Gerard at her induction.

When she and Don reached the altar, Gerard whispered, "You're beautiful."

"So are you," said Erica.

"Shh! Behave!" Don whispered.

"Good afternoon, and welcome," Franco said to the assembly. "Gerard and Erica would like to thank you for joining them on this blessed day. As their closest friends and family, you have shared your lives with them and will do so from this day forward. I charge you, the members of the House of Blevins, to bless and support the union between Gerard and Erica, encouraging and assisting them in nurturing their love and devotion to one another. Do you, as their friends and family, so pledge?"

The garou and the monks of the House of Blevins said, "Yea."

"Who presents this woman to be married to this man?"

"I do," said Don. He kissed Erica, took her hand, and placed it in Gerard's, patted Gerard on the shoulder and then took his place next to Grace.

"My friends," said the Aleph, "we often speak of perfect love and perfect trust. When we say these words, we're not speaking of perfection, but rather the acceptance of one's imperfections. We are flawed beings, and as garou we live with shortcomings that no human can understand. While we do not promise to stand beside each other in sickness and in health, we do take into consideration the good and the bad, joy and sorrow, violence and peace. Your life together will not always be smooth; conflict is the way of the garou. But today you promise that your love and trust shall be stronger than any discord you may experience, and that you will live with, for, and beside each other through your best and worst."

Franco retrieved six colorful cords from the altar. "These cords are used to symbolize your promises to each other and the binding of your souls."

The vows were simple and standard, with Franco asking for their promise to love and cherish for better or for worse, with the added vow to lead the House of Blevins together. As each vow was completed, the Aleph wrapped one of the cords around their clasped hands.

When the rite was completed, Franco slipped the cords from their hands, which remained clasped. "My friends, the knots of this binding are not formed by the cords," he said. "They are formed by your vows. The cords are merely symbols, and you now hold in your own hands the making or breaking of this union. Who holds the rings?"

"I do," said Peter. He handed Gerard and Erica each a gold ring, then returned to his place.

Gerard and Erica exchanged rings, and Franco pronounced them husband and wife. They kissed, then walked up the aisle together, and Erica blinked back a tear. That kiss fulfilled all her hopes and dreams, but at 102 years old, she felt like her life was just beginning.

* * *

Though the garou were usually uncomfortable with pomp and ceremony, the females tended to go a little crazy when it came to weddings. Rhea, Aeron, and Abigail had covered the chapel with flowers, and Mary, Grace, and Maria had hung so many ribbons and streamers in the common room that the ceiling was barely visible. The monks prepared a feast, and the celebration lasted into the night.

Teresa Bianco was less than impressed and advised Erica that the great hall would have been a better venue for the party. Although most of the garou were fond of Teresa, Erica had never cared for her. In Erica's opinion, she had spent too much time as a ruler and had forgotten what it was like to be a fighter. She had once overheard the Alephey tell someone she hadn't killed a vampire in fifty years. How could a garou spend so much time detached from the mission and her charges and understand anything about them? Let alone the fact that in Ireland, they just did things differently from in Italy, especially the commoners.

"We rarely use the great hall," Erica said. "We don't stand on ceremony much here, and the grandeur of the great hall makes us uncomfortable. I'm much happier celebrating in here."

"But it is your wedding and you have important guests," Teresa protested. "Surely you could have made better arrangements."

Several eyes turned their way as the garou waited to hear Erica's response, and she didn't intend to disappoint them. She hadn't wanted the Biancos at her wedding to start with, and this pompous shrew was complaining because the preparations weren't to her liking? Oh, no.

"I'm terribly sorry you're dissatisfied," Erica said. "I was under the impression that the celebration was for Gerard and me, not our 'important guests.' If you would be more comfortable in the great hall, do feel free to go there. Oh, and by the by, if you feel it necessary to remind someone that you're important, you may have a problem."

She turned her back on the Alephey and went to dance with her husband.

Teresa glared at Peter and Don, who stood close by, laughing. "Oh, shut up," she snapped.

"Do you ever wonder why people say that to us so much?" Don asked Peter.

"No sense of humor?" Peter suggested.

"That must be it."

13

And the Cradle Will Rock...

You are the bows from which your children as living arrows are sent forth. — Khalil Gibran

The females went into heat a couple of years after Gerard and Erica married. When one of them went into heat, they all did, and the topic of children came up for the first time in nearly seventy-five years.

Wolves have historically been better at birth control than humans. In a conventional wolf pack, only the Alpha Pair mates, and if food is scarce, even they don't produce offspring. While garou had no restrictions on sex, even in the 1400s, they tended to do the same with regard to having children, especially in light of their long lives. A mortal woman in her prime might give birth once every couple of years, but a garou female stayed in her prime for hundreds of years. A baby every couple of years would result in fifty children in a century with a nearly 100-percent probability of becoming effectively immortal themselves. If several females in each house had that many children—not to mention if other preternaturals reproduced at such a rate—they would overrun the world.

Nature had offered a solution to the problem. Garou females could only conceive when in heat, and they only came into heat for a single lunar cycle every few years. They also couldn't conceive in wolf form. The relative predictability of the cycle allowed them to plan, and careful consideration was given to each birth. If children weren't practical, precautions were taken to prevent unwanted pregnancy.

While the Alpha Pair primarily had the children, if subordinates wanted children they could petition for permission or leave and start their family on their own. Living independently was not an option in the White Guard, so permission was usually granted, especially if the Alpha Pair wasn't actively producing children or if they weren't mated to each other. Adam and Mary Quinn had been born when Gerard and Rhea, brother and sister, were the Alpha Pair.

When the females came into heat, the Masterses, Williamsons, and Quinns took birth control precautions, as did Peter and Aeron. Gerard sent word to Rome that he and Erica were interested in having children. Technically, they were asking permission, but it was only a formality. The White Guard needed to know about children because it meant changes in structure and number of garou available for combat. Couples rarely waited for approval, and usually by the time word came from Rome, the female was already pregnant.

When Erica read the letter saying that the White Guard had approved their request to have children, she rubbed her swollen belly and said, "Well, my child, it looks like we'll not have to hide you in the bulrushes. Their timing is impeccable." She was already in the early stages of labor.

"You know they would not have denied our request," Gerard said.

"Wouldn't have done them any good if they had. Do you think it's ever happened? Would Rome say no to a female who was already with child? And what would they expect if she were? In truth, Gerard, it is a silly tradition."

"The way you dislike the traditions, I wonder sometimes that you ever advanced in rank at all."

"Just because I don't like them doesn't mean I don't follow them. I just think the White Guard would be better served by affording us more autonomy. But we do what we have to do."

The letter also announced that the House of Blevins would be augmented. A garou from the House of Westchester in England had died in childbirth, and her husband wanted to relocate with the infant. They would arrive at Ballybrook within the year.

A baby boy was born the next day after several hours of screaming and swearing on Erica's part. According to Mary and Rhea, the delivery was routine and relatively easy, but Erica didn't agree.

"That child must way a tonne!" she cried as Mary cleaned the boy off.

"He does not, and he's perfect," Mary replied. She handed the baby to Erica. Then, "Go get Gerard," she told her mother, and Abigail left the room.

"What will you name him?" Rhea asked, sitting on the next cot.

"Aidan Corbin," she replied.

"Aidan?" Gerard said as he walked into the room. "You're still determined not to him for a saint?"

"Must we have this discussion again?" she said. "How many garou in the House of Blevins have saints' names?"

"Most have them as second names."

"If all children were given saints' names, there would be too few names in the world. Besides, don't you want to name him for your best friend? Don's second name is not a saint's name, is it? Or is there a St. Corbin that I've not been made aware of?"

"Actually, I'm fairly certain there is a St. Corbin," said Mary, "and a St. Aidan, for that matter."

"Who knew you had so much knowledge of the saints?" Gerard said to Mary.

"Some of us pay attention to our religious teaching," Mary teased him.

"Well, there you are," said Erica.

Children were born fully human, and their parents brought them across on the Full Moon after their twentieth birthday. The whole house was involved in raising the children, and the House of Blevins had the added assistance of the monks as well. As a baby, Aidan never knew what it was like to be alone. If he wasn't on Erica's hip, he was on someone else's. He was a bright child who said his first word at six months and was walking without assistance at nine months. After he learned to speak, he rarely cried unless he was in pain. He was forming complex sentences by the time John Easton and his son Will, who was a couple of months older than Aidan, arrived at Ballybrook.

John and Will were both stocky, with strawberry-blond hair and grayish-blue eyes. John's accent hinted that he had lived in England for a short while after spending decades in Eastern Europe. He confirmed that he had been born in Moldavia and had only joined the House of Westchester about ten years ago after meeting his wife at an induction.

When father and son arrived, Erica suggested that they put Will in the nursery with Aidan while she and Gerard showed John around the monastery. The instant Aidan and Will saw each other, they screamed and reached out to each other.

"You're here! You're here!" Aidan shouted.

John placed Will on the floor next to Aidan, and the toddlers hugged each other as if they were old friends who had been apart for a long time. Aidan took Will's hand and started showing him around the nursery.

"This is where we sleep," he said, pointing to the crib. "Don't climb out. You will hit your head. Call for *Má'r*, and she will let you out. This is the table where *Má'r* changes us."

"Ooh, stinky," said Will.

"She'll take the stinky away soon. She always do."

"Did you tell him Will was coming?" Gerard asked Erica.

"Nae. I didn't think he'd understand, so I thought to introduce them when they arrived."

"Well, it seems they're going to get along," said John. "How old is Aidan?"

"Just over a year," said Erica.

"He speaks better than Will."

"Hey!" Will cried indignantly. "I speak good!"

"Yes, you do, son."

"Don't talk too loud," Aidan whispered to Will. "It hurts the 'rou's ears."

"Brother Marcus set up a nursery for Will next door to your room," Gerard told John. "It's at the end of the—"

"*No!*" Aidan and Will cried in unison. They clung to each other, screaming at the top of their lungs.

"Will, it's just down the hall," John said.

"No, no, no!" Will shrieked.

"Please don't take him away," Aidan begged.

The adults eyed each other with concern, and Erica tried to pick Aidan up, but she couldn't pry them apart without hurting them.

"I think we can let Will stay in here, no?" said Erica.

Before long, the lads were more dependent on each other than they were on the adults. While Aidan rarely cried before Will came, he screamed in agony when they were separated, even if Will was only in the next room. Will did the same, and they usually cried until they were reunited. Thus, the adults let them stay together all the time.

"I bet they're soul siblings," Erica said as she and Gerard played with the lads one evening while John was out in the stable.

Soul siblings possessed an extraordinary emotional bond, and it was widely believed that they actually shared a soul.

"'Tis possible," said Gerard. "I don't know any, but I hear they're common among garou."

"We had a pair in the House of O'Shea. I used to think Peter and Don were soul brothers before I got to know them, but there are distinct differences."

"Like what?"

"For one thing, soul siblings feel each other's pain."

"But pain is of the body, not the soul. How is that possible?"

"I don't know. Also, they often think the same thoughts, have the same emotions, finish each other's sentences, even share mates." She took a toy Will handed her. "Thank you, Will." When he sat back down next to Aidan, she said, "I've never seen any who found each other so early."

"And fully human, at that," Gerard remarked.

"I've heard of soul siblings who weren't even born into garou families. They found each other after one or both of them became garou. It follows no reason that I can see."

Aidan said something unintelligible to Will, and Will replied in the same gibberish.

"What say you, lads?" Erica said. "Do you share a soul?"

"Aye!" they yelled in unison. Then they covered their mouths with their fingers and said, "Shh!"

* * *

Though they both spoke well, after a few months Aidan and Will abruptly stopped talking. The garou spent hours trying to engage them in conversation, only to have them smile and turn back to each other, babbling incoherently.

"I knew it was too easy," Erica complained as she practiced two-handed fencing with Rhea. "I'd heard child rearing was demanding and a babe would cause no end of worry, but Aidan was so perfect. John said the same of Will. Why have they backslid so?"

Abigail, who sat nearby, said, "Methinks someone is unaccustomed to failure and frustration."

Erica turned and glared at Abigail, leaving a rib open for Rhea to cut a shallow wound in her side. She turned on Rhea. "Oi, that hurt!"

"Keep your mind on the task at hand, then."

"You are not helping!"

Rhea smugly sheathed her weapons. "What do you think, Abigail Quinn? Have we finally found the great Erica Blevins's weakness?"

"A babe does tend to cloud a mother's sensibilities."

Erica turned to Abigail, rubbing her rib painfully. "So sayeth the voice of experience," she said.

"I know not what you're talking about," Abigail said haughtily.

"Adam and Mary. Are they not yours?"

A coy smile crossed Abigail's lips. "Your point?"

"Was there ever a problem like this with them?"

"Nae," Abigail admitted, "but I did notice things when they were small, in-jokes that only the two of them understood. If you listen carefully, you may recognize patterns in the lads' speech. To us it's nonsensical, but there may be more to it."

"Eh?" Rhea asked with a curious turn of her head.

"How do we speak in wolf form?"

"We use the language of—" With that, she brightened. "The language of the wolf!"

"Aye," Abigail said. "A flick of the ear, a nod of the head, a whine, and we can discern each other's meaning. And the birds, when they sing, does their song not have a design? We can tell what type of owl is in a tree by his call, no? 'Haps Aidan and Will have created their own language."

"If such is true," Erica said, "how will we get them to talk to us?"

Abigail sighed. "That's the question, then, isn't it?"

* * *

Aidan's *má'r* and the other *máthairs* were right. Will and Aidan could speak very well. They just didn't have anything to talk to the grown-ups about. Together, they never ran out of things to talk about. Besides, if the grown-ups didn't think Will and Aidan understood what they were saying, the lads got to overhear all sorts of things they weren't supposed to know. For instance, they knew the grown-ups fought vampires, because they talked about it when they thought he and Aidan weren't listening.

"Here, you take this one," Aidan said in their secret language as they played in the nursery one afternoon. He handed Will a wooden horse, then got another and marched it around the nursery.

"Let's fight vampires!" said Will.

"You be the vampire."

"But I *always* have to be the vampire. I *never* get to kill you."

"That's 'cause the vampires never kill the 'rou."

Will peered speculatively at his soul brother. "What do you think a vampire is?"

Aidan started to answer but stopped short. "You know what? I don't know what a vampire is."

"I bet it's a big, hairy monster with a lot of teeth and sharp claws."

"With one big red eye in the middle of its head."

"Aaarrgh!" Will growled.

"See? You do that real good. That's why you're the vampire, and that's why I get to kill you."

"But I don't want you to kill me anymore. I don't like it when you kill me."

"I know—why don't we *both* be 'rou, and we can kill made-up vampires."

They killed make-believe vampires for a while before getting bored and moving on to the next game.

"Let's shift and be 'rou," said Aidan.

"But we can't shift," said Will. "It's the New Moon."

"I saw Peter and Don shift on a New Moon."

"You did not. If you saw it, I would have saw it, too."

"I did! I'm not making it up."

"Maybe they *can* shift and they just don't like to."

"I wonder why."

Will shrugged in response.

"Let's go ask *Athair*."

Will followed Aidan downstairs to his *athair's* office. They stood before his desk, trying to appear grown up, and waited for him to finish whatever he was writing.

"Hello, lads," Aidan's *athair* said, looking up.

"*Athair*," Aidan said, "why do the 'rou not shift on the New Moon?"

Aidan's *athair's* mouth dropped open and his eyes got really big. He said, "Oh, uh, well, we're closer to our human selves when the Moon is new."

"So you *can* shift, but you don't like to?"

"That's right."

"Thank you, Aidan's *athair*," Will said before following Aidan out the door and back up to the nursery.

"He acted like he didn't know what to say," Will said, reverting to their secret language.

"Do you think he made it up?"

"Maybe, but what he said made sense. They *always* shift when the Moon is full. They like her a real lot then."

"I don't know why," Aidan said. "She just hangs up there and doesn't do anything."

"And then they sit out on the lawn and don't do anything except stare up at her."

"Maybe they're looking at the lass. They see better than us. Maybe she's really pretty, and they like to look at her."

"Hmm. Maybe we should ask your *athair* about that. Or no, we'll ask your *má'r*. She's a lass."

Will followed Aidan to the common room, where he asked his *má'r* about the lass in the Moon. Funny. She gave them the exact same expression as Aidan's *athair* did.

* * *

Vampire activity was heavy, and Erica did not have another baby for several years. Ian Luke was born when Aidan and Will were ten years old, and the boys carried him everywhere. Erica rarely saw him except when it was time to nurse or when they couldn't find someone else to change him. Their refusal to change a diaper aside, they were good caretakers and teachers, and Ian learned to speak and walk even faster than Aidan. In fact, "Aidan" was his first word.

Ian was a good-natured baby, but when he turned two, he started acting out. He didn't want to be held, he didn't want to be changed anymore, and whenever anybody called him "the baby," he stomped his foot and marched from the room.

Erica sat him on her lap in the courtyard one sunny summer afternoon after a particularly nasty tantrum and said, "How now, Little John?"

He muttered something about a ball and started into some lengthy tale he had made up, but Erica stopped him.

"Nae," she said, "why are you in so bad a mood these days?"

Ian stuck his lower lip out. "I nae bad!"

"Nae, you're a good lad, but you're in a bad mood. Why?"

"Aidan said I was the little brother."

"You arc."

He set his jaw in frustration and growled. It was all Erica could do to keep from laughing.

"Why does that bother you so?" she asked. "Being the little brother is good. People take care of you and bring you things, and you get loads of hugs and cuddles."

With that, Ian threw his arms around her neck and hugged her. When he pulled away, he said, "But I want a little brother to take care of and bring things and give hugs and cuddles."

"Well, don't fret, Little John. A new baby will come soon."

Ian's little face lit up. "He will? When?"

"Winter. A baby is growing in my belly, and this winter, when it's very cold and snowy outside, it will be too big—"

"*He'll* be too big, *Má'r!*"

"It could be a she."

Ian shook his head vehemently. "No, no, no! I want a little brother!"

"I can't choose, Ian. But you could take care of a little sister."

Ian eyed her dubiously. "All right," he said finally, "but I'd rather have a little brother."

"I'll do my best," Erica said, kissing his forehead.

"Má'r?"

"What is it, Little John?"

"How did he get in there?"

Before she could figure out how to answer the question, Aidan and Will came to her rescue. "Come, Ian," Aidan said from the doorway. "Let's go skip rocks on the river."

Ian joyfully held his hands up to his brother, who lifted him onto his shoulders and headed off toward the river with Ian chattering about a new baby brother.

* * *

Erica screamed. Gerard Blevins, Alpha Wolf of the House of Blevins, high-ranking member of The Order of the White Guard and hardened veteran of over 400 battles with deadly vampires, nearly crumbled. He had more influence than the majority of Alphas in the world and more control than most, but the cute little redhead down the hall could make him forget all that and wag his tail like a puppy. Or tuck his tail and go whimpering. Or want to tear her throat out.

She cried out again, and he actually stood and took a step toward the door, but his services weren't required at this time.

They loved to say that males and females were the same, but the fact was there were some things that one sex or the other just didn't do. Childbirth was for the females.

"Your screaming is not helping," he heard Rhea say.

"It may not be helping you," Erica said, "but it's helping me loads." She cried out again and unleashed a torrent of curses.

"Well, it's giving me an earache, so shut up. You are trained to withstand pain, you know."

"When you shite a pumpkin, you can talk to me about withstanding pain."

Peter laughed. "Maidens throughout Ireland are blushing."

"Her cries are worse this time," Gerard said.

"No, they're not, although she has been in there longer than with Aidan and Ian."

"Something is wrong."

Peter stood up and placed a hand on his shoulder. "Sit yourself, brother. Mary'll take good care of her."

Gerard reluctantly sat back down.

Don and Grace herded the boys into the common room, drew mugs of ale, and sat with Gerard and Peter. Ian climbed into Gerard's lap, and Aidan and Will stood respectfully next to his chair.

"Is he here yet?" the toddler asked.

"Nae, Ian, he's not here yet." Gerard could hear Mary coaching Erica, instructing her to push and counting to ten. "It shouldn't be long now, though."

"When your *már* stops screaming," Peter said, "the baby will be here."

"A new baby!" Ian squealed and clapped his hands. The three-year-old wriggled on his father's lap so that his mounds of dark curls bounced all over.

"Ian," Aidan complained, rolling his eyes.

"He's just glad not to be the youngest anymore," Will said.

The screaming stopped, and a baby began to cry. Abigail came in a moment later. "'Tis another lad, Gerard," she said.

Ian squealed with glee. "Dar! Dar!"

Aidan sighed and said, "*Deartháir*. Not Dar."

"See? I told you. A baby brother! You see? I *told* you!"

Aidan held his arms out to the toddler. "Come, Ian. *Athair* will want to go see *Már* and the new baby."

"I go too!" Ian demanded.

"Later," Gerard replied. "Let them rest awhile first."

Ian pouted. "He's had enough rest. He's slept in *Máᵈr*'s belly for a long time!"

"But *Máᵈr* hasn't been sleeping, and she needs *her* rest. Soon, Ian." He handed Ian to Aidan, and the lads left the room.

Gerard stood, as did Peter, Don, and Grace.

"Cheers," Peter said, clapping him on the shoulder.

"Thank you, brother," Gerard replied, his voice breaking. "Oi," Don said, "is weeping allowed when a third son is born?"

"Try and stop me."

"Kiss them for us," Grace said as she hugged Gerard.

He left the common room and headed to the infirmary. Mary had just finished cleaning the baby when Gerard arrived, and she brought him to Erica and placed him in her arms.

Erica tapped at the baby's chin until he opened his mouth and then forced it to her nipple. He caught on right away and latched on, and she gasped.

"He's strong," she said. "And smart."

Gerard sat on the cot and stroked a gentle finger across the baby's head, which, like his brothers' heads, was covered with dark curls. "I was worried," he said.

"'Twas a long labor, but we're fine."

"Next time, can you give me a red-haired beauty?"

"Must all Blevins males try to tell me what child to bear?"

"So, my love, what will he name him?"

"I was thinking of Logan Peter."

"A strong name. I like it, but Brother Herschel won't like the name of Logan."

Erica gave him what he had come to refer to affectionately as *that look*. "Peter is a saint's name. Besides, if we only gave children the names of saints—"

"We'd all have the same names."

"'Haps he'll be a saint someday."

Gerard laughed and said, "Well, welcome to the world, Saint Logan."

14

Fortunate Son

From childhood's hour I have not been as others were—I have not seen as others saw. — Edgar Allan Poe

"It's squishy," Logan said as he peered into the cradle at his new brother, Ryan James.

"He's not squishy," Ian replied.

"It's fat."

"He *is* a big baby, but they all look like that."

"How do *you* know?"

With an air of superiority uncharacteristic for a six-year-old, Ian said, "I know many things."

"Do they all look like that?" Logan asked his *máthair*, who knelt on the other side of the cradle.

"Aye, they do."

"I didn't look like that!"

Ian laughed. "You were even squishier than he is."

Logan glared at his older brother. "You said he weren't squishy. *Má'r*, why is he so squishy?"

"Babies are born with extra fat to help keep them warm. And to make them more fun to cuddle."

"I think you just like the word, 'squishy,'" Ian said to his younger brother.

Logan stuck his tongue out at him.

Erica picked Logan up and carried him out of the room.

"Come, Little John," she called. "Let Ryan sleep."

Ian took Logan and Ryan into his care in much the same way Aidan had taken him. Over time, he all but abandoned the older boys' companionship and spent most of his time with the younger ones.

The lads all resembled Gerard, but where Aidan and Ian had inherited his cold glare, Logan and Ryan had warm, expressive eyes like Erica. The lads looked so much alike that sometimes Erica marveled at how different they all were.

Aidan was determined and serious like Gerard. He adored his father and tried to be like him, often going out of his way to use Gerard's words or mimic his mannerisms.

Ian was willful and most likely to get into trouble. He was closest to Logan but went his own way much of the time and often disappeared for hours, to be found a mile away playing make-believe in a cave, or napping atop one of the outer towers.

Ryan was gentle and sweet, full of love and concern for others. When any of the garou was injured, Ryan went to the infirmary and held his or her hand while Mary treated them. This endeared him to Mary, who had done the same thing as a child, and she often carried him around with her.

As for Will, for whom Erica had become a de facto mother, he was still Aidan's shadow. At times, he didn't really seem to have a personality of his own, but then he would say something so logical and reasonable that it made one believe there was more going on in his mind than adoration for Aidan.

Even at three years of age, Logan possessed an incredible curiosity. Abigail had told Erica about what she liked to call "The Wherefores," when a child asked "why" about everything, but Erica hadn't really experienced them. Aidan and Will asked a few "whys," but Ian rarely questioned anything they told him. He would rather find his own answers, and if he asked something, it was usually in the form of a request for help rather than a why. Logan, however, questioned everything. He asked, as Aidan had, why no one shifted on the New Moon, but the queries went much deeper. Why, when she had red hair, did Erica shift to a white wolf? Why, when she was pregnant with Ryan, didn't she shift, even on the Full Moon? Why did the monks and the children get sick but none of the garou, and why were some of the monks so white and wrinkly? Why did it rain? There was an endless stream of whys and hows that bordered on annoying, but she answered every question as well as she could. She was also careful to say, "I don't know" when she really didn't know an answer instead of making up some white lie in an attempt to satisfy his curiosity. He wouldn't have believed her anyway. He was smart, maybe too smart for his own good.

Erica knew she wasn't supposed to have a favorite child, but she had to admit she was closer to Logan than the other lads. She didn't love the other lads any less, but she had a special bond with Logan. When Logan wasn't asking why about everything, they had meaningful conversations. He was intelligent and practical, and even at age two or three he could be reasoned with. He was most likely to be found sitting on a hill somewhere, contemplating something he had learned from the monks or Peter, whom Logan asked as many questions as he did Erica. Logan seldom got upset or cried, and when he did, it was usually because someone had insulted his intelligence or treated him like a baby. Logan was no baby, and Erica thought maybe he never had been.

* * *

At times, Logan thought the same thing. He was too busy to be a baby. There were so many things to learn, so many things to do, that sometimes he couldn't sleep because there was just too much to think about. It wasn't always that way, though. When he climbed into his *má'r*'s lap, he turned back into a bright-eyed toddler. Aidan called him a baby when he did that, but he didn't care what Aidan said.

Logan didn't like Aidan, and he was pretty sure the feeling was mutual. Aidan picked on him from the time he could walk, and Logan could never understand why. Maybe when he was smaller, he committed some offense he just didn't remember. It must have been bad for Aidan to stay mad for so long. Ian said Aidan was scared of him, but that didn't make sense. Aidan was so much bigger that he could squash Logan into a greasy spot on the ground if he wanted.

Will didn't have much more interest in Logan than Aidan did, but at least he was nicer. Where his brother would shout and scold, Will would wink and say, "That's just gonna get you into trouble, you know." At times, he would even defend Logan when Aidan was being unreasonable.

Logan became conscious of the Moon very early on. The adults were obsessed with her. He would have thought of the Moon as an "it," but the garou referred to her as "she," as though she were an actual person. When the night was clear, he could see dark spots that looked kind of like a face; maybe that had something to do with it. He admitted that she was fun to watch, especially on clear nights when she was surrounded by millions of stars or when the northern lights provided an ever-changing rainbow as a backdrop. At times, he would go into the yard outside the keep as the Full Moon approached and sit with one of the garou as they stared at her. Some of them even did it when she was nowhere near full. Logan studied her a lot and asked dozens of questions that the adults tried to answer, but they ultimately referred him to Brother Herschel, who gave him several books. He learned to read by studying the books the monk gave him.

The initiation chamber lay beneath a trapdoor in the hallway outside the infirmary. A rug covered the trapdoor, and Logan had never even known it was there, but when Will turned twenty, the monks opened it up and aired it out. Will's twentieth birthday was two months before Aidan's, and he asked if his initiation could be delayed so that he could be brought across at the same time as his soul brother.

Though Brother Marcus expressly told the lads the room was off limits, Logan and Ian went exploring anyway. Thinking they were being stealthy and forgetting that the entire pack could hear them open the trapdoor, descend the steps, and whisper to each other to be quiet, they crept into the chamber one night. The room was empty except for two sconces and two sets of shackles bolted to the wall.

"What are those for?" Logan asked his brother shakily.

"I don't want to think on it," Ian replied.

Several stains darkened the walls and floor.

"Who was the last one brought across?" Logan asked.

"Mary, I guess. Think that's her blood?"

"I don't like this place."

"Let's away from here," Ian said uneasily, and they climbed back up the stairs and replaced the rug.

The next day, their *athair* sat down with them in Ian's bedroom.

"You got quite a scare last night, no?" he said.

"Are you going to punish us?" Ian asked.

"For sneaking into the initiation chamber?"

"Well, *trying* to," said Logan.

"One would think ye'd have learnt by now that you can't do anything secretly in this house. I've already punished you just by letting you go. Ye learnt the hard way that when we tell you something is forbidden, we do it for a reason."

"*Athair*, what goes on down there?" Logan asked.

"What do you think goes on down there? You've been told how a garou is brought across, and I'm sure you already have ideas, but now they're even worse 'cause of what you saw. Are you sure you want more knowledge than you already have to live with for the next ten years?"

"Well, not when you put it like that," Ian said.

"We're sorry, *Athair*," said Logan. "We won't do anything like that again."

"Of course, ye will."

Ian shrugged. "Aye, we probably will."

* * *

Logan sat on Ian's bed the first night of the Full Moon and listened for sounds coming from the rooms below. Mary's room, which was near Ian's, was directly above the infirmary and could be accessed by a spiral staircase. She often forgot to close her bedroom door, so it was easy to hear sounds coming from below. Tonight, she had remembered, and Logan and Ian couldn't hear what was going on all the way down in the initiation chamber.

"Do you think they chained them to the wall?" Logan asked.

"They probably did."

"Maybe they lock them up so they can't run away before they bite them."

Ian regarded him grimly. "Someday we'll be the ones chained to that wall."

Logan tried not to cry, but his lip trembled and he couldn't contain his tears.

"I'm scared too," Ian said bleakly.

"Maybe they won't make us do it."

"If we don't, we'll grow old and die like Brother Finnius."

After a while they heard movement, and Ian and Logan went to Mary's door and put their ears close. Will whimpered, and Aidan, his own voice thick with pain, told him to shut up.

"They're alive," Ian said.

"They wouldn't have killed them."

"Not on purpose, but Don says accidents happen."

"Say you didn't believe him," Logan said. "It was Don! He was making fun or trying to frighten you."

"'Haps. The garou are out of the monastery, you know. Do you want to go back?"

"No!" Logan cried. "You can go by yourself this time."

* * *

As alarming as the initiation chamber was, it was nothing compared to Logan's horror when Ian told him the garou would leave for Rome soon.

"That was *surely* Don telling you tales," he said, but Ian shook his head.

"You don't remember it, but *Athair* and the rest of the pack went after Ryan was born. They go every fifth year. *Má'r* didn't go 'cause we were too young."

Logan shook his head in denial. "Nae," he said. "She'll not leave us."

"She will," Ian said. "And she'll be gone for a long time."

"You're lying!"

"I will never lie to you, little brother," Ian promised.

Logan worried over it for days and even tried to distance himself from his *má'r* in case what Ian had said was true, but when she looked at him with sadness in her eyes, he couldn't help jumping into her arms. She finally confirmed what Ian had said.

"Why, *Má'r*? Why must you leave us here?"

"You're too young to go," she said. "The trip would be hard for you, and you wouldn't comprehend the goings on."

"But you said I'm smart. I would understand."

"Nae, dear heart. Besides, the garou don't take children to inductions. 'Tis a time for us to be together as grown-ups."

Logan had to walk away without saying anything else, although she pleaded with him to stay. He left the monastery and ran until he couldn't run anymore and then threw himself to the ground and cried. How could she do this to him? She had all but said she didn't want him to go.

Peter showed up a while later and sat down next to him. Peter was his godfather, and he had taken the role of mentor very seriously. He had never treated Logan like a child and had always spoken to him like a little adult. When others chided and coddled him—even Gerard and Erica—Peter reasoned with him. He could make Logan understand when others could not.

"Your *máthair* is upset," Peter said.

"She's not upset. She doesn't even care."

"You know better than that, little brother."

Logan sighed. "I know. But she's gonna be gone so long."

"You'll have Ian and Ryan and the monks. This is important to your *máthair*. She hasn't gone to an induction since before Ian was born, and this year, Aidan and Will are to be inducted into the White Guard. Would you want her to miss such an important event? How would you feel if it was you and she didn't attend?"

"That's different. Aidan wouldn't care 'cause he has no feelings."

Peter laughed. "Of course, he does. He just shows them different. Erica isn't abandoning you, Logan. Indeed, she'll miss you more than anything. And what of your *athair*? Won't you miss him?"

"I will! I'll miss you and the others too."

"But it's different with your *máthair*, no?"

"Is that wrong?"

"Not at all. Most children are closer to one parent than the other."

"Who were you closer to?"

"My father. He was very proud to have sons, and he took us everywhere."

"How many brothers did you have?"

"I had one."

"Tell me about him. What was he like?"

Peter shook his head. "I've told you too much already, and we're not talking about me, anyway. I know it's hard to let your *máthair* go, but it's something you must do. Erica is a soldier in an elite militant order, and she set her duties aside while you and your brothers were small, but it is time to take them up again. We all have things we have to do, even you. Your *má'r* expects you to pick up after yourself, take care of your brothers, keep up with your studies, even go to Mass."

"I guess."

"What do you do when we leave for a mission? She has gone with us then."

"But those are only for a few weeks. She has never gone for so long. I do understand, Peter. Her duty is to go to Rome, and mine is to stay here and take care of my brothers and be patient. But it's hard, and I'm afraid."

Peter put his arm around Logan's shoulder. "I know, little brother. But you're a brave lad, and you'll be all right."

They sat for a while longer, and Peter told him about a few of the events that would take place in Rome. By the time they returned to the monastery, Logan felt better about Erica's impending departure.

Will and Adam were fencing in the courtyard, and Don and Aidan observed from a nearby bench. Logan and Peter sat down with them.

Adam stepped past Will's sword and slapped his face. "You'd best watch leaving yourself open in such way," he said. "They'll bury you in Rome."

"How did he err?" Don asked Aidan.

"He let his blade swing wide, and Adam was able to come in too close. He could have as easily run him through as slapped him."

"I'd have run him through," said Peter.

Will practiced the technique, and Adam said, "Better, but watch your lead foot. You don't want to lose your balance when a blade is aimed at your heart."

"I know, I know," Will said.

"If you know, then put it into practice."

"You're no better than he," Aidan told him.

"'Haps not," Adam admitted. "But what I lack in talent I make up in experience. If I see an error, I shall point it out. Even with you, my dear superior wolf."

Logan had heard it before. Logan liked Adam, but Aidan couldn't stand him. In fact, neither could Peter and Don. A fortnight after his initiation—even before he had shifted the first time—Aidan had challenged Adam and easily defeated him, and he never let anybody forget it.

Peter patted Logan's knee. "I'm going inside," he said. "Will you go or stay and watch?"

"I'll stay."

"Don't stay too long. You'll want to go find your *máthair* soon." When Peter left, Logan scooted over next to Don and watched as the match continued. Aidan criticized Adam whenever he made a mistake, but he never said a word to Will. He didn't even say anything when Will made an error so obvious that Logan spotted it.

He stood up and pointed at Will, his eyes open wide. "He left his rib open!"

"'Tis not your place to say, little one," Aidan snapped.

"Why not? It was a mistake. I saw it."

"You saw no such thing! How would you even know it was a mistake? Stick to your childhood games, Logan."

"He was right, you know," Don said.

"It doesn't matter. He's overstepping his bounds."

"He doesn't have those bounds, and you know it. And why does it matter to you? I would have thought you'd be proud that your brother is already starting to pick up our ways."

"Well, if he's old enough to criticize our fencing, he's old enough to start learning our other ways, too, and that means watching his mouth."

"You're overreacting."

"And I think you're not reacting enough. Truly, Don! Erica spoils him, and Ian and Peter drag him everywhere they go. You needn't do it too."

Don slapped the back of Aidan's head. "And you need to remember *your* place, 'little one,' 'cause your attitude will get you into trouble. It would be unseemly for the Alpha's son to go to his induction in the position of Omega Wolf."

"You wouldn't!"

Don raised an eyebrow and glared at him. Aidan glowered back at him for a moment before looking away. "I'm sorry."

"Tell *him*," Don said.

"You were right," Aidan said to Logan. "I was jealous 'cause you said it before I did."

"'Tis all right," Logan said casually. In truth, though, he wondered again why Aidan disliked him so.

15

Who Knew?

Don't Kill the Messenger. — The Messenger

Ardis and Pippa sat in a pub in Calais listening to a group of drunken Englishmen ranting about the French. The war had been over for years, but the English still loved to blather about it. Pippa, for one, wished they'd just shut up.

"Know what I think I'll do?" Ardis said.

"What's that, my love?"

"See that skinny mortal over there? The sickly, pale one who looks like he couldn't kill a mouse?"

"I see him." The man was young, maybe twenty. There were dark, puffy circles under his eyes, his skin had an ashen hue, and his scent was sour. A plague raged through Europe—a plague was *always* raging through Europe—and the young man evidently suffered from the disease.

"I think I'll bring him across then tell him all of his friends are spies for the enemy," Ardis said.

"Which enemy?"

"Does it matter?"

"He's ill, too. You would be doing him a great favor. We can make up an elaborate story for him. Make him think the French are going to invade England."

Ardis smiled approvingly. "Very creative! See, this is why I love you, Pippa. You understand me. We'll work him into a lather, bring him across, and then turn him loose. He'll be cured of his disease, and we'll have amusing entertainments."

They had to hold off on their plans when Wilhelm, a vampire who scouted for Ardis, walked into the pub. Wilhelm was tall and skinny, with sharp, hawkish features and pale blond hair. In the gloom of the bar, the lavender glow of his eyeshine was quite noticeable. He wore the clothes of a commoner: brownish tunic, leather pants tucked into soft boots, and a worn wool cloak. It had been years since they had seen him, but Ardis rolled his eyes and grunted in annoyance at the intrusion, as if he were tired of being bothered. Wilhelm stood at the table, waiting for Ardis to acknowledge him. Ardis snapped, "What!"

"I have come from Ireland, *mein* master," Wilhelm said.

"Really, now? That's encouraging, seeing how that is where I sent you. I wouldn't expect you to come from, say, India, if I'd sent you to Ireland, now would I?"

"*Nein*, Master."

"And I would be able to ascertain on my own that you've come, because you are standing here before me. Am I correct?"

"*Ja*, Master. I apologize for my inane remark."

"Right, then. What do you want?"

"Want? I ... naught, Master."

"Then why are you here?"

"I am here to report."

"Ah, of course! What's happening on my favorite island?"

"Naught of any import. Life goes on as usual. Vampires still come and go in large numbers and the garou hunt them. Few live tell the tale. The White Guard never replaced the pack you destroyed. Only the House of Blevins guards Ireland now."

"Any deaths?"

"*Nein*, Master. They are all well. There have been a few births, though."

"Births?" Wilhelm didn't notice the edge in Ardis's voice, but Pippa did.

"I believe I told you before that the Alpha Pair had married," Wilhelm continued. "They are breeding, and she has given birth to five sons. Three are still small, but the other two are old enough for combat. They are—"

Ardis stood up and loomed over Wilhelm. "You think this is not important news? Can you really be that stupid? Pippa, can he really be that stupid?"

"But they are only children," Wilhelm protested. "How can they affect you?"

"Apparently, he *can* be that stupid." He started speaking very slowly. "Listen carefully, Wilhelm, and I'll use small words. Infant ... garou ... grow up ... to be ... what?"

Wilhelm's eyes widened with fear, but he answered. "Adult garou?"

"And ... what ... do ... infant ... *White Guard* garou ... grow up ... to be?"

Realization dawned on Wilhelm's face. "Ah. I am sorry, Master. I didn't think."

"*Nein*, you didn't. And if two are old enough for combat, why am I just hearing about it now? That's more than twenty years. Why is it that every vampire I bring across completely loses all brain function?"

"I do not understand, Master."

"Exactly!"

"Again, *mein* apologies."

"What else?"

"They travel to Rome. This is why I came when I did. After the garou left, I could not bear to be within ten miles of the monastery."

Ardis groaned. "Those damned inductions." To Pippa, he said, "What do you think the Church does to keep our vampires away while they're all off to Rome?"

"I don't know, my love. Some strange magic. The faithful have powers we do not understand."

Ardis pounded his fist on the table. "But I have powers *they* don't understand! I should be able to circumvent them easily, even if no other vampire can. I'm practically a god myself, Pippa!"

"I know, my love."

Pippa smiled up at Wilhelm, who smiled halfheartedly back at her. He was clearly afraid of what Ardis would do to him; the elder vampire was unpredictable, and Wilhelm had brought bad news.

"Is there anything else I can do for *mein* master?" he asked timidly.

Ardis folded his arms and considered. He was so beautiful when he was pondering something that Pippa couldn't contain herself, and she got up to wrap her arms around his waist.

"What do you think, my dear?" Ardis asked her warmly as he gazed into her eyes and stroked her hair. "Should we give him some other task or send him on his way?"

"If you want to pay Gerard a visit when he comes home, you may want some other vampires with you. Wilhelm could help you bring them across."

Ardis kissed the top of Pippa's head and let her go. "What do you think of that, Wilhelm? You've not brought anyone across before; here's your opportunity to give me a dozen."

"I—I would be honored, Master!"

Ardis made a face as though trying to decide what to do. Finally, he said, "Nah, I don't think so."

He grabbed Wilhelm and bit into his throat, and the younger vampire screamed. None of the humans noticed because Ardis was very good at hiding himself, but it amazed Pippa that they didn't notice all the blood. Ardis was never tidy when he fed. The messier the kill, the happier he was. Before long, he had all but chewed Wilhelm's head off. He smiled at Pippa as he dropped the lifeless body. It made two hollow thumps as it hit the wooden floor, the first from the body and the second from the barely attached head, and Ardis nodded with satisfaction. His face and clothes were covered in blood and gore now, and his eyes were wilder than before, but oddly, his hair was still perfect.

"That's too many Blevinses, don't you think?" he said.

"Yes, especially if they grow up to be as adept as their parents."

He sighed sadly. "Something will need to be done about it, I guess."

"What about the wards?"

"People leave the castle all the time, don't they?"

"Indeed, they do, my love."

"That will mean killing Gerard, though. Probably Peter and Don, too. I hate that."

"You knew it would have to happen sooner or later."

"I know. We could kill all the rest and leave them alive."

"But you would still have too many Blevinses."

Ardis thought it over. "You know what would be really fun? If we could break into the monastery and bring their children across before they had the chance to do it. Especially if they're still young like you. Why, we could have a whole coven of tiny vampires!"

Pippa laughed. "I like it, but there's no easy way to get in."

"We've done it before."

"Yes, and after that raid in County Cork, you promised not to put me through that again. You might be able to get past those wards of fear, but they put knots in my stomach. Have you ever tried to fight a werewolf with knots in your stomach?"

"Well, it's not like you have to fight. You can just sit back and watch. I'll think on it for a while. I mean, how hard can it be?"

"How hard, indeed."

"Ah, well. I guess for now we'll just have to go with what we've got, and that means killing the ones we can draw out."

"You'll kill the whole pack, then? That will take fighters."

"Then we'll just have to bring some fighters across, won't we? So. What of our immediate plan?"

Pippa had long since become used to Ardis's cruelty, and she barely regarded Wilhelm's ravaged body as she turned her gaze to the sickly man on the other side of the pub. He coughed.

"I still think it is a good plan," she said.

"Would you like to go get him and bring him to our table?"

"Of course, my love."

Ardis kissed her, then sent her off, spattered with blood from his face and clothing, to get the human.

16

The End of the Innocence

If a man will begin with certainties, he shall end in doubts; but if he will be content to begin with doubts, he shall end in certainty. — Sir Francis Bacon

A few months after the garou returned from the induction, word arrived regarding vampire activity in County Down. It was only a couple of days' ride, so Gerard saw fit to send scouts instead of taking everyone. He thought it would be a good chance for Aidan and Will to get their feet wet, so he sent them to investigate with Don and Peter along to train and supervise.

Peter was less than happy about it.

County Down was crawling with O'Neills, families conquered by the dynasty, and factions who had allied themselves with them. Peter doubted if there was a soul in the area who hadn't somehow been influenced by the O'Neills.

"What exactly did I do to incur your wrath?" he demanded.

"Come, brother," said Gerard, "you haven't been there in more than a century. What are the chances you'll run into someone you know?"

"You're a villain, Gerard."

"It gets worse. You're going to Belfast. Castleraegh."

Peter's face turned red. "I'm seriously considering running you through."

"Killing me would make you Alpha, and then you could send someone else."

"Don't tempt me."

"You live here and you never see them."

"That's different."

"How?"

Peter growled in frustration. "Brother, don't do this to me. Send Owen. He's been itching for a good fight."

"You've taught them everything they know. They need the experience, and truly, who better to lead them into their first battle?"

"You're certain we can't just let the vampires have Castleraegh?"

Gerard gave him a rare laugh but would not relent.

As they left the monastery and headed east, Aidan said, "I take it you've been to Castleraegh before."

"We're not gonna discuss it on this journey, except to say that no one—*no one*—is to use my surname. Understood?"

"Understood."

The party camped by the road for two nights and arrived at Belfast the third afternoon. They got rooms at a local inn and began their investigation the next morning. Fortunately, Peter didn't come face to face with any of the nobles of Castleraegh during their stay, and by talking with the peasants and merchants, they were able to track and locate a coven in a few days.

Ireland's vampires usually had one of two different types of lairs: they either holed up in a crowded city or invaded a remote farm, killed the residents, and moved in. These vampires had tried something new. They had taken over a castle.

It was small as castles went and didn't even have a wall, obviously not meant to be the stronghold of a clan chief, but it was larger than most other vampiric lairs. The house had three floors in three wings in addition to several outbuildings. The furnishings were luxurious, with lots of elaborate tapestries, overstuffed chairs, and tiled floors. Crown molding, blue velvet, and gold trim were everywhere.

"Did Ballybrook once look like this?" Will asked.

"It did," Peter replied. "It was God-awful."

Whereas most lairs they encountered smelled of blood and decaying bodies, there were few unpleasant scents in this castle. There was some spoiled food in the kitchens, but nothing more sinister. The castle didn't even have the ubiquitous chamber pot odor that Peter hated so much. Someone had cleaned.

The garou started with the cellar, which was the most likely place for vampires to spend the day, but it was empty. They went up from there, searching overly decorated ballrooms, music rooms, libraries, and bedchambers. They discovered four vampires in a salon on the second floor.

Three males and a female slept in large boxes that looked for all the world like coffins. The boxes had lids, but they hadn't closed them, choosing instead to draw the heavy curtains at the windows. Aidan reached for his sword, but Peter put a restraining hand out and motioned for Aidan and the others to follow him outside.

When they were safely out of the house, Peter said, "Don't forget they hear nearly as well as we do. As quiet as we are, they still might hear us. Most of our fights occur when we wake them up by making too much noise, and it's easy to do. We must check the whole house and grounds before we kill them. We can't afford to leave any of it unchecked, especially one this large. There may be more of them."

The rest of the castle was unoccupied, but when they explored the outbuildings, they finally happened upon the odor of death and decay. Seven bodies, a family of four and three servants, were piled in the gardener's shed.

"Relatives?" Don asked.

"Don't know," Peter said. "Don't really care to."

"Do we bury them?" said Will.

"Nae, we take their heads and burn the bodies," Don replied.

"Why?"

Don bent and turned the head of the nearest corpse to show fang marks. "They may have been turned."

"But they're badly decayed," Aidan said. "They've been dead at the least a fortnight."

"Peter, do you hear them arguing with us, or is it just me?"

"Nae, they're arguing."

"Sorry," Aidan said.

"Never take that kind of risk, little brother," said Don. "If they've been bitten, no matter how long they've been dead, you take their heads."

"Let's get rid of the vampires first," Peter said, "and then we'll come back and take care of these poor bastards."

They went back inside, ascended the stairs and listened carefully at the door to the salon. When they were confident there was no movement in the room, they drew their swords, and Peter opened the door.

Before they even saw that the boxes were empty, one of the vampires leapt onto Will's back and bit his neck. Aidan gasped with pain. Will's sword flew out of his hand and crashed into a wall. He curled his fist and punched the vampire as close to its nose as he could manage, and it snarled and let go of his throat. He grabbed its hair and yanked its head back, then hit it again.

"This is why we teach you unarmed combat," Don said as Will engaged in a heated brawl with the female. He went to a window and jerked a curtain down, letting in the sunlight.

"*Allons-y,*" someone said, and the other vampires moved from behind tapestries, brandishing swords.

"*En garde!*" another one exclaimed.

"*En garde?*" Peter said incredulously.

"'Haps it's been taking fencing lessons," Don suggested.

"It'll need them." Peter confronted the nearest one.

Aidan had waited all his life for the day he would kill his first vampire, but when he'd seen them sleeping in their boxes he'd begun to have doubts. They didn't look anything like big, hairy monsters with one red eye in the middle of their heads. Spending years training to kill them didn't mean he would actually be able to do it when the time came. Fencing for sport or rank wasn't the same as actual combat. He knew what he had to do and was perfectly willing; he just hoped he didn't choke. As his neck throbbed with Will's pain, he knew it wouldn't happen. He advanced on one of the vampires.

"We should thank you for waking up," Peter said to the vampire he fought.

"Indeed," said Don. "We were just saying that our young companions needed to contend with some live vampires. 'Twould be a shame to have to behead you in your sleep and go back home without a proper fight."

Will punched the female in the abdomen and kneed it in the face.

"Nicely done," said Peter. "Now, I would say 'twas wrong to hit a lady, but I'm betting that's no lady."

"Pretty, though," Don said. "Methinks it won't be so pretty without a head."

One of the vampires said something in French, and Don said, "Oi, lads? I don't think these fiends understand a word we're saying."

"Well, that's no good," said Peter. "Do you recall any French?"

"Hmm, let us see. *Elle n'aura pas l'air si jolie sans tête.*"

Don's pronunciation and grammar were off, but the vampire got the point. It screamed and ran for the door with Will in pursuit.

"And that's why we teach you to speak the Romance languages," Don said.

Aidan felt a sharp pain in his forearm, and somewhere out in the hallway Will cursed. A moment later, the female shrieked and hit the floor with a loud thump. Aidan's vampire turned toward the doorway, called the female's name, and left its chest wide open. Aidan lunged, and his aim was perfect. He pierced the vampire's heart and it dropped to the floor.

"Well done!" Peter said proudly.

Aidan couldn't answer. He stood there, staring at the creature where it lay, and he couldn't breathe. It looked too human, and the sight of it with his sword sticking out of its chest was paralyzing.

"All right, brother?" Don asked.

"Not sure," Aidan replied.

Will came into the room, bloodied silver dagger in hand, looking unsettled. "How'd it feel?" he asked Aidan.

"As though I'll never be the same again."

"Aye, for me, too."

"You get used to it," said Don.

Peter and Don were still fighting the last two vampires. How he and Will had been able to make their kills before the older garou was incomprehensible until he watched them. His packmates' skills were so far beyond those of the vampires, it was almost funny. Blades clanged as Peter and Don parried swing after awkward swing, rarely making attacks of their own. They remained on the defensive for several minutes, and Aidan realized they were toying with the beasts.

"Why are ye prolonging the fight?" Aidan accused them.

"Do you think they're in a hurry to die?" Don retorted.

Peter's opponent found an opening and almost made contact with his side. "Good show," Peter said appreciatively. "I didn't even give you that one."

The vampire said something in French.

"Ooh, bad form!" Don said.

"What did it say?" Peter asked.

"It told you to eat shite."

"The French have no manners."

The vampire fighting Don breathed heavily, and Aidan and Will watched in amazement. "It's getting tired," Don said.

"He's breathing!" Will cried.

"Aye, they do that."

"But they're dead."

Peter said, "Boggles the mind, no? Hey, Don."

"Eh, brother?"

"Are you ready to end this?"

"Now is good. It's near lunchtime and my belly is starting to rumble."

In perfect unison, Peter and Don tipped the points of their blades low, inviting a high attack. When the vampires obliged, they stepped back and beat down their blades, then lunged and delivered quick slashes to the vampires' throats. They came in with a second stroke to decapitate the creatures.

"Now you're just showing off," Will said.

"Aye, we do that," said Don. "Shall we burn the house?"

"Nae, let's take them to the shed and burn them with the humans," said Peter. "'Tis a nice house; someone may want it."

"If you weren't armed, I'd say something about you thinking like a noble."

"Good thing you didn't say anything like that, then."

"What about those ... coffins?" Will said.

"I don't think they'll fit in the shed," said Don.

"Damnedest things I've ever seen," Peter mused. "Well, the peasants thought it was vampires. If anybody comes in and discovers the coffins, they'll have something to gossip about."

Each of them took a body and carried it to the shed. "It was fortunate there were four of them," Peter said. "Ye lads got your first kills, and Don and I got to enjoy a good fight."

"I'd hardly call it a good fight," said Don. "I all but had to coach the damn thing. I think they just took decorative swords off the walls, 'cause they didn't know how to use them."

They placed the bodies in the shed, Don administered a simplified version of Last Rites to the humans, and they set about taking the heads of the remaining two vampires and their victims. Aidan had no trouble with the creatures, but he balked at decapitating the mortals. Peter laid a hand on his shoulder.

"Think of it this way," he said. "If it were you, would you want to awaken as a half-living monster obsessed with a thirst for blood, or would you hope someone would see to it that you were spared such a fate? You won't hurt them, little brother. You'll save their souls."

With that, Aidan found it easier. It still made him a little nauseous, and Will's face said he felt the same way, but they took the heads of the dead without further hesitation, doused the bodies and the shed with fuel oil, and stood back as Peter set the fire.

"Do you think they left any food in the kitchens?" Don said.

"Can't hurt to check," said Peter.

Aidan and Will gaped at them.

"What?"

"How can ye be so callous about all this?" Aidan said.

"When you've been fighting them for three hundred years, you'll see things differently," Peter said. "The first few times it's hard, but you'll soon become accustomed to the fact that they only *look* like people."

"I don't think we've reached that point yet," Will said.

17

Bad Day

No one can confidently say that he will still be living tomorrow. —
Euripides

1492

The two years after the battle at Castleraegh were slow. There
was minimal vampire activity, and the House of Blevins's newest
soldiers only had two missions. One was a tough fight, but the
other was a simple extermination. Boredom set in, and Gerard had
to contend with some in-fighting. As the dry spell wore on, the
garou traded rank very often.

Don became Beta Wolf for a few months before Peter took the
rank back. Don and Peter rarely fought—in fact, they seldom
disagreed—but their battles for rank were especially brutal,
usually with both of them ending up in the infirmary.

"Why do you two do this?" Mary asked Peter after their second
duel, in which Don had punctured Peter's lung before sustaining a
massive concussion from which he still hadn't regained
consciousness.

"It's the only time we don't feel we have to hold back," Peter said.

"'Haps you should. You're gonna kill each other."

"And if you don't," said Grace, who stood next to the table on
which Don lay, "I think I might kill you both."

"We're not gonna kill each other. We know each other's limits
and how far we can push."

Mary glared at him.

"What?"

"You can barely breathe, and he's been unconscious for over an
hour."

"I'm awake," Don mumbled.

"You're an idiot."

"Aw, I love you, too, Mary."

* * *

The females went into heat in the spring, and Gerard and Erica were hopeful that some of the garou's tensions would be relieved. If nothing else, they would at least be in a better mood.

Less than a week into the females' cycle, they got an assignment.

"Now?" Gerard said incredulously to Brother Marcus, who sat across the desk. The monk had brought documents passed on from the monastery in Derry with news of vampire activity in County Clare.

"You can't tell me those vampires weren't drawing attention to themselves a month ago," said Erica, who sat next to Brother Marcus.

"It stands to reason that they will still be there a month from now," Brother Marcus said helpfully.

"It's tempting," Gerard admitted. "Very well, tell the pack. We'll leave tomorrow morning."

Brother Marcus got up and left the room, and Erica gave Gerard an exaggerated pout.

"Don't do that to me," he said. "You know we have no choice."

"I know. I'm actually glad, for the most part. There's not much I would rather do than fight a vampire. But bloody hell, Gerard!"

"Cover your ears." Erica did so, and Gerard shouted, "Peter!"

The Beta Wolf came in a moment later, and Gerard passed the documents across the desk.

"Now?" Peter cried.

"So we're all in agreement that the timing could be better," said Gerard, "but just look at it."

Peter looked over the papers with growing interest. This wasn't a standard note with rumors of a blood disease, disappearances, or strangers lurking in the shadows. This was detailed documentation of actual vampire sightings, complete with a map. The coven had killed a family, moved into their home, and set about terrorizing the countryside.

Peter looked up at Gerard with a raised eyebrow. "Ardis?"

Erica narrowed her eyes. "Bloody son of a whore!"

Gerard laughed. "Breathe, love. It doesn't matter if it's him or someone else, but it does feel like a trap."

"If it's too easy ..." Peter said.

"So we'll be more cautious."

* * *

The last day of the weeklong trip was a rare one. The sun was shining, the breeze was crisp and cool, and everyone was in high spirits. The married couples shared horses, as did Peter and Aeron, who had rekindled their on-and-off relationship, and John and Maria. Aidan and Will lagged behind as they jousted.

"If ye knock each other off your horses and get hurt," Peter called back to them, "none of us is gonna carry you home."

The soul brothers rode up next to Peter and Aeron. "You are no fun," Aidan accused him.

"War is never fun, little brother."

"Oh?" said Will. "Then why are you sporting that grin?"

"It's 'cause he likes the way the saddle feels between his legs," said Don.

As the sun rose to its daytime peak, they passed a farm with a large pentagram painted on the barn.

"Hex mark," Peter said, riding up next to Gerard. "They know vampires don't fear the cross."

"They don't fear the hex mark, either," Aeron pointed out.

"'Haps the farmer doesn't know that. If it is not of Christ, 'tis of the devil, no? 'Haps they see the evil of the hex mark is more than the vampires' own."

Gerard gave Peter a wry grin. "Since when do you think a hex mark is evil?"

"Our Lord is the *greatest* good, not the *only* good, but tell that to yon farmer."

"Blasphemy," Aeron singsonged.

He pointed to another barn as they passed, this one showing a cross *and* a hex mark. "Or is it just superstition?"

They reached their destination just after noon. The farm was very small. The house was whitewashed with dark shutters, a thatch roof, and a matching barn. A wagon stood in the yard. Several types of beans grew in the back. There were a few cows and a couple of horses in the barn, but they had been dead for weeks. They found no human bodies outside the house.

The doors were locked and the windows were shuttered. After listening carefully at the doors and windows and concluding that all was quiet, John used a skeleton key to open the lock. Erica and Mary scouted the inside, throwing open the shutters as they went.

The kitchen and living area were spotless; a vase even held fresh flowers. There were plenty of signs of recent use—a floor free of dust, an open book lying on a table, a blanket crumpled on the floor at the foot of a chair. The house had a homey, lived-in quality, although the current residents weren't exactly living.

Connor found a trapdoor in the kitchen. Gerard took hold of the rope and pulled it up, revealing stairs leading to a root cellar. The only scents wafting up from the cellar were those of potatoes and dust, but they couldn't rely on scent to determine if vampires were sleeping down there. Or lying in wait.

Gerard looked up at Peter and Don, who stood nearby, swords at the ready. Don shrugged, and Peter nodded. Gerard descended the stairs with Erica and Don following.

The cellar was large for so small a house. Several low shelves and nooks were piled with quilts, tapestries, and pillows; others were stocked with jars containing food. It was a great storage area for the residents who had once lived there, but it afforded too many hiding places for Gerard's comfort.

The trapdoor slammed shut. The cellar plunged into darkness, and before Gerard had the chance to react, Erica screamed.

The light returned when someone reopened the door and the rest of the garou rushed down the stairs. A crossbow bolt hit Gerard in the side. He yanked it out and looked up to see Ardis standing ten feet away amongst a crowd of vampires and garou, giving him a huge, fang-laden grin. He waved a small crossbow at Gerard.

"Hello, Gerard! How's your day?" Ardis said.

Gerard charged Ardis, but the vampire disappeared—just vanished from view. Over the din of battle, Gerard could hear Erica swearing at someone.

The room may have been large, but there were at least a dozen vampires in addition to the garou, to say nothing of all the shelves. Their enemies were well armed; Ardis had evidently brought some soldiers across. Gerard engaged a vampire, but the room was so crowded, it was nearly impossible to make a swing wide enough to take the creature's head with his longsword. He didn't have time to switch weapons, though, so he did the best he could. The vampire was having trouble hitting him, too. Someone bumped Gerard from behind, and his sword happened to be in the right position. It sliced through the vampire's head and pinned it to another vampire who fought behind it. The blade barely injured the other creature, but Gerard's opponent shuddered and perished. He pulled his blade out of its head and prepared to engage another.

Don practically screamed in anguish. Gerard whipped his head around to see him nearby, uninjured but locked in a furious struggle with a vampire. His scent emitted blind rage. When Gerard saw Grace's headless body lying at his feet, he discerned that Don was perilously close to a shift to *faol mòr* form. *Faol mòr* was a Gaelic term for "big wolf," but garou in *faol mòr* form were more monster than wolf. They went berserk, and one could only get out of the way and try not to get hurt. Gerard had never seen a garou in *faol mòr* form; it was incredibly rare, and even Don had never surrendered to it. Gerard almost felt sorry for the vampires if he did it now. He wouldn't need a silver sword; he would just rip them to shreds.

Pippa had wrestled Adam to the floor and was sitting astride him. Before Gerard could get to them, Pippa dug into Adam's chest and wrenched his heart out. The small vampire saw Gerard, giggled, and tossed the heart at him playfully. He lunged at Pippa, but a bolt hit him in the shoulder, and before he had time to pull it out, another vampire attacked him. He snarled and turned on it just in time to see a flash of blonde hair as Abigail fell to the floor next to him with blood spurting from her chest.

Three vampires stood in the corners with small crossbows like the one Ardis had, taking potshots at the garou. They hit their mark often, and though most of them didn't kill the garou with one shot, multiple bolts spilled a lot of blood and wore them down for the vampires with swords. Ardis appeared again as well, plucking his crossbow as if it were a lute with invisible strings. A quick scan of the room showed that in addition to Adam and Abigail, Maria, Owen, and Aeron were dead.

"Fall back!" he called as he saw John hit the floor. "Aidan, Will, out!"

As the youngest garou headed for the stairs, one of the vampires took aim at Will with its crossbow. Rhea was close enough to deflect the shot but not fast enough, and the bolt sailed across the room and caught Will in the arm. In her effort to protect

Will, she didn't see the bolt flying at her own head. It hit, and she went down.

Don dragged Mary, who had refused to leave, out of the cellar while Erica guarded the stairs. In her effort to protect Don and Mary she didn't see the sword that came at her head from behind. Connor, who was halfway up the stairs, dove for the vampire, throwing it to the floor before it could hit Erica. Ardis picked Connor up by the head and snapped his neck with a violent jerk.

"Guess I showed him," Ardis said smugly.

Connor's death left only Erica, Peter, and Gerard in the room alive. Peter and Erica were near the exit, but five vampires stood between Gerard and the stairs, two of whom were using ranged weapons, and Ardis and Pippa were nowhere in sight.

"Peter, now!" Erica called.

"I'm not going anywhere," he said. He dodged a bolt as he decapitated one of the vampires who wielded a sword.

Gerard started to charge one of the archers but stopped short when Erica made a soft gasp, almost like a hiccup. He turned to see her standing in the middle of the room with a bolt protruding from the center of her chest. He reached her and pulled it out before she collapsed in his arms. The fighting stopped, and even the vampires watched in silence as Gerard and Erica stared at each other. Then the light left her eyes, her face went slack, and she died. Gerard's heart wrenched as if the bolt had penetrated his own body. He couldn't breathe, couldn't move, and he found he didn't want to, because nothing would ever be all right again.

At the edge of the room, Ardis waved his crossbow at him and smiled with what Gerard could only describe as sympathy.

Gerard rested Erica gently at his feet, then looked up at Peter.

Don, who had come back after seeing Mary safely outside, stood next to him.

"Take care of them," he whispered to his brothers. They stood and stared at him for a moment before nodding and starting up the stairs.

The vampires weren't just going to let them go, though, and Peter stumbled as three bolts slammed into his back. Gerard couldn't tell if Peter made it to the surface alive because the vampires with swords rushed him. He took them both out before the others converged around him, but not before sustaining several more wounds. He was beginning to weaken; blood loss was starting to take its toll. Ardis stood before him with a broadsword in his hand and a melancholy expression on his maniacal face. They were all covered in blood, but it seemed different on Ardis, almost like he was wearing it. Pippa peeped out from behind him as if she were a timid child hiding behind her father. She was taller than Gerard had thought, and older, maybe in her early teens.

"You know, Gerard," Ardis said, "I'm really going to miss you. I put this off as long as I could, but your pack was getting entirely too big. I hope you understand. I mean, if I let the White Guard rule all of Ireland, how would that look? Imagine what people would say. 'Oh, that Ardis is going soft!' We can't have that, can we? You're easier to get to than your children, so it had to be you instead of them. I figured you'd probably rather have me kill your wife instead of letting one of the others do it, so I took care of it for you. Good-bye, my friend."

The last thing Gerard saw was Ardis swinging the blade toward him.

Part II

Rebuilding

18

Shattered

Pain is no evil, unless it conquers us. — Charles Kingsley

Peter passed out just as he reached the top of the stairs, and Don carried him outside and laid him on the ground. Don was in charge now, and that worried Mary. His emotions ran hot on a good day, and this was about as far removed from a good day as they could get. His skin was ashen and his eyes were black. He trembled and gritted his teeth as he fought off a shift.

"Don, I need you," Mary said meaningfully.

"I'm all right," he assured her. He went back inside and moved a piece of heavy furniture over the trapdoor.

Don, Mary, and Aidan all had shallow wounds where they had been hit with bolts, but they had removed them during the battle and hadn't even slowed down. Aidan removed the bolt from Will's arm quickly and painlessly. The bolts in Peter's back were more complicated. They didn't seem to have penetrated any vital organs, but one was so deep it went almost all the way through, and another appeared to be lodged in bone.

"This is not too bad," Mary said when Don came back out. "He's not gonna like us getting them out, though."

"Can we get them out here?" Don asked. His voice was steadier, and his eye color had returned to normal.

"Aye," she replied, "but it will give us less of a head start."

"The sun won't set for another half a day," she heard Gerard say. She raised her head to see Aidan standing over her. She had never noticed how much he sounded like his father. "Get the bolts out while Will and I hook a couple of the horses to that wagon," he said.

"Set about burning the house while you're at it," said Don.

"But the garou—" Will began.

"Do you think Ardis will let us go back inside so we can retrieve our dead?"

Will said no more, just turned and followed Aidan to the wagon. Don squeezed his eyes shut and breathed heavily.

"Don?" Mary said.

"Don't," he replied quickly. "I know now is not the time to lose control."

She watched him carefully until he opened his eyes and nodded to her. "Very well," she relented.

She got a medical kit from her horse, retrieved some bandages, and folded one of them into a tight bundle. "You pull the first bolt out," she said, "and I'll put pressure on the wound."

Don took hold of the deepest bolt and pulled it out, jolting Peter into consciousness.

"Damn it!" he cried. "How long was I out?"

"Not long enough," said Don. "You're about to wish you were still unconscious."

"I'm sorry, Peter," Mary said. "There are two more."

"How bad is it?"

"One's not bad, but I think the other one is stuck in bone, and we can't do anything about the pain."

"I'm not worried about the pain. Let's get on with it."

Mary called to Aidan and Will, who had finished hooking the wagon up and were on their way to douse the interior of the house with fuel oil. "One of you sit on his legs to keep him still. He's brave, but even so, if he moves too much, he'll suffer that much more."

Aidan sat on Peter's legs. Will sat next to Peter and took his hands.

It infuriated Mary to think that Ardis was standing no more than a few feet away, probably laughing at them. She loved Peter almost to the point of idolatry, and causing him this much pain rent her heart. Her life as Omega had been hard, but without him and Don to defend her, it would have been unbearable. As terrible as Connor was to her, it was Adam who had gone too far. He had tried to rape her once, and Peter had come to the rescue. He stuck his silver dagger in Adam's scrotum and threatened to castrate him if he ever touched her again. Mary had convinced Peter not to tell Gerard about the incident. Thinking back, she wasn't sure why she did. If she had let him tell Gerard, he might have demoted Adam to Omega and her life might have been a lot easier.

Mary loved Don, too, and he was her best friend, but with Peter it was different. She would marry him if he asked her, but he never would. He had always treated her like a sister and no more. Even Don wasn't above taking her to bed, and they had slept together a dozen times, but Peter had never laid a hand on her.

She stood ready with the bandages. Don took hold of the second bolt, and Peter winced.

"Try to relax," Mary said. "Tensing your muscles will only make it worse. Don will pull on the count of three. One—"

Don tugged on one, hoping for it to be over before Peter had the chance to tense up, but the bolt didn't budge. Peter stifled a scream and squeezed Will's hands as Don struggled with the bolt. Don mustered all his strength and jerked hard enough to free it, losing his balance and falling into Aidan's lap in the process. Peter wailed.

"I'm sorry, brother," Don said despairingly.

Mary studied Don as he got to his feet. He was pale and distraught, and his lip quivered. His eyes had turned black again; he was starting to falter.

"I'll take out the other bolt," Aidan offered.

"No!" Don shouted.

"Don," said Peter. Don knelt so they were face to face, and Peter said, "I know what you're thinking, brother, and it's all right. We've been through worse."

"Have we?"

"Well, no, but we have to keep ourselves together a little while longer, 'cause if we don't, we're dead. Don't think of it as torturing me. Think of it as giving me fodder to torture *you*."

"You're not helping," Don said shakily.

"Of course, I am. Now, suck it up and get the last bolt out so we can leave here before Ardis decides to come after us."

Don stood up and eyed Mary, and she caressed his cheek. He held her hand for a moment then took hold of the third bolt.

"And no pulling on one, you bastard," Peter said. "I'm not falling for it again."

"'Haps I'll just leave it there."

When Peter started to retort, Don tugged on the bolt. It met with little resistance and came out much easier than the other two.

"Bloody hell," Peter groaned. "A silver cross is naught compared to that."

"Quit your whining," said Don, his voice still unsteady.

"It's over," Mary said.

"Not till we get him in the wagon," said Aidan.

"I can walk. Help me up."

Peter got to the wagon on his own, but he had to have help climbing in.

"Ride with him, Mary," Aidan instructed, and Mary climbed into the wagon. Peter laid his head in her lap, and she stroked his hair.

"My God, you smell good," Peter said, and a hint of desire seeped into his scent.

Lovely, she thought. Leave it to the one male in the pack who wouldn't touch her to notice she was still in heat. And having him lying in her lap wasn't helping.

"You saw it, too, no?" he asked her.

"Aye, love," said Mary. "I saw it, too."

"Saw what?" Don asked.

"Nobody touched the trapdoor," she said. "It slammed shut of its own accord."

"Doors don't just slam shut by themselves."

"That one did," said Peter. "Brother, we were right there. One minute it was flat on the floor, and the next it swung over and closed. I had to jump out of the way or get hit."

Mary held Peter while the others finished splashing the house with fuel oil and set it afire. Don climbed into the driver's seat of the wagon, but they didn't leave yet. They just watched it burn. The vampires weren't the only ones being incinerated in the blaze.

When the house began to collapse, Don made the Sign of the Cross and said, "Let's go home."

19

The Aftermath

They who go feel not the pain of parting; it is they who stay behind who suffer. — Henry Wadsworth Longfellow

The garou rode to the farm where they had observed the cross and the hex mark, and the farmer and his wife were happy to offer them hospitality. They didn't ask many questions, either. In Mary's experience, oftentimes the more superstitious people were, the less curiosity they showed in regards to the supernatural. Fearing what they didn't understand was preferable to having those fears confirmed. Thus, they gave them a bed for Peter, water to clean up with, and food and shelter for the horses with little more than confirmation that yes, they gotten rid of the "bad elements" that had plagued the countryside.

The House of Blevins had burned houses with Ardis in them before, so they would never be certain he was dead until they saw his severed head. Thus, acting on the notion that he and his coven might get out and come after them, Will and Aidan stood guard while Mary tended to Peter's wounds. She and Don took over the watch sometime toward morning. They saw no vampires that night, and by noon the next day, Peter was ready to travel.

Riding a horse would be uncomfortable, but he would manage it. His pain was unusually distracting, especially for Peter, whose tolerance was even higher than the others', but he wanted to get home more than he wanted to take time to heal, so he endured it the best he could.

The trip back to the monastery was one of the fastest they had ever taken. They rode hard, and since they had the extra horses from the fallen garou, they were able to change mounts often to give them a rest from the burden of having to carry a rider. This allowed them to travel faster, and they cut the trip nearly in half. There was very little talk during the journey, but it wasn't hard for Mary to tell what the other garou were feeling.

Peter slipped into his role as Alpha of the new House of O'Neill without a second thought. He ignored his grief, using the pain of his injury to keep him focused on the ride and holding the others together. Mary was strong; after living with her family's abuse for so long, she had almost as much emotional control as Peter. She would be fine, but the others were falling apart.

Will was nervous and edgy. He startled easily, jumping at the slightest noise. Aidan brooded, and the closer they got to home, the testier he grew. He even snapped at Will. As for Don, he was barely hanging on. He was ghostly pale, with dark circles under his eyes, and when he spoke there was a tremor in his voice. At times, especially at camp or when they were stopped for a break and he wasn't otherwise occupied, Mary would catch him staring off into space with an expression so bleak and hopeless that she couldn't help but wrap her arms around him. None of them slept much, and by the time they rode through the gate at Ballybrook, they were exhausted.

Brothers Marcus and Lawrence met them at the gate with horror on their faces.

"What happened?" Brother Marcus asked.

"Ardis," said Peter.

"And the others?"

Peter shook his head. The monks made the Sign of the Cross and muttered a short prayer.

"You buried the bodies?" said Brother Lawrence.

"No," Don replied desolately.

They made the Sign of the Cross again and said another prayer. Aidan rolled his eyes and tried to push past them, but Peter put a hand out to stop him. Brother Marcus noted Aidan's impatience and said, "Go. Talk to your brothers. We'll care for the horses."

Aidan stalked toward the keep, and Peter ran after him.

"Aidan, wait," he said. "Think about what you say before you say it. You don't want to make it even worse."

"Why don't you let us tell the lads?" Mary said.

"Nae," said Aidan. "'Tis my office. I'll tell them."

Ian, Logan, and Ryan waited just inside the northwest entrance. When Ryan saw Mary, he ran to her and hugged her. Ian and Logan, sensing something was amiss, stood fast.

"Where is everybody else?" Ian asked with apprehension.

"Let's go to the common room," said Aidan.

At seven, Ryan was too big for her to carry, but Mary picked him up anyway and followed Aidan and the others to the common room.

Ian and Logan sat on the floor in front of the fireplace, and Mary put Ryan down next to them. Aidan sat in a chair before them, and Mary perched on the arm.

"The battle didn't go well," Aidan said, trying to be gentle, but he was having trouble figuring out what to say. Mary placed a supportive hand on his shoulder.

"Gerard and Erica fought bravely," she said.

"They did," said Aidan, "but in the end they ... they were killed."

The boys didn't react, just looked up at Aidan as though they were waiting for him to say more. When he didn't, Ryan got up and ran out of the room. Mary followed him out the door and caught his arm before he started across the yard toward the stable.

"Ryan," she said, "they're not in the stable, dear."

The boy grimaced, sighed, and said, "They're just late. They'll be home soon." He turned and went back inside, skipping to the common room, where Logan and Ian still sat staring at Aidan.

"How did it happen?" Ian asked finally.

"You don't need to know that, little brother," Peter said.

"But I do."

"Nae," Peter said again.

Aidan's scent flared with anger, and he said, "Why would you even *want* to know that?"

"'Cause he doesn't believe you," said Ryan.

"Why would we lie about something like that?"

"It's not true," Ryan said, shaking his head vigorously.

"Grace? Rhea? The Quinns?" Ian asked.

"Everyone but us," said Mary.

"Nae, they're just late," Ryan insisted.

"Didn't ye hear me?" Aidan said, his voice starting to rise. "Our parents aren't late. They're not coming back 'cause they're dead."

Don silently left the room. A moment later, the outer door slammed shut.

Peter said, "Aidan, you're not helping."

"There is no help," Aidan retorted. "That's the point. Why are ye lads just sitting there? Why aren't ye crying? You're children. Children are supposed to cry!"

Ryan continued to shake his head in denial.

"Did ye kill them?" Ian asked. "The ones who did it. Are they dead?"

"Most," said Mary. "The rest, we don't know for sure."

"Then I'll hold on to my grief. After all, we may meet them again someday. I'll use it to make me a better fighter."

Logan remained silent.

When the lads still didn't give him the reaction he expected, Aidan yelled, "I don't believe this! Ye act like ye don't even care. You're so ungrateful, ye don't even deserve to have parents."

He got up and stormed out of the room. Will shrugged helplessly, then turned and followed.

Logan sat silently and listened as Aidan's footsteps faded. When he could no longer hear his brother, he got up and went to Peter, threw his arms around his waist, and bawled.

* * *

Don lapsed into a crippling depression. He stopped eating and barely spoke, and he awoke screaming every night. Mary began sleeping in his room to comfort him, but more, she wanted to keep an eye on him. Don was so often ruled by his emotions, and he was completely demoralized. Mary was afraid he would do something to hurt himself, or worse. But she couldn't watch him all the time, and a couple of weeks after the root cellar, he took his horse and left the monastery in the middle of a rainy night.

Mary and Peter tried to track him, but the rain washed away his scent and obscured any trail he might have left. They searched for several days, but they finally gave up and prayed he would keep himself out of harm's way.

A little over two weeks after he left, Don returned to the monastery. He walked into Peter's office just before noon, sat down and said, "Right, then, let me have it."

Peter and Mary obliged.

"Where the devil did you go?"

"Why would you do that?"

"Especially after all that's happened."

"Did it even occur to you that we would worry ourselves mad?"

"You could have at least left word so we wouldn't think you had gone off to die."

"We didn't even know where to look."

"And believe me, we looked."

"Don, don't ever do something like this again."

"It was bad enough that we had to contend with setting things in order here, plus the lads not knowing how to handle their grief—"

"To say nothing of the fact that Aidan has become a veritable ogre."

"I mean, did you even think about what your leaving would do to the two of us?"

"We've hardly slept since you left."

Don sat quietly as they railed at him. When there was a lull in the shouting, he said, "I'm sorry I worried you. You're right: I should have left a note or something, but I wasn't thinking straight when I left, and it didn't cross my mind."

"Where did you go?" Peter asked him again.

"I brought them home."

"Don, why didn't you let us go with you?" Mary asked him.

"I don't know. I just needed to do it myself."

"How bad is it?"

"It's bad. The fire didn't even reach the cellar. The floor was still intact."

"Oh, dear God."

"Ardis got out. I didn't need to tell you that."

Peter laid his head on the desk. "All that for naught."

"All the better that I went back and got them."

"Where are they?"

"In a wagon in the stable. Now we can give them a proper burial. I ran into Brother Marcus on the way in. The monks are going to start making coffins for them today."

* * *

The House of O'Neill buried their dead three days later. Though Brother Marcus wanted to have a funeral Mass, Peter felt a simpler ceremony would serve to honor them better.

"When they were alive, they weren't much for formalities," he explained. "I think they would prefer us to just remember them and move on."

In the end, the abbot administered Last Rites and then said a few words at the gravesite. Afterward, they gathered in the common room and drank a toast to their fallen comrades. Before long, Don felt the need to share a particularly embarrassing story of an adventure he, Peter, and Gerard had experienced before Gerard had ascended to Alpha. Once started, they had an almost endless stream of anecdotes to share about the times they had spent with their friends. The boys and the younger garou listened long into the night as Peter, Don, and Mary offered a far more fitting tribute to their packmates than anything they could have said at the gravesite.

It would not last, but for at least that night, there was laughter heard again in Ballybrook.

* * *

After they buried the garou who were killed in the root cellar, Don's nightmares dropped off and he began functioning normally again. He wasn't the clown he had been before, but he was still good for a wisecrack when the occasion warranted it. For Peter's part, he had never had any interest in running the house. He had ruled in the past, but it had been very different from what was expected of him now. A wise man had once told him there was a difference between ruling and leading, but he had never understood what it meant. In the months after the root cellar, he finally got the point. Ruling was easy. Leading, however, was hard. Leading a White Guard pack was even harder, because there were administrative responsibilities that a normal Alpha would never have to handle. He had no taste for tending to details and was more in his element as an advisor, teacher, and fighter. He had known that being Beta Wolf put him in a position to become Alpha, but he had been too cocky to believe Gerard would actually be killed. But here he was, in charge of four traumatized garou, three children without parents, and a monastery full of monks.

"I think you would be better suited to this office than me," he confided to Don, who sat across the desk from him.

"Why not let the monks help you more?" Don asked. "How much of the day-to-day affairs can't be handled by them?"

"More than one would think, but the day-to-day matters are not what concern me most. The vampires aren't gonna go away just 'cause there are only five of us, and in faith, I don't know that any of us is in condition to fight. I also have to think of the lads. They're young and need a mother, and I need to figure out a way to keep Aidan from taking out his frustrations on them."

"Mary will take care of them. She already said as much."

"She didn't say anything to me."

"She probably assumed you'd know without her having to tell you."

Peter grimaced with pain and shifted in his chair.

"Is your back still bothering you?" Don asked.

"Nae, it's fine. I've more pressing matters than a sore back."

"You know, my lord, the House of O'Neill may not be such a burden as you think, once you get used to it."

The House of O'Neill. The name alone made him nauseous.

"There's no way I can get you to stop calling me 'my lord,' is there?"

A pensive look came over Don's face. "Hmm, what was that thing Gerard did that made me stop? Oh, that's right. Nothing!"

Peter glared at him.

"Hey, if it makes you feel better, you can say 'don't call me that' all you want."

"Thanks so much for that. I still think you'd do a better job than me. You're doing awfully well these days."

"Aye, 'cause I sit here and you sit there. It chills me to think how close I came. I was gonna challenge you again next New Moon."

"You wouldn't have won anyway."

"You keep telling yourself that. I haven't cracked your skull in a good, long while."

Peter was so busy that he never took time of his own to mourn. He kept pushing the grief to the back of his mind, along with the nagging back pain that never quite went away, and over time it became harder to do so. Most days he managed to make it through, but one New Moon he lost his resolve.

Since the root cellar, Aidan had become angry and bitter. He directed his wrath at his brothers, and there was only so much Peter and Don could do to prevent it. Peter was seriously considering demoting Aidan to Omega in an effort to humble him and even out his temperament. This particular day, Aidan had struck Logan when the boy had spilled a bag of horse feed, leaving him with an ugly bruise on his cheek and a black eye. Don had retaliated against Aidan, giving him a black eye of his own. A severe storm had taken out part of the stable's roof and killed two of their horses. Ryan, who was acting more like a four-year-old than a seven-year-old since the root cellar, had engaged in no less than three temper tantrums since breakfast. A host of other small things built up until Peter gave up and fled to his room.

Don found him lying on his bed, head covered with a pillow, sat silently next to him, and laid a hand on his shoulder.

"Do you know why he stayed in that cellar and sent me out?" Peter said after a while. "I'll tell you why. So he could sit up there in the heavens and laugh his arse off at me struggling to be a worthy Alpha."

"Well, he didn't laugh much while he was living. 'Haps it was time for some humor."

"It's not funny."

"Then you're doing something wrong."

Peter emerged from under the pillow and eyed him angrily. "Really? Do you think?"

"The Moon is new, my lord."

"Don't call me that, Don."

"This is a hard time, and we're all out of sorts. No one really expects you to be strong all the time, but you've always lived up to your name. You will this time too. You're the rock, brother. You use reason when the rest of us act with emotion."

Peter sat up next to his friend. "Times I don't want to be the rock. Times I think I can't do this at all, much less excel."

"Do you think Gerard didn't struggle? He struggled with it till the day he died."

Peter sighed with resignation. "I know he did. I'm just frustrated right now."

"Aye, but it won't last. Tomorrow you'll go back to being the rock again. You may hate it, but you'll do it. For now, feel free to whine a bit. You've earned it." Don thought for a minute and added, "This is very strange. I can't remember ever reasoning with you about anything."

"That's 'cause you're the unreasonable one."

"I don't like this reversal. You should get back to yourself quickly before I get some common sense."

"I miss them, Don. I keep expecting to look up and see Gerard walk in and tell me to get out of his chair."

"I miss them too. I can't sleep without holding onto Grace's pillow. Hell, I even miss Connor."

"I can't help thinking about what would happen if you or Mary had been killed," Peter said grimly. "I couldn't bear that."

"But we weren't, brother. You can't dwell on what could have happened, lest you neglect the here and now. Mary and I aren't going anywhere, and we'll do what we can to help you." He regarded Peter for a moment, then said, "You know, you haven't said anything about Aeron since the root cellar. You didn't even mention her the night we buried them."

"I didn't think I'd miss her so much. Most of the time, we were only together 'cause we were bored or because she was in heat, but she was so lovely. Next to Mary, she was the most beautiful lass I'd ever seen."

"How do you think we came to have so many lovely females in the pack?" Don asked. "Every one of them was beautiful."

"Abigail smelled the best, though."

"That, she did. Too bad she was an insufferable harpy."

"She wasn't so bad after she became Omega."

"That's true," Don admitted.

"All right, all right, I'm done whining. What now?"

"Ale," Don said resolutely. "Loads of ale."

* * *

With superior senses, it was often hard not to eavesdrop. Thus, the rest of the garou heard everything Peter and Don said. Will ignored them; they usually did when they weren't actively participating in a conversation. Mary did, too, for the most part, but it didn't escape her notice that Peter had said she was the most beautiful female he'd ever seen. Aidan found it very difficult to ignore them. How could Peter be so disheartened? Nothing bothered him. Aidan had heard the monks talking, and he knew that Peter had been some kind of nobility, somebody with real power, but he had lost it. Now he had power again, and he didn't want it. He could smell Peter's distress and hear the fear in his voice, and he didn't understand. Surely Gerard had never been so afraid or overwhelmed. Don said he had, but he was just trying to comfort Peter.

Peter couldn't handle running the house. Don didn't want to do it, either. Who else was there?

Aidan knew exactly who.

He couldn't tell anyone his idea, not even Will. Will talked him out of doing a lot of things, and this was one thing from which he did not want to be diverted. He stayed awake into the night, long after Will had gone to sleep, formulating a plan.

20

Big Mistake

It is better to deserve honors and not have them than to have them and not deserve them. — Mark Twain

The next day was warm and sunny, and Peter, Mary, and Don took the boys down the hill by the river before supper. Aidan put on his sword belt, went to Peter's room and retrieved his rapier, and then went to find Will.

"Come," he said. "Let's go down to the river with the others."

Will handed him a cup of wine, but Aidan shook his head. "Hold onto it for me, can you?"

"Surely," Will said as he followed Aidan.

Mary played tag with Logan and Ryan, and Peter watched while Don gave Ian archery instruction. Aidan stood over Peter, staring at him.

"What's the matter?" Peter asked, noticing the weapons.

"It's you." Peter looked at him quizzically, and Aidan said, "*You're* the matter."

With that, the others took notice. Peter got up, and Mary sent Logan and Ryan inside and stood protectively in front of Ian, who watched in confusion.

"What is this?" Will asked.

Aidan ignored him and glared Peter in the eye. "You have no idea what you're doing!" he roared. "You said it last night. You cannot abide as Alpha Wolf."

"You've got a lot of nerve, little boy," Peter said.

"I am not a little boy."

"You keep telling yourself that."

"Peter, I formally challenge you for the Alpha rank."

Will's scent changed. Not only was he surprised; he was

furious. It stung, but Aidan had suspected it would happen.

Don stepped between them and pushed Aidan backward. "Are you daft? Gerard would beat you black and blue!"

"But he's dead, is he not? And Peter won't do it. He's already said that since the root cellar, he hasn't the fight. He said none of us did, but he was wrong."

"Peter had the fight a century before your father was born, you witless dullard. Besides, there are traditions. You have to challenge Mary and me first, or is your tiny mind so muddled you forgot? I must have hit you harder yesterday than I thought. And even if you defeated us, as Alpha, Peter is not compelled to accept your challenge. More than one hot-tempered and reckless garou has stood up to an Alpha, only to be beaten soundly and lowered to Omega."

Years later Aidan would tell someone a plan would never work unless its architect took all parties into consideration. When laying out his plot, he had forgotten he would have to go through Mary and Don before he fought Peter, but it was too late to back down. "It's a risk I'm willing to take. Besides, you threaten me with that all the time. You can't make me Omega, and I don't think Peter will do that, either. I'm not afraid to fight you, Don. I outgrew you years ago."

Don smiled at Peter, then turned to Mary.

"You do realize you're about to get hurt badly, no?" Mary asked Aidan.

"You won't hurt me."

Mary laughed mirthlessly. "You know what? You speak right. I shan't hurt you. I'll let them do it. I concede. Don?"

Don's eyes bored into Aidan's. "Do you think you're ready, boy?"

"I just told you I was ready—" he began, but he never got the chance to finish his boast.

Don's first blow flashed out with greater speed than Aidan had thought the smaller garou possessed. It wasn't a heavy blow, but it snapped his head back and threw him off balance. He reset and brought his eyes back to focus just in time to see Don's other fist come crashing into the center of his face. All the power that seemed to have been missing from the first blow came riding along on the crest of the second. Aidan couldn't remember ever being struck so hard. Everything slowed around him as the world started to spin. He barely noticed the impact of his back hitting the ground, only that he was suddenly looking up at the sky.

Something warm dripped into his ear. He reached up to see if his nose was bleeding and flinched. It didn't feel much like a nose anymore; Don had crushed it.

"Still think you've outgrown me?" Don said, placing a foot on Aidan's chest.

"You gave me no warning," he said. It hurt his nose to talk.

"Very well." Don removed his foot and stepped back into a fighting stance. He stood a full head shorter than Aidan, yet he was more imposing than a giant as he glared into Aidan's eyes.

Aidan wouldn't be intimidated, though. He had too much to lose. He got up and took the stance, and they began to circle each other. Aidan's fatal mistake was thinking he had even the remotest chance. He tried to use the height difference to bear down on Don, but Don leaned in and threw a powerful upper cut to his abdomen. Aidan doubled over, and Don brought a knee up to connect with his shattered nose. The next thing he knew, he was on his back again, and Mary was shaking him, imploring him to wake up. Will lay close by, groaning in agony.

Don stood at Aidan's feet with his arms folded. "Tell you what," he said magnanimously. "I'll concede my rank to you, 'cause it's time for you to learn what our Alpha is truly capable of and 'cause you need another beating. When your schooling is done, I'll take back my rank before you can wipe your bloody nose."

Don reached out to help Aidan up, but when he was on his feet, the older garou didn't relinquish his grip. "And what have we learnt from this little activity?"

"That you fight dirty?"

"Of course, I fight dirty! I always have, and if you're just learning that now, I've been lax in your training. Never underestimate your opponent, Aidan, and never *over*estimate yourself, especially when you're already injured. You must rely on more than skill, little brother. If you are not prepared for the unexpected, your skills mean nothing."

"Do you think I don't know that?"

"I know you know it. But you sorely needed reminding."

Don released his hand, and Aidan turned to Peter. "Now that that's out of the way ..."

Don rolled his eyes.

"And why should I accept your challenge?" Peter asked as he put his sword belt on.

"You will, or I'll subscribe you a coward."

"And you're the only one who will believe it. More likely, they'll call you a fool for drawing on me and laud my infinite mercy for letting you live."

"There's no need for a moot. Everyone's here. Will'll never stand against me, and Mary and Don have already assented. Now, draw!"

"'Haps you should wipe your nose first," Don said mildly.

"Have you any idea what being Alpha entails?" said Peter.

"I can do no worse job than you."

To Don, Peter said, "Remember what I said last night about Gerard laughing at me?"

"I doubt he's laughing now," Don replied. "I, however, am finding this all quite amusing."

"You're twenty-five years old!" Peter cried. "You've been in three real battles, and you're still so young, I wonder that your beard doesn't wash off when you bathe! You *are* bathing yourself these days, no? Or does Mary still have to go in and wash behind your ears? And let's not forget that all your formidable skills were taught you *by me*. What makes you think you can defeat me? Don't forget, little one, I taught you everything *you* know, not everything *I* know. You're gonna learn something new today, and that is to think twice before you start calling people out that you can't possibly beat. Or did you mean to let Don break your nose to give me a false sense of security? I'll keep that in mind and try not to tremble in my boots as you stand there, bleeding."

Aidan's face turned red, and he trembled, trying to control his temper. Peter was taunting him, trying to throw him off balance, and it was working. Well, he could taunt, too. He took a deep breath and collected himself, then said, "Even you can be defeated, Your Highness."

Aidan rolled his eyes. Your Highness? That was all he could come up with? If he was going to get under Peter's skin, he would have to do a hell of a lot better than that.

He was wrong.

In an instant, Peter changed. His face went slack and his scent flared with anger. His eyes took on an expression cold enough to rival the harshest of Blevins glares, fierce and cruel, the eyes of a battle-hardened male who was capable of anything. Aidan couldn't help taking a step back. Even Don backed up. Aidan marveled that Peter had gotten so furious over such an innocuous barb.

If he hadn't been looking at Peter, he might have missed it, because his ire didn't last more than a few seconds. Then, as quickly as it had come over him, it was gone.

"Indeed, I can," Peter replied evenly, as though his brush with rage hadn't even occurred, "but by you? You hadn't even the courage to tell your own soul brother what you planned today, and you want to subscribe *me* a coward? Tell me, Aidan, who was first out of that root cellar and who was last?"

It appeared that Peter would win the pissing match after all. Aidan's resolve gave way and he seethed. *"Draw!"* he shouted, ignoring the pain in his nose.

Mary pulled Ian away and Peter drew his sword. Before Aidan could even make his first swing, Peter yanked the sword out of his hand and kicked him in the chest. Aidan fell to the ground, and Peter placed the tip of his blade at his throat.

"Look at that," Don quipped. "On his back thrice in five minutes."

Peter sheathed his sword, retrieved Aidan's, and tossed it to him. "Get up," he said. "We're not done." He turned his back on Aidan and moved away.

Aidan was indignant. Was Peter so arrogant that he thought Aidan needed such an advantage? Now Peter was underestimating *him.* He got his weapon and leapt up into a lunge, attempting to skewer Peter before he turned around.

Peter twisted to the side so that Aidan's thrust passed through empty air, and then he brought his elbow up to smash into Aidan's nose. Will screamed. Aidan's world was momentarily one of unprecedented pain, flashing lights, and shadows. When his vision cleared, he was staring at the tip of his own sword, now held by Peter, pointed at his heart. He had no idea when Peter had taken it.

"Nae, I didn't underestimate you," Peter said, "but any opening you see is one I've shown you in order to lead you to pain and defeat. After another few decades, or a century, you'll learn the difference between brandishing a weapon and being one."

Peter threw Aidan's sword at his feet. "This fight's over, but I'll consider it for a month. If, on the next New Moon, you still think you're capable of being a worthy Alpha—and more importantly, if *I* think you're capable—I shall accept. But in that time, little brother, you had better learn some control. An Alpha who cannot control his temper isn't worthy of the title. If you can't handle a little taunting from me, who's to say you'll survive Ardis again, or that any of us will?"

"I'll learn," Aidan promised.

"You'd better hope you're right, 'cause when we're done, if you're not Alpha, you'll be Omega. And you were wrong: I *will* do it. Now, go on. Get back to the monastery and do whatever it is you're supposed to be doing. You're Beta Wolf for now, and you're gonna have more to do anyway."

Aidan picked his sword up and started to walk away, but Peter stopped him. "Oh, and Aidan? If you ever call me 'Your Highness' again, I will *end* you."

Don and Mary gaped at Peter, and Aidan stood rooted to the spot. It wasn't a taunt or banter; Peter was deadly serious. Such threats were practically unheard of in White Guard packs, but Aidan had seen Peter's eyes, and he had no doubt Peter would carry through on the threat without hesitation.

"Go on," Peter said again, and Aidan turned and headed up the hill.

* * *

"What the devil were you thinking?" Will demanded in their secret language as he followed Aidan. It seemed he was always the one following.

"It had to be done."

"How do you figure?"

"I can do a better job than Peter, and you know it."

"Nae, I don't know it. And by the way, next time you plan to do something really bloody stupid like that, try to keep in mind that I feel your pain."

"Sorry, I forgot."

"Aye, you forgot 'cause you were only thinking about yourself."

"I said I'm sorry, all right?"

"No, it's not all right. I need to go for a walk or something. You go to the infirmary and wait for Mary. And tell her to give *you* something for the pain so *my* nose will stop hurting."

"Will—"

Will put a hand up to stop him and walked away.

He climbed the stairs of the tower on the southeast corner of the outer wall. The outer towers had been favorite play areas for all of the lads when they were young, and Will and Aidan had spent a lot of time up there, plotting and planning, making up stories, and inventing game after game. As they had started to get older, they had sat up there talking about Aeron, upon whom they had developed a crush.

Will stood at the wall awhile, looking out over the countryside, trying to piece together what had just happened and how Aidan could betray him so. This was the first time in their life that one had done something without talking with the other first. The fact that it was something as monumental as a challenge to the Alpha only made it worse.

"Will won't stand against me," Aidan had said. If he had bothered to ask, he would have gotten a rude surprise: Will would have said no.

Aidan had advanced in rank pretty easily, but Will had struggled. He wasn't the fighter Aidan was. In fact, Aidan did a lot of things better than he did. It didn't matter. Aidan had never made him feel inferior about anything. Besides, Will wasn't *totally* inferior. He was more reasonable and levelheaded than Aidan, and he had kept them out of trouble many times growing up. And now Aidan had taken Will's one real strength and used it against him. He hadn't told Will what he was going to do because he knew Will would talk him out of it.

For the first time in their life, they were truly at odds. They were both totally alone.

Will collapsed to the floor, curled into a ball, and wept.

21

Falling

The greatest glory in living lies not in never falling but in rising every time we fall. — Confucius

"Why did he do that?" Ian asked as they watched Aidan and Will walk back up the hill toward the monastery.

"Is he out of his mind?" Peter said, still reeling from shock at Aidan's audacity, not to mention the fact that the young garou had inadvertently hit upon one of the few things that would threaten Peter's control. Mary was still staring at him with her mouth open. He reached under her chin and closed it.

She finally recovered and said, "At the farmhouse, when you were unconscious, he took over with nary a thought. He sounded so much like Gerard that I thought he had made it out of the cellar. He's his father's son, Peter. He's young, and he has much to learn, but he could make a good Alpha, if given time."

"Given time, aye, but now?"

"What would he do to you if he became Alpha?" Ian asked.

"He could kill him," said Don. Ian gave him a wry look, and he said, "I'm in earnest for once. But don't worry; it's not gonna happen. White Guard packs are not like others. Besides, if the impossible did happen and Aidan actually defeated Peter, he'd need help. He might make him Omega Wolf, and that's more likely, especially in light of Peter's threat to do the same to him and the beating we just gave him. Come to think of it, he could make *me* Omega. I beat him worse than Peter did."

"Mary, you should probably go in and see if you can do something with his nose," Peter said. "I don't think swift healing's gonna do much for that one."

"Did ye have to break it three times?"

"He had it coming," Don said dispassionately.

Mary sighed with resignation. "Aye, I guess he did. Peter, are *you* all right?"

"Of course, I am. Why wouldn't I be?"

"The comment about—" Peter raised an eyebrow at her, and she decided to let it go. "Right, then."

She turned and walked back to the monastery, and Don turned to Ian. "Shall we continue?"

"Can we stop?" Ian asked. "I'm not feeling so good."

"You don't have anything to worry about, little brother."

"I hope you're right. Can we still stop for now?"

"Aye, go on," Don relented.

* * *

Ian left Peter and Don by the river and ran to his cave. He had found the cave when he was little and spent countless hours there. He'd heard his *athair* and Don talking about playing there as children, but he enjoyed pretending that he was the first to have ever discovered it. It was his playhouse, but it was also his place of refuge, where he went when he needed to get away from the monastery. He loved Ballybrook and the House of Blevins, but sometimes he just needed to be alone.

The entrance was wide and opened onto a large room with several passages branching off. He had explored and mapped the tunnels extensively and believed they came out on the other side of the River Foyle, but he had never found a passage under the river. If he could locate it, he could get farther away from the monastery. If Aidan ascended to Alpha, Ian figured he'd be escaping there even more often. Maybe someday he'd use it to run away altogether. He might have left already if not for the idea that he would never be brought across and would therefore grow old and die. Also, truth be known, he couldn't bear to leave Logan and Ryan at Aidan's mercy, especially today, when the evidence of Aidan's cruelty was so clear on Logan's bruised face.

They said he and Aidan had been close when Ian was very young, but he didn't remember and didn't really care to. Aidan had been harsh and spiteful, either ignoring them or yelling at them throughout their childhood, and since their parents died, he had gotten even worse. Peter and Don stepped in often, but even they could only do so much because they couldn't watch him all the time.

If Aidan became Alpha and Peter and Don couldn't stop him, Ian fully expected Aidan's cruelty to get worse. If it did, he didn't intend to be around for it. He'd take Logan and Ryan with him if he had to. Even growing old and dying would be better than living with Aidan tormenting them for the next several hundred years. Maybe they could find another pack and join them.

Ian made his way through the cavern using a lantern he kept in the front room to light the way. He went farther today than he had ever gone before, and he discovered a leg that veered abruptly to the right. Water rushed nearby, and he briefly thought he had finally found the tunnel under the river, but the channel reached a dead end.

"Bloody hell," he muttered. He started to turn back, but a shadow caught his eye. The lantern hadn't cast its light at the proper angle so he had missed it before, but there it was: a crevice just big enough to squeeze through. Hoping his size didn't betray him and get him stuck, he stepped through the crack.

The way on the other side wasn't much wider than the opening, and Ian had to move sideways, holding the lantern out in front, but at least he could walk. The walls were damp and water trickled from the ceiling. Ian walked carefully so he wouldn't slip on the wet floor. If he fell and cracked his skull on a rock, they would never find him. Two hundred years from now, one of Logan's grandchildren would be exploring the cave and discover his bones.

The passage finally opened up into a wide room. Ian took a step and fell into nothingness.

He screamed and clawed for the walls, but there were none. He plummeted through thin air, and the ground, or maybe Hell, was coming up fast. He still had ahold of the lantern, but it offered no assistance, waving about as it was.

The ground wasn't at the bottom of the shaft, nor was Hell. Ian splashed into an underground lake. Unfortunately, so did the lantern. He could not feel the bottom; he was in over his head, and with no light, he couldn't tell if he was near a shore or if there even was one. He panicked, kicking and flailing his arms wildly, and he quickly began to grow tired.

He was going to die.

Instead of increasing his terror, the realization calmed him. There was no point fighting it; that would just tire him out and make him die sooner. He stopped thrashing and began treading water more deliberately.

The water was cool but not nearly as frigid as he would have thought. He could still hear water rushing overhead; it seemed he had indeed found the tunnel under the river. It was too bad nobody would ever know about it, except for maybe Logan's grandchildren.

As his eyes adjusted to the light, he began to look around for a foothold. Then it dawned on him: there was *light*. Light probably meant a way out. Maybe he wasn't going to die after all.

* * *

Peter watched Aidan closely over the next few weeks as he handled his duties as Beta Wolf. He usually worked in tandem with Will, and although Aidan had been the one who made the challenge, Peter thought it wise to evaluate Will, too. If one of them became Alpha, it wouldn't matter where the other was in the hierarchy; they would lead together. Will was Aidan's grounding influence, his quiet, reasonable bearing a good balance for Aidan's brashness. Aidan made an effort to control his temper, and he handled any tasks Peter gave him with careful attention. If he had trouble, he asked for help. He even exercised more patience when dealing with his brothers. But there was still something missing, and Peter couldn't allow him the chance to lead the house without it.

The night before the New Moon, Peter sat down with Aidan over a pint of ale. "Have you still got a mind to take my place?" he asked.

"I do," Aidan replied.

"Do you believe I'm such a bad Alpha?"

"Nae," Aidan said, "but I heard you say you couldn't do the job. You're not happy. Am I wrong?"

"Nae, you're not wrong," Peter admitted. "If I were, we probably wouldn't be having this conversation. If you're capable, then I'm more than willing to let you do the job. But ambition doesn't make an Alpha, little brother, and being Alpha doesn't make you better or above the others."

"That's not why I want to be Alpha."

"Then why?"

"I never want to see anything like we did in that root cellar again. Gerard lost focus, or we would not have gone in like that."

"Why do you say he lost focus?"

"Erica was in heat, and Gerard could think of nothing else. And it got eleven of them killed."

"All the females were in heat, not just Erica."

"Aye, and all the males were distracted. But Gerard was responsible for keeping the rest of us focused. How many times had he said he knew Ardis and his methods and that he always expected an ambush?"

"And he did then. He wasn't so distracted as you might believe. When he went into that cellar, he didn't do anything he hadn't done many times. If anything, he was *more* alert. He knew it was a trap."

"Nae," Aidan insisted, "he barged into that root cellar, too busy thinking with his member and not his head. If I were Alpha, nothing like that would ever happen again."

"Bloody hell, Aidan, are you hearing yourself? You were just as preoccupied with the females as the rest of us, no?"

"Well..."

"Well what? Maybe it was you thinking with *your* member, and you can't fathom that Gerard, or any of us, could have more control over those impulses than you."

Aidan didn't reply. He couldn't deny it. All the males had been worked up over the females, but he had the willpower of a teenage boy with flourishing, unchecked desire.

"You're right," he said sheepishly.

"Little brother, you haven't learnt a damn thing."

"Nae, I have. As you pointed out, there is more to being Alpha than battle prowess. You may well be the best swordsman who ever lived. You know tactics and strategy, and you know how to teach others to fight, but you haven't the more mundane skills. If we go into battle while you're preoccupied with details as you've been these past months, you might not be able to keep your mind on the fight. You might lose focus due to all the other burdens weighing on your mind."

"And what makes you think you won't?"

"Because I think of nothing but killing vampires. My parents sacrificed their lives in that cellar so I could get out. When that vampire shot Will, my arm was wracked with pain as well. Imagine what it would have been like if he'd been killed. Then after all that, I had to hold you down while Don plucked bolts out of your back when he was barely able to contain his despair. I've turned the matter over in my mind so many times that it's burnt there. Do you think I want to see my brothers killed like that, or in that much pain? Or see them have to pick up the pieces 'cause the only way I could save them was to die myself? I'll do anything to prevent that. I'll make certain they don't lose focus, and I'll ensure that if we ever encounter Ardis again, he dies."

"But you have to have both," Peter said. "You can't focus so single-mindedly on the mission that you neglect the details. It is the Alpha's burden to keep the garou focused on their mission, but he also has to make sure the children are cared for, the monastery stays in good repair, we stay in touch with Rome, and a host of other functions. It's not one or the other. The secret is being able to balance the two. And you're wrong: I may hate it, and I may struggle, but I do know what I'm doing."

"Saying that was wrong," Aidan said humbly. "I apologize."

"Apology accepted. You know your brothers are afraid of you."

"I know. But better afraid of me than the fight."

"A cruel Alpha does not long keep his house together."

"I won't lie and tell you I'll not be hard on them, Peter. But I'll not hurt them."

"You've hurt them before."

"I assure you it'll never happen again."

Peter weighed his words. Aidan cared about the pack, but he still had no idea how to lead it. He dreaded asking his next question because the answer was probably going to make him and Aidan enemies, but there was no other way to do it. He leaned over the table and stared Aidan in the eye. Aidan stared back for several minutes before finally turning away, making Peter dread the question even more.

"No matter what other things the Alpha must do," he said finally, "there is one that supersedes all others. He cannot perform his other offices without it. Do you know what that duty is?"

Aidan didn't reply right away, seriously considering the question.

Peter sighed. "Wrong answer, little brother."

"You didn't even give me a chance to think about it."

"'Tis not something you should have to think about. You either know it or you don't."

"What's the answer?"

"Tell me after you've been Omega awhile."

Aidan's jaw dropped. "Damn it, Peter, how can I learn to be Alpha if I'm Omega?"

"There's no better place. When you figure it out, then you can challenge me."

Aidan bit his lip and breathed hard, trying to control himself long enough to get out of the room. "Can I go now?" he asked through clenched teeth.

"Aye, go find a place to cool your anger."

* * *

Aidan stormed out of the common room. He threw open the back door and burst through, slamming it shut behind him. Peter hadn't said a word about control, and he hadn't had to. Aidan already knew he was losing it. He'd spent the last month trying to control his temper, and what did he get for it? He got busted to Omega. Where was the justice in that?

He ran across the yard and pounded his fist into one of the stable doors, putting a hole through it.

"Bloody hell!" he growled, his hand smarting.

Peter was right. He had no business being Alpha.

He opened the broken door and went inside, where he went to his horse, grabbed a brush, and began to groom it. The horse nuzzled him, and he patted its nose.

The horse didn't even have a name. All the rest of them did, but Aidan hadn't bothered to give him one because he was just a horse. Yet when he felt alone, this was where he came. He hadn't gone to Will; he'd come to a horse.

"What do you think, horse? Should I give you a name? Or do you even care what I call you as long as I care for you? I bet I'm going to spend more time out here in the next few months.

"What does he want? And why didn't he let me answer? Maybe there *was* no answer, and he just used it as an excuse to make me Omega."

The horse snorted.

"You're right; it's not in his nature to be petty. I don't understand it! He's miserable being Alpha—everybody knows he's miserable—but he won't even give me the chance to take the position. There's no better place to learn to be Alpha than Omega? What the devil does that even mean?"

"Aidan, you're talking to a horse," Will said.

Aidan looked up to see his soul brother standing at the door of the stall. He must have really been distracted; he hadn't even smelled Will entering the stable. "I guess I knew the horse wouldn't try to reason with me," he said.

"I won't either if you'd rather I didn't." He picked up a brush and went to work on the other side. "What did he have to say?"

"Weren't you listening? He made me Omega."

"I meant the horse."

Aidan actually managed a chuckle.

"You know what I'm enjoying in all this?" Will said.

"What?"

"I outrank you. That's never happened."

"Well, don't think I'm going to let you order me around."

"Never would."

"He asked me one question. What was so important that he would make me Omega 'cause I didn't know the answer?"

"Do you think he'll promote you if you figure it out?"

"Do *you* know the answer?"

"If I did, I don't think I would tell you."

The remark was devastating. Aidan's head swam, and he could barely hold himself up. "What, are you just gonna abandon me now that I'm Omega?"

"Brother, you know better than that. All I'm saying is that you got into this on your own and now you're gonna have to get yourself out."

"Damn it, Will, are you ever gonna forgive me for that?"

"I do forgive you, but I'm not ready to forget. I tell you everything. *Everything.* And up to now, I thought you had told me everything, but you kept something this important from me 'cause you didn't trust me not to talk you out of it. How can I trust you not to do that again? Even now, you're talking to a horse instead of me. What am I supposed to think of that?"

Aidan couldn't breathe. He sat down with his back against the wall and covered his head as if he were protecting it from falling objects. Will sat next to him and put an arm around him.

"I didn't mean to hurt you," Aidan said.

"I know, and I don't want to hurt you, either, but I can't lie to you and say it didn't mean anything."

"How can I make it up to you?"

"You can trust me with your secrets just like you always have, and you can talk to me instead of the horse."

He looked up at Will. "Is it control? Is that the answer?"

"I don't know. Ask Peter."

After they finished brushing the nameless horse, they went back inside the keep. Peter was in the common room, playing chess

with Don. It was his move and he was concentrating hard, so he
didn't acknowledge Aidan when he and Will came in and sat down.

"How's your hand?" Don asked.

"It's fine."

"You're gonna fix the door; you know that, right?"

"I guess I do."

"And what have we learnt from this little activity?"

"Not to punch a hole in the stable door?"

Don chuckled in response.

"The answer is control," Aidan said.

Peter moved his bishop and said, "Check," then looked over at
Aidan and shook his head. "That's not it, little brother. All garou
need control. It's the hardest thing any of us has to do."

"Bloody right," Don said. He moved a knight and took Peter's
bishop. "Checkmate."

"Goddamn it!"

"What were you thinking, moving there in the first place? You
checkmated yourself, you know."

"Nae, I'm fairly certain it was you. Rematch?"

"I'll just obliterate you again. Times I think you like getting
punished."

As he reset his pieces, Peter said, "It's not something you can
guess, Aidan. You're gonna have to learn it, and then you're gonna
have to accept it."

"Accept it?"

"When you learn it, you'll understand."

Aidan and Will didn't have anything better to do, so they
stayed at the table and watched the game. Many soul siblings not
only shared a soul but a mind as well. They had met a pair of
females at their induction who finished all of each other's
sentences. He and Will definitely did *not* share a mind; they
disagreed on a regular basis. But he had never knowingly hurt
Will before the day he had called Peter out. It was the worst thing
he had ever done, and even if Will had forgiven him, it would be a
long time before he forgave himself. He briefly considered
abandoning his challenge to Peter, but even guilt didn't make it
acceptable to stay Omega.

Omega Wolf. He was in for a rough time.

22

Lessons Learned

He who is not a good servant will not be a good master. — Plato

Aidan didn't know what he expected, but life didn't change all that much. The others gave him a few more menial tasks, they told him to shut up more often, and Don wouldn't let him correct his brothers in any manner whatsoever, but he came to realize after a couple of weeks that they weren't going to make his life hell. If anything, they were more affectionate, at times treating him as they had when he was a child or as they might treat a pet.

He made a real effort to learn what Peter expected of him. He watched and waited for some realization, some epiphany that would explain everything, but the only thing he learned was that it wasn't going to be that simple.

Not long after he became Omega, three garou arrived at the monastery. Cicero Parvisi, a burly Arab, and a robust Scottish couple named Charles and Devon McCabe had been dispatched from a nearby house to augment the pack on an emergency basis until more permanent arrangements could be made. Though they lived at Ballybrook, they technically were not members of the House of O'Neill and would not be allowed to vie for position. All other privileges and responsibilities would be afforded them.

"A female!" Mary cried with delight when she met Devon. She hugged her new companion warmly.

"What?" said Don. "You don't like our company?"

"Of course, I do, love, but I've no one to talk about the males with. I can't very well talk with Peter about the shape of your bum, can I?"

"Well, I guess you could if you wanted to," Peter muttered. "It would be awkward, though."

"I don't know why. You've seen him naked too."

Peter and Don both raised their hands and walked away.

Peter called a formal meeting to welcome the new garou and familiarize them with practices and traditions specific to the House of O'Neill. Mary gave Aidan some paper and a quill pen. "Just note everything that is said," she told him. "You don't have to write it word-for-word; just record the general flow and any important decisions made or orders given."

Taking notes was easy; sitting alone at the end of the table wasn't. He'd never realized just how long that table was. Not used to keeping silent, he began to speak, only to have Peter say, "Aidan, as Omega you're not permitted to address this assembly."

When Peter adjourned the meeting, Mary came to the end of the table and sat next to him. She took the page and read it over. "You did a better job than I ever did. Come with me and I'll show you where the log is so you can record your notes."

She took him to the office and got a heavy volume from a shelf. She turned to the first blank page, which was about halfway through the book. "I'd say to summarize as best you can, but I think you can copy what you have. You've always been so smart."

Aidan thumbed through the pages of the archive. It was dry reading, little more than a tally of meetings, events, changes in hierarchy, and orders and decisions of the Alpha. Mary leaned on the desk. "Are you doing all right?"

"I'm coping."

"Peter shushing you today hurt, though, no?"

"I can't deny that. 'Haps I should just call him 'Your Highness' again so he'll kill me."

Mary chuckled. "I know you have Will, but just remember he hasn't been Omega. I have." She reached up and kissed him, then left the room.

Aidan decided then and there that he was in love with her.

After he finished recording the minutes, he put the logbook away and went back to the common room. The garou were drinking and socializing, and Will waved him over. He stopped at the keg first to pour himself some ale, but as he reached for the tap, Cicero Parvisi grabbed him roughly and pushed him out of the way.

"Wait your turn, Omega," he said.

Irritation boiled up inside Aidan, and he took a step toward Cicero. He opened his mouth to retort, but Don stepped between them and placed a hand on Aidan's chest.

"Stop," he said to Aidan. Then he turned to Cicero and said, "We don't do that here. The Omega shall not be the target of abuse."

"Are you in jest?" Cicero said. "That's what Omega is for!"

"That is not what *our* Omega is for. If you mistreat him, you'll answer to me."

Cicero laughed. "Yah, I'm going to like it here. Tiny little Beta Wolf trying to protect the Omega from big Cicero." He patted Don on the head.

Don didn't reply, just smirked and turned back to Aidan. "Are you all right?

"Aye, I'm fine."

He turned to the keg and poured a mug for Aidan. "Go on," he said. "Get out of here."

Aidan took the mug and joined Will by the fire. He overheard Don say, "Let's you and me take a walk," to Cicero.

Aidan didn't know what Don did or said to Cicero, but the big Arab never laid another hand on him, or anyone else in the House of O'Neill, for that matter.

Aidan went to Peter later that night when the party was breaking up.

"It's respect," he said. "The Alpha has to treat his packmates with respect."

"'Tis not the answer I want, but it is a good lesson, and an important one. You need to learn to treat others with more respect. 'Tis one reason I made you Omega. It hasn't been easy for you, and you can't expect to get it if you don't give it."

Aidan leaned close to Peter and whispered, "Even Cicero?"

"Even Cicero."

"Damn."

* * *

The House of O'Neill went on three missions in the next several months, only one of which resulted in a fight, and otherwise life was uneventful. Aidan began following Peter around when he was working. Peter didn't mind; in fact, he encouraged it and often called on Aidan to accompany him. He watched everything Peter did, and the Alpha explained what he was doing and offered instruction when appropriate. In addition to learning a lot about the office, Aidan learned a lot about the man.

Don liked to call Peter "the rock," and the Alpha Wolf lived up to it. He had always been the most levelheaded garou in the pack, even more so than Gerard, and he was adept at calming even the most irate garou. He loved to say, "Think of it this way," and offer an explanation with logic so sound that it couldn't be denied. Aidan came to believe Peter could convince the garou of almost anything. Much of the silliness he and Don had before the root cellar was gone now, a fact he attributed to being forced to grow up by taking the Alpha rank. He possessed more determination than Aidan could have imagined, and he thought nothing of staying up all night if something needed to be done. He was fiercely devoted to those in his charge, but his affection for Don and Mary came very close to Aidan's bond with Will. It was almost impossible to get him angry, but Aidan never forgot the rage that had nearly broken the surface when he had called Peter "Your Highness." Peter's threat had frightened him, and even now, he was afraid to ask why it had bothered him so.

He was afraid. He recalled how scared Peter had been when he had first taken the Alpha rank. Maybe that was it.

He went to Peter one afternoon as he sat in his office writing in one log or another.

"It's fear," Aidan said as he sat down.

Peter looked up at him, eyebrows raised.

"Fear is the thing an Alpha must possess," he said.

Peter shook his head. "Not it."

"Courage, then."

"Fear and courage go hand-in-hand."

"So they're the same lesson?"

Peter nodded.

Dejected but less upset than he would have expected, Aidan did the only thing he could do at this point: he went back to shadowing Peter.

Peter still hated being Alpha with a passion. He good-naturedly cursed Gerard for dying and leaving him with the job and even threatened to concede his rank and make Don Alpha. Occasionally, Mary went into his office and told him to stop whining. Whether he was happy or not, though, Peter wasn't about to give the position to somebody who didn't understand what it meant. Unfortunately, for all that Aidan learned from Peter, he still couldn't figure out what that elusive puzzle piece was.

One night when Aidan was sitting in the common room with Will, Peter came in and dropped a heavy tome in his lap. "Read it," he said.

"What is it?"

"It's Gerard's journal."

"Why do you—?"

"Don't ask me why. Just do it. Now."

"The whole thing? It's hundreds of pages."

"You'd better get started, then."

Will patted his shoulder and left him alone, and Aidan took the book to the table and started to read. The first entry was an eye opener.

> *23 October 1330*
> *I cannot believe he actually made me Omega. I've done everything he's ever asked of me! I know he only did it so the others wouldn't accuse him of giving his own son special treatment. I'll never forgive him for this.*

Gerard had been Omega Wolf! But there was more to it than that. He had been impetuous, hot-tempered, and arrogant. It was as if Aidan had written the journal himself.

He read into the night and was still sitting at the table when the monks brought breakfast in the next morning. Peter came in and sat across from him.

"Any questions?" he asked.

"I can't believe he was Omega Wolf."

Peter snickered. "Aye, and Don and I never let him forget it. 'Twas a great time."

"Not for him."

"Stephen Blevins made Gerard Omega to teach him a lesson, not to torment him. The only ones who ever mistreated Gerard were Don and me, and we'd have done that anyway. And you know we never really hurt him. Well, Connor and his *athair* tried, but Stephen put a stop to it. Gerard's time as Omega could have been much worse. It was a lot like yours, actually. Stop and eat, then get some rest. You can finish the book later. I would recommend you start writing one as well."

"Why?"

"So I can give it to your son to read after you die."

Aidan showed him his middle finger, and Peter chuckled.

"Writing your thoughts down helps you sort things out. Helps you remember things, too. Mary, Don, and I, we've all done it for years. I've filled two of those things and am working on a third."

Aidan ate, but he didn't go to bed. He was committed and had to finish the journal before he did anything else.

The book reminded him how much he had loved his father. He'd idolized Gerard and had aspired to be like him. After reading the journal, he realized how much they'd had in common. Gerard's attitude and arrogance had gotten him reduced to Omega when he was twenty-five years old, and he had learned so much from the experience that he'd grown to be one of the greatest White Guard Alphas of all time.

Over the years, the tone of his writing changed. When he was younger, the entries were full of emotion, usually anger and frustration, but as he got older, especially after he became Alpha Wolf, they evolved. They were mostly accounts of battles he'd fought and thoughts about pack life, but there was very little sentiment. He detested Ardis, and the vampire's affection bewildered him. He had lovers every once in a while and even had a brief flirtation with Mary, but it hadn't developed into anything because of some comments Connor had made to Mary.

Aidan had always believed Connor was a bully, but apparently he had been much worse when younger. Gerard couldn't stand him, and he struggled to remain detached and not let his personal feelings affect his job.

Gerard expressed a tremendous amount of regret over demoting Mary to Omega. It was the worst mistake he had ever made, and he resolved to find an excuse to promote her as soon as possible without unjustly demoting someone else.

When he met Erica, the tone of Gerard's writing changed again. For a brief time, the entries held some of their previous emotion. He went from irritation to wide-eyed adoration for the cute little red-haired pixie, even before they got together. While her audacity annoyed him, he couldn't help admiring it, and her strength made him love her even more. It was torture to remain neutral and detached during her advancement through the ranks, but with so much contention, he felt he had no choice. He poured his heart out in those entries, expressing all the emotions he couldn't share with Erica.

As their relationship settled in and they started having Aidan and his brothers, the entries became more objective again, but his happiness infused even the driest accounts. He ended every entry by asking God to bless his wife and his sons.

The last entry opened Aidan's eyes even more.

> *21 April 1492*
> *We got word of activity in County Clare. It was the most perfect report we've ever received, and I can't help being suspicious. I won't be surprised if we see Ardis when we get there. We'll exercise more caution in anticipation of an ambush. It's a damned inconvenient time, what with the females all being in heat, but we do what has to be done. God bless Erica and the lads, and protect us as we go into battle.*

After the root cellar, Aidan's bitterness had consumed him, and he had refused to believe Gerard hadn't made any mistakes. But Aidan had fabricated those mistakes. The night Peter had made him Omega, Aidan had said things he never should have *thought*, much less uttered. No wonder Peter had demoted him.

He closed the book and held it close to his chest. Peter had given it to him to teach him a lesson, and when he gave it back, Aidan knew he'd better have an answer to Peter's question or he was going to be Omega for a long, long time.

There was still something missing, something he couldn't put his finger on, but he thought he knew where to look. He opened the book again and turned to the entry for the day Gerard became Alpha Wolf.

> *20 January 1380*
> *Today's fight was terrible. We lost three garou: Ben Williamson, Anne McFee, and Patrick O'Halloran. Don is pretty broken up about losing his athair, but he still managed to remind me that this is no longer the House of O'Halloran. I am Alpha Wolf of the new House of Blevins. What in God's name am I going to do now?*
> *If we'd had the battle five weeks ago, Don would be in my place now. If I didn't know better, I'd think*

he knew what was going to happen and let me win so
he wouldn't have to be Alpha.

Alpha is a lonely place. Don and Peter say they'll
help me, but I know I'm on my own. Patrick was a
strong Alpha and a good friend. I can only hope that
I'm able to serve as well as he did.

To serve. Now he knew what Peter had been trying to tell him. The Alpha didn't rule his pack; he served it. Aidan could see now how Peter served the House of O'Neill. He didn't give orders or lord over the garou; he tended to their needs and took care of them. But could Aidan do it? Was he able to do the one thing that would make him a worthy Alpha? What if he became Alpha and found out he couldn't serve? He didn't think he would have the fortitude to concede his position once he had it. It didn't matter anyway; he'd never defeat Peter in a duel, and Peter wouldn't even let it get that far if he didn't think Aidan was worthy.

The keep was quiet, so he left the common room and went to find the others. Cicero, Charles, and Will were in the stable, and Devon was working with Brother Elgin in the vegetable garden. Mary and the lads were in the courtyard playing with a ball.

His brothers were afraid of him. He supposed they weren't quite as afraid these days. He'd said before that he'd rather have them be afraid of him than the fight, but things were different now. One couldn't be a worthy leader by striking fear in the hearts of his charges.

Aidan went back to the common room to get the journal and found Peter and Don sitting at the chessboard, just beginning a game. He sat down next to Don.

Peter grimaced. "You look like shite. When's the last time you slept?"

"When's the last time you took a bath?" Don added.

"Couple of days. I'll get a bath and go to bed now."

"Anything you want to tell me?" Peter asked him.

"The most important task an Alpha must perform is to serve." For the first time, his answer wasn't a guess or a question; it was a statement of fact.

"Huzzah!" Don exclaimed.

"Do you think you can do that?" Peter asked.

"I don't know," Aidan admitted.

"Good answer. Come back when you do know."

Peter had denied his petition again. He should have been furious, but he wasn't ready and he knew it. He resolved to find the part of himself that would determine whether he would be a great Alpha like Gerard or remain Omega for the rest of his life.

* * *

By the year's anniversary of his demotion, Aidan still didn't know if he was capable of serving as the pack's leader. He certainly served a lot as Omega, but his temper still threatened to betray him and he had trouble swallowing his pride. Humility was the hardest obstacle he'd had to face, and he still hadn't conquered it. He had to bite his tongue to keep from talking back to Cicero or avert his eyes in a staredown, and every time he had to do it, he wanted to scream.

He still shadowed Peter, but he followed Mary too. He had never thought he'd be the type to go all starry-eyed over a female, but he couldn't help himself. As Omega, he couldn't make any advances, and controlling those impulses was harder than anything he had to put up with from Cicero. Will was in love with her, too—what one of them felt, they both felt—but he hadn't said anything, either. He wouldn't, though. He followed Aidan's lead, even when he was of higher rank.

Because he spent more time with Mary, Aidan in turn spent more time with his brothers. He tried to interact with them, but they usually avoided him. Most of the time, when Aidan was around, Ian left the monastery and went to hide in his favorite cave. He wondered what Ian did there. He often came back wet, and Aidan figured his brother was swimming in the river.

The lads, being mortal, got sick from time to time, and Mary wiped a lot of runny noses and nursed cuts and scrapes so they wouldn't get infected. Aidan didn't like to think about the times when it had been his nose she had wiped. He had only been garou for a few years, but he had already forgotten what it was like to get sick. Then Ryan contracted pneumonia.

Mary banished the garou and put Ryan to bed. She closed the infirmary door but left her bedroom door open, and Aidan could hear what was going on in the infirmary from his room. He stayed awake for three nights, listening to his brother's raspy chest cough and Mary's soothing voice as she comforted him. She rarely left Ryan's side, and after a while, Aidan could detect signs of fatigue in her voice. Somebody needed to care for her so she could care for Ryan.

After dinner on the fourth evening, Aidan caught sight of Brother Elgin taking a bowl of broth to the infirmary. He stopped the monk.

"I can take that," he said.

"Thank you, Aidan."

He knocked on the infirmary door and Mary called to come in. He stuck his head into the room and said, "Suppertime."

Mary sat next to a cot, upon which lay a child Aidan barely recognized. Ryan was pale and gaunt with dark circles under his eyes. His breathing made a rattling sound, and each breath seemed to drain what little energy he had. He glanced up at Aidan when he walked into the room, coughed, and closed his eyes.

"Sit up, dear," Mary said. "You must try to eat."

"He's not eating?"

"Not for days. He usually minds me. I don't know what else to do."

"I'm not hungry," Ryan said.

Aidan knelt next to the bed. "You should try to eat," he told his brother. "You need to keep your strength up so your body can heal."

He sat on the next cot and got a glimpse of Mary. She was nearly as pale as Ryan.

"You should rest," he said.

"Nae, I'm fine."

"You're not fine; you're exhausted. At least get something to eat. I'll abide here."

Mary looked at him as if he had grown horns.

"What?"

"Nothing. I'll only be gone a few minutes. If you need me, just call."

"I think I can care for my brother long enough for you to take a rest, Mary."

"Very well. Make sure he stays warm. And make sure his head is raised. And make sure—"

"Mary."

She smiled and got up to leave, stopping to kiss his cheek on the way out.

Aidan got the bowl and sat in Mary's chair. He sniffed the broth and said, "Smells good. It'd be a shame to waste it. Are you sure you wouldn't like some?"

"Mm-mmm."

"You know, it would make Mary happy if I could get you to eat something."

Ryan smiled.

"Come, little brother. Try and sit up."

Ryan sat up, and when the blanket fell away, Aidan saw just how frail Ryan had become. He was eight years old, but he looked five. He was emaciated and barely strong enough to sit up on his own. Aidan moved over to hold him up so he could eat. He dipped a spoonful of the broth and held it out for Ryan, who took the bite and the next few that Aidan fed him.

"I don't think I can eat anymore right now," he said.

"That's fine. 'Twas a good start."

He set the bowl aside and started to get up, but Ryan laid his head in his lap. He hadn't noticed his brother's fever before, but heat poured from his little body. Garou's body temperatures ran higher than humans' so if Ryan felt hot to Aidan, his fever must be dangerously high. Ryan began to cough with deep, ragged spasms that rumbled down in his chest.

"We need to raise your head," Aidan said. He got a pillow, and Ryan sat up long enough for Aidan to place it on his lap, and then lay back down. Aidan pulled the blanket up to Ryan's chin.

He held Ryan for a long time and didn't really know when he went to sleep, but he roused when Mary squeezed his hand.

"How late is it?" he asked drowsily.

"Almost morning."

"Wake me when it's time for breakfast."

Ryan's hacking woke him the next time. Though the cough wasn't much better, the pillow was wet with sweat and Ryan's skin was cooler. Aidan opened his eyes to see Mary sitting in her chair.

"His fever's broken," she told him.

"I got him to eat a bit last night."

"So I see. I'll spell you if you want to get some breakfast."

"I'll be back later."

He went back to the infirmary at lunchtime, and again he was able to get Ryan to eat when Mary couldn't. He sat with him most of the afternoon and even read to him awhile.

Aidan had never really paid much attention to Ryan before, but now he found himself with an almost desperate need to protect his sick little brother. He'd gone from one extreme to the other overnight.

He and Mary spent the next three days taking turns sitting with Ryan until the lad started to get up and around. The night Ryan moved from the infirmary to his own bed, Aidan tucked him in. When he left Ryan's room and went to the common room, Peter was sitting by the fire.

"Challenge accepted," he said when Aidan sat down next to him.

"That's not why I've been caring for him, Peter."

"I know. That's why I'm accepting."

23

Leader of the Pack

Be careful what you wish for. You may receive it. — Origins Unknown

Peter's argument with Cicero and Charles was epic. When they had come to assist the pack, Peter hadn't bothered telling them about Aidan's unique circumstances. All they saw now was the Omega challenging the Alpha and a scandal that would rock the foundations of Rome herself. They barged into Peter's office and slammed the door, but everyone heard them anyway. The rest of the garou sat in the common room, eavesdropping.

Peter explained the situation and his promise to Aidan, but they refused to let the issue rest.

"He must not be allowed to duel you!" Cicero bellowed. "He is Omega! He is nothing!"

"Lower your voice, Cicero," said Peter.

"It is simply not done," Charles said, more quietly but with no less force.

"'Tis done now, 'cause I'm doing it."

"You made him Omega because he was impertinent and disrespectful," said Cicero, "and he still is such because you and your Beta Wolf allow it."

"I've seen no such impertinence," Peter said. "He has spent the last year and a half learning humility and patience, and that is what I see. If ye have seen otherwise, why am I only hearing about it now?"

"It was not our place to interfere."

"And how has that changed?"

"His ascendance to Alpha will affect the White Guard. It will look bad."

"It will *look* bad? Are you telling me that the reputation of the House of O'Neill is more important than its ability to carry out its mission? Truly, lads, I don't give a good goddamn if the House of Bianco likes us or not. I care that Ireland has more vampires for its size than any other country in the world and we're tasked with fighting them. If I didn't believe Aidan was capable of leading us in that fight, I wouldn't allow him to oppose me."

"At least make him go through channels," Charles said.

"He went through channels when this began, and I made a promise to him. I'll not go back on it now."

"Only a weak Alpha would bend to this!" said Cicero.

In the common room, Don said, "That was a mistake."

"What, exactly, do you think I'm bending to?"

"You're letting your Omega lead you!"

"A pack's hierarchy is set up as such for a purpose," Charles said. "The Alpha is not deposed unless he's a poor Alpha."

There was silence behind the office door.

"I know that silence," Mary said. "I wouldn't want to be on the receiving end of that silence."

"First of all," Peter said, his voice steady—

"He's mad, isn't he?" said Devon.

In unison, Don, Mary, Aidan, and Will all said, "He's not mad."

—"I shouldn't need to remind you that you're not members of the House of O'Neill. You're guests here, and as such have no right to object to anything I do as Alpha. If you're unhappy with what happens here, you're perfectly welcome to leave anytime, 'cause truly, neither of ye is a good enough fighter to be missed when you leave."

"That'll leave a mark," said Don.

"That being said, if you're still of a mind to question my strength as Alpha, I'll gladly accept your petition to join the House of O'Neill, and then ye can learn firsthand whether I'm weak. In the meantime, get the hell out of my office and mind your own bloody affairs!"

Cicero left the next day. Charles and Devon decided to stay awhile. They didn't petition for acceptance into the pack, but Charles did agree to keep his objections to himself.

At noon on the first day of the next New Moon, Aidan and Peter met in the courtyard. A handful of monks sat among the garou, as did Ian.

Don stood in the circle between them. "Aidan," he said, "hast thou challenged Peter for the rank of Alpha Wolf?"

"I have."

"And Peter, hast thou accepted?"

"I have."

"I call a duel with rapiers. The match will continue until one of you submits and verbally acknowledges the other as Alpha, or one of you is rendered unconscious or is killed. Begin."

Peter waited for Aidan to initiate the first attack. Cognizant of Peter's skill, Aidan proceeded cautiously, advancing in a spiral path with deliberate steps and careful footing. He kept his eyes slightly unfocused in order to track the tip of the Alpha's sword, hand, shoulders, and hips simultaneously. Peter turned to the side as Aidan approached and kept his blade up between them.

Aidan delivered two quick feints, thrusting high and then low. Peter tapped the foible of the younger garou's rapier lightly the first time and more solidly the second. Had the thrust been more forceful, his sword would have been knocked out of position. Peter stepped forward quickly, and his blade began to flash out but slowed at the last instant. Aidan was able to parry and then riposte easily.

The initiative changed several times over the next minute or two with each duelist thrusting, being blocked, and then drawing back to stop his opposite's counterattack. Aidan noticed Peter flinch several times. At first, he thought the movements were feints, but he soon realized they weren't threatening enough for that. Aidan grew more aggressive, striking faster and with increasingly intricate routines, but no matter where he struck, Peter's blade was always there to intercept his and deflect it harmlessly to the side. It gave him no small measure of pride to realize he was doing the same when his superior assumed the offensive.

Neither of them scored a point on the other in the first few minutes. Aidan began to think it strange that they were so evenly matched, given the difference in their experience and skill. There was nothing easy about the duel, but he'd expected to be overwhelmed as he had in his earlier contests with Peter and Don. He remembered how Peter had toyed with the vampire at Castleraegh. His temper flared, but then he realized something was off. Peter took every fencing exercise seriously and wouldn't demean him that way in an official duel. With sudden comprehension, he knew Peter wasn't toying with him but testing him. He was evaluating Aidan's performance as he had in all things since his initial challenge to the Alpha. The more experienced swordsman was pushing him and escalating the fight to see how long he could keep up. The flinches he had noticed were Peter's reflexes instinctively starting an attack when he saw an opening, only to be overruled by his intent to keep the match going while he gauged Aidan's abilities.

So be it, Aidan thought. I'll be judged by my capabilities and skill and my determination to give my all. It will have to be enough, and I'll hold out as long as I can.

* * *

As Peter lunged, he felt something give way, and white-hot pain shot through his back. He cried out and fell to his knees. Aidan thrust his rapier at his chest, and though Peter was able to partially deflect the blade, it still went through his shoulder.

Another spasm wracked Peter's body, and for the first time in his adult life, he dropped his sword. Up to now, Don pulling the crossbow bolt out of bone was the worst pain he'd ever experienced. This far surpassed it.

With confusion on his face, Aidan removed his blade but kept it pointed at Peter. He said, "Do you yield?"

"Aidan, he can't continue the fight," Mary said.

"Then he must acknowledge me as Alpha."

"Acknowledged," Peter croaked, and Aidan sheathed his rapier. He held his hand out to help Peter up, but Peter didn't move.

"Peter?" Mary said, her voice breaking.

"I'm all right. Just give me a minute." He took five. When he started to get up, he recoiled. "Bloody hell," he groaned.

"I know it's not your shoulder," Aidan said. "What is it?"

"It's my back. It feels as though I've been stabbed with a blade that was struck by lightning."

"Let's get you to the infirmary. Ian, get his rapier."

Aidan and Don had to help him get to the infirmary. Mary sent everyone out, and Peter sat on the operating table and took his shirt off, which caused another burst of intense pain.

"Let me see that," she said, pressing gently on the hole Aidan had made in his shoulder.

"That's nothing," Peter said. "I've been run through before; there's one in the back just like it."

Mary scowled at him.

"What?"

"You're my worst patient, Peter O'Neill."

"Why, 'cause I don't whine and moan like everyone else?"

"Precisely."

He leaned over and kissed her. "Well, if it'll help, I'll whine and moan when you treat my back."

"That would be magnificent, thank you."

She walked around the table, and when she saw his back, she said, "What in God's name is that?"

"You aren't instilling me with a lot of confidence, love."

"There's a spot as big as my hand near your spine that's swollen and purple." She pressed on the area and said, "Something hard is moving beneath the skin."

"What is it?" Peter asked.

"I'm not sure, but it's right underneath where you were shot. I think a piece of a bolt may still be in there."

"That explains it."

"Explains what?"

"It's been hurting since the root cellar."

"And you didn't tell me? Peter!"

"I'm trained to ignore pain, remember?"

"You're trained to *withstand* pain, you idiot. If there's something I can do to fix it, you're supposed to tell me. And if you say you were too busy to worry about it, I'm just gonna leave it there."

Mary retrieved a knife from a side table and sharpened it on a whetstone, then wiped it clean. "Lie down." He complied, and she stretched the skin and sliced deep into his back.

"Oh, me, the pain," Peter said, deadpan.

"Come, Peter. You can whine better than that."

"I'll see what I can do."

"There it is. Tiny piece of metal less than half an inch from your spine. I don't have tongs that small; I'll have to get it with my fingernails." She grasped the shard, but it slipped and pain shot up his back. He flinched.

"Are you all right?" she asked.

"My God, it hurts so bad."

"Oh, just give it up." She cut deeper into the muscle so her fingernails could get a better grip. Once she thought she had it, she yanked hard and it came out. "What the devil?"

"What?"

"Hold out your hand."

She placed the shard in Peter's hand. It stung.

"Bloody hell, that's silver!"

"I guess Ardis thought we had a good idea. That must be why your body didn't push it out on its own. I shudder to think what would have happened if it got into your bloodstream and went to your heart."

"Well, that's disconcerting. Hey, Don!"

"Don't do that to him," Mary whispered.

"Are you daft? I can use this against him for centuries."

Don came into the room. "Will he live?"

Peter tossed the shard at him. Don caught it and quickly dropped it. "Oi, what'd you do that for?"

"I thought you might want it back."

"It's a piece of one of the crossbow bolts," Mary said.

"Aye, a piece that you left in me."

"That's it. Make me feel worse."

"I'm afraid I'm gonna do just that. It's silver," Mary said.

"Ardis was using silver?" Don said incredulously.

"Here's another one for you," said Peter. "That little bugger cost me the Alpha rank."

"You didn't want it in the first place!"

"Lads, need I separate you?" Mary said as she prepared to stitch the incision.

"Nae, it's all right. You're about to stick needles in him; I'm satisfied."

"She wouldn't have to if you had got the whole bloody bolt out to start with," said Peter.

"Peter, you know this is killing me," Don said earnestly.

"It's nothing you did, brother; you know that. But I couldn't let it go without jibing you a little bit."

"So, Beta Wolf. What now?"

Peter rubbed his shoulder. The hole Aidan's blade had made had scabbed over. "I guess we'll see, no?"

* * *

Though he had agreed to stay out of the matter, Charles complained anyway. "The duel wasn't fair," he told Peter. "He took advantage of you when you were unable to fight. At the very least, he should agree to duel you again."

"He speaks right," Aidan said. "I'll not deny you a rematch if it's what you wish."

Peter shook his head. "In our last duel, I turned my back on you and told you any opening was one I gave you. You had no reason to think my fall wasn't a bluff. You reacted as I taught you, and you did it fairly. I'd have done the same to you. The result stands; you are Alpha. I'd prefer you had gained more experience before shouldering the burden, but you'll have to pick that up as you go, and we will help you. But know this: I'll hold you to your word. You will serve this house, and you won't harm the lads."

Peter's meaning was patently clear to Aidan. He was Alpha on approval. If he got too far out of line, Peter would depose him.

"You won't have to worry, brother. I'll not let you down."

* * *

The pack took the name of House of Blevins again, and at the age of twenty-seven—decades, even centuries, earlier than his predecessors—Aidan ascended to Alpha Wolf. It was rare but not unheard of that soul siblings became Alpha, and they essentially shared the position. Will maintained his rank and would advance and fall in the normal course, but as the Alpha's soul brother he asserted more authority than he typically would. At present, he didn't see himself advancing at all because everyone in his path had decades of experience on him and he had no hope of defeating them in the near future. More likely, Don would break Will's nose just as badly as he broke Aidan's. Will wasn't sure why they had done it, but he felt that Don and Peter had allowed Aidan to become Alpha. Whatever the reason, there was no way they would permit Will to become Beta Wolf.

It took Aidan two whole hours to realize he had made a mistake. The issues that had piled up on Peter still existed, but now they were his problems, and he couldn't remember a thing he had learned while shadowing Peter. He was caught in the same trap as Peter, but he didn't have the experience to help work his way through it. He had once believed that to be Alpha was to have power. Peter had been right: He had been out of his mind.

During Aidan's first winter as Alpha, there was an unprecedented snowstorm, and Aidan and Will got their first glimpse into the wonderful world of snow removal. Mary came into the office where they sat speculating on which was more intimidating: a snarling vampire or a foot of snow.

"Word has come from Rome," she announced. She laid a piece of paper on the desk. "They'll send several garou home with us after the next induction. I also believe Charles and Devon are going to petition to stay with us."

"After the whole trouble with Aidan's rise to Alpha?" Will said.

"Aye, they think he's doing a fine job."

"Well, they're the only ones," Aidan muttered.

"I put the messengers in a couple of the guest rooms. They had enough trouble getting here. I don't want to send them back out until the snow melts."

"Very well," said Aidan.

They waited for her to leave, but she didn't. "I want to remind you why you're Alpha," she said.

"I'm Alpha 'cause I won the fight against Peter," Aidan said defensively.

"Nae. Try again."

He furrowed a brow, trying to figure out what she meant. "Peter thought I was worthy to challenge him?"

"Come, Aidan, you aren't daft. What started the whole matter up in the first place?"

"Gerard was killed?" Will offered.

She nodded. "And do you know why?"

"Why?" they asked together.

"Gerard died 'cause he was too far from the door. He didn't sacrifice his life to save you. He would have escaped if he had been able, but the cellar was overcrowded and too many vampires stood between him and the stairs. Likewise, when you dueled Peter, you defeated him when he succumbed to an old injury."

"What's your point, Mary?" Aidan asked impatiently.

"My point is that things happen. We don't always know why, but we have to live with what God gives us. You wanted to be Alpha, and now you are. You may not have known what you were getting into when you opposed Peter, but by doing so, you freely accepted your fate. Unless you do something incredibly heinous, he'll not likely challenge you to take back the Alpha rank. It's time to grow up and rise to the task, 'cause you have no choice."

Though he knew she was absolutely right, Will said, "Tell me, then, who exactly are you to instruct him in how to run the House of Blevins?"

Mary sat on the desk. "With only five of us, and especially since I was the only female, no one said much about the Alpha Bitch rank. But the pack is growing now, and rank will come into play more for all of us. As the female who has been here the longest, that makes me dominant, and it makes me Alpha Bitch. *That's* who I am to tell you how to run the house. Any questions?"

"Oh my God, I'm Omega," Will said grimly. An Alpha with an Omega for a soul brother. He couldn't think of anything more miserable.

"You might want to talk to Don about that," Mary said.

* * *

The garou tried to talk him out of it, but Don conceded his rank to Will, thereby demoting himself to Omega. He said he was tired of the politics and vying for one position or another.

Peter took him to a pub in Derry so they could talk without the other garou eavesdropping. "What are you doing, brother?" he asked. "You're the most aggressive garou in the pack. Why put yourself in this position?"

"I told you why. I'm weary of fighting for rank."

"It isn't as if there would be much of a fight. Will doesn't have the stones to challenge you, and me—well, you trying to take the Beta Wolf rank from me would just be silly."

Don didn't laugh, and he didn't come back with a smart remark.

"You're serious," Peter realized.

"I am. That's all there is now, but others will be joining us soon, no?"

"No, there's more to it than just not wanting to fight for rank."

Don didn't say anything for a while but sat quietly, drinking his ale. Peter waited. Don was weighing his words, trying to decide what and how much he was going to say, and there was no point pressing the issue. They were best friends and blood brothers. They had told each other nearly everything for two centuries. Don had told him about going back to the root cellar, but Peter knew him well enough to know he hadn't told him everything. When Don was ready to tell him, he would.

"All right," Don said. "After the root cellar, I considered taking my life."

"My God, Don."

"I couldn't live with what had happened."

"But you weren't at fault."

"Nae, it wasn't that. I couldn't get the pictures out of my mind. That vampire taking Grace's head, Pippa yanking Adam's heart out, Ardis shooting Erica, us leaving Gerard down there to die. We could have gotten him out; you know we could have. But he didn't want to get out. He didn't want to live without Erica, and I knew how he felt. And then we had to leave them there to burn. I knew we couldn't help that, either, but it didn't stop the nightmares."

"And that's why you brought them back."

Don nodded.

"Bringing them home saved your life."

"Maybe."

"But not your spirit."

"I don't know. I'm still a soldier, but I don't know if I'm a fighter any longer. At least for now. I'm tired, Peter."

"Then heal, brother. Take your time, and heal."

Don glowered at Peter. "He's out there, you know. Laughing his arse off."

"I don't think he's laughing. Not this time. He didn't want to kill Gerard."

"Well, I'm not laughing, either." Don raised his cup. "Know what I'm thinking? I'm thinking that the next time I meet Ardis will be the last. He dies or I do."

Peter tapped Don's cup with his own. "Or I do."

24

Family Snapshot

I wish they would only take me as I am. — Vincent van Gogh

Mary knocked on Aidan and Will's bedroom door one night not long after she declared herself Alpha Bitch. Afterward, she spent more nights with them than she spent in her own room.

Aidan struggled, but he wasn't afraid to ask for help, and with the assistance of the other garou, he became a decent Alpha. He recognized that diplomacy wasn't his forte, and he allowed Mary and Will to handle any conflicts or social issues that came up.

Devon and Charles officially joined the pack, and upon their return from inductions, the garou brought Kristoff Amundsen, an imposing Norseman who towered over everyone, and a husky Bohemian named Erlich von Reinman. Later that year, Michael and Gwendolyn Blevins arrived with their daughter Amanda. Michael, a distant cousin of Gerard's, looked like the family, with the ubiquitous Blevins dark curls and brooding eyes. Gwendolyn had sandy hair, pale blue eyes, and an infectious smile. Amanda had Gwendolyn's smile and eyes, and they were a startling contrast to her dark Blevins features. She had never cut her hair, and her nearly black curls hung to her waist.

Amanda's arrival turned the House of Blevins on its ear. When Aidan and Will showed the family to the common room to introduce them to the garou, jaws dropped and several of the males gawked shamelessly at Amanda. Amanda, however, gawked shamelessly at Ian, who was celebrating his seventeenth birthday.

"Happy birthday," Peter said to Ian.

Although Aidan had allowed Don to take the rank of Omega Wolf, he had refused to treat him or allow him to be treated as a standard Omega. The garou who had met him at inductions were used to it, but Don's situation caused controversy the first day Michael, Gwendolyn, and Amanda spent at the monastery. During the meeting to formally welcome the Blevinses, Michael mentioned Aidan's broken nose.

"'Twas during a fight for the Beta rank," Aidan told him.

Peter pointed at Don, who sat at the end of the table taking notes. Don waved. Michael's eyes widened. "*He* did that?"

"He's stronger than he looks," Aidan said drily.

"You had it coming, and you know it," Don said.

Michael was outraged. "You dare talk to your Alpha in such manner? And at a formal proceeding!"

"I told you you should have said something beforehand," Peter said to Aidan.

"Don is Omega only in the most basic sense of the word," Aidan said. "When there were only five of us, he sacrificed his position so as not to put others in a bad situation. He performs the normal Omega's duties and doesn't compete for rank, but it's by his choice, and otherwise he's afforded the same courtesies as the higher-ranking garou, including having a voice in meetings and formal proceedings. Besides, he's right; I did have it coming."

"This is unheard of," said Gwendolyn.

"Actually, it's not," Mary pointed out. "We even went so far as to ask the House of Bianco about it at the last induction, and they said it was perfectly acceptable. Several White Guard packs don't even *have* Omegas."

"The only reason we even use the title is 'cause he's stubborn," said Peter. "Oh, and by the way, not only will there be no abuse, Don is allowed to defend himself."

"And trust me," said Aidan, "he will."

"Can we stop talking about Don like he's not here?" Don said.

Michael still looked offended but voiced no further objections.

* * *

Although Aidan was closer to Ryan than before, Ian and Logan still tried to avoid him. As they got older, especially after they began training, contact was inevitable. Aidan usually treated them fairly, but his patience slipped occasionally and he was harsh with them. He hadn't quite mastered the ability to apologize, but he was working on it.

He was overly protective of Ryan, and whereas they had always let the boys play away from the monastery, Aidan admonished Ryan to be careful, not to go too far, to stay away from the river and other things that might put him in danger. He actually lost sleep when Ryan began fencing. He had nightmares of him falling dead with someone's blade piercing his heart and thus made sure he was present every time his little brother picked up a weapon.

"You never let me do the things Logan can do!" Ryan protested. "You won't even let me touch a sword when you're not around. How am I ever supposed to learn to fence if I can't practice? Especially when you leave for inductions."

Will cringed. "Ooh, you shouldn't have said that."

"Oh, no!" Aidan said. "You don't go near a sword while we're gone to inductions."

"But that's more than half a year!"

"Aye, half a year that I don't have to worry about Ian or Logan accidentally killing you."

Ryan growled with frustration and stormed off.

"You're overreacting," said Will.

"Better to overreact than to bury him."

* * *

Aidan brought Ian across, and the initiation was traumatic for both of them. Michael gave Aidan extensive instruction on how to initiate Ian properly without hurting him too badly, but he still botched the job and nearly did permanent damage.

After Ian's wounds healed, Logan bombarded him with questions about the initiation. He had always been honest with his brother, but he found himself hedging rather than giving him direct answers.

"He wants some sort of comfort," he confided to Amanda, "but I can't give him any. How am I supposed to tell him I don't have anything good to say about it?"

"Just like that," she said. "You've never lied to him before; don't start now. Be truthful, and don't pretty it up."

"That's easy to say, but I can't scare him like that. He trusts me."

"Would you rather scare him or lose his trust? What if you tell him it's not so bad and Aidan hurts him worse than he did you? He needs to know what to expect, love. You might try to make it sound worse than it is, 'haps even show him the initiation chamber."

"Amanda, have you *seen* the initiation chamber? Besides, he's been there before. He and I snuck in when we were small. I remember talking about the dark spots on the wall and floor and wondering whose blood it was. If he went down there now, he wouldn't have to speculate. It's my blood he would see."

In the end, Ian leveled with Logan about his initiation, and though he assured him that Aidan had hurt him worse than usual and the injuries weren't typically so bad, his words didn't give Logan much comfort.

On the journey to Rome, Ian got a surprise. He was relaxing by the campfire one evening when Aidan sat down next to him.

"Logan's pretty scared," he said.

"Understandably so, don't you think?" Ian replied.

"Do you think it would be easier on him if you brought him across?"

"What's that?"

"I asked Peter to bring you across," Aidan confessed. "I thought it would be easier on you since you're closer to him than me."

"But he said no?"

"He said it was a family member's office. But now we're in the same situation, not to mention the fact that I'm skittish after nearly killing you."

"I think you're right," Ian said. "Logan would be more comfortable if I did it, although I'm not sure how comfortable *I'll* be with it."

"I feel your pain, brother."

* * *

Logan sat on the stone floor of the initiation chamber on the Full Moon after his twentieth birthday, and Ian encased his arm in a manacle. Fear dominated Logan's scent, and he trembled. Truth be known, Ian was pretty damn scared, himself.

The garou crowded into the room and converged around Logan in a half circle. They were lined up according to rank, except for Ian, who stood on the end next to Aidan. Michael murmured a complaint about the cold floor. He was right: it was the middle of January, one torch wasn't enough to provide warmth, and except for Logan, they were all naked. Ian was freezing. He would have thought all the body heat would help warm the room, but it didn't help much, if any.

In order to bring Logan across, Ian had to remain in human form long enough to vote, and it was with supreme effort that he did so. The mixture of scents in the room was seductive. Most of the garou would normally be in wolf form by now, and Ian wasn't the only one trying to suppress the shift. He wasn't certain he possessed the control to do so long enough to initiate Logan. Aidan had assured him that he would step in if Ian couldn't manage it, but he prayed he wouldn't have to rely on the Alpha to bring Logan across.

Aidan knelt before Logan. "Logan Peter Blevins," he said, "upon having reached the age of twenty years, thou hast requested admittance to the House of Blevins. By what right doth thou so petition?"

Logan said, "I, uh, it is my birthright as third son of the House of Blevins and brother of Aidan and Ian."

"Hast thou employed a sponsor who shall speak for thee?"

"Yea, I have brought Amanda Blevins, member in good standing."

Aidan turned to Amanda, who stood outside the circle. "Amanda Blevins, step forward. Wilt thou speak for Logan?"

Peter and Mary separated, and Amanda stepped through and knelt next to Aidan. Logan swallowed hard, and desire flared in his scent. Ian's relationship with Amanda was the only source of tension with Logan, who'd had a mad crush on her since she had joined the pack. Ian and Amanda had tried to be considerate of Logan and not flaunt their relationship, but it wasn't easy to keep quiet, especially since Amanda tended to make a lot of noise when they were in bed together.

"Yea, I shall," Amanda replied to Aidan. "He is my cousin, known to me these six years. He shall make a fine addition to the House of Blevins."

She winked at Logan and backed out of the circle.

"Petition and affirmation having been made," said Aidan, "I call for a vote." He called on Don, who stood at Logan's far left.

Each of the garou approached Logan on all fours, sniffed his throat, and voted before returning to their place. All the votes were "yes," which didn't surprise Ian. Logan was the perfect one, the paladin. The only one Ian worried about was Aidan. He had the nagging suspicion that Aidan had asked Ian to bring Logan across not to make him more comfortable but so he could vote "no."

Then again, if Aidan voted "no," Peter would probably say something. Peter let Aidan have his head, but if Aidan was unreasonable, Peter jerked him back.

This had to be the strangest pack in history. They had an Omega Wolf they didn't treat like an Omega, an Alpha who rose from Omega in one step, a Beta Wolf who would slap the Alpha silly if he got out of line, and a twenty-three-year-old garou who was already bringing someone across.

Aidan crawled forward and paused for an unusually long time before sniffing Logan's throat, but he did ultimately give a "yes" vote. He returned to his place and said, "One vote remains. If that vote is yea, thy initiation shall commence forthwith. Now is the time to object."

"I have no objection," Logan said shakily.

"Ian Blevins," Aidan said.

Ian crept toward Logan. He had been concerned that if he actually managed to make it this far without shifting, he wouldn't be able to bite Logan like he was supposed to. The initiation of a new garou was violent, and he didn't want to maim his beloved brother, but it was just the way it was done. Now that he was here, with the tingling sensation that accompanied the shift spreading over his body, he knew he would have no trouble. Suddenly, it was perfectly natural. He just hoped he didn't hurt Logan as badly as Aidan had hurt him.

Logan turned his head, and Ian nuzzled his throat. He sniffed, whispered, "Yea," and then he shifted and bit into Logan's throat. With the bite, Ian swallowed some of Logan's blood, and for a moment, it was as if he and Logan were linked and he could see into Logan's mind. His brother was in terrible pain and was about to throw up, but his fear was gone and he was glad the anticipation was finally over. He was also glad Ian had initiated him instead of Aidan, and he desperately wished he would lose consciousness. He was vaguely aware of Ian, but the pain was so great he barely noticed.

A draft blew the hatch shut and the torch went out, and Mary screamed. Erlich was closest to the door and still in human form, so he climbed the stairs and threw the hatch open. Logan finally passed out, and Ian checked to make sure he was still breathing before following the others up the stairs.

* * *

When Logan awoke, he was in the infirmary with Brother Marcus standing over him. His throat was stitched up, and he was in very little pain.

"How late is it?" he asked in the whisper that was all he could manage.

"Nearly dawn," the old monk said. Ballybrook's abbot had been old and gray when Logan was small. He had to be at least 150 years old by now. He handed Logan a cup. "Drink this. It'll temper the pain."

Logan drank and gagged. "Dear God, that's worse than the initiation!"

"It is stronger than the medicine you were accustomed to as a child."

Within minutes his head began to swim and the pain subsided even more. "Brother Marcus, how old are you?" he asked groggily.

"Logan, what a question! I suppose I should be glad you can speak at all. Aidan did so much damage to Ian's throat, I was afraid I could not repair it effectively with Mary gone. As it was, he was mute for three days."

"I remember. Are they back?"

"Nae, they'll not return till the morrow, perhaps not till the day after. They're not far, though. I hear howls on the occasion." Brother Marcus smiled. "Next Full Moon, you'll join them."

"What happens till then?"

"I know not," the old monk replied. "Every garou's first month is different, and not being garou myself, I've no frame of reference. Ian and Peter shall give you whatever help you need."

Brother Marcus left the room, and Logan turned to face the wall. As he began to drift off to sleep, he smiled. The worst was over for now, and the only thing left to do was go forward.

* * *

Ryan sat shoulder to shoulder with Ian and Aidan on a bench in the courtyard. Will and Don sat at Aidan's other shoulder, watching Logan fence with Peter. It was chilly and damp, ten days after the frosty night when Ian had brought Logan across, and Logan was back to health and ready to step up his training.

The steel blades flew, at times so fast that Ryan's eyes could barely keep up. Ian and Aidan spouted words at him, terms like parry and thrust, feint, riposte—things he was sure were important, but all they were doing now was distracting him. Across the courtyard, Amanda fenced with Mary while Kristoff, Michael, and Gwendolyn watched. Ryan spent more time watching them, Mary in particular, than Logan's match with Peter.

Ryan's feelings for Mary were complicated. After his *máthair* was killed, Mary took over raising him and Logan, but Ryan could never think of her as a mother figure. These days, he just wanted to see her naked. He was pretty sure she had slept with every male in the pack except for him, so he still had hope.

But here he sat, surrounded by males trying to hurt each other, and he was supposed to pay attention. He would much rather watch the women try to hurt each other. One time Amanda's shirt had been torn by an errant swipe of Don's sword, and Ryan had slept on that one for weeks.

Logan's cry tore Ryan's gaze away from the females. He realized with chagrin that Logan was on the ground bleeding and he had no idea how it had happened.

"You ass!" Logan exclaimed. "What did you do that for? I just healed from that damn initiation, and here I am needing stitches again."

"You'll live," Peter said glibly.

"Small comfort. You gored me right through."

"Probably ruptured your kidney as well."

"Aye, thanks for that."

"What did he do wrong?" Aidan asked Ryan.

"He, uh, the tip of his blade was out of position, and his feet were placed so he was off balance."

Ian laughed. "Oi, wasn't that insightful! Why didn't you just say, 'He got stabbed'?"

"Try again," Aidan said.

Ryan sighed. "I don't know."

"Don, pray enlighten my brother."

"Logan tried a circular parry, engaging Peter's blade in a circular motion—hence the name—spiraling outward to throw his blade out of guard position. He immediately followed up with a fast lunge. Sadly for Logan, Peter had already countered with his own circle and had his sword back in place. In essence, Logan lunged onto Peter's rapier all by himself. And that is bound to leave a mark."

Aidan glared at Don. "You are not helping."

"What? Was that not what you wanted?"

"Speaking of not helping," Peter called, "can one of ye lads help me get your brother into the infirmary? He is gonna need stitches."

"Thanks to you," Logan griped.

"Next time, be better."

Ian went to help Peter get Logan to the infirmary, and Aidan said, "Now that the fencing lesson has been so rudely interrupted, let's work on the history lesson."

"Might we quit for the day?" Ryan pleaded.

"Not now. You must learn to stay focused, little brother. Give me an account of the founding of The Order of the White Guard."

Ryan recited the history monotone, as if he were reading from a book. "Vampires and lycanthropes maintained an uneasy peace for centuries. Neither race made itself widely known to outsiders, and each policed the actions of its own with few altercations between them. In the twelfth century, a group called the Cartha started to bring across thousands of vampires around the world. Many of those vampires were insane. It was uncertain whether the change had driven them crazy or if the Cartha vampires had chosen the mad to bring across to start with. In any case, the creatures were like animals, their minds so impaired that most of them couldn't even speak. They had neither the mental capacity nor the self-control to bring their victims across, so the death toll was actually much higher than the number of new vampires. Early in the thirteenth century, Cardinal Angelo Benetti formed The Order of the White Guard. He recruited a handful of garou, but over time, the number grew to several hundred."

"Did you memorize that word for word?" Don asked.

"I think he did," said Aidan.

"Why did he choose garou?" Will asked him.

"He chose garou 'cause humans could have been easily overpowered and brought across or killed outright, to say nothing of the fact that most of them couldn't be made to believe or understand anyway. Lycanthropes could take the worst punishment most any vampire could hand out and heal quickly, and they were resistant to their mind-control tactics."

"What about the Bast?" Aidan asked.

"What about them?"

"Why didn't he use them instead of garou?"

"Three reasons: the Bast shift to leopards, mostly black panthers, and there aren't any panthers in the northern countries, so they would draw more notice than garou. Also, the Bast are more susceptible to mind control than the garou, and they turn their noses up at the other preternaturals, so they probably wouldn't help anyway."

"Who told you that?" said Will.

Ryan pointed at Don. "He did."

"Again," Aidan said, "not helping."

"Tell me I'm wrong!" Don retorted.

Aidan rolled his eyes and turned back to Ryan. "Talk about Cardinal Benetti."

"There's not much to tell. He and the rest of the original White Guard pack are all dead. It isn't even known whether he was garou or not. It really hasn't been that long. You'd think somebody would know what happened."

"There are many secrets in an order such as the White Guard," Will said. "No one knows everything. We can only educate you to the best of our knowledge. If there is ever anything you need to know, someone will find a way of telling you."

"So somebody does know what happened and they're just not telling?"

"Somebody knows and they're just not telling," Don confirmed.

"Do you know?"

"Nae, but if we did, we probably wouldn't tell you," Aidan said.

"I know what happened," said Don.

"Damn it, Don—" Aidan began.

"I know, not helping."

Aidan regarded him with sudden realization. "You really *do* know, don't you?"

"I've no idea what you're talking about."

Peter called to Mary from the infirmary, and she and Amanda walked across the courtyard, distracting Ryan again. Sometimes he wished he could forget about Mary long enough to concentrate on his studies. Fawning over her didn't do any good anyway. She still treated him like a child, which he supposed he was. There were no younger children, and Mary had often called him "the babe," which was absolutely the worst thing Ryan could think of to be called. He was almost seventeen, for pity's sake!

Of course, when sleeping between two males such as Will and Aidan, as she was these days, it was probably easy to forget a scrawny, wide-eyed teen like Ryan, and it wasn't like he would ever be Alpha. He wasn't cut out for leadership. He was quiet, introverted, and tended to let others tell him what to do. But that wasn't the biggest problem.

The biggest problem was that anything associated with The Order of the White Guard terrified him. He wasn't a killer. He wasn't even a fighter, even though Peter liked to tell him he was a natural with a sword. He understood the need to rid the world of vampires, but he couldn't imagine actually killing one. Maybe he could be a surgeon or something, stay behind and take care of the wounded. Mary could teach him. Then Aidan wouldn't have to worry about him getting hurt all the time.

"Pay attention," Aidan snarled, and Ryan jumped.

"You've been at him since dawn," said Don. "Why don't you let him go?"

Aidan glanced at Don and back at Ryan, his stern visage softening somewhat. "As you wish," he said reluctantly. "Go on, then."

Ryan didn't need to be told twice. He got up and went inside, Don following. Mary passed them in the hallway on her way to the infirmary with a bucket of water.

"Is he all right?" Ryan asked.

"Come and see for yourselves," she replied.

They followed her to the infirmary, where she put the water on a side table. Logan lay on his back on the operating table. Ian sat on Logan's feet to hold him still, and Peter leaned against the next table with a smug expression on his face. Logan clutched the pillow beneath his head and yowled as Amanda's needle pierced his side.

"Amanda!" Logan cried. "You're spearing me worse than he did!"

"Your whining is not helping, so hush yourself and try to relax. Tensing your muscles only makes the pain worse."

"Did I ever tell you about the time I took three crossbow bolts in the back?" Peter asked. "Three *silver* bolts, by the way. I didn't complain nearly as much as you, and I was in agony for months."

"Agony?" Don said with a raised eyebrow.

"Well, not agony, but it hurt."

"Aye, and you had been used to enduring pain for three centuries," Mary said.

Logan looked up at Ryan. "When you're brought across, mind Peter's blade. As soon as you're off the operating table, he'll put you back."

Peter said, "You can't expect to become the best unless you train with the best. Improvement comes by opposing those better and more experienced. Besides, I told you we'd no longer go easy on you after you were brought across. Do you think any of the others would be more merciful than I?"

"Did he rupture his kidney?" Don asked.

"Of course not," Mary replied.

"Are you sure?" said Peter.

"Stop trying to scare him." She kissed Peter on the nose and left the room.

Amanda drew her last stitch, tied the thread off, and bit it. Logan recoiled, then reached up and kissed her cheek. She batted him playfully away, and he flinched again. She kissed him on the mouth, then dipped a rag in the water bucket and cleaned the wound off.

"Move over to one of the cots and get comfortable," she said as she exited the room.

Ian moved off Logan's legs. Logan sat up and swung his legs over the side of the table, then hobbled to a cot.

"Come on, then," Ian said to Don and Ryan. "Let him go to sleep."

"We'll be along shortly," Don said.

"Don't tarry too long," said Peter. "Let him get his rest so I can gore him again tomorrow. 'Haps I can work on rupturing that kidney."

Logan rewarded him with an obscene hand gesture. When Peter and Ian were gone, Ryan and Don sat on the cot next to Logan's.

"Blade went clear through," Logan said. "I'm sewn front and back. And she wants me to get comfortable? I can barely move."

"Did she give you a sleeping draught?" Ryan asked.

"Aye, but I don't think it was enough. She didn't know how much to administer with my body changing like it is."

"Shall I go get her?"

Logan shook his head. "She or Mary will be back shortly."

"Can I ask you two something?" Ryan said.

"Anything," Logan replied.

Ryan paused, choosing his words carefully. He knew he could trust Logan and Don with what he was about to say, but it still wasn't easy. "Did ye ever have doubts?" he asked, barely above a whisper, hoping Aidan and Will were still outside and less likely to overhear.

"About what?" Logan said.

"All of it. Any of it."

"Only in the instant before my *athair* tore into my throat," said Don. "At that moment, I wasn't so sure."

"Why?" Logan asked. "Have you doubts?"

"I don't think I'm cut out for killing vampires."

"That could be a problem," said Don.

"I'm in earnest, Don."

Logan shifted uncomfortably. "I don't really have doubts, but I am nervous about it. I think it's normal."

"It is," Don said. "There's uncertainty now. Your time is only a few years away, and you have much to learn, to say nothing of watching Logan get his arse beaten on a daily basis." He turned to Logan. "I think Peter enjoyed stabbing you today."

"He'll not always be better than I, and then I'll make him pay."

Don laughed. "I think I said those exact words when I was your age." He patted Ryan's shoulder. "We all have doubts from time to time, little brother. Courage slips in even the bravest of us, and you're a gentle soul to start with. You won't be so gentle after you're brought across."

Logan grimaced and sucked in a breath. "'Haps ye should go get Amanda or Mary for me."

"Sleep well, brother," Ryan said.

"I'll try."

They left Logan and delivered the message to Amanda and Mary, who had gone back outside and were watching Michael and Will fence, then went to the common room and sat down at the chessboard. Don was a master chess player and Ryan had yet to defeat him, but he was improving. They sat silently over the board for an hour, and though Don offered instruction and advice, it was a sound defeat as usual. It hadn't helped that Ryan was preoccupied.

Don and Logan hadn't helped much, and Ryan was more afraid than ever. Yes, he was afraid of the pain of the initiation, but who wouldn't be? He had accepted that, though, because he couldn't imagine not becoming garou. Unfortunately, in this pack, being garou meant being a soldier in The Order of the White Guard.

There was no choice; he knew that. Nobody had ever asked if he wanted to join the White Guard, and nobody ever would. Ryan didn't have the spirit to rebel, so he would do as he was told. He just hoped he didn't get himself or anyone else killed in the process.

25

Diana

Wolves have howled at the Moon for centuries, yet it is still there. — Proverb

After Ian brought him across, Logan's training intensified, and in the next few years it would do so even more. Now that he was harder to break, the garou did their best to do just that. Before he went into battle, he would know how a broken bone felt, what a sword through his side meant, how to nurse a vampire bite, and he probably would end up with a ruptured kidney or damage to some other vital organ. He began to learn what real pain was and how the garou lived with it. He also learned rudimentary first aid, how to apply a field dressing, and how to stitch a wound in case Mary and Amanda were unavailable or unable to treat an injury.

The garou didn't let him near silver yet, but there was a lot of it in the monastery. The garou never removed their silver crucifixes except to shift, and they all had deep scars on their chests where the crosses rested. Though Logan figured they must be in constant pain, they didn't complain. When they practiced, however, they used steel weapons, because, as Peter put it, "If I'd put my silver sword into your belly, you'd spend the last few minutes of your life screaming in agony. You know how painful steel is. Imagine if it were set afire."

The changes to his body were almost instantaneous, and he had trouble getting used to them. He hadn't expected to be completely different when he woke up the day after his initiation, and it was alarming.

Logan experienced a new intimacy with his family members that he wasn't prepared for. His enhanced senses caused more problems than the injuries the garou inflicted. The improvement in his sense of smell was immediate and profound. Because smell had influence over taste, there were food items he could no longer stomach and some he craved desperately. Everything had a scent, even if it was just that of the person who had last touched it. He could smell the horses, the barn, the garbage, even the outhouses, when he was inside the keep with the doors closed. The pack was fastidious and very aggressive about keeping everything clean. In an area where the nights could get cold, each of them bathed daily and changed their clothing regularly, as did the monks. Logan had always thought good grooming was just a custom, and he had never thought to question why. Now it was clear. They were bombarded with enough odors already without letting the stink of their own bodies permeate their lair.

Everyone had a unique scent, and it changed with mood. Logan could find anybody just by following his or her scent. There were few secrets, simply because it was so easy to tell if someone was lying, what they had eaten, where they had been, if they had been having sex, or if they wanted to.

His enhanced hearing was the most disquieting of the changes to his body. The garou were normally soft-spoken, and they weren't shy about letting someone know when they were speaking too loudly. They would complain about noise hurting their ears when they ignored all other pain, and Logan had always thought it was odd until he learned just how sensitive their ears were. Loud noises often hurt more than any of the blades the garou were sticking in him.

Ian and Amanda's relationship caused Logan a lot of distress. He had been able to ignore their love affair throughout his teens, but it was impossible to ignore now. Their passion for each other was always present in their scents, even when they weren't together, and thanks to his improved hearing, nighttime was agony. Throwing a pillow over his head did nothing to suppress the sound of Amanda's moans, and he found himself hating Ian just a little bit.

Ian and Amanda weren't the only ones he had to listen to.

There were several couples in the House of Blevins—even a threesome with Mary, Will, and Aidan—and Logan couldn't imagine how modesty didn't keep them from touching each other at all. But they didn't let the lack of privacy bother them, and none of the other garou seemed to pay attention.

Logan had always been mild-mannered, never quick to anger, but now little things set him off and made him snap at others. Or just snap. He was watching Peter and Don playing chess one evening when Michael and Kristoff came into the common room, discussing an altercation between Gwendolyn and Amanda.

"Gwen made a comment about grandchildren, and Amanda didn't take it well," Michael was saying. "She hadn't even been in earnest, only making fun, but Amanda got angry and stormed out of the room."

Peter glanced up, noticing that Logan's scent had changed. The thought that his emotions were so transparent—and always had been—irritated Logan.

"What?" he demanded.

"Nothing," said Peter.

Michael and Kristoff drew mugs of ale and sat down by the fire, continuing their conversation.

"Amanda has a temper," said Kristoff.

"Yes, and she has no sense of humor."

Logan looked in Michael's direction, and the other garou glanced up at him. "Sorry, Logan. If you'd rather we go somewhere else—"

"No need. I'm all grown up now, and you don't need to worry about pampering me."

"All right," Michael said patiently. "I just understand that you have much to get used to."

"But you don't. Nothing about my reactions has changed. If I get jealous or angry, my scent still changes the same as it always did, no?"

"Logan," said Peter.

Logan ignored him. "Nobody said anything before, but now that I'm aware of my own reactions, everybody wants to coddle me."

"You're overreacting," said Michael.

The comment infuriated Logan. He got up and went to Michael's chair, looming over him. "Am I?"

Michael stood up to face him. "Yes, Logan, you are. You should calm yourself before things get ugly."

"Too late," Don muttered.

Logan didn't know what came over him, but he pushed Michael, who fell backward over his chair and came up swinging. Kristoff grabbed Michael and held him back, and Peter did the same to Logan. Logan instinctively fought to get free, and his elbow connected with Peter's nose. The next thing he knew, he was on his back and Peter had him pinned to the floor.

"Are you done?" Peter asked.

"I'm done. Sorry, Michael." Peter let Logan up.

"No worries," said Michael. He was still angry, but he was cooling off quickly.

Don stood off to the side, grinning wickedly.

"What's so funny?" Peter asked.

"Logan just broke your nose."

"It's not funny," said Logan.

"Sure, it is," Peter said. "Let's go get Mary and get her to set it."

"I hate this," Logan said as he accompanied Peter to the infirmary. "I've never had such a temper before. Michael didn't even say anything, and I was ready to tear his head off."

They walked into the infirmary to find Mary standing at the bottom of the spiral staircase, arms folded, waiting for them.

"You heard?" Logan asked.

"And I smelled the blood." She smiled at Peter. "Logan did that?"

"While he was holding me back from Michael," Logan clarified.

Mary patted the operating table. "Come sit."

"Don't worry too much about your temper," Peter said as he climbed onto the table. "We're all aggressive, and we have nasty—"

Mary jerked his nose back into place with a loud crunch.

"—tempers. Bloody hell, Mary, couldn't you have waited till I finished my sentence?"

"Nae, 'twas funnier that way."

"You've been spending too much time with Don." He hopped off the table and kissed Mary on the cheek. "My thanks, little sister."

Mary batted him away. "Stop it. You'll get blood all over me." To Logan, she whispered, "Good job, love."

Logan followed Peter outside to the well, where Peter drew some fresh water to wash the blood off his face.

"You're not so bad," said Peter. "All new garou have trouble with their emotions, and some never get over it. You have more control than most."

"I don't *feel* like I'm in control," Logan replied. "I know it's silly, but I'm always afraid I'm gonna lose control and shift to *faol mòr*."

"You're not gonna shift to *faol mòr*. You probably never will. You won't even lose control of the shift to wolf form before the Full

Moon. Every new garou worries about that, but it just doesn't happen. I've been garou almost three hundred years, and I've never seen a garou shift to *faol mòr*. Even Don has never done it, and he's the most likely to lose control of the shift."

"What's it like? Do you know?"

"Just what I've heard. Your face is generally lupine, but your teeth are longer and your eyes take on a yellow glow. The top of your body is mostly human and the bottom is mostly wolfen, except you walk upright and your hands and feet end in long, sharp claws. You're covered in fur, but there's a thicker main going down your spine. It's also said that your size and strength increase tremendously."

"Sounds terrifying," Logan remarked.

"I wouldn't want to meet up with one."

"But even if that's not a danger, all this is still so frustrating. I don't know myself anymore. It's not just the temper. I start to run, and I trip over my own feet. It's like I'm going too fast for myself to keep up. I'll open a door and pull the handle off. Yesterday I nudged a chair with my foot, only to have it fly across the room."

"Here's something to consider: think about how difficult it was for us to train you while you were still a clunky, awkward mortal."

Peter was right. Logan had never been injured, hadn't sustained so much as a bruise, and he marveled at the great care the garou must have taken not to hurt him. Aidan's overprotectiveness of Ryan made more sense now. It worked the other way too. Fighting with someone as inexperienced and clumsy as they had been as human teens was just as dangerous for the garou, because the student was more likely to make a mistake and accidentally harm the teacher.

After all his studying and the vague answers he had received growing up, Logan finally understood the mysteries of the Moon, and he could see why they referred to her as if she were a person. She didn't just affect the garou's moods and the shift; she took an active role in their daily lives. She was always there, and they sensed her even when they couldn't see her.

As the Moon waned, Logan grew out of sorts and felt almost lonely, and he noticed differences not only in himself but in the others as well. They weren't as graceful or as passionate, they were more likely to ignore pack hierarchy and disobey orders, and those who gave the orders were less likely to offer retribution.

Even Aidan tended to sigh and say, "Oh, very well," about things that normally would have sent him into a tirade. The only real signs of aggression they showed on the New Moon were the competitions for rank. Two matches took place on Logan's first New Moon as garou. Charles and Erlich traded rank, and Ian tried unsuccessfully to take Gwendolyn's position.

When the Moon began to wax, the garou started to come back into themselves. With each day they behaved more like a pack of wolves than a family of humans, and they spent more time sitting outside, staring up at the Moon. They also shifted more often.

Three nights before the Full Moon, Logan sat in the yard outside the keep, contemplating the glowing orb. Tonight he was particularly fascinated with a starburst pattern near the bottom. It was huge, and Logan wondered what could have hit her hard enough to make such a splatter. The air was so cold that his cheeks stung, but he was so mesmerized by the Moon that the cold didn't matter. He barely even noticed when Ian came out and sat next to him.

"So," Ian said. "What deep, philosophical question doth thou ponder this e'en?"

Logan chuckled. "You're making fun of me."

"Not at all. Well, 'haps a bit."

"I was just thinking about the Moon."

"Granted. What else?"

"What's it like? Killing a vampire, I mean."

"The first time is disturbing. You think, 'Oh my God, I've killed someone.' And then somebody reminds you that they only *look* like people, and after that it gets easier. Now it doesn't evoke any sort of emotion from me. It's just something I do."

"I wouldn't say it's deep and philosophical," Logan said, "but I do want to ask you something. When you brought me across, for just a moment, I felt like you were in my head, like I knew what you were thinking and you knew what I was thinking. Was I just delirious, or did you feel that too?"

"Aye, I felt it too. I asked Peter about it, and he said it's not common, but it does happen, especially if the garou swallows blood. He said that one time when they were younger, he and Don decided to become blood brothers. When they cut their hands and mingled the blood, they felt a huge rush of emotion, and they were in each other's minds for days. They could hear each other's thoughts, feel each other's emotions; he said it was almost like they were soul brothers. He said part of it went away after a while, on the surface, at least, but the bond never did."

"That's why they're so close?"

"I guess so."

"In that case, I'm even happier that you brought me across. I don't know that I'd want that kind of bond with Aidan."

"Might not have happened anyway. I don't have it with him."

"Still. You know, I can't believe I never asked before, but why did you ask to bring me across?"

"Why do you think *I* requested it?"

"I assumed—"

"Nae, 'twas Aidan's idea. He said he was reluctant after hurting me so bad and he thought it would make you more comfortable. But I also think he didn't want to do it 'cause he's jealous of you."

"Jealous? Why?"

"I've thought about this a lot. The others say I spent most of my time with him and Will when I was little and that when you were born, I stopped following them and spent all my time with you. Then there was *Má'r*. We all knew you were her favorite, and it hurt Aidan."

"What about you?"

Ian shrugged. "A bit, I guess, but it wasn't as if she didn't love us. She was just closer to you. I'm closer to you than Ryan, but that doesn't mean I don't love him."

"I don't know how to feel about that."

"There's no need to feel anything about it. It's nothing you did; it's just the way it was. There's more, though. Times I think Aidan sees you as a threat."

"A threat to what?"

"I don't know. Maybe his rank."

"What? I would never do that. Disputes for status are only among the lower-ranking garou. The Alpha is not deposed."

"Challenges to Alpha are more common among garou outside the White Guard. Indeed, they're not unheard of in the House of Blevins. It's how Aidan became Alpha."

"I remember, but those were special times. If he were cruel or abusive, the Beta Wolf would oppose him. It'll be a long time before I'm Beta Wolf, if ever, and besides, Aidan is not cruel or abusive. *Abrasive*, aye, but not abusive."

Ian chuckled. "You have it in you to be Alpha, brother," he said, "'haps even a ranking officer in the White Guard, and Aidan can sense that. It's not so much that he fears you; he just can't help seeing you as a rival. When we were small, it was for *Má'r*'s and my attention. Now it's for power. The fight is in all of us, but you have the mind too. And the control. That combination makes you a likely Alpha."

"Aidan has them too."

"Aidan has Will. I don't believe he would have the control if not for him. Times I think they couldn't function at all without each other."

"Careful, they'll hear you."

"I don't care. Besides, they're busy with Mary."

"I was trying to ignore it, but thanks for pointing it out."

"You'll get used to it soon enough."

"Will I ever get used to you and Amanda?" he asked bluntly.

Ian sighed. "I hope so. We'd not want it to cause a rift between us."

"Not gonna happen. It's just ... uncomfortable. I can't get used to the lack of privacy."

"You have to learn to make your own privacy. Say you're hunting. You spot a pheasant in the brush, but the pheasant isn't all you see, right? You see the brush, the sky, the ground, even your bow and the arrow you're peering down. But you filter out all those other things and focus on the pheasant. Or, if you're in a crowded room with a lot of talking, you tune out everything but the person you're trying to listen to. It's the same thing, just on a grander scale."

Logan's hand started to cramp. He tried to work out the cramp, but the pain sharpened as the bones began to change shape.

Ian took his hand and studied it. "You should wear loose clothing for the next day or two. You may shift early."

"What is the shift like?"

"There is some pain the first few times, but it hurts less the quicker and more often you shift. After a while, it causes more pleasure than pain. It's as though your body *wants* to shift. It wants to be in wolf form, and you're letting the wolf become."

"Become what?"

"Just *become*."

As if in response to his statement, a wolf howled far off in the distance and another joined in.

"Peter and Don." Ian threw back his head and howled in response.

Inside the monastery, howls, mostly human, rose up, and Logan himself was unable to keep quiet as the urge to sing welled up inside him. He howled with the rest of them, expecting an awkward human sound and surprised by just how wolflike his voice was.

"Can you abide by yourself?" Ian asked, his voice guttural and his human scent mixed with his lupine.

"Aye."

"I'm off, then." Ian pulled off his clothes, left them on the ground next to Logan, then shifted and ran for the gate.

* * *

During the next two nights, more of the garou joined Logan in the yard, sitting with him and musing about the Moon before running to the woods and surrendering to their wolf forms. Logan didn't shift early, and by the first night of the Full Moon the longing was agonizing. Ian didn't leave him tonight. He stayed close by, fighting the shift so he could be there when the time came for Logan.

He still hadn't shifted by midnight. Howls arose from the woods, but he was too anxious to sing along with them. One call came from nearby, and desire flared in Ian's scent.

"How can you tell one howl from the other?" Logan asked, surmising the call was Amanda's.

"Each voice is different," Ian replied, "just like our human voices."

Ian was having trouble suppressing the shift, and he trembled with the effort. The scent of his wolf form surrounded them both, as did hints of the power Logan had felt when Ian had brought him across. His breathing was quick and shallow, more of a pant, and his eyes were black.

"Maybe you should have let Peter sit with me," Logan said.

"Nae, I want to be here," Ian replied in a husky, lustful tone.

They sat listening to the winter wind rustling through the trees and the river rushing by. At times, the garou would howl or an animal would dart through the woods. Once or twice, Logan could have sworn he heard someone whispering his name.

"Hear it?" Ian said, as though the call hadn't been Logan's imagination. "The night cries out for the garou. It longs to embrace us. These are our nights, brother. Vampires, the White Guard, everything about our human lives mean nothing on these nights. All that matters is Diana. That's what the Romans called her. Or was it the Greeks? I get them mixed up. On these nights she's our goddess, our lover. There is only Diana and the freedom of running across the countryside. These are the nights we can be who we truly are."

Logan recognized that Ian was trying to help him shift, but his brother wasn't just tempting him. He believed and felt everything he said. His words were poetic, but his speech patterns, his tone, and even his voice were different, more guttural, part growl, and the more he spoke, the more feral he sounded.

"I can show you parts of the hills and the forest you never knew. The scents so much stronger in wolf form. The beat of your heart as you chase a deer through the wood. The scrape of the bramble. The wind as it blows through your fur. The smell of fish close to the river. Things no human knows. No human could ever understand." He reached a hand out and pointed. "Look with your mind's eye. Imagine a stag standing in front of you. Over there."

Logan imagined a magnificent, sixteen-point buck grazing on the hill just outside the gate. Ian crept forward, and Logan followed, vaguely realizing he was on all fours and panting.

"Sense it," Ian whispered. "Feel it. The wolf feels his prey, becomes one with it. The stag feels you, too. Watch the muscles in his shoulders. Smell his fear. Gauge whether he will run left or right. Whether he will try to trample you or gore you with his antlers."

Ian made a fist, as if grabbing for the animal. "You lunge. He bolts. He's too late. You take him! Taste the flesh. Smell the blood. Feel it trickle down your throat."

Logan felt it, all right. Goose bumps covered his back and legs, and his hands and feet began to cramp. His vision improved abruptly, as if it were suddenly daytime. The scent of blood reached his nostrils, but it wasn't the blood of a deer. It was Ian's.

Ian held his up hand, which had begun to shift. He had made such a tight fist that his fingernails had dug into the flesh of his palm. Logan grabbed his brother's hand and breathed in the rich coppery scent.

A cry broke from his throat, and his body started to spasm. Sharp, stabbing pains shot through his limbs as his bones broke and mended themselves in a new position. His trousers ripped as his body contorted. The shift started with his legs and worked its way upward. Later, when he thought about his first shift, he would remember growing a tail above all else. It was the only part of the shift that didn't hurt, but it was the weirdest sensation he'd ever had. It tingled, almost tickled, and felt as though his skin was stretching, which, he supposed, it was. He rode the pain, holding onto Ian's bloody hand until his own hands began to shift. All of it was bearable until his face started to change, and Logan screamed as his jaw elongated into a muzzle. But it wasn't a scream at all— it was a howl—and the pain ended abruptly. It had taken no more than a minute to complete the shift.

He stopped howling and regarded his brother, who was still fighting the shift. Logan's ravaged tunic clung to his body, and Ian pulled it away.

"How's it feel?" Ian asked.

Logan tried to speak, and it came out as a soft whine.

Ian looked him over. "You're a true creature of the night, brother. Your fur is black as pitch. Try to stand up."

Getting to his feet proved more difficult than he would have thought. He tried to stand, but he wasn't used to the way his back legs bent, and he faltered a couple of times. Once he was up, he took a few tentative steps around the yard and discovered that walking was easier than standing. He broke into a run but stumbled and rolled end over end.

Ian laughed. "Don't worry. By the time this night is over, running will be easy. Now, pray tell me you're ready to leave this place."

Not knowing exactly how Ian expected him to answer, he nodded his head.

Ian laughed again. "I did the same thing when Peter asked me that question. All right, then. Let's away."

He stripped off his clothes and shifted, then loped off into the moonlight with Logan trailing behind him as best he could.

26

The Kids Aren't Alright

All happy families resemble one another, but each unhappy family is unhappy in its own way. — Leo Tolstoy

Ian had indeed discovered the tunnel under the river, and after further exploration, he had found a way out on both sides. It also turned out that the drop into the underground lake wasn't nearly as far as it had seemed that first time, only about twenty-five feet, and he made the jump on a regular basis to enjoy a swim in the lake. He could get to the lake more easily through the second entrance, but it was about two miles farther, and besides, he preferred the trip through the tunnels and the leap into the darkness. Ian liked the darkness. He didn't really know why, but he had always felt safer and more comfortable in the dark than in the light.

He had never told anyone about the tunnel, the lake, or his scare when he was thirteen—not even Logan—except for Amanda. He had taken her there shortly after she had joined the House of Blevins. It had ceased to be *his* cave, and now it was *their* cave. There may have been no real privacy in the monastery, but they could truly be alone in their cave. They even stashed some blankets and lanterns in a nook to make their secret place more comfortable. They spent a lot of time there, talking, swimming, making love, or just holding each other.

They sat together on a rock just outside the exit a few days after Logan's first Full Moon. The air was frigid, and they snuggled together inside a heavy blanket with Amanda leaning back in Ian's arms. They watched a hawk circling overhead, tracking a hedgehog that had awakened early from hibernation.

Amanda giggled.

"What?"

"That hedgehog should have slept a while longer."

"Hardly fair, eh? He emerges from hibernation only to be eaten by a hawk."

She rested her head on his shoulder. He wrapped his arms tighter around her and smelled her hair. Amanda complained about her hair a lot, but Ian couldn't resist it. It was soft and lustrous, and once in a while, a stray curl would fall over one eye, giving the impression that she was peeking at him from behind a fluffy curtain. Then she would run her hand through it, throw her head back, and say, "I've too much hair!" It made Ian crazy, and he was pretty sure she did it solely for his benefit.

"Aye," she said, ripping his mind away from her fantastic hair, "but the hawk must eat as well, no?"

"Oi, the cycle of survival!" Ian laughed. "You've been listening to Brother Edward teaching Ryan, no?"

"'Tis interesting. The beetle eats the plant, the hedgehog eats the beetle, the hawk eats the hedgehog—"

"We eat the hawk."

"And nobody eats us."

"Vampires," he noted.

"That makes sense," she agreed. "But it's a cycle, so who eats the vampire?"

Ian thought about it, then said, "The beetle. The vampire dies, its body rots or burns and feeds the seed, which makes the plant, which the beetle eats."

"Did you get that from Brother Edward?"

"Nae, I just thought it up."

Amanda laughed.

"What are you giggling at now?"

"We talk about such inane things."

"Nothing we talk about is inane. Besides, who else can I talk with about beetles and hedgehogs and not have them think I'm daft?"

She turned and kissed him, caressing his cheek with her delicate hand. "I love you so," she said.

Though they'd been together almost six years, being with her still made Ian as giddy and breathless as he had been the night she had stolen into his room and said those words to him for the first time.

"Methinks Ryan would rather learn about hedgehogs and beetles than vampires," Amanda said.

"Aidan doesn't care what Ryan wants. He cares only for Will and the White Guard."

"Yet he had you initiate Logan instead of doing it himself because he was worried about him."

"So he said. Aidan has always been hard on Logan. It's better now, but he used to be cruel to him—well, he used to be cruel to all of us."

"He's not so these days."

"Nae, but the memory is still there, and I can't forgive him. I don't know. Times I think I would be happier somewhere else. There are places I want to see, not just those 'tween here and Rome."

"You'll see them someday. 'Haps you'll take me with you."

"I'd not go without you."

"We could go and take Ryan with us," she said.

"Are you in earnest or just imagining?"

"Just imagining, I guess, but I'd consider it if you did."

"I'd not leave Logan, either."

"'Tis fortunate our lives are long. We can decide another time, and until then, we have each other. The sun is sinking. Are you ready to go back?"

Ian kissed her soft curls. "Nae, but I guess we better."

They held hands as they walked back toward the monastery, and in the quiet of their journey, Ian thought again about leaving. He'd considered it so many times, and yet he stayed. For now, he had duties and he would fulfill them, but someday he and Amanda would use the passages in their cave to leave forever.

* * *

Because The Order of the White Guard only inducted soldiers every five years, Ryan's induction would take place the year he was brought across. He wanted to wait until the next one. He really didn't see how one little induction would make such a difference, but Aidan refused to consider it. They couldn't afford to have Ryan wait another five years. Thus, his training paralleled Logan's. He wouldn't be as accustomed to pain and injury as Logan by the time they were inducted, but he would have the same training.

He did well enough with a bow and arrow, but Ryan was gifted as a swordsman. Put a sword in his hand, and if he was paying attention, he executed each move flawlessly, as if he had been born with the weapon curled in his fist. It reminded Don so much of

Gerard that at times he had to blink to make sure he wasn't seeing hallucinations of his old friend.

Don was Ryan's godfather and had assumed the role of mentor since Ryan was an infant. He understood Aidan's compulsion to be overly protective of Ryan. It was difficult to let him go his way to explore and learn on his own because there was always the sense that he was fragile. He was no smaller or weaker than his brothers, but it was easy to forget. Don had never said anything, even to Gerard and Erica, but there were times he wasn't sure Ryan was suited to be garou. He was too gentle, too quiet, and though some of that would be tempered when he was brought across, Don feared that Ryan would become the least aggressive garou who had ever lived.

Ryan never asked questions about the pack, the hierarchy, or even the shift, and he displayed a suspicious lack of curiosity about the White Guard. He studied and answered all questions posed to him, but he rarely asked any of his own. He never even asked about the battle in which Gerard and Erica were killed. When it was brought up to him, he responded with disinterest.

When his twentieth birthday approached, he finally started to ask questions, and he asked them all. Why did the garou have to bite him? Why didn't a scratch work? Why did it have to be in wolf form? What was the shift like? Why didn't size and weight remain the same when they were in wolf form? The anxiety he expressed was normal, but Don couldn't help being concerned. Ryan was easy to worry about.

The day after his birthday, just over a week before his initiation, he and Don were practicing hand-to-hand combat, and Ryan kept getting distracted and asking questions to which he already knew the answers—everything from voting procedures to the mechanics of the bite.

When he asked, "How bad will it hurt?" Don gave up.

"Very well, sit down," he said.

"It's gonna hurt that bad?"

"You know we've told you these things a hundred times."

"You've told me, but you haven't told me everything."

"Or is it that you just weren't paying attention?"

Ryan didn't respond, just stared at him.

"All right, no more going easy on you, but don't say I didn't warn you. Imagine the worst pain you've ever felt and know that you'll have to rethink it when you're done."

"Thanks for that."

"It's a rite of passage, little brother, and your life will never be the same. It's terrifying, it's brutal, it's screaming agony, and then it's over and you get on with your life."

"Well, I asked, didn't I?"

"It could be worse. I've heard that the Bast actually hunt their initiates."

"I don't think I like the Bast much."

Don chuckled. "Few garou do. Have you chosen anyone to speak for you?"

"Nae, I don't know who to pick."

"Pick someone who will come on and say what an asset you'll be to the house. You know, lie through their teeth for you. If I were you, I'd pick someone from your family, someone sentimental and likely to embellish in your favor. Aidan can't do it 'cause he's bringing you across. Ian and Logan are both good. Amanda is a good choice, too. She vouched for Logan and didn't even break a grin."

"Who did you pick?"

"Who do you think I picked?"

"Peter. Of course. Will you do it?"

"Hmm, let's see. What would I say? Ryan would be a good garou 'cause he already knows how to eat without using his hands.'"

"Don."

"I'm not exactly high in rank, little brother."

"So you like to point out, but you still exert more influence than most of the others. You could be Alpha if you wanted."

"God, wouldn't that be a nightmare! I don't have the control to be Alpha. I still don't know what I was thinking, competing for the Beta Wolf rank all those years. But you've made your point. I can probably speak for you. Ask Aidan, though, and choose someone else in case he says no. The Omega usually doesn't speak in a ceremony."

"What of the other garou?"

Don shook his head. "You should stay with someone you can be sure will speak well of you."

"What do you mean?"

"It wouldn't do to ask someone to speak for you and have them decline. It would put a strain on your relationship, and that's not a situation you want to be in when fighting alongside each other. Or worse, ask them and have them recommend that you not be brought across. It would be shameful for you to get eaten after coming this far."

"I doubt that's gonna happen."

"I'm almost certain of it."

"Will you stop that?" Ryan cried in frustration.

"Why is everyone always saying that to me?"

"I can't imagine."

"You daydream too much, little brother. Though *I* know you hear every word, you appear to pay no attention when others are speaking, and it's disrespectful. Aidan says you don't live up to your potential, and the others take note of that. Now. Above all, you must promise me something."

"Anything."

"Never breed."

"You're just doing it to get on my nerves now, aren't you?"

"Is it working?"

"Oh, definitely. Besides, somehow I doubt breeding will be a problem, seeing how I'm not cut out to be Alpha."

Don shrugged. "If the Alpha Pair are not mated, it does happen. Mary's parents weren't Alphas, and neither were mine. All right, no more frivolity. Be careful the next few days. Keep your mind on business, and whatever you do, show respect. Even one 'no' vote could hurt, and more could make things very difficult for you, especially if they're from members high in the ranks. You've reached adulthood. Though you're not yet a full member of the pack, you're still a subordinate, and you must start acting like one. Make no one unhappy. In fact, do your best to make everyone happy."

"Do you think it's possible I'll not be brought across?"

"About as likely as you bedding Mary."

"Now, that was unnecessary."

"I doubt you could get enough 'no' votes to put you out of the pack, but there are other forms of retribution. Aidan has wanted a reason to promote me for years. Don't be that excuse."

"What do you mean?"

"I don't get treated like an Omega 'cause I didn't lose my status as a punishment; I engineered Mary's rise to Alpha Bitch and conceded my rank to Will, thus relegating myself to Omega. Peter and Mary like to say it's not so much that I'm low in rank but outside the ranks. But if enough people vote 'no,' or if you are made Omega due to some transgression, you won't get the same treatment. If you wonder what it's like to be such an Omega, ask Mary. Her life was a veritable hell until Peter and I grew weary of it and began defending her, and even we couldn't prevent all of it. Oftentimes, when we stepped in, we only made it worse. We never could figure out why her family seemed to hate her so. Physical abuse is not allowed, but life will still be hard for you, and you may never get a chance to prove yourself worthy of a promotion. 'Tis rare, but I have heard of Omegas dying at the hands of superiors. Times I was astonished Mary's family didn't kill her. I want none of that to happen to you."

Ryan heaved a long sigh. "I don't really understand."

"Little brother, I fear that if you don't get your head out of the clouds, you shall come to understand all too soon."

* * *

Aidan permitted Don to speak for Ryan, and the initiation went well. Erlich gave him a "no" vote, but one dissent wasn't enough to get him Omega status. It was a relief for Aidan to finally bring Ryan across. He had never been able to get the image of the sick little boy out of his mind. He had actually thought of asking Ian to bring Ryan across because he wasn't sure he would be able to hurt him. A bite was a bite, but it could be considered a dishonor if Aidan went too easy on him. He managed to do it without injuring him too badly, but he thought he did a thorough enough job that no one would complain that he was coddling Ryan. Now that his little brother was sturdier, Aidan wouldn't have to worry about him so much. He would probably worry anyway, though. Habits were hard to change.

After Ryan healed and his training intensified, Aidan was glad to see that he was really trying to keep his mind on business. He still daydreamed, but he did so less often, his enhanced senses forcing him to pay more attention to the world around him.

Many new garou went a little crazy and made frequent challenges, but Ryan made no attempt to advance in the hierarchy. Logan, on the other hand, leapfrogged through the ranks so quickly that by the time the pack started to prepare for their trip to Rome, he was fifth in line of succession to Alpha. Peter and Don teasingly called him Erica. None of it surprised Aidan. He had seen it coming. There was a lot of their mother in Logan, not so much an ambition to rule but a need to overcome the next obstacle, whatever it was, and Aidan didn't trust Logan not to see *him* as the next obstacle. Aidan didn't complain much, but being Alpha was hard, and it seemed to get worse all the time. What if Logan could see that he was plagued with self-doubt and thought he could do a better job?

Although he cared about his younger brother, Aidan had never really liked Logan. Those thoughts were always there, even when he was a child. Erica had doted on Logan, and although Will had assured Aidan that it was in his mind, he knew she gave Logan preferential treatment over the rest of the lads. He guessed he envied Logan, but whatever the reason, he couldn't keep from picking on him even now. Logan followed the traditions to the letter and never questioned an order unless he was prepared to back his argument up. There were so few real infractions for which to correct him, Aidan started making things up. He didn't even realize he was doing it until Logan pointed it out.

On an icy March evening during the New Moon, Logan sat down next to Aidan in the common room, where he lounged in front of the fireplace with a tankard of ale. Logan took a sip and held the mug up.

"Brother Hiram outdid himself on this batch."

Aidan nodded. "Indeed, it is one of his greater works. The cask of wine he brought out at dinner was excellent as well. Only monks can make good ale and wine. All others make barley water and grape juice."

Logan sat quietly for a while, watching the fire. Aidan was uncomfortable with the silence. He and Logan rarely socialized, and he couldn't imagine why his brother had chosen tonight to become pals.

Finally, Logan said, "I look forward to seeing Rome."

"You'll not have much time to see it. We'll come home as soon as inductions are done."

"I pray a word in earnest."

There it was. "Aye, speak your mind."

"Would it be better if I were to leave the House of Blevins and join another pack?"

"Where did you get a notion like that? You can't leave."

"Why not?"

"Well ... we're brothers."

Logan gave a weary sigh and took a drink of his ale. "Aidan, we are brothers in name only. We've never been friends, and even if we *are* brothers, there's no tradition forcing us to remain together."

"Do you wish to be Alpha? Is that what compels you to leave?"

"I'm twenty-three years old. Why in God's name would I wish to be Alpha?"

"I wasn't much older when I decided I wanted the post."

"Aye, and you've been miserable since you took it up, no? I don't want to be Alpha, and I don't wish to leave. But I pray you stop treating me like an Omega."

"Do I do such things?"

"You know you do. I don't intend to challenge you. We may not be friends, but I think you're a good Alpha. Besides, it is not done that way, and the way I follow all the other traditions, I'm amazed you'd think I would break that one."

"You're right, of course."

Aidan considered Logan's proposal. Maybe his departure wouldn't be such a bad idea. Then again, if Logan left, chances were Ian would leave, too. Amanda would go with Ian, and he couldn't discount the notion that Peter and Don might go as well. If they left, Mary would leave. The thought that without even trying, Logan carried more influence than he did irked Aidan, but if letting him go meant losing half the pack, he couldn't have that.

He laid a hand on Logan's knee. "If you must go, you have my blessing," he said, "and we will part friends. But I would like it very much if you stayed."

Logan gave him a wry smile. "So you enjoy making my life hell."

"Nae, my brother. Gruff, I am; it is my way. But I'll do my best not to single you out."

"I would be grateful."

Aidan regarded his brother. Did he enjoy making Logan's life hell? Perhaps he did. He'd have to be careful not to enjoy it too much.

27

This is the Day

Remember tonight, for it is the beginning of always. — Dante Alighiere

Rome was alive with activity. Soldiers and clerics hurried about, moving between churches, homes, and the marketplaces. Men and women of various nationalities descended on the city, many of them wearing one type of uniform or another and others wearing simple robes of brown or white. A layman might take no notice, or they might comment on the crowd or the fact that women were wearing military uniforms, but they would see nothing out of the ordinary in the men and women themselves. The more sensitive might know that they were anything but ordinary. Rome was teeming with garou.

The city bustled as more garou arrived and began preparing their postulants for the formal induction that would take place in St. Ambrose Cathedral on the second night of the New Moon. The postulants competed in numerous tournaments, including fencing, unarmed combat, footraces, and other tests of strength and speed, but these weren't the only contests. Other activities were organized to measure the intellect, as well as trials that tested the postulants' ability to function in tandem with other garou, to trust and be trustworthy.

Peter told Logan that the White Guard's ranking garou used the tournaments and other activities to evaluate the postulants and that they would use their observations to determine the order in which they were inducted. Nearly every Alpha in the White Guard had been inducted first or second, Aidan among them. Ian and Devon had also been inducted first, and Mary had been second. Logan appreciated the explanation because he had felt like someone was watching him. All the competitions were crowded, but even when he wasn't competing, the hairs on Logan's neck would stand on end, and he would turn to see no one there. It made sense, though, that the ranking garou would observe him when he wasn't expecting it. People acted differently when they knew they were being watched.

It didn't escape Logan's notice that Aidan and Ian had both been inducted first, thus putting a tremendous amount of pressure on him and Ryan. Nobody had to tell him that the ranking garou would have high expectations and be studying them closely. However, Ian advised Logan and Ryan to ignore the observers and try not to worry too much about being the best. Many postulants got so caught up in vying for the elusive first position that they did poorly. Ian had done well by just enjoying himself and doing the best he could—and, as Peter humbly pointed out, having been trained by the best fighters in the world.

Ryan performed well, not only in combat but also in the more intellectual contests. He even won the chess tournament and one of the fencing events. Logan, however, outshone the competition. He did not win every contest, but he placed consistently in the top two or three. Amanda said she overheard an Alpha from another house call Logan "a force to be reckoned wit," and compare him closely to Gerard. Logan tried to ignore the talk. He simply did what Ian had suggested and enjoyed himself.

The night before the induction, the postulants were made wards of the House of Bianco. Logan, Ryan, and thirteen others stood along the wall in the ruling house's initiation chamber with their sponsors beside them. Franco Bianco approached each of them in wolf form, and his wife Teresa accompanied him in human form. Teresa asked each sponsor to speak for the postulant and then called on the garou of the House of Bianco for a vote. The vote was only a formality, and they always said yes. The postulant held out a hand, and Franco bit it hard enough to draw blood. Teresa kissed the postulant's cheek and presented a leather scabbard, which had been tooled and embroidered with the coat of arms of The Order of the White Guard.

Mary hadn't had many positive things to say about Franco and Teresa, but Logan thought they were very amicable. Teresa was sweet and warm, and she even mentioned that she and his mother had been good friends. When she turned her back, though, Mary caught Logan's eye and shook her head "no."

After the ceremony, the attendant monks took the postulants away, scrubbed them from head to toe, shaved them, and doused them with some sort of fragrant oil. The process was a ritual cleansing in preparation for the induction ceremony, but Ryan complained that he smelled like a girl.

"You needed a bath, anyway," said Don. "They thought it proper to purify you while they were at it."

"Very well, I'm pure, but as soon as mass is over, I'm shifting so I'll smell like a wolf again rather than some perfumed fop."

The next day, Logan and Ryan waited in the staging area of the cathedral with Peter and Don, who wore the dress uniforms of The Order of the White Guard. In battle, the garou wore no uniforms, only clothing that would protect them or that would not be missed if they shifted. Most of them rarely even bothered with armor, and never more than extra padding or leather. The uniforms were strictly for formal occasions, and Peter and Don were resplendent, albeit uncomfortable, in their finery. The postulants were dressed in white hooded robes that were belted at the waist and wore the scabbards given to them the night before.

Don and Peter joked around as usual, flirted with the females, and teased Ryan about the scented oil that offended their nostrils even now. Logan gazed silently out the window, ignoring them.

"Nervous?" Ryan asked.

"Not really," Logan said softly.

"What, then?"

Logan shrugged and gave his brother a half smile. He couldn't explain what he was feeling because Ryan simply would not understand. He may not have taken the competitions as seriously as the other postulants, but now the profundity of the occasion struck Logan forcefully. This was, to date, the most important event of his life, and frivolity was out of place.

A girl stood in the square below. She was fresh faced and pretty, with pale blonde hair that hung straight to her shoulders, and she wore a golden bodice over a sky blue chemise. The beauty stared at the church with a pensive expression. She looked up, saw Logan, and waved. He smiled and waved back.

The chimes in the church's tower rang, and Cardinal Giuseppe Caprese came into the staging area. Logan turned away from the window.

"The music shall begin in a moment," the cardinal said in Italian, "and we shall enter the cathedral. Have you any questions?"

No one asked questions, so the cardinal said, "Then I shall assume you have all been schooled on the ceremony and that you are versed in Latin and Italian. Let us bow our heads and pray."

Cardinal Caprese offered a prayer in Latin, and the music began in the church. Logan made the Sign of the Cross as he took his place in line with the other postulants.

As the congregation sang, a deacon marched up the aisle carrying a crucifix mounted atop a long staff. Cardinal Caprese went next, flanked by two altar boys, and the sponsors walked behind him. As they entered the cathedral, each sponsor selected a sword from a rack just outside the door. The swords were all different, having been designed by the sponsor with the postulant's history and abilities in mind. Most were longswords, but there were a couple of shortswords, a rapier, and even one scimitar. Logan didn't see much after that, only his feet, as he walked into the church behind Alicia Bianco, Franco and Teresa's daughter.

The sponsors knelt before the altar and made the Sign of the Cross, then moved to the side to stand on a marble step. The postulants did the same and stood on the floor in front of their sponsors, keeping their heads lowered. When everyone was in place, the cardinal spoke.

"*In nomine, Patris, et Filii, et Spiritu Sancti,*" he said. "*Dominus vobiscum.*"

The congregation made the Sign of the Cross and said, "*Et cum Spiritu tuo.*"

When he spoke again, the cardinal spoke in Italian. "In the Year of Our Lord 1223, Cardinal Angelo Benetti formed a militant order whose mission was to cleanse the land of a band of unholy abominations that spread their desecration throughout Europe and Asia, killing and stealing the souls of the innocent and preying on the young and the virtuous. The Order of the White Guard has become the scourge of the undead, despised and feared by their vile hosts. They are the last bastion of defense for the righteous against the evil creatures. Today, we welcome fifteen new garou into our hallowed order. Let us pray."

The congregation recited the Kyrie, and then Franco Bianco approached the lectern, bowed, and read from the Scriptures.

The reading was an account of the story of Samson from the Book of Judges. The other readings followed the same theme: that the righteous could prevail with God's help. When Franco finished, he bowed to the altar and returned to his place in the first row. Cardinal Caprese took the lectern.

"A garou in The Order of the White Guard accepts his charge willingly, without reservation, and vows to offer up his life in the eternal struggle against evil. From the time you were brought across, you have been instructed in the ways of the order. Like Samson, you are charged to use the strength that God has given you to go forth and do battle with the enemies of the Lord. You have proven yourselves worthy to carry the coat of arms of the White Guard and defend all mankind against foes existing outside of God's most holy natural order."

Out of the corner of his eye, Logan noticed Ryan smirking.

The cardinal turned to the congregation and said, "Do the commanders of The Order of the White Guard accept these postulants as novitiates into the Order, with full rights, privileges, and duties commensurate with said title?"

One by one, the ranking garou responded, "Aye." As before, the exchange was just a formality and there were no negative replies. The cardinal continued.

"Logan Peter Blevins, step forward with your sponsor."

Logan's heart felt as if it would burst through his chest. He raised his head and approached the altar with Peter at his side.

"Logan," said Cardinal Caprese, "do you vow to uphold the traditions of The Order of the White Guard, the House of Bianco and your own house?"

"On my oath," Logan replied as he had been instructed.

"Do you vow to offer up your life to the fight against the unclean, to expose and destroy evil wherever it arises?"

"On my oath."

"Do you pledge fidelity to the Holy Catholic Church, The Order of the White Guard and the precepts upon which it was founded?"

"On my oath."

"Turn to your sponsor."

Logan turned to Peter, who stood proudly next to him.

"Logan," Peter said, "accept this sword as my charter to thee, as a symbol of our brotherhood and our common mission. Wield it justly and well in the cause of righteousness."

Logan held out his hands, and Peter placed the sword in them. He gasped as the blade, which was made of a steel/silver alloy touched his skin. He tried to ignore the pain as he bowed to Peter and then walked over to the cardinal and knelt, offering the weapon up with his gaze lowered humbly to the floor. The cardinal made the Sign of the Cross over the sword, then placed his fingers lightly on the blade. The act was twofold. First, it offered God's holy benediction. Second, it symbolized Logan's offer of the weapon to the Church, its acceptance and return, with the charge to use it in the Church's work.

"Stand, Logan, and take your place amongst your brothers and sisters in The Order of the White Guard."

Logan rose and turned toward the congregation. Cardinal Caprese removed the hood from Logan's head and said, "Welcome your brother."

A resounding "Amen" rose up through the congregation. Logan raised the sword in salute, sheathed it, and went back to stand with Peter, who had returned to his place on the step.

After all the garou were inducted, Cardinal Caprese celebrated the Liturgy of the Eucharist and then led the novitiates and their sponsors, this time walking side by side, from the Church.

As soon as they were outside the cathedral, Peter grabbed Logan and swung him around gleefully.

"Well done, brother!" he cried.

Logan held his hand up to show Peter the burns on his fingers. "Could you not have warned me that the silver would sting so badly?"

"Should I have had to, fool?"

"Maybe if you had bothered to let us touch the stuff while you were busy impaling us on your blades and breaking our arms, we would have known. By the time we got here, we knew what everything felt like save silver on our skin."

"Well, we had to leave some amusements for Rome, no?"

"Are you serious?"

"Not truly, no. It's just the way it's done. But in faith, brother, were you in such a hurry to be in pain?"

"If you are, just wait," Don said as he joined them, his arm around Ryan's shoulder. "By dusk, you'll be covered with silver."

"Cheers," Ryan said to Logan.

"Well done."

"I don't know. Fourth to be inducted isn't all that good."

"Nae, fourth is good," said Don. "I was inducted fourth."

"Out of how many?" Ryan asked him.

"Four," said Peter.

Don gave him an obscene hand gesture. "Out of twenty. Gerard was first."

"What about you?" Logan asked Peter.

"Let's just say they did things differently when I joined the White Guard," he replied cryptically.

"Well, go on then," said Don. "Have a look at your swords."

Logan drew his sword first. The coat of arms of The Order of the White Guard and his name were engraved in the blade of the longsword. The hilt was black leather with steel roping, and a sapphire was inserted into the pommel.

"'Tis modeled after your *máŕ*'s sword," said Peter. "The sapphire came from a decorative sword she owned."

"I love it," Logan said. He turned to Ryan, who drew his weapon, also a longsword.

The blade was similar, bearing the coat of arms and Ryan's name. The hilt was steel, engraved with a crosshatch pattern, and a golden crucifix that looked exactly like the silver ones the garou wore was worked into the pommel.

"Also your *máŕ*'s," said Don. "When you were small, whenever she picked you up, you took hold of the cross. Oftentimes, you would kiss the mark on her chest to make it feel better."

"Aw, isn't that cute?" Peter said.

"I don't even remember that," said Ryan.

"You wouldn't." Don replied. "You couldn't have been more than two or three, but it was one of her favorite memories of your childhood. I thought she'd want you to have it. I had it layered in gold so it wouldn't interfere when you were wielding it."

"I'm honored. But Don, how'd you get her cross?"

"Magic."

Ryan glared at him.

"She took it off to fight," he said, "so she wasn't wearing it when she died. I asked Aidan for it and put it away."

"I don't know what to say."

"I think 'thank you' is the appropriate phrase," said Peter.

"Thank you!"

* * *

The House of Blevins held a private celebration that night, and Aidan presented Logan and Ryan with their uniforms and other appointments.

"As we are allergic to silver," he said, "vampires are even more so. Thus, The Order of the White Guard uses silver as its most powerful weapon." He handed Logan and Ryan each two silver daggers, a vial of holy water, and a golden chain, from which dangled the silver crucifix. "Wear the cross next to your skin at all times," he told them. "Take it off only to shift. You can also take it off when going into battle if you wish."

"Don mentioned that earlier," Ryan said. "Why then?"

"For the same reason the females tie up their hair. Jewelry, long hair, a sash, they all make a good handhold for an enemy."

"Your *má'r* was bad about tying her hair up," Don said, "and it was used against her more than once."

"Believe it," said Amanda, stepping amongst them. "I learnt that the hard way the first time I engaged a vampire. It used my hair to sling me clear across the room. You have no idea how hard it is to tie this mess up so it doesn't hang loose, but I do it."

"Poor baby," Logan teased. She playfully slapped his cheek.

"They tell me that over time, we get used to silver and the allergy goes away," said Aidan. "I have worn this crucifix for some fifteen years, and it still stings my skin. However, you will get used to the pain."

"No, you won't," said Peter, whose 280-year-old scar was nearly as raw as Aidan's.

Aidan laughed. "You're not helping," he told Peter.

Don tapped Aidan on the shoulder. "When were you planning on leaving?" he asked.

"A couple of days. Why?"

"After the induction, I heard Teresa Bianco suggesting to someone that Logan might be a suitable match for Alicia. We might want to leave as soon as we can so we don't have Teresa trying to arrange a marriage."

Aidan and Peter both laughed, but Logan glared at Don. "Was that the best you could do?"

"See, this is what I get for making a jest or two. No one believes a word I say. I speak the truth, brother. Unless you *want* to be heir to the House of Bianco, we ought to get home."

"That's the best thing I've heard all year!" Peter said.

"Just shut it," said Logan.

"Alicia is quite fetching, you know. It might be worth considering."

"Still not helping."

After the others moved away, Logan and Ryan hung the crosses around their necks. Ryan sucked in a gasp. "That's gonna smart for a while," he said.

Logan nodded. "Now I see why our brothers drink so much. What say you *we* go find something to drink that will numb the pain?"

Ryan started to follow, but Logan stopped, eyed his brother critically, and said, "What did you find funny during Mass?"

"Not funny as much as ironic. He spoke of our foes that exist outside God's natural order."

"Aye."

"Don't we exist outside of God's natural order as well? And he never once said the word 'vampire.'"

Logan laughed. "Someday, you are gonna get into so much trouble."

"Aye, but it won't be today."

28

Things that Make You Go Hmmmm

Nature has given women so much power that the law has very wisely given them little. — Samuel Johnson

Word of vampiric activity came less than two days after the garou returned to Ballybrook, and the House of Blevins got very busy. They were used to a few missions a year, but in the year after the induction, they went on no less than seven operations, four of which resulted in bloody battles. Although no one was killed, several garou sustained serious injuries.

After the profound no-going-back moment that most garou experienced when they made their first kills, Logan took to his task easily, as if he had been a White Guard soldier all his life. In a way, he supposed he had. One of his earliest memories was of Peter sitting with him in a meadow near the monastery and telling him that they all had responsibilities. The admonition had stuck in his mind. It had become his mantra, his philosophy of life. He had a holy mission, and he meant to carry it out to the best of his ability. He never thought twice about cutting a vampire down. They taunted, they begged, they fought like mad, but none of it affected Logan. He remained calm and cool, and he did what he knew was right. Peter had taught him well, and he continued to hone his skills and improve a little bit every day.

Ryan improved as well, but unfortunately, all he got better at was faking it. He fought, somehow, he always managed to arrange it so that someone else was on hand to administer the killing blow. Aidan was smart and Logan couldn't see how he didn't know, but the Alpha seemed oblivious to the fact that Ryan never killed a vampire. What if Aidan *did* know and was keeping quiet in anticipation of Ryan making a terrible mistake?

Logan discussed his concerns with Peter as they rode into Derry one afternoon. The Full Moon was approaching, and even with all the fighting they had been doing, tensions were high, so he suggested a run to town. He and Peter could pick up supplies while they were there and have a few drinks at the pub, any excuse to get out of the monastery and away from their packmates for a while. Also, he wouldn't have to worry about Aidan or Will eavesdropping on the conversation.

"I know you don't believe me," Peter said, "but you and Ian are overly sensitive to Aidan's moods. He cares too much for the pack to do something so petty. He's been overwhelmed; 'haps he's hoping the problem will work itself out. You might say something to Ryan. You do outrank him."

"I fear I'm not yet used to asserting my authority."

"You'd best get used to it, brother. You advance with your mother's ambition, and you will continue to gain authority. Someday you'll be telling me what to do."

"Not gonna happen."

"Bloody right," Peter declared with a chuckle. "Five hundred years from now, I'll still be coaching your swordsmanship, making sure you to clean up after your horse, telling you what you're doing wrong as Alpha—"

"Ye gods! I can't even count to five hundred! Have you ever known anyone so old?"

"None, save Ardis. The oldest garou I know is twenty or twenty-five years my senior."

"Who is he?"

"*She's* in the White Guard. She wasn't at this year's induction, and word had it that she's living with a house in the Orient. Sweet lass, name of Bronwyn."

"Sweet lass who's three hundred-some years old?"

"As the years pass, you won't think so much in terms of age but of experience. Someday even our age difference will seem insignificant."

On the outskirts of town, Logan saw a familiar face. A lovely blonde sat on a cart by the road, swinging her crossed legs over the side. She wore no shoes. She had no horse, either; she had evidently been walking, but her bare feet were as clean as if she had walked only on carpet. Her eyes were blue, her cheeks and lips were pink, and her pale hair hung just past her shoulders. One errant wisp blew in the breeze. To say she was fetching was an understatement; she was exquisite. And he had seen her before.

He wasn't sure it was her at first, but she was eerily similar to the young woman he had seen standing outside the church in Rome. She even wore a similar dress. When she smiled at him, he was positive.

"Hey, Peter?"

"Hmm?"

"Do you see her?"

"Have the Normans invaded again?"

"She was in Rome."

"What's that?"

"'Twas likely my imagination. It's been months after all. But she looks just like her."

Peter stopped his horse and said, "Are you needing help, lassie?"

"Nae, gentle traveler, I've just stopped to rest a bit. Do go on your way."

Peter nodded to her, nudged his horse, and moved on, but his scent flared with anxiety and he stiffened as if he were on alert for enemies. A knot formed in the pit of Logan's stomach. If it was bad enough to scare Peter, he should probably be afraid, too.

Peter remained all but silent as they rode through town, put their horses up, and went into the pub. He went to a corner and sat with his back against the wall, facing the door. The serving wench brought two large tankards of ale to the table without having to be asked, and Peter paid her, guzzled the drink, and asked for another.

"You're thirsty today, my lord," she said.

"Don't call me that, Colleen."

The wench smiled and leaned on the table toward him. "And what shall I call you, then?" she said.

Logan had heard the exchange before. They bantered and teased, and Peter had stayed in town with the barmaid a few times, but he wasn't up to flirting today.

"I'm not in the mood for our usual joust today, love," he said.

She furrowed her brow with concern. "Are you all right, Peter O'Neill?"

"Just make yourself useful and bring us more ale, will you?"

Colleen smiled. "Anything for you, dear." She kissed his cheek and waited until he patted her bottom, then went to the bar to draw more ale.

Unable to stand it anymore, Logan said, "*Are* you all right?"

"Not sure yet."

"Are you gonna tell me, or need you be drunk first?"

"I'm considering being drunk for it, be assured." He waited for Colleen to bring his third mug of ale and then sipped at it, his face pensive, as if he were trying to figure out a difficult problem. Peter was unflappable; it was hard to get under his skin. The blonde had done so just by sitting on a cart beside the road.

"I've seen her once as well," he said finally, "also in Rome."

"When was that?"

"Even before your *már* came to the House of Blevins. The lass was on my arm for a week. I recall her speaking in riddles; I even said I didn't understand a thing she said. But she was garou. I saw her shift. I bedded her, for God's sake!"

"Then what has got you so frightened?"

"She had no scent."

"What? Of course she did."

"Nae, she didn't. Now that I think on it, I don't believe she had one in Rome, either."

"That didn't give you pause?"

"I barely noticed."

"But it's daylight."

"Aye, and it confounds me."

"But if she is a vampire, why doesn't she attack? And why didn't she attack you in Rome? And how did hundreds of garou not detect her nature? And how did she shift? And how can she go out in the day!"

"Take a breath, Logan. She would have to be ancient. Ardis doesn't fear the sun and he's over a thousand years old. But my God, what of your other questions?" Peter gathered his thoughts, then said, "I'm gonna tell you a story. 'Tis a secret one, and I've not told anyone in many, many years. Don knows it, but I would trust no one else with it. Indeed, I don't know if I should even tell you, but if I don't say something, it will weigh on me."

"I'm honored that you trust me enough to even consider it," Logan said.

"Mind this, though, brother: you can tell no one else what I'm about to tell you. Ever."

"I understand."

Peter lowered his voice to a whisper. "Angelo Benetti killed himself."

Logan's eyes widened. "You know that?"

"In Rome, you asked what order I was inducted in. The truth is, I was never inducted. I was a charter member of the White Guard."

"Good Lord! Peter, what a secret!

"You have no idea."

"But you're all supposed to be dead."

"We're not *all* dead, obviously."

"Wait a minute. Does this mean you're responsible for all the silver?"

"Nae, I had nothing to do with that tradition, although I have to admit I've always thought it was a good idea."

"Why did Cardinal Benetti kill himself?"

"This was in Rome, mind you, ten or twelve years after we formed the White Guard. He disappeared for three or four days. When he came back, he rarely spoke, and what he did say made no sense. He spent many weeks in his room, writing in his journal and mumbling incoherently, and when the Full Moon came, he didn't shift. One night after a few months, we heard him in his room, weeping and praying, and then we smelled his blood. We found him dead, impaled on his silver sword. Had it been anyone else, the Church might have deemed it a mortal sin and refused to bury him on holy ground. As it was, he was administered Last Rites, beheaded, and buried with other deceased priests."

"Beheaded? Had he been bitten?"

"Aye, he had."

"But garou are immune to the bite of a vampire."

"His journal was on his desk when we found him, and the things he had written made us question many of the things we thought we knew. One of the things he said was that he had met up with a vampire during the day."

"The lass we saw?"

"Could be. He said she was tall, golden, lovely, enchanting, the most beautiful creature ever to walk the earth, he said. A few pages beyond in the journal, he spoke of more than just her beauty and resistance to sunlight. He spoke of demons, monsters, images she had put in his head, and he said she had forced him to drink her blood. Then the last few entries changed. They conveyed remorse and regret for his sins. He began to speak about how wrong he had been and that his mission was a sham. His final entry was an apology to the White Guard and an assurance that he had found peace."

"Just before he killed himself."

"This is one reason we say garou are *largely* immune to their mind control. The age and the power of a vampire who can go out in the day and have that kind of effect on a garou's mind ... it mystifies. Truly, it terrifies."

"And now you think she might have done the same to you."

"I'm older now than Angelo was—he was just over a century old at the time—but if she's an ancient, who can tell?"

"And who knows what else she can do?"

"'Twas chilling, brother. The things in that journal were ... they were ..."

His voice trailed off, and Logan placed a hand on his friend's shoulder. "It was long ago, Peter."

Peter regarded him with confusion. "What was I saying?"

"You were talking about Angelo Benetti and the vampire."

"Vampire?" He furrowed his brow and took a drink of ale, but he said nothing else.

"Peter?"

"Anyhow," he said, "I think Ryan will be all right. He's only taking longer to adjust than you are. But don't worry about Aidan. He'd not put the pack at such risk. Or Ryan, as far as that goes."

"Ryan? But we had—"

"You're overreacting. He'll be fine."

* * *

Logan tried to get Peter to talk more about the vampire, but he didn't remember anything. He didn't even remember the girl sitting by the road. He did believe Logan, however, especially when Logan repeated some of the story about Angelo Benetti.

They went to Aidan.

"We may have a problem," Peter said.

Logan didn't tell the story about Cardinal Benetti, but he told them about the girl, Peter's sudden memory loss, and his concern that she might be an ancient vampire.

"You're certain it was the same lass?" Aidan asked Logan.

"Aye, as was Peter."

"And you don't remember anything?"

"Nothing," said Peter. "We were on the road to Derry, and the next thing I knew we were in the pub, I was half drunk, and we were talking about something else."

Aidan didn't respond for a long time, and Logan began to think his brother hadn't believed him, but he finally said, "If not for your confusion, Peter, I might say Logan was mistaken, but you're stronger than all of us."

"So you believe me?" Logan asked.

Aidan nodded.

Will said, "There's been so much activity, we can't afford not to believe you."

"Just 'cause she was in Derry doesn't necessarily mean she knows the location of our lair," said Aidan.

"Nae," said Peter, "but it was obvious which direction we came from."

"'Haps we shouldn't leave Ballybrook for a while," said Will.

"We can't neglect our duties," Aidan said. "If we're called, we have to go. We'll have to remain alert and watch for anything else out of the ordinary. And Logan, keep an eye on Peter. His loss of memory concerns me more than anything."

"You're not the only one," said Peter.

"My question is, if she took your memory, why not Logan's?" Will said.

"Who knows? 'Haps she's as demented as Ardis, or 'haps she did it to cause confusion."

"It worked," Logan muttered.

29

Flirtin' with Disaster

The great proof of madness is the disproportion of one's designs to one's means. — Napoleon Bonaparte

Ardis Cmineralo. Hated and feared, blah, blah, blah, totally insane, blah, blah, blah.

Pippa was not pleased.

She rarely got irritated with Ardis. In addition to being hated and feared, he was brilliant, talented, cunning, all the fine things one could say about a vampire, so normally the insanity didn't bother her much. This was not one of those times.

In most cases, Ardis was well-nigh indestructible. Even so, he hardly ever got them into anything that put them in real danger. Occasionally, though, he came up with an idea so radical and boneheaded that Pippa had to shake her head in dismay.

The last time had been when he had tried to raid some Egyptian pyramid that his father used frequently. It was the only time Pippa had ever seen the elder vampire, and she wasn't likely to forget him. He was big, blond, and beautiful like Ardis but with more chiseled features. He also looked a bit older, as though he had been brought across in his early thirties. He wore clothing from the Orient and wielded a long, curved sword. He was as frightening as he was handsome and struck a figure so commanding, it made Ardis, who was actually taller, seem small. He had such an aura of foreboding that Pippa couldn't believe Ardis didn't run screaming.

But no, Ardis confronted him, and Pippa sat next to his father's lover and watched a very one-sided duel. The lover, Francesca or something, was Greek or Italian, with olive skin and dark hair. She was incredibly old, and the lavender eyeshine had faded, leaving her eyes the lovely dark brown that the gods had given her. The beautiful vampire was the polar opposite of Ardis's father and exuded spirit and energy. Her warm smile was infectious. Frangelica grinned at Pippa, rolled her eyes, and said, "Oh, just ignore them. How do you like Egypt?"

Ardis made swing after swing at his father, who blocked every single one with barely a thought. They had different fighting styles, and Ardis had to work hard to keep up. The older vampire exacted a terrible, slicing blow across Ardis's chest that, had it gone much deeper, would have cut him in half. Ardis would never admit it, but Pippa knew the blade had cut just as deeply as his father had intended.

"It is time for you to go now, Ardis," was all he said to his son. Pippa would never forget his voice. Where Ardis could be flighty, even giddy, this vampire was the epitome of control. His voice was soft, almost gentle, but those nine words carried more force than anything she had ever heard.

He stood and glared until Ardis faltered, turned to Pippa, and said, "What say we see what goes on in Europe?"

Felicia squeezed Pippa's hand, said, "It was a pleasure meeting you," and actually waved as she and Ardis fled the pyramid.

They didn't make it to Europe. Ardis was hurt badly, and it took him two years to fully recover. During his convalescence, even he admitted that going up against his father wasn't the best idea.

The fight in Egypt had occurred about two hundred years ago, so Pippa figured Ardis was overdue for something stupid. They were in Ireland again, joyfully terrorizing the countryside and having a great time feeding, killing, and bringing hapless victims across. They could have gone on for decades, but a friend of Ardis's had shown up and given him a terrible idea.

Pippa couldn't stand this vampire. She called herself Isis, as if she could even think of comparing herself to the goddess whose name she used. She was sarcastic and superior, and she treated Pippa like a foolish child.

Isis had been in Derry a few weeks back and had seen a couple of Ardis's "friends" in town. They had recognized her for what she was and had been troubled by it. Isis had gotten quite a laugh over it, as did Ardis.

After Isis left—thank the gods—Ardis decided that it was time to meet the Blevins lads. This would have been nothing—after all, he had come up against Gerard time after time and hardly even broken a sweat—but Ardis had no intention of an ordinary meeting.

"I'm a legend to them, you know," he said as they sat on a knoll overlooking some little fishing town. He had reverted to his wild look, and Pippa couldn't remember the last time he had bathed. Even Isis had grimaced and said he needed to clean up.

"This meeting should be special, memorable—spectacular! You know, Pippa? Just think of all the amazing tales Peter and Don and that one female—Mary?"

"Mary," Pippa confirmed. "That one I remember."

"Just imagine the tales! I think it's time to get to know the young Blevinses personally, don't you?"

"Of course, my love. What did you have in mind?"

"We know where they live, you know," he said with a mischievous glint in his eye.

"Yes, I do, but what about the magical aura that surrounds the place? Or did you intend to draw them out again?"

"Nah, we've done that a dozen times. I'm going to figure out a way to get inside. The aura causes fear. We can ignore fear. We'll bring more soldiers across. They're brave."

"Ardis, I don't think this is such a good idea."

"Why not? I think it's a great idea! Besides, it's not like we haven't done it before."

"Do you remember how hard it was to get all of us into that inn in County Cork? And we're not talking about your quotidian White Guard pack here. The House of Blevins is known as one of the best in the world."

"You make it sound like we've never fought them before. We won last time, you know."

"By using silver. And do you remember how traumatic *that* was for all of us? You also promised never to do that again."

"We still killed most of their pack last time. Most of their fighters are young and inexperienced."

"Except for Peter, Don, and Mary. I heard you say once that you were afraid of Peter."

"I never said that. Oh, come, Pippa, don't tell me you're not up to it."

"Don't bait me like that. It's unbecoming. You're not going to give up on this, are you?"

"Don't worry, my love. I'll take care of you. If the wards are like the ones around the inn, we should be fine once we get past them.

We'll have to think of something really creative for after we get inside, though." He laughed. "I know. We could sneak in and rearrange all their furniture."

Pippa laughed, but Ardis frowned.

"You don't like that idea."

"It seems kind of silly, really."

Ardis scoffed. "Well, of course, it's silly. That's why it would be so funny. How about this: We can bring all their monks across and watch *them* fight!"

"I like that idea. We could rearrange their furniture while we were at it. You know, just for laughs."

Ardis laughed. "I love you so, Pippa. Just imagine their faces when they come in and ..."

He stopped and stared off into space. He didn't move for the longest time as he watched some scene taking place in his warped mind. Pippa just waited. Whatever was going on in there had him so consumed that if she said anything, he wouldn't hear her anyway.

The last time they had invaded a White Guard lair, the terror had been practically unbearable. True, she had been fine once she got inside, but after the massacre in County Cork, the White Guard had probably strengthened the existing wards, and the fear would be even worse. He could deny their fighting ability all he wanted, but Pippa knew better. If Peter ever got ahold of them, she and Ardis would die.

After maybe an hour, Ardis turned and gazed down at her. With narrowed eyes and a wicked grin, he said, "I have an idea that will indeed be spectacular, my Pippa."

Spectacular. Lovely. Ardis's scheme was going to be a disaster, and Pippa didn't think a father's mercy would save them this time.

30

When Death Calls

In God's world, for those who are in earnest, there is no failure. No work truly done, no word earnestly spoken, no sacrifice freely made, was ever made in vain. — Frederick William Robertson

Ryan sometimes wondered at the way things worked out for him. He had been a soldier in The Order of the White Guard for nearly two years and as of yet had avoided killing anything bigger than a cockroach. There were plenty of opportunities. The House of Blevins had routed a dozen covens and killed more than forty vampires. Ryan had done his share of the fighting, but when it came to the actual killing, one of the others, usually Don or Mary, was there to finish the job. It was as if they knew instinctively that Ryan wasn't ready to kill and arranged it so he didn't have to.

Don had been wrong when he had said Ryan's gentleness would lessen after he was brought across. Although he was able to concentrate better with his enhanced senses, he didn't develop the hot temper or competitive nature the other garou had. He would still rather watch the others fight than do so himself.

He had been thinking about talking to Aidan and asking if he could be a fulltime medic, but he was afraid the others would deem him a coward. He wasn't afraid; he just didn't have the fight. But until he found the right time to talk to Aidan about it, he was going to have to fight anyway.

He found his opportunity one afternoon when Aidan called him to his office.

"Is there anything you wish to tell me?" he asked Ryan.

"I have a feeling you already have something in mind."

"'Haps you'd care to tell me why Don and Mary always happen to take your kills."

"I don't know what to say," he said sheepishly.

"It's been two years, Ryan. Sooner or later, your luck's gonna run out and you're gonna have to kill a vampire or die yourself. Or get somebody else killed."

"Ye all make it seem so simple, like it's nothing. Times ye even taunt them just for fun. I can't do that, and times I think I never will."

"I blame myself. I should have taken it upon myself to oversee your first kill, but I've been so preoccupied, I let it slip. I waited too long to broach this subject with you, but now I'm fearful of letting you go into battle."

This was it, his chance to discuss his concerns and maybe find a way for him to serve without fighting. But he lost his nerve. "If you don't let me fight, the garou will deem me a coward."

"Then what can I do to help you, little brother?"

"I don't know. Just have faith in me. Don says if someone hears something about himself enough, he begins to believe it. You've always thought of me as a weak, sick little boy you needed to protect. 'Haps I started believing it, too."

"If that's so, then I beg your forgiveness. But Ryan, you can't afford to be weak, or even think you are. Like it or not, you're a fighter, and fighting usually leads to killing."

Aidan's eyes bored into Ryan's, and Ryan had to turn away. It wasn't the glare of the Alpha asserting his dominance; it was the gaze of an overly protective caretaker who had trouble letting his protégé go out on his own. Ryan didn't remember the cruel Aidan his brothers spoke of. Aidan had been kind to him as far back as he could remember, and while he tended to be a mother hen, he left no doubt that he had Ryan's best interests at heart.

"I'll do my best not to disappoint you, brother," Ryan said.

"And I'll do the same," Aidan replied. "Next time we go into battle, I'll stay with you. 'Haps that will help."

Ryan didn't think that was the kind of help he needed, but he didn't argue.

* * *

As the garou surrounded a house on an overcast autumn morning, Ryan knew this would be the day he would finally have to kill a vampire. Today's operation was a standard surround and ensnare, nothing out of the ordinary. The house was in the shadow of Dunluce Castle, fewer than forty miles from Ballybrook. They had ridden up the day before, and they planned to eliminate the vampires and get back to Ballybrook by late afternoon.

Ryan stood at the front door next to Aidan and waited for Will to pick the lock. Most of the others were gathered around them, with three or four posted at the windows and back door. Will unlocked the door, and they went inside. The home had belonged to relatives of the McQuillen clan—dead now, word had it—and it was well appointed with plush furnishings and decorations, whitewashed walls, and thick rugs covering polished hardwood floors. The front rooms were empty, as expected, and the garou spread out to search the rest of the house. While the garou couldn't smell the vampires themselves, they could smell stale blood and other trappings they carried with them, but no such scents were present.

Aidan followed closely behind Ryan, having resolved to stay with him for his first kill. They came to a closed door, and Ryan listened for sound on the other side. When he heard nothing, he opened it cautiously.

The room was empty.

Further investigation revealed that all the rooms were empty. There was no indication that vampires had ever been there. Either they had cleaned up after themselves with uncharacteristic thoroughness or the pack had been sent to the wrong place. Such mistakes were all but unheard of, and it was more likely that the mission had been a ruse.

As if finding an empty house was not enough, it rained all the way back home. The weather put the garou in a bad mood, and it didn't help that Aidan was annoyed with himself for making the mistake of bringing the whole pack on such a short mission. He had been overly cautious after Logan and Peter's encounter in Derry, and his reluctance to send a few garou had turned into a big waste of time for everybody. By the time Ballybrook came into view on the horizon, everyone was grousing at each other.

They rode through the back gate to the stables, where they unloaded their belongings and left the horses in the care of Erlich and Michael. As they approached the keep, Peter stopped dead in his tracks, causing Aidan to collide with him.

"That's a hell of a place to stop, brother," Aidan said as he tried to pass him.

Peter said, "Stand fast. Something's amiss."

"What is it?"

"I don't know; it just—it feels ... wrong."

"'Tis only your imagination," Aidan said. "We're all in a foul mood and ready to be home."

"Nae, wait. Just think about it. Why would someone intentionally send us to the wrong place? And listen. Where are the monks?"

Aidan stopped and listened. There was usually a lot of noise in the monastery at this time of day. The monks of the House of Blevins took no vows of silence. They sang, told stories, prayed, and were always moving about, cooking, cleaning, performing maintenance and other tasks. They would be going back and forth to the outbuildings or working in the yard. But an eerie stillness had settled over the castle. There were no unusual scents, nothing to indicate fear, injury, or death, but the tension in the air was palpable, as if the castle itself were holding its breath in anticipation.

"How could we have missed that?" he said, his voice sounding too loud in the silence of the yard.

"'Cause it's not something we're used to. Ballybrook has always been safe, and we had no reason to think someone would invade it."

"We should have," said Don. "Grace, Erica, and Maria came here after *their* lair was invaded."

"Let's go back to the stable," said Aidan.

Nothing was out of place in the stable. The garou stored their gear in an empty stall and met at the north door to organize a search. Aidan deferred to Peter's experience and gave him the floor.

"We'll split into three groups," Peter said. "I'll take Logan, Ian, and Michael through the northwest entrance and up the stairs to the third floor. Don, take Ryan, Kristoff, and Charles in the northeast door and do the same. Aidan and Will, take the rest of the pack through the front. Split up at the doors, three of you taking one set of stairs and four taking the other. When we've all reached the third floor, we'll clear the castle from the top down. Work your way toward the stairs to your left, checking rooms as you go, then do the same for the second and first floors, but make sure we all stay on the same level, and make sure no one gets past us on the stairs."

He paused, then said, "Now. Something each of you must keep in mind: if someone has breached our lair, it's likely a very powerful vampire. If humans had done it, we'd be able to smell them by now. I only know of one vampire who would be strong enough to locate the monastery, let alone get into it, and the last time we saw him he was using silver. He's mad, and he's unpredictable, but he's clever. Expect to see something you've never seen before, and don't lose focus, not for a second."

Ryan, Charles, and Kristoff followed Don into the northeast entrance and up the stairs. They met the others on the third floor and began their search. Kristoff and Charles watched the east hall as Ryan and Don checked each room, swords at the ready, closing doors behind them as they went. They waited at the top of the southeast stairs until Peter's and Aidan's groups made it to their destinations and then descended to the second floor.

Kristoff's, Erlich's, and Amanda's bedrooms were located along the south hall. Ryan and Don took the hallway and stairs while the other two checked the bedrooms. Each went in and came right back out, motioning for Don. What awaited them inside was an enigma. While no intruders were in the room, the furniture was clearly out of place.

They closed the doors and waited at the top of the stairs for the others to finish, and Ryan could see that the garou moving up the west hall were finding the same thing. When Don caught sight of Peter, he signaled for him, and Peter came to meet him. Aidan and Will approached from the other corners.

"The furniture in every room has been rearranged," Peter said.

"Could it be a prank by the monks?" Will asked.

"Nae," said Don, "it's more something *we* would do."

"Then at this point, the mission hasn't changed," said Aidan. "We continue the search on the first floor."

Peter, Aidan, and Will went back to their places, and the four groups went downstairs.

Ryan and Kristoff checked the infirmary, which hadn't been touched. They came out prepared to move to the abbot's office next door, but Don and Charles stood frozen, peering down the hall at the chapel doors. The doors were always open. Ryan couldn't remember ever seeing them closed before now.

To be thorough, they checked Brother Marcus's office, which was clear except for displaced furniture, and then they moved to the chapel doors.

"Oh my God," Don whispered with horror. He made the Sign of the Cross.

"What is it?" Ryan asked, but his senses caught up before Don could answer. A stench had begun to seep under the doors in a putrid miasma. Ryan didn't know what possessed him, but he reached for the door handle.

"Nae," Don said, laying a restraining hand on Ryan's forearm. "Wait for the others. Whatever's happened is over and done. If he's still in there, we'll want the others beside us."

"Why couldn't we smell it elsewhere?" Charles said.

"There's only one reason I can think of."

Peter's group came around the corner, and Don waved them over.

"Holy Mary, Mother o' God," Peter muttered when he picked up the odor.

"It's him," said Don.

"Gotta be. If he's strong enough to get in, he may be powerful enough to somehow mask the scent until we were right on top of it. We should have expected him to turn up."

"We did," Don said. "We just didn't expect him to turn up *here*."

The others gathered behind them over the next couple of minutes. Aidan and Will were the last to arrive. They pushed their way to the front of the group, and Aidan placed a hand on the chapel door. The silence inside was just as complete as the rest of the monastery, but no one had any illusions that it was empty. They knew what was behind the door.

Aidan sighed and said, "Well, I guess we'd better get on with it."

He pushed the doors inward.

The hinges squealed in protest at the force of his entry. The thunderous impact of the doors against the walls of the chapel accompanied a fetid gust of noxious air that rolled over the garou like a wave of effluent, carrying the odors of blood and urine, bile and excrement. They painted an image of terror, torture, and death in the minds of the garou, a picture that was all too quickly brought to life in the light of the chapel. A few of the garou gasped, and Ryan had to hold his breath to keep from vomiting.

The tableau that lay before them was as profane as it was grotesque. The sculptures representing the Stations of the Cross had been shattered, and pews were overturned. Statuary and icons in wall niches were covered with blood and feces. Not a square foot of the room of worship had escaped destruction or defilement, but the worst travesty awaited them at the front of the room. The life-size crucifix attached to the far wall behind the altar had been brutalized. The cross had been taken from the wall and leaned against the altar, inverted, and its arms broken. The sculpture of Christ had been roughly hacked from the cross and tossed into the font. In its place, Brother Marcus hung upside down, crucified and disemboweled.

Standing next to the abomination was a huge vampire. His wide face and square jaw spread around a prominent nose. His matted hair splayed out in all directions. He wore tan breeches and a vest made of some sort of fur. Taken as a whole, his appearance was almost primitive, but his eyes shone with a malevolent intelligence. A tiny blonde sat at his feet. He leaned nonchalantly against the altar with a chalice in one hand and a bottle of wine in the other. As the garou looked on, stunned by the unbelievable atrocity before them, the vampire added his own personal affront. He poured some wine into the chalice, then held it under Brother Marcus's still dripping throat, as if the monk were a tapped barrel. When the goblet was full, he downed the blasphemous cocktail in one swallow.

"Hello, Peter!" the vampire called amicably. A trickle of red ran down his chin.

"Hello, Ardis," Peter replied.

Ryan's blood ran cold at the name. He had wanted to believe Ardis was just a myth or that they had exaggerated when describing him, but the reality was even more terrible than he had imagined.

"And Don as well! My friends, how are you? It has been a long time."

"Not long enough," Don murmured.

"On the contrary. It's about time you joined our little soiree. Your tardiness shows a deplorable lack of courtesy and etiquette. And after we worked so hard to redecorate for you. Ah, well." He casually wiped his lips with the back of his hand. "Breeding will tell. Now, speaking of breeding ..."

Ardis nodded toward Aidan. "Looks just like his father, doesn't he, Pippa? He ran out of that basement so quickly I didn't get a good look before. Let me see if I can pick the others out." He pointed at Logan and Ryan. Ryan shuddered under the great vampire's gaze. "Uh huh, those two are Gerard's, except they have their mother's eyes. What was her name, Pippa? I can never remember."

"Edwina, or something," the little female replied.

"Erica," Logan said.

"Ah, yes, Erica. And let's see." He looked around some more until his eyes settled on Ian. He nodded, then glanced at Amanda, who stood next to him. "Hmm," he said. "You look like the family, but you smell like him. Boy, have you been naughty with your sister?"

"I'm not his sister," Amanda replied coldly.

"Oh, then you must be his," he said, pointing at Michael. "You're not Gerard's son," he said to Michael. "I've seen you before. England, right?"

"That's right," said Michael.

"All you Blevinses look alike, and there must be a hundred of you, because you're everywhere. What, it's just the four brothers, then? Wilhelm said there were five."

"Maybe he thought the soul brother was the fifth," said Pippa.

"Because he looks *so* much like the others. Wilhelm wasn't very smart."

"He does have reddish hair," said Pippa. "Maybe he thought he looked like Edwina."

"Erica," said Logan.

"Erica."

Ardis shrugged. "You know, lads, I loved your father dearly. Gerard was a worthy opponent. But I'd be willing to bet my soul that the four of you will never measure up. So, Don and Peter. No children? Oh, wait, I killed your wife, Don, didn't I? Sorry about that, really."

"Nae, Ardis. You couldn't do it yourself. You had to have somebody else do it for you because you ran away to hide like a coward after you shot Gerard."

"*Touché.* You're probably still upset over that, aren't you?"

"You have no idea."

"Yes, I can see why you would be, I guess. You're right. I should have honored you by killing her myself as I did for Gerard. Ah, well. Shall we give it a go, then? Enjoy yourselves, my children, but don't hurt my friends Don and Peter."

Vampires emerged from their hiding places among the piles of debris that were all that remained of the chapel's furnishings. Others descended from the shadows above. A melee ensued while

Ardis watched with a joyous smile on his face. Peter rushed the big vampire, but Ardis vanished. He looked anxiously around the room, but Ardis was nowhere to be seen. He growled in frustration.

"See what I mean?" Don said. "Coward!"

Ryan alone stood still, stunned by the sheer vileness of what had been done to the sacred place. It couldn't be real. He had to be imagining it. Maybe he was dreaming, but couldn't manage to wake himself up. He was jarred from his paralysis by a weight striking him soundly on the back, reminding him that the scene was all too real. A figure clung to him, slashing at him with some sort of blade. The vampire was strong but small, and it hadn't tied its hair back. Ryan grabbed a fistful of thick, curly hair, whipped it over his head and slammed the vampire to the floor. It squealed like a little girl.

Ryan was taken aback when he saw that it was indeed a little girl. It couldn't have been more than ten or twelve years old. It was the one Ardis had called Pippa, but in the initial shock of the destruction, he hadn't noticed how young it appeared. It wore a loose-fitting white dress and golden shoes of a kind Ryan had never seen before, and it even had a bow in its hair. In his logical mind, Ryan knew that the vampire was not a child, but he wasn't yet accustomed to thinking logically about vampires.

Why did she have to look like a child? *It*, he corrected himself. *It's not a she.* And of everyone in the room, why did this one have to choose him?

But he knew why. He was the easiest target, and it showed. He would have to do his best to prove her wrong.

The innocent, childlike visage was suddenly shattered by a feral snarl. "You pulled my hair out, you bastard from Hell!" The vampire lunged with her dagger, and Ryan brought his sword to the fore to ward off the attack. Seeing herself at a disadvantage with the comparative sizes of their weapons, the vampire, moving so rapidly that Ryan saw only a blur, reversed her grip and threw the knife at his head. He instinctively dodged to one side to avoid the blade, but the attack accomplished its purpose and gave Pippa time to arm herself with one of the standing sconces used to light the room.

Brandishing the sconce with a speed and strength that was wholly unnatural, Pippa put Ryan on the defensive, but her advantage was short lived. The makeshift staff was taller than she was and had never been meant to be used as a weapon, and Pippa couldn't maintain her balance. Ryan recovered and took the offensive, forcing her to slowly give ground. He methodically struck at and past the sconce, jarring Pippa's hold and making her practically leap away in attempts, at times unsuccessfully, to avoid his blade. She grew more frantic as she continued her retreat. She swung her improvised weapon wildly, trying desperately to connect with Ryan's head. Her back finally touched the wall and she reflexively turned away. Her distraction provided Ryan the opportunity for a quick upstroke that cut deeply into both of Pippa's wrists. She screamed and dropped the sconce as she yanked her arms back and held them against her chest.

Oh, lovely. His first kill was going to be a little girl. But he couldn't balk now; it had to be done, and no one else was close enough to do it for him. He had asked Aidan to have faith in him, and now was the moment of truth.

As he advanced, Pippa slumped to the floor, curling herself into a ball. Her expression softened and her frightened eyes welled with tears. Ryan's sword stopped as he was overcome with the realization that he was about to end the life of a scared child. She was not the fierce, fang-bearing beast he had perceived but a small, painfully thin little girl. She was even younger than he had thought before, no more than five or six years old. Her eyes no longer glowed but expressed only fear, and she stuck out a quivering lip.

But she wasn't a child, and he knew it. He raised the sword to strike.

The little girl whimpered and shut her eyes.

Ryan stopped midstroke and noticed Pippa was trembling and her breathing was heavy. She was *breathing*. If she was dead, why was she breathing?

"M-m-mama," the girl whined.

He haltingly took a step back, the tip of his sword drifting toward the floor. He clenched his eyes shut and shook his head in an attempt to regain some clarity. When he lost sight of Pippa, she changed. Again with that unnatural speed, she picked the sconce up, knocked the sword from Ryan's hand, and leapt for him. Her weight, slight as it was, backed by her supernatural strength, bowled him over. His head crashed to the stone floor, and bright flashes of light passed across his vision as intense pain shot through his skull. He caught sight of the girl's face, no longer innocent and frightened but in all her vampiric glory, a mask of hatred and evil delight in her triumph, fangs bared and eyes glowing. She straddled his chest and raised a limb that looked more like a claw than a hand.

* * *

As usual when fighting Ardis's covens, Don marveled at how easily his followers died. These vampires were fighters, but they didn't have two hundred years of experience. Don had killed two of them and was looking for a third when he caught sight of Pippa sitting on Ryan's chest with her hand curled into a claw. Don had seen that pose before and knew what Pippa was about to do, and he was too far away to prevent it. The garou who were close enough were engaged in struggles of their own, and dividing their attention could be fatal.

The thought of watching helplessly—again—as a loved one was slaughtered sent Don into a frenzy, and even as he dashed toward the back of the chapel, he began to shift. He fought as hard as he could to hold back the impulse. If he could just get back there, all it would take was one swing to kill the little monster, but the outrage over what Ardis had done to the chapel was too fresh. That, combined with the smell of blood, Ardis's barb about Grace, panic at seeing Ryan about to be slain, and the fact that he had repressed a lot of emotion over the last several years conspired against him. As he leapt for the vampire, he lost the struggle.

* * *

Through a fog, Ryan saw that one of the garou had jumped on Pippa. The garou had shifted before tackling the vampire, knocking her off Ryan, and now he went for Pippa's throat as she struggled to deflect his muzzle. It was one of the pack's three gray wolves, which meant it was a male, but in his daze, Ryan couldn't tell which one. When he couldn't reach her throat, he grabbed her arm and started gnawing on it, eliciting several expletives from the creature. Ryan tried to get to his feet and rejoin the fray, but the slightest movement brought back the flashes of light and burning pain, and he collapsed again. Waves of nausea rolled over him, and it felt as if the inside of his head was being gouged with sharp rock. He was helpless to do anything but watch as the vampire managed to get a hand free.

The wolf gave a pitiful yelp as Pippa dug her hand into his chest. He made no other cries as she yanked her hand out again, holding his heart and part of his ribcage. She wriggled out from underneath him and laughed wickedly. "I love to do that," she said.

"Damn it all, Pippa," Ardis said with annoyance, "you killed Don!"

Pippa gasped. "Oops! Sorry about that. But he deserved it, Ardis. Look what he did to my arm!"

Pippa got up and ran toward Ardis, and they disappeared as Don's body reverted to human form.

Peter shouted, "*No!*" and Mary shrieked.

Ryan screamed and scrambled across the floor, trying desperately to reach his friend, but the pain overwhelmed him and a haze obscured his vision. The last thing he saw was several shadowy figures standing over him.

Part III

Soldiering On

31

No Mercy

Every tiny step in the world was formerly made at the cost of mental and physical torture. — Friedrich Nietzsche

Ian had never been squeamish. He had never been the kind to worry or be horrified by a situation. Horror was a way of life in the White Guard, a fact he had accepted at thirteen when the garou had returned from a mission without his parents. He had channeled his wrath into the fight as he had planned, but over time, the anger at what had been done to his family had waned, and now, killing vampires was just what he did. Thus, he had experienced no real shock when he saw what the vampires had done to the chapel. Considering their enemy, it was typical. He was angry, yes, and bewildered that they had managed to circumvent the wards around the castle, but he felt no personal insult at having his home invaded. After all, he and the others had just returned from doing the same thing, hadn't they? Or at least trying to. Besides, that was what Ardis wanted. He had desecrated the chapel for effect, to demoralize them for his own entertainment, and Ian refused to give him the satisfaction. Though he had smelled Amanda's indignation, he had seen Ardis's taunt for what it was and refused to take the bait.

Ian had carried out his mission to the letter, killing every bloodsucker that came within reach with very little emotion. Yes, they were evil. Yes, they were monsters. But somewhere in the back of his mind, Ian thought that, just maybe, they thought the same thing of the garou, making them enemies in the most basic sense of the word.

Of the House of Blevins, two were dead and three more were seriously injured. Ian didn't know how many vampires had attacked, but fourteen of them lay dead on the floor. One remained alive, conscious and relatively healthy, lying on its back with Peter's sword pointed at its throat. Power flowed from Peter, and his eyes were solid black. Ian hoped his friend could suppress the shift long enough take care of business.

"Get up slowly," Aidan instructed the vampire, "and sit."

He pointed to a nearby chair, one of the few pieces of furniture in the room that remained intact, and Peter let the vampire up. He held the blade at its throat as it sat in the chair, and Amanda bound its hands and feet with never-used silver shackles she had gotten from the armory. The vampire wailed and tried to kick free, but when Peter's fist connected with its jaw, it fell blissfully into unconsciousness. When Amanda finished her task, Erlich threw a bucket of water in its face, waking it with a start.

"Let me go, girl," the vampire said, insinuating its will into Amanda's mind.

"You needn't bother," she said. "Your mind control doesn't work on me."

"Bitch!" the vampire cried.

"Oh, me, you had to think long and hard on that one, no? Now, don't run away. I think our Alpha may have a few questions for you."

Mary wouldn't let Peter go near Don's body. She said it would be better if he guarded the vampire and let the others take care of Don, and he didn't argue. He and Ian watched the fiend while the other garou took the injured and dead to the infirmary. Erlich and Kristoff set about the grim task of taking Brother Marcus off the cross, putting him back together as best they could, and wrapping his body before taking it to the infirmary as well.

Ian guessed he was a good choice for intimidation. His height combined with his muscular build and his cold Blevins eyes made him very scary. Peter stood behind the vampire, but Ian stood directly in front of it—loomed over it, really—and fixed it with a malevolent stare. The vampire was clearly uncomfortable. It squirmed fitfully beneath the shackles and Ian's glare, and by the time the garou started to return and Aidan was ready for the interrogation, the normally scentless vampire actually smelled of fear.

Aidan tapped Ian on the shoulder and motioned him out into the hallway.

"I've not done this before," he said, "and I don't know what it will take to get it to talk. Can you do what's necessary to assure that it does so?"

With a chill, Ian realized Aidan was asking him to torture the vampire. Killing them was one thing, as was intimidation. But hurting them just for the sake of hurting them was quite another.

"I'll do it," Peter said ominously.

Amanda had just come into the hallway, and she fixed the Alpha with a venomous scowl. Ian almost said no, but he knew that if he did, Aidan would let Peter do it. He peered at Peter over Aidan's shoulder. His expression was bleak, his eyes were dead, and he was still fighting a shift. He had only seen Peter angry once, and he had never seen him this close to losing control.

"Nae, Peter," he said. "I'll do it." He pushed past Aidan and walked into the chapel. Amanda called Aidan a foul name.

"Are you sure you want to do this?" Will asked.

"Do we have a choice?"

"Aye, we could just kill it."

Aidan hesitated but said, "Nae, we can't pass up an opportunity like this. He may know where t find Ardis." He drew a quivering breath, walked into the chapel and stood before the vampire.

"They'll come back, you know," the vampire said shakily to Aidan. "They'll keep coming back until you're all dead. They'll rip out your hearts by hand and eat them just for pleasure."

Peter's lupine scent flared. Anger burst into Aidan's scent, and he seized the vampire by the collar, pulling it and the chair it was shackled to off the floor. "I'm going to rip *your* heart out, you evil bastard!"

"Stand down, Aidan," Will said coolly, placing a hand on his soul brother's shoulder. "The vampire must answer some questions, and *then* you can rip its heart out."

"And why the devil did you rearrange the furniture?" Aidan shouted.

"Ardis thought it would be funny," the vampire croaked.

"Funny? That's it?"

"Yes, that's it."

Aidan let go, and the chair dropped to the floor with a thump. The vampire cursed.

"Funny," Aidan said to Will. "He thought it was funny."

"He was wrong," said Will.

"Actually, it was pretty funny," said Peter.

"You're not helping," Aidan said to him.

"I'm not laughing, either, am I?"

The vampire struggled with its bonds.

"Don't worry," Will said. "We haven't forgotten you."

Aidan shut his eyes and curled his hands into fists, trying to control his anger.

"Why don't you let me do this?" Will said.

"Nae, it's my office. I'm fine now."

"I'll answer none of your questions," the vampire said.

Silently, Ian started twirling one of his daggers in his hand.

"I don't fear your blade, werewolf," said the vampire.

"You do know it's silver, no?" Logan said.

The vampire faltered, but then it mustered its courage and said, "It doesn't matter. I'll not be broken."

"Bet on it," Peter said, his voice full of menace.

Aidan leaned toward the vampire. "Where are the rest of the monks?"

"Your monks are dead."

"Where?" Aidan repeated with a slight edge to his voice.

The vampire remained silent.

"Ian."

Ian said a silent prayer for forgiveness, then grabbed what remained of the vampire's shirt and tore it roughly from its torso. He took the silver dagger, made a small incision, and sliced a thin piece of skin about the size of his thumb from the vampire's chest. The flat of the silver blade was like molten lava, and the vampire howled. By the way the vampire howled, Ian figured the flat of the silver blade must have felt like molten lava. Ian ceased his ministrations but held the knife directly in front of the vampire's eyes so it had a clear view of the bloodied silver blade.

"Where?" Aidan repeated.

"Get this butcher away from me, and I'll tell you."

Butcher. There was a title that would stick.

Ian bit his lip to keep it from trembling. Amanda's scent turned to pure hatred, and it wasn't for the vampire. Doubt pierced Aidan's scent, but he didn't hesitate with his next words.

"Tell us, or he'll skin you alive."

Ian's eyes never left the vampire's. He didn't even blink, but he desperately hoped it wouldn't come to that.

The vampire hesitated before saying, "In the village to the east. Down the well."

"Derry is too public a place for such acts," said Will.

When the vampire didn't answer, Ian took his dagger and slammed it through its forearm, pinning it to the arm of the chair. Anything other than slicing off more skin.

"They're here!" the vampire cried when Ian produced another silver dagger. "Ardis knocked down a wall in the cellar and put them in the dungeon."

Peter walked out into the hall. He leaned against the wall and took several deep breaths. His wolf scent was still close to the surface, but so was another, more feral scent. He was fighting a shift, but not to wolf form.

Aidan followed Peter into the hall and placed a hand on his shoulder. Peter jumped, startled. "You don't need to be here, brother," Aidan said softly.

"I'm not leaving," Peter growled. He went back into the room and took his place behind the vampire.

"Smells to me like somebody's having trouble keeping control," it said.

Peter pulled the chair over backward, and the vampire hit the floor with a grunt. He bent over and grabbed it by the throat, his nails digging into its flesh. "Say something else," he dared it, his voice gravelly and inhuman.

"Peter," Aidan said, "if you tear its throat out, it can't answer questions. Set it back up, please."

Peter glared into the vampire's eyes for a moment before releasing it and righting the chair.

"And what have we learnt from this little activity?" Will asked.

"Don't make him mad?"

"Don't make him mad," Will confirmed.

"I have to wonder why it would be cheeky under these circumstances to start with," Kristoff commented.

"It's bravado," said Amanda. "It's stupid, but that's what it is."

"It's trying to keep us on edge," Logan said, "threaten our control. It knows we've never done this before, and it's hoping somebody will make a mistake and allow him to get away."

"Not gonna happen," said Kristoff.

"How many vampires escaped?" Aidan asked the vampire.

"I can't betray my coven," it said fearfully.

Aidan leaned over and placed his hands on the creature's shackled wrists. The pressure rocked the dagger, and the vampire whimpered. "Your coven is evil, the kind that take pleasure in defiling a church. Loyalty is a foreign word in such a group."

"They'll kill me."

"*We're* gonna to kill you. It can be quick, or we can make you suffer for weeks. Ian has many silver daggers, and he would like nothing better than to use them on you until each and every one is dull and worn. I'm sure Peter here will be glad to take over then, and if it were me, I'd rather be tied out for the sun."

"No, please."

"Then tell me what I want to know. How many escaped?"

The vampire didn't answer.

Aidan stood back and said, "Ian."

Bile rose in Ian's throat, and he found himself unable to move toward the vampire. It sensed his hesitation and laughed, and that was all Ian needed. He grabbed the creature by the hair and slowly inserted the dagger into its eye. Cold blood and viscous fluid sprayed from the wound, spattering Ian's face as his victim shrieked and writhed in pain, begging for release, but Ian held him firm. Several of the others turned away, but he stifled the impulse and maintained his icy gaze on the vampire's good eye.

"Tell me what I want to know, and we'll release you," Aidan said.

"Two!" the vampire cried. "No, no, three, I think there were three!" He took a deep breath, trying to focus around the agony. "Ardis, the master, the ... uh, Agnes and Pippa. The little one."

"Where did they go?"

"Not far."

"How can they go out in daylight at all?"

"Some of us can go out during the day if it's overcast enough. Pippa's drunk a lot of Ardis's blood, so she's stronger. Ardis gave the rest of us some of his blood and covered us up."

"What about the aura of fear around the monastery?"

"We were ... more afraid of Ardis."

Peter grunted.

"Where are they?" Aidan asked.

"There are some caves a mile hence. N-near the river."

Ian and Amanda's cave.

"We've been staying there. The master found some blankets there, and he thought it would—"

Amanda's scent flared with sorrow. Ian nudged the dagger and the vampire screamed.

"Kristoff, Amanda," Will said, "go."

They left without argument, but the hatred in Amanda's scent exploded.

"Anyone want to ask it anything?" Aidan asked the others.

"Why there?" Ian said.

"I don't know."

"How'd you find our lair?" said Will.

"I don't know." Ian nudged the dagger again. "Please make him stop," the vampire begged.

"How?"

"He's known for years. Pippa heard it from the mind of a garou in Dublin."

"Dublin?" Peter said incredulously.

"She was in pain, thought she was going to die."

"He's known all this time?"

"When was that?" Aidan asked Peter.

"More than fifty years ago. It was when Abigail tried to kill Erica before she ascended to Alpha Bitch."

"Dear God."

"Why now?" Logan asked.

"I don't know." Ian nudged the dagger. "No, please! No one knows why Ardis does these things. He's mad. Please, I've told you everything I know, I swear."

"Very well," said Aidan. "Peter, release him."

Ian withdrew the dagger from the vampire's eye and stepped back. Peter bent and whispered, "See? Broken." With a swing of his sword, he released the vampire's head from its body.

They all stood silently for a few moments, looking at the decapitated body, its arms still pinned to the chair. They had crossed a line today, and none of them, even those who merely stood by and watched, would ever be the same. Ian made the Sign of the Cross, and Erlich patted him on the back.

"You did what you had to do," Erlich said. "I concede my rank."

With that, Ian turned and ran for the outside door. Once he was in the open air, he threw up.

* * *

Don's, Michael's, and Brother Marcus's bodies lay covered on the floor of the infirmary. Gwendolyn sat next to Michael's body, crying. Charles was on an operating table, in shock and unconscious after losing a hand. Devon, having received a serious vampire bite, lay sleeping on a cot. Ryan lay on another cot, wishing he could return to unconsciousness.

Mary stayed by his side, and together they listened to the interrogation. She cried when she heard that Ardis had put the dead monks in the catacombs beneath the monastery. Ryan was unable to contain the nausea brought on by Ian's retching, and he vomited in a bucket Mary shoved under his nose. She wiped his forehead with a cold cloth.

"Don't," he said, pushing her hand away.

"I'll not have you passing out on me."

"God, let me pass out."

Aidan and Will came into the room and stood at the end of the cot.

"He'll be all right," she said softly.

"Indeed," Aidan said.

"Tomorrow, Aidan."

"Stand aside, Mary."

Mary glared at Aidan but went to check on Charles.

"Do you remember?" Aidan asked Ryan.

"I'll never forget."

"You're a coward, Ryan."

Ryan recoiled as if Aidan had struck him.

"You couldn't bring yourself to kill, and because of that, Don had to trade his life for yours."

Hot tears poured from Ryan's eyes, along with a fresh rush of pain. "She put ideas into my head," he said. "I tried to resist her, but she was too strong."

Aidan knelt down and put his face close to Ryan's. Ryan expected a thrashing, a long tirade of cursing and yelling so loud it would give headaches to all those who *didn't* have concussions, but Aidan did none of those things. Very quietly, almost gently, he said, "It seems we're without an Omega."

"Aye."

"You aren't worthy to take Don's place, but you can succeed him as Omega."

Ryan sniffled and nodded.

Aidan and Will left the room. Mary sat down on the cot and put her arms around Ryan, and he buried his face against her and wept. He relished her touch, fearing this might well be the last time she ever even said a kind word to him, let alone held him in her arms.

He didn't mind being Omega. The demotion was probably the best thing that had happened to him all day. He had lost his best friend, his honor, and any chance he would ever have to win Mary's affections, all with one misplaced act of compassion. He deserved that and worse. But it still scared the hell out of him.

Ryan knew what he had to do. He would do what he hadn't been able to do in the chapel. There would be no more mercy.

32

The Void

Either thou, or I, or both must go with him. — William Shakespeare

Mary gave Gwendolyn a sleeping draught and took her to her room, and Ryan took the opportunity to sneak out. He got his sword, which someone had leaned against the wall when they had brought him to the infirmary, and then slipped out before anyone noticed his absence. His steps were unsteady, but he was determined, and by the time Mary came back to the infirmary and noticed he was gone, he was too far away to hear her cry of alarm.

He encountered Kristoff and Amanda, but he ducked into a thicket to hide. They caught his scent and looked for him briefly, but when they didn't find him right away, they headed back toward the monastery, with Kristoff saying something about bringing Aidan to the cave anyway. They smelled of fear, and Ryan figured they had found Ardis. He would have to hurry.

There was less than an hour of daylight left when he arrived at the cavern. He heard steady breathing inside the cave. The vampires were in there somewhere, breathing, but that still didn't make them people. He'd never make that mistake again. He drew his sword and crept inside, hoping no one was up. He was in luck; they were all sleeping in the front room.

The first vampire lay on a mat about twenty feet from the entrance. There had been no attempt at subterfuge; it slept right out in the open, curled around a cushy pillow. A few personal items were stored at the end of the mat. The other two slept nearby, also on soft mats surrounded by their things.

Ryan didn't stop to think about the vampires' attempt at making the cave homey or the fact that he was about to commit his first murder. He just did it. He drew his sword, raised it over his head, and swung, decapitating the vampire with a single blow. It never even woke up as the blade sliced through its neck, the pillow and the mat and crashed to the stone floor, clanging and raising sparks. Blood sprayed, and Ryan gasped. Miraculously, neither his gasp nor the clatter of the weapon woke Pippa or Ardis.

He didn't have that moment of horror that the others had experienced with their first kills. There was nothing but conviction and the throbbing in his head.

Pippa lay on her back, mumbling in her sleep. On closer inspection without her insinuating herself into his mind, he saw that she looked much older than she had when they fought in the chapel, maybe twelve or thirteen years old, and far from the helpless child he had thought. Ryan stepped over the body and approached her. As he raised his sword, she opened her eyes and sat up. She stared into his eyes, and all the remorse and uncertainty came back in a rush. Again, she was just a scared little girl. The wave of guilt was so powerful that Ryan couldn't maintain eye contact. He saw in his peripheral vision that she had already begun to form her hand into a claw, a claw that, not two hours ago, had held the dripping heart of his best friend.

The memory of Don's yelp rang in his ears, and the image of his broken body and the blood from the gaping hole in his chest pooling on the floor brought Ryan back to the here and now. In an instant, Pippa ceased to be a "her" and became an "it." There would be no more guilt, no more hesitation. Ever.

With more strength and speed than he knew he had, he swung his sword. The blade didn't even slow when it hit Pippa, and thinking he had missed, he readied for a return stroke. Before he could follow through, however, the vampire's head began to topple, and its body crumpled to the mat.

When Pippa died, Ardis awoke with a gasp. He sat up and peered at the little vampire's body.

"Pippa?" he said softly. When there was no answer, he crawled to the headless body and dragged it into his lap. He cradled and rocked it, weeping wretchedly. Ryan wasn't sure why he waited, but he didn't advance on Ardis while he held Pippa. He still refused to believe that the creature could possibly experience love or grief, but somewhere in the back of his mind he hoped Ardis *was* feeling pain, and he wanted to make it last as long as possible.

The vampire finally looked up at Ryan, fangs bared and eyes burning. "You have no idea what you've gotten yourself into, you insignificant maggot."

Ryan didn't respond. He raised his sword and stared at Ardis.

The vampire got to his feet. "You want a fight, puppy? I'll give you a fight. Come on, nip at my heels. Which one are you? Ryan? Well, by the time I'm done with you, Ryan, you'll wish I had been as merciful with you as I was with your abbot. And your parents."

Ryan said nothing.

"How old are you, werewolf? Eleven? Twelve?"

He waited for an answer, so Ryan gave him one. "Twenty-three."

"My, my, you're practically an ancient. I haven't seen twenty-three in two thousand years, little one. How long do you think you'll live? You're going to feel pain like you've never imagined for the rest of your very, *very* long life. You'll learn to beg for the sweet release of death, and it will never come. You're different, you know. Most garou are immune to a vampire's mind control, but Pippa got into your head easily, didn't she? You know why? Because you're *weak*, that's why! You're not fit to lick your own father's boots, and I thank all that's holy that he's not here to see how weak you are! You wouldn't believe the pictures I'm going to put into your pathetic little mind."

With that, the image of Ardis taking Gerard's head flashed through Ryan's mind, followed immediately by that of Pippa yanking Don's heart out. He ignored them and continued to glare at Ardis, all guilt and fear replaced by a cold fury. Let him talk. Let him throw images at his mind. The monster standing in front of him spewing venom just made it easier.

Peter's scent filled the room, and Ardis looked over at the entrance where he had just appeared. "Come to fight his battle for him? Again?"

Peter was desperately fighting a frenzy, but his voice was as calm and rational as ever. "Nae, I came to watch."

"You lie, Peter."

"You speak right. I came to take Pippa's head and hang it as a trophy over my mantle, but alas, he got here first."

"So he did. And what of me?"

"Don and I made a pact once that our next meeting with you would be our last."

"Well, give me about a minute and a half and it'll just be you and me." Ardis went to his mat and picked up his broadsword.

"What happened to all those years of torture?" Ryan asked.

"Change of plans," he said.

"Peter?" Ryan said.

"He's all yours."

"He's nothing!" Ardis cried. "He's a weak, measly coward. If it wasn't for him, Don would still be alive."

"Nae, Ardis, if it wasn't for *Pippa*, Don would still be alive. But now she's dead, too, no? You keep telling yourself he's weak right up until he sends your head flying across the cave. I thought to do it myself, but I'll enjoy watching him do it even more."

Ryan started to advance, and Ardis stood and let him approach. Ryan swung, and at the last possible instant, almost too late, the vampire raised his weapon to block. Ryan could tell that he'd surprised Ardis with his speed, but any satisfaction that realization might have brought was swept away by the stinging in his hands from the clash of the blades. It felt as if he'd tried to cut down a stone column.

As the battle ensued, Ryan moved and reacted without conscious thought. He found himself striking at openings he wasn't aware of until after his sword was already in motion. He instinctively parried every riposte, often as a side effect of his own attack. Every strike led into the next block; each block flowed smoothly into the following strike. But for all the skill he possessed, he could gain no ground. Ardis's attacks and counters, while not as sophisticated as Ryan's, were still not the techniques of a novice, and they were backed by a speed and strength that far surpassed his own. For all his determination, Ryan was nearing the limit of his endurance. Sorely injured, he functioned on willpower alone. When it ran out, he would be finished. Ardis seemed to sense his failing strength and pressed his attacks harder, forcing Ryan to expend more effort defending himself than attacking.

No. It couldn't end this way. He had to—nae, he *wanted to*— kill this vampire. Once that realization set in, there was only one possible outcome.

* * *

Aidan entered the cavern expecting to find Peter fighting Ardis, but Peter stood by with his sword sheathed while Ryan fought the vampire. Ryan, though hard-pressed against Ardis, was holding his own. The impact of swords jarred Ryan violently with every stroke, but the young garou never faltered, his face a mask of grim resolve. Aidan's heart soared with pride and love for his brother, but as several of the other garou arrived, he remembered all too quickly why they were there.

"Ryan!" Logan called as he attempted to push past Aidan.

"No," Aidan said, placing a hand on his chest to restrain him. "This is his battle. Let him see it through."

"Have you any idea how old and powerful that vampire is?" Mary said angrily, resisting as Peter held her back.

"He doesn't want your help," Peter said.

"Stay out of it!" Ryan snarled. His voice was a mixture of a human cry and a wolfen growl.

Aidan watched as blow after blow hammered Ryan's sword. He didn't know how many more his brother could take before his hands numbed and Ardis knocked the weapon from his grasp. Ardis was swinging so hard that if Ryan failed to block even one stroke, he'd be cut in two.

Peter kept his hand on the hilt of his sword. His eyes were black, and his breath came in shallow pants. He was barely keeping it together, and Aidan hoped the Beta Wolf would have the control to rescue Ryan if necessary.

Aidan wondered what would happen if Ardis's sword suddenly met no resistance. As if hearing his thoughts, Ryan swung his sword around hard to intercept the vampire's blade as it hurtled around toward his head, but instead of stopping the blade, Ryan shoved the hilt upward, letting the tip drop toward his shoulder. Ardis's blade deflected above Ryan's ducking head, but it barely slowed it in its flight. Aidan had been right: Ardis, expecting firm resistance, overextended and didn't recover fast enough from his swing. Ryan pivoted to the turning flank of the ancient vampire and brought his sword down cleanly on Ardis's neck. The blade caught in bone and sinew, but Ryan pulled back and down, and the sharp edge of his blade completed its grisly task. Ryan swayed as he watched the body drop to the ground.

Aidan expected Ryan to fall, and he almost reached out for his younger brother when he dropped to one knee, but Ryan wasn't falling. He picked up the head, then got up and approached Aidan. He held it by the hair, and ridiculously, it brought to Aidan's mind the incense pots the monks carried during special masses. He absently made the Sign of the Cross.

Ryan held the head out to Aidan and stared him in the eye, silently compelling him to take it, and Aidan did so. It was strangely heavy, the hair stringy and blood-matted, and the eyes stared up at him vacantly. Ardis's face had a confused expression, almost as though he was having trouble believing he was actually dead. Aidan was tempted to drop it in disgust, but he held onto it.

"It's done," Ryan said, "they're all dead. I'm gonna take a nap now."

With that, the color drained from his face, his eyes rolled back into his head, and he crumpled to Aidan's feet in a dead faint.

33

Dire Wolf

Passion and shame torment him, and rage is mingled with his grief. — Virgil

Peter removed his sword belt and silver crucifix and handed them to Mary. "Take these home for me, will you?" he asked. He turned and walked out of the cave, and she followed.

"Where are you going?"

"To the woods for a while. Don't worry. I won't do anything stupid."

Mary sobbed. "Please, Peter, I can't lose both of you in one day."

Peter wrapped his arms around her and held her while she cried. "You're not losing me. I'll be back by morning; I just need to be alone awhile."

"Promise me!" she demanded. Her scent was filled with desperation and terror.

He pulled back and looked her in the eye. "I promise, love. I won't do that to you."

She nodded, reached up, kissed him, and went back to the cave.

Peter went into the woods. He walked for a minute and then broke into a run. He ran as hard as he could, trying to cool some of the rage that threatened to overwhelm him, but it continued to build. He had never been so full of anger and hatred. He hated Ardis for—well, he just hated Ardis. He hated Pippa for killing Don, even more for doing it so brutally. And he hated Ryan more than any of them for killing Pippa and denying him the opportunity. He had already been losing control when he had walked into that cave, and he couldn't discount the notion that he had allowed Ryan to fight Ardis in the hope that Ardis would kill him. In fact, had he stayed much longer, Peter might have lost it all right then and there and killed Ryan himself.

What little rational thought he had started to slip away, and Peter collapsed to the ground. He leaned against a boulder, panting.

He wept. Then he screamed. Then he shifted. Then he picked the boulder up and hurled it as if it were weightless.

* * *

Throughout the night, the land resounded with howls and otherworldly cries that could be heard for miles. Every so often, the garou heard small animals screaming or timbers breaking and falling. None of them had ever seen or heard a garou in *faol mòr*, but there was little doubt they were hearing Peter. He had known what was coming and had the presence of mind to leave before his fury got the better of him, and he spent the night tearing up the forest and killing anything that got in his way.

* * *

Gwendolyn had told Amanda she had fallen in love with Michael the moment she had met him. Amanda hadn't believed such instant love was possible until she had first walked into the monastery two weeks before her thirty-fifth birthday. It had been Ian's seventeenth, and the second she had met his eyes, she had vowed to love him till the day she died. Not long after that, he had vowed the same to her.

All the Blevins brothers had something that made them unique. Ryan was the sweet one, the dreamer. Logan was smart and levelheaded, always the one to do the right thing. Aidan, although Ian refused to see it, was conscientious, knew his shortcomings, and worked hard to overcome them.

Ian was special because he could separate the two parts of his life. When training and fighting, he was the consummate warrior. He did have a rebellious streak, and he thought nothing of defying Aidan, partly because he despised him. Aidan usually let him get away with it, although he had demoted him once or twice. The Alpha had tried many times to patch things up, but Ian never forgave him for his cruelty when they were younger.

In private, Ian was loving and gentle, more sensitive than anybody knew, and he had a unique, poetic view of the world.

Some of his ideas and tales he told her were so beautiful that she had started writing them in a journal.

Today, when he had put his dagger into that vampire's eye, he had ceased to be able to separate the two parts. For the rest of his life, every time he closed his eyes he would see the eyeball burst, hear the vampire scream, feel the fluid as it hit his face, and fight back the bile that rose in his stomach. He would do it again if he was asked, but he would never be able to leave it behind, and it would taint his amazing view of the world forever.

And then Will had sent Amanda away when Ian had needed her standing beside him. There had been no reason to send her other than to get her out of that room, and she knew it. And she hated Will for it.

Why did it have to be Ian in the first place? Because he was big? Kristoff matched him in size and strength; he could be just as menacing as Ian. And what about Peter? He would have done it. In fact, he had *wanted* to do it. He had fixed his eyes on the vampire with an expression so baleful that it had frightened her. Will would have done it, too, but Aidan wouldn't have dared ask him. For that matter, Aidan could damn well have done it himself.

Amanda could hear Mary now, hurling insults at Aidan and Will. She called them everything from villains to barbarians who were no more human than the poor creature they had forced Ian to hurt, to some things Amanda didn't even recognize.

Their argument was, of course, very logical. Those vampires had encroached upon their home and defiled their place of worship, thereby justifying any punishment the garou wanted to inflict. But more, they had left an opportunity to find Ardis. And hadn't it worked? Ardis was dead now.

True, he was dead, but that wouldn't bring her father and Don back. What Aidan didn't know was that he had killed Ryan and Ian, too.

Ian lay on Amanda's bed, staring up at the ceiling. He was uncharacteristically silent. There was no real privacy in the castle, but behind a closed door, there was the illusion of it, and he had told her many secrets in this room. They would have even less privacy now because they could never go back to their cave again.

"What can I do?" she asked.

"Nothing," Ian replied.

"Ian, please talk to me."

He looked up at her, his eyes full of grief and pain, and she would have given anything to restart the day. She would have done anything, even died herself, not to have to see that expression. Tears welled in her eyes, and she blinked them back.

"Don't weep, love," he said softly, stroking her cheek. "It'll be all right."

"Will it?"

"You can't worry about me. You lost your father today. *I* should be worrying about *you*."

"I don't really feel like he's gone. Not yet. You can care for me tomorrow when it finally strikes me that he's not coming back. For now, I'll care for you."

Ian rolled over on his side with his back to her. She snuggled up to him and wrapped her arms around him.

"Amanda, what have I done?" he said.

"You did what was necessary, and because of what you did, a vampire who has plagued Ireland for hundreds of years—and killed your parents—lies dead. It will never hurt anyone again."

"The one today. He called me a butcher. *He* called *me* a butcher."

"Aye, it did."

"Maybe he was right."

"Never think that. You're a good man. Even the best of us have to do horrible things."

"Fighting them was different," he said. "It was a battle, skin against skin, blade against blade, me or them. But the vampire we captured was helpless, and what I did to him was wrong."

"I agree with you, love, but do you think any of the rest of us would have backed down from it?"

"Why do you think I agreed to it? I'd rather have done it than put you or one of the others through what I go through now. Did you see Peter's eyes? I don't think he'd have ever recovered from that. He's going through hell out there now. Imagine if he had that to live with."

"Will *you* ever recover?"

"I don't know. Better me than him. But now, I don't know how to feel."

"Ian, if you let today's episode cause doubt, it may cost lives in the future. Grieve if you must, hate yourself and tell yourself all sorts of terrible things, but put it to the back of your mind when the time comes, because we'll need you."

"Amanda, I think I lost my soul today."

Amanda squeezed her eyes shut to hold back the tears. "I know, love. I know. But you can't let this one incident, this one horrible day, define you."

"How can I not?"

"It's something you did, not something you are. You're more than that."

Ian didn't respond, and she knew he didn't believe her. She only hoped that over time, he would forgive himself.

* * *

Aidan and Will sat on the floor in the corner of their room, bawling. They had stayed strong until business was taken care of, and then they had fallen apart.

Aidan had done things today he could never take back. He had incited Ian to commit an unspeakable act. There was no denying that it was a good strategy, but it was still evil, and asking someone else to do it was even worse. He should have done it himself. He had called Ryan a coward, but he was the coward.

He had also broken his promise to Peter never to hurt his brothers. Ryan was the lowest-ranking garou, so he became Omega with Don's death anyway. But Aidan had made a point of reducing him to Omega while he lay in the infirmary, suffering from a concussion, with the horror over the destruction of the chapel and remorse over what had happened to Don still fresh. Aidan had done it out of anger, and he had known exactly what he was doing. Now he was trying to figure out how he could ever make it up to his little brother.

It wasn't just Ryan, though. He had made so many mistakes lately, not the least of which was letting Ryan's reticence go for too long. He had already begun to doubt his ability to be a worthy Alpha. Then today, taking the whole pack on a mission only forty miles away was stupid. If he had taken just a few and left the rest of the garou at Ballybrook, Don, Michael, and the monks might still be alive. Perhaps he should concede his rank to Peter, because he just couldn't do it. He was no Alpha. He didn't deserve the rank.

"Will?"

"Eh?"

"Do you think we'll go to Hell for what we did today?"

Will sniffled and wiped his nose on his sleeve. "Aye," he said, "I think we probably will."

* * *

Mary was still in the infirmary when Peter came in just before dawn. He went straight to his room and slammed the door, and Mary went inside without knocking.

He was lying facedown on the bed, naked and covered with scrapes and bruises. She sat next to him and stroked his back. "Do you feel better?" she asked softly.

He turned over, and Mary couldn't contain a gasp. He was pale and exhausted, and his arms and torso were covered with deep scratches, as if he had been in a fight with a bear. What was more, his eyes still had the yellow glow of the *faol mòr* form. Blood dripped from a gash in his left temple. She used a kerchief she had in her pocket to blot the blood.

"Do you feel better?" she asked again.

"No," he said, his voice still not completely human. He sat up and kissed her—not the brotherly kiss she was used to but a deep, sensual kiss that took her breath away and raised goose bumps all over her body—then pulled her down on the bed.

34

Someone Else's Story

I said there was but one solitary thing about the past worth remembering and that was the fact that it is past—and can't be restored. — Mark Twain

"Damn it all, Pippa, you killed Don!"

Peter awoke with an anguished cry, gasping for breath, his heart hammering with terror. It took a minute to figure out where he was. The battle was over, he was in bed, and it had just been a terrible nightmare. The realization didn't help. The real nightmare had occurred the day before, and it was no dream.

His mind drifted to the aftermath of the battle, the heinous act they had committed, and the overwhelming rage that had taken over his mind and body. *Faol mòr* form had been far more extreme than any of his preconceived notions. He'd been totally aware of what he was doing, but he'd had no control whatsoever. It was surreal, as if he were in a half-waking dream where even the impossible seemed perfectly normal. He hadn't even been able to control the shift back to human form, which happened so abruptly that it was jolting.

He'd come home, still not feeling like himself. The dream he'd had afterward was intense, erotic, and more realistic than anything that had happened while he was in *faol mòr* form. And it changed everything he'd ever felt about Mary Quinn.

He suddenly realized her scent was all over him. It was no dream, either.

"I'll be damned," he said with wonder. He got out of bed, dressed, and went to find her.

The monastery was too quiet, and Peter stopped at the door of his room, almost afraid to go any farther, but then he picked up

Gwendolyn's scent and heard her moving around in her room, so he continued on, hoping everybody else was just outside.

He went to Mary's room, but she wasn't there, so he took the spiral staircase to the infirmary. She wasn't there, either, only Ryan and Charles, who slept on the cots.

One of the bodies had been placed on the third cot, and the operating tables held the other two, all covered with sheets. Peter went to the nearest one and drew back the sheet. It was Don.

Someone, probably Mary, had removed his tattered clothing and redressed him, and the hole in his chest was covered. Good. That was one image he wouldn't have to remember for the rest of his life.

Don's silver crucifix lay outside his shirt. Peter's hand went to his own cross. He took it off, then threaded the chain of Don's pendant through his fingers until the clasp came around where he could reach it. He unclasped the chain, pulled it off and hung it around his neck, then placed his cross around Don's.

He stood next to the table for a while, holding Don's hand. It still didn't seem real. It didn't even look like him.

Somewhere in the deep recesses of his mind, he knew it was irrational, but Peter couldn't help feeling he was to blame. He was a warrior. He had lived and breathed combat since he was a child. There must have been something he could have done to prevent Don's death.

He'd known about the trouble Ryan was having, even before Logan mentioned it. He trained Ryan; of course, he knew. When Aidan hadn't done anything, he should have stepped in. Ryan's readiness for battle was his responsibility, and he had failed. It should never have gone far enough for anyone to feel the necessity to protect Ryan. As it was, Peter should have been the one protecting him.

For that matter, he should have protected Don as well. Don was too far away to reach Ryan safely. Peter was nearby and knew he had shifted, but he hadn't even looked away from the vampire he was fighting. He was toying with it, prolonging the kill, hacking at it in an effort to cool some of the frustration he felt over losing Ardis yet again. Don was vulnerable in wolf form, and they all knew what Pippa was capable of, but Peter had been distracted.

Distractions would get you killed.

Mary stepped into the room. "I knew I couldn't keep you away," she said. "I'm glad I cleaned him up and dressed him before you got in here. You didn't need to see him like that."

"I had to see him, touch him, or I'd never be able to accept it," he said.

"Did it help?"

"No. I still can't accept it."

"You're blaming yourself."

"Of course, I am."

"Uh-huh. Logan, too, and Kristoff. Aidan has been in here twice. I even took the blame for a few minutes. There was nothing you could have done, love."

"Not true."

"Peter, you did the best you could. We all did."

"Nae, I didn't. I knew Ryan wasn't ready to kill, but I let it go. And that vampire I was fighting, I was playing with it. If I'd just killed the damn thing and got it over with, I might have been paying more attention."

"You knew that Ryan needed to come to terms with killing on his own and that to force him into it before he was ready could do more harm than good. And you had no way of knowing that he would be as susceptible to Pippa's mind tricks as he was. You always do your best, Peter. You would accept nothing less of yourself. Would you do anything different, knowing what you do now? Aye, of course, you would. We all would. But you didn't know. All you can do is the best you know how, and when you find out afterward that there might have been a better way, you make sure you remember it for the next time."

Peter considered what she said, and he wanted to believe her. Mary had grown so much since the day she had defeated Connor, and somewhere along the way she had gained unparalleled strength and wisdom. But he couldn't believe her because he wasn't ready for wisdom just yet. Better to change the subject.

"I'm sorry I abandoned you," he said.

"Don't be. You needed to be out there more than I needed you here."

She sniffled, and Peter looked up to see her sweet face wet with tears. He took her in his arms, and they held each other and cried. When they finally pulled back, Mary covered Don back up.

"Your eyes are still yellow," Mary said.

"Well, that's troubling."

"How do you feel?"

"Fine, except I woke up alone."

"I had to check on our injured, and I didn't know how you ... I figured last night was just part of your frenzy, and I didn't want to make things awkward by seeing something that wasn't there."

"Mary—"

"Peter, I've loved you since I was fourteen years old—"

"You what?"

"—and I've always known you didn't feel the same way—"

He placed a finger over her lips to shush her. "I do now," he said, then bent his head and kissed her.

Charles groaned behind him.

"Don't go away," Mary said, "and don't uncover Don. You're just torturing yourself."

Torture. Poor choice of words.

"How are you feeling?" Mary asked Charles.

"Like I lost an arm."

"Are you in a lot of pain?"

"Some. Not too bad."

"I'm gonna give you something for it." She picked up a cup that she had set on the nightstand earlier and held it to his lips.

He drank the concoction and then looked up at Peter. "How do you feel?" he asked.

"Like I lost an arm."

"Is Devon all right?" he asked Mary.

"Aye, she went into town with the others. She said you wouldn't rest if she were sitting here worrying over you."

"She's right. And Ryan?"

"He'll be fine. Now, close your eyes and get some rest."

Charles closed his eyes, and Mary turned back to Peter.

"Where is everybody?" he asked.

"They went into town to get burial supplies."

"All of them?"

"Except for Gwendolyn. Aidan said they needed to get away from the monastery for a while."

"Can you get away from your patients for a while?"

"I think so."

"Come back upstairs with me?"

"Oh, definitely."

* * *

The garou cleaned up the chapel, buried their dead, and burned the vampires' bodies. They didn't bother repairing the wall in the basement; they didn't intend to use the initiation chamber again anyway. Instead, they nailed the hatch closed and put a piece of furniture on it. Aidan sent word to Rome, and they began the wait for new orders. It was possible the White Guard would require them to stay in Ireland, but Peter expected a transfer. The location of the lair would have to change, and the House of Bianco would likely say a pack who had not witnessed the horrors of the past few years should replace the House of Blevins.

Whatever the reason, Peter would be glad to go. He didn't care where they went, really, as long as it was away from there. He'd be perfectly happy if he never saw Ireland again.

They had lost so much the day the monastery was attacked. Some might say that those who had died had lost the most, but no. They were the lucky ones.

Peter briefly considered leaving altogether, but he couldn't bring himself to go. He had developed a love and respect for Logan and Ian so profound that he didn't want to live without them. It didn't equal his affection for Don and Mary, but he expected that over time, it might. They had inherited the best of Gerard and Erica, and sometimes when Peter was with them, it was as if his friends were still alive. Logan had both Erica's ambition and Gerard's control, and he possessed tremendous inner strength for one so young. Ian was a free spirit like his mother. The tribulations he suffered would not break him, even though Ian wasn't so sure. Then again, Peter supposed they were all pretty broken.

Peter might be certain that Ian would recover, but he wasn't so sure about Aidan. He feared that Aidan had lost what had made him a good Alpha. He had come so far since the day he had first challenged Peter, but now he was uncertain and reluctant. He had always been dominant over Will, but he had begun to follow his soul brother's lead more often, and he deferred to him when any but the most basic decisions needed to be made.

Conversely, Will was stronger and more self-assured than he had ever been. Where he had usually let Aidan do the talking and give the orders, he asserted the authority of the Alpha much more than before, and more often than Aidan. The garou generally went along with it, except for Mary, who refused to do anything Will said, even if the order was justified.

Peter kept his head during the day when there were things to do, but nights were utter hell. Some nights he didn't sleep at all, and when he did sleep, it was fitful and filled with nightmares. Then Mary would reach out and hold him, and it would be a little better for a while.

Mary was the one bright spot in his life these days. He had thought of her as no more than a little sister for a century, but he suddenly found himself head over heels in love with her. When he stopped to think about it, he had to wonder if his change of heart was really all that sudden. He had always been unusually protective of Mary, even before Adam had tried to rape her, and he had said many times that she was the most beautiful female he had ever seen.

The garou liked to talk about love at first sight, but Peter hadn't thought much about it. He had figured it would happen when the time was right. But maybe it had been right in front of him the whole time and he just hadn't recognized it for what it was. It had taken a devastating tragedy and a loss of control to open his eyes. Mary had recognized it. To his utter amazement, she told him she had always been in love with him. In a culture where there were few secrets, especially with regard to one's emotions, the fact that she had kept her feelings to herself for so long was astonishing.

Equally surprising was Peter's willingness to tell her secrets he hadn't shared with anyone other than Don. One afternoon as they sat by the river, well out of earshot of the others, Mary asked him about the day Aidan had called him "Your Highness."

"I'd seen you angry before," she said, "but this was so abrupt. It frightened me."

"I'm sorry."

"You threatened to kill him."

"You know I wouldn't have done it."

"Peter, I truly wasn't sure. What did he say to elicit that kind of reaction?"

"I don't want to talk about it, Mary."

"You should. It'll make you feel better."

"It's not something I dwell on, so telling you isn't gonna make me feel better."

"Well, it'll make *me* feel better. Please, curiosity is killing me."

"No, it's not. You'll live."

Mary tackled him and knocked him back, and she sat on him and placed her hands on his shoulders. "As Alpha Bitch, I order you to tell me."

Peter turned over, easily overpowering her, bearing her to the ground and pinning her more effectively. "We're of equal rank, my love," he reminded her.

"Oh, shite!"

Peter laughed, kissed her, and let her up. "Are you sure you want to know all this?"

"Aye, I'm sure!"

"All right, all right. Well, you probably figured it had something to do with my family."

"I did."

"Here's something that'll shock you. When I was human, I was a prince. Niall Ruad macAedo O'Néill, Second Prince of Tyrone and Prince of Ulster."

"Quite a name."

Peter chuckled. "When I told Don, he said, 'No wonder you hate your family.'"

"So you mean to tell me I've been in love with a prince all this time?"

"Boggles the mind, no?"

"Not really."

"The O'Neill dynasty owned half of Ireland at that time, but we were in Tyrone. My father willed Ballybrook to me to be transferred upon my marriage. I married when I was sixteen and moved here, but my brother didn't like it. He wanted me close so he could keep an eye on me. He thought that if he didn't watch me, I would try to take his throne."

"Would you have done it?"

"Ye gods, no," he said. "I had a good life. I had all the privileges Aed had but few of the responsibilities. He couldn't imagine that I didn't want to be king, though, so he had spies watch me all the time. One would have thought that after a while, he'd have accepted the fact that I was perfectly happy in Derry and didn't have designs on the throne, but he had people watching me for years. I had people watching him, too, of course. I may not have wanted to be king, but I wasn't stupid. After a while, though, we settled into a routine, and I think spying on each other became more of a habit than anything. Then I met Angelo Benetti."

"You knew Angelo Benetti?"

"Of course, I did."

"I guess it makes sense. You are three hundred years old. How did you meet him?

"He was in Derry hunting a coven. His name kept coming up, so I had him arrested and questioned him. He told me everything."

"A bold move."

"You have no idea."

"But you didn't believe him."

"Not at first. I thought he was mad. But his tale was amusing, so I figured I'd let him talk till I got bored and then I'd kill him."

"But you didn't get bored."

Peter shook his head. "He started telling me about some things he'd seen and heard, and they were things I'd seen and heard as well. The more he told me, the less amusing he got, but no, I most definitely didn't get bored."

"You started to believe him?"

"Not yet, but I did start to think there was more to it than just madness."

"When did you finally start to believe?"

"When he shifted."

Mary's eyes widened. "He didn't! For a human?"

"As you said before, Angelo was bold. He was lucky I wasn't superstitious, 'cause I might have thought he was a demon and had him killed anyway. As it was, my *máthair*'s family had ties with Druids and the ancient Celts, so I hadn't been raised to instantly believe that if it wasn't of Christ, it was of the devil. I decided to let him live and see what happened. He persuaded me to go to Sligo with him, and that's where I killed my first vampire."

"As a human?"

"Aye."

"Even then, you were a great swordsman."

"Not to boast, but I was the best in all of Ireland. I think that scared Aed, too."

"Why did Angelo do all that?"

"He wanted my help. I think he figured I could help him 'cause I ruled Derry, but it didn't turn out quite the way he had hoped."

"Why not?"

"Aed's spies had told him I left Ballybrook with a group of soldiers and suggested that he was correct in thinking I was plotting against him. While I was gone, he came to Ballybrook to leave the message that if I was planning to overthrow him, he would crush me. I came home to discover my wife dead and my sons gone. I found out later that Aed had convinced them of my treachery and won them over."

"Oh, Peter."

"It gets worse. Before he killed Nuala, he had his way with her."

"You loved her."

"Nae, I couldn't stand her. It was an arranged marriage, and we never got along, but that wasn't the point. Our *athair* taught us many terrible things, but he also taught us to be kind and to women. He did love our *máthair*. She was sickly and kind of frail and weak, and he believed in treating all women as if they were as delicate as she was. I had done some bad things, but I had never harmed a female. Aed not only harmed Nuala, but he broke and humiliated her and then left her on the floor of the great hall to bleed to death. And not only had my sons allowed him to do it, they allied themselves with him afterward."

"No wonder you hate the great hall so much," Mary remarked.

"And Adam. If he'd raped you, I would have killed him. And I would have made him suffer."

"Peter, you shouldn't say such things."

"I'm not just saying it, love. I came very close to losing control and killing him anyway."

"What did you do to your brother?"

"Nothing."

"Nothing?"

"I left for Tyrone, planning to kill him. I was halfway there when Angelo caught up with me and talked me out of it. Aed had raped and killed Nuala to draw me out, and if I went to exact revenge, he would be ready and would likely kill me instead. Angelo gave me an alternative. He brought me across, and I faked my death, went to Rome, and joined the House of Benetti."

"Angelo Benetti brought you across?"

"Indeed, he did. Here's another secret that you'll love: I helped form the White Guard."

Mary gasped. "No!"

"Aye."

"Did Don know that?"

"He did. Logan knows, too, but no one else. And he doesn't know about my mortal life, so let's keep it that way."

"Of course, love. So you're responsible for all the silver?"

Peter laughed. "Logan said the same thing. Nae, that was all Angelo's idea. All the traditions came from the clergy; I just did the fighting."

"It was a good idea, though. One might not think so all the time, but the pain tolerance does come in handy. You donated Ballybrook to the Church before you left?"

"Aye, I wanted to make sure Aed didn't get it. I couldn't let his offense go altogether; I had to take *something* from him. I demanded in the will that the dungeon be walled off and the great hall be razed. I have no idea why it's still standing. Had I stayed Alpha much longer, I really would have torn it down."

"Why did you change your name?"

"Partly for anonymity, but also 'cause Niall was arrogant and cruel. He killed, stole, committed adultery, pretty much broke all ten of the Commandments. After spending several months with Angelo Benetti, I ceased to be that man. Angelo suggested calling me Peter 'cause I hadn't broken under the weight of all that had befallen me."

"The rock."

"I had loved my father, so I couldn't bear to change my surname, but I did take the name Angelo gave me. I didn't feel I was worthy to be named after St. Peter, but Angelo said he had faith that I would live up to it." He chuckled. "I never even knew he was a priest until we got to Rome, let alone a cardinal. *He* was the rock. He was the strongest person I had ever met. He had a righteous mission, and he never wavered. To a point, anyway."

He told her about the cardinal's encounter with the vampire and his subsequent suicide.

"But word has it that you're *all* dead," said Mary.

"Nae, only Angelo and two others who were killed in battle. Most of them left to form other packs. I stayed in Rome as Beta Wolf of the ruling house."

Mary laughed.

"I know, I know. It's my biggest flaw. I'd rather be second than first. Anyway, over time, the rumors started about us being dead, and we just let them fly. Better that than answer questions about Angelo."

"Do you know what happened to your sons?"

"For the most part. When Aed was killed, there was quite a bit of jockeying for the throne. Official records even show that *I* was king for a short time, which was quite a feat, seeing that I'd been dead seven years. Aed's son Og took the throne."

Mary laughed. "Tell me that was a nickname."

"I wish I could. It's a family name, actually. I'm just glad he got it and not me."

"If we ever have children, we are *not* naming one of them Og."

"You have my word. Og was apparently killed by my eldest son, Brian, who kept the throne until he was killed in a battle with the Normans. I don't know for sure what happened to my second son, Ruadiri, but rumor has it that Brian had him killed."

"Let me guess: He posed too much of a threat."

Peter nodded. "Uncle Aed had taught him well. Aed sent Conchobar, my third son, to County Down. He and his family had quite a bit of influence in Belfast, particularly the district of Castleraegh."

"Isn't that where you and Don took Aidan and Will for their first battle?"

"Aye, that would be the place. That's why I was so irritated that Gerard made me go."

"Did he know?"

"He knew I had family there. He didn't know they were direct descendants."

"Peter, how do you know all this?"

"Oh, I kept track," he assured her. "After I returned to Ballybrook, I made sure I knew where my family was and what they were doing."

"When did you come back?"

"Not for nearly a hundred years."

"But your brother and sons were all dead by then. Why did you still keep track?"

"It wasn't just the O'Neills. All the clans were dangerous. Most still are. The Alphas have always kept track of the nobility; I would have thought you knew that."

"I knew there was some, but I didn't know you went into that much detail. Or is that just your family?"

"Nae, it's all of the more powerful noble families, here and in Britain. Better to know what they're up to than have one of them suddenly decide to take Ballybrook and lay siege. The notion that always disturbed me was how many of them knew about the White Guard. It's hard to keep a secret with the nobles gossiping so much."

"They don't seem to know we're garou, though."

Peter grunted. "Thank God for small favors. I've had nightmares of hordes of townspeople storming the monastery, ready to burn the monsters. At times I wonder that it hasn't happened somewhere."

"God is protecting His own. Or 'haps it has something to do with the wards around White Guard lairs."

"'Haps."

"Why did you come back to Ireland? I can't believe you'd *want* to come back."

"I didn't. The Aleph persuaded me to come back. Ireland was crawling with vampires, and I was the best fighter in the order. I dreaded it, but I came anyway. If I hadn't come back, I never would have become friends with Don and Gerard. Or you. But walking back into that castle was the hardest thing I'd ever had to do."

He lay back in the grass. "Do you want to know why I have nightmares? Not just because of what happened, but what *could* have happened. After Ardis attacked and pretty much until I came home the next morning, I was Niall again. I was full of wrath and hate, and I wanted nothing more than to kill Ryan."

"Peter, my God."

"That's one reason I had to get away."

"You don't still feel that way."

"No. God no. But there's more. If Aidan had asked me to torture that vampire, I wouldn't have hesitated for a second, and I would have been more creative than Ian. I'd done it before, right down there in that dungeon. I didn't have others do it for me; I did it myself. What does that say about me?"

Mary laid her head on his chest, and he wrapped his arms around her. "I would think less of you if it *didn't* give you nightmares," she said. "Every single one of us would have tortured that vampire if we were asked to. If you hadn't done the things you said you did, you wouldn't be the man you are now. You touched evil, and then you learnt to fight it. No matter how terrible the things you did were, they made you *you*. As for Ryan, you said you wanted nothing more than to kill him, but I don't believe that. You did what you had to do to ensure that you wouldn't. You saw that you were in danger of losing what you had become, and you got away before you could hurt anybody. You weren't Niall again, Peter. Not even close."

He kissed the top of her head. "'Haps. I know one thing, though: I don't want to be in this castle anymore. I'm ready to leave, and this time, I'll never come back."

"I agree that we should leave. Too many ghosts."
"How many do you think will follow us when we go?"
"I fear it'll be many."

35

Hope for the Future

*The hour of departure has arrived, and we go our separate ways, I
to die, and you to live. Which of these two is better only God knows.*
— Socrates

Amanda's hands shook as she approached the entrance to their
cave. She hadn't been there since Ryan had killed Ardis nearly
three weeks ago, and she hadn't ever planned on going back. But
then she had missed Ian, and she had followed his scent to the
cave. She couldn't imagine why he had returned.

She stopped at the door, reluctant to go in. The last time she
was there, she was carrying out the decapitated body of Agnes, the
first vampire Ryan had killed. The front room was filled with the
personal belongings of more than a dozen vampires, and
everything was strewn about or kicked over after Ryan's fight with
Ardis. Many of the items and much of the floor were covered in
blood. As far as she knew, those items were still in their cave. The
garou had taken the vampires' bodies back to the monastery and
burned them, but they hadn't cleaned up the rest. She dreaded
going through the door, but she steeled herself and went in.

Someone had cleaned the room. All of the vampires' things
were gone, and the worst of the blood had even been cleaned up. It
was almost as it had been the last time she and Ian were there
together.

A lantern had been placed on the floor at the back of the room
where the tunnels and channels started. It was as if Ian had
expected her to follow him. She picked the lantern up and started
navigating through the caverns. After a while, she came to the
narrow passage that led to the shaft to the underground lake, and
she worked her way through. She stood at the edge of the shaft,

squinting into the darkness of the room beyond. Amanda had always felt it contained something very important that wasn't meant to be found. Every once in a while, when she held her torch or lantern just right, she could detect a faint shimmer in the darkness. She and Ian had explored extensively, but they had never found a way into the room. The chasm was too wide to throw a torch across. Ian had even tried to shoot flaming arrows into the room, but the arrows either fell short or burned out when they hit the floor. Thus, the room remained a mystery.

"Are you coming down?" Ian called from below.

"On my way!" She blew the lantern out and jumped.

She couldn't hold back a squeal of glee as she dropped through the shaft, the thrill of free fall and the sheer joy of doing it again sending delicious chills up her spine. She plunged deep into the lake, the cool water muffling the sound as she floated upward. When she broke the surface, Ian was waiting for her. She reached out to him and kissed him.

"Did you clean the cave?" she asked.

"Nae, I think Gwen did it. I caught her scent when I was coming through."

"I wonder why she did that."

"Maybe 'cause she knew we'd come back eventually."

"Why *did* you come back?"

Ian let go of her and swam toward the shore, which was about thirty yards from the shaft. It was more a ledge than a shore, really, and it led to a wide room and more channels. High overhead, the afternoon sun shone through a narrow crevice. It didn't provide much light, but it was more than enough for their enhanced eyesight. He climbed onto the ledge and reached out to help Amanda up.

"I didn't think I'd want to come back," he told her, "but then I got to thinking about it. The day Ardis attacked the monastery, so much that I cared about got turned to shite. The more I thought about it, the angrier I got. I can't change what I did; I can never take that back. But I *can* take our cave back. I was able to find peace here when I couldn't get it anywhere else. If this is the only place I can have peace, by God, I'm not gonna let Ardis take that away, especially since we might not stay in Ireland long."

"Do you mind some company?"

"I left the lantern for you, didn't I? It's *our* cave, love, not mine."

She leaned in and kissed him. "I love you so."

"And I love you. I'm sorry if I've been distant. I haven't been myself."

"Who of us has? 'Haps you can get some of that back here."

"I hope so."

"Hope. That's a big word these days."

"It's a foreign word."

"Not down here," Amanda declared.

* * *

"Concentrate!" Will barked at Ryan.

"He *is* concentrating," Mary said as she walked through the courtyard. "Stop shouting at him."

"And you remember who you're speaking to."

Mary stopped and glared at him. "You're a bastard, Will," she said. "Lest you forget, I outrank you, so you remember who *you're* speaking to."

"What did I do?" Will asked Aidan as she stormed away and went inside. Aidan merely shrugged.

Mary had been right: Ryan was concentrating, although his mind wasn't on the lesson. Ryan was reliving the battle with Ardis, as he did every time he fenced these days. He was hitting hard, and when their blades clashed, a shockwave radiated up Peter's arm.

Peter tried a new tactic he had seen while watching Ryan's duel with Ardis. As Ryan was striking overhand toward his center, Peter took a half step forward, moving his back foot to the fore and thereby pivoting just far enough to step out of the way, and then he brought the blade down at Ryan's shoulder. Ryan had mimicked the move perfectly when Ardis did it and was able to defend against it. When Peter did it, he laid a gash from Ryan's shoulder to his belt. Had Peter been using a different sword, he might have hurt Ryan much worse.

Ryan handed Peter his sword and pulled off his torn shirt. Peter scrutinized the wound critically. "Oi, that's some tactic! You should have Mary see to that."

"It's fine." Ryan replied as he took his sword back. "Let's go again."

Peter shrugged, took Ryan's shirt and wiped the blood from his blade, and then began again. It was a mystery. During the fight with Ardis, Peter had seen Ryan do things he had never been taught. Ardis had been handling a sword for centuries, and Ryan shouldn't have been able to best him or even survive so long, but he had returned every advance with an attack of his own, never missing a step. Ryan was skillful, but he had achieved mastery that day. Achieved it, and abruptly lost it. He was back to his previous skill level, although his determination had increased immeasurably. Though Will shouted at him about concentration, he no longer needed to do so. In fact, he didn't have to make Ryan practice or even stay on while he did. Ryan trained for hours on end, and if he had no one to fence with, he trained on his own.

Later that evening, long after Aidan and Will had stopped paying attention, as they made their way through the halls toward their rooms, Peter asked him about it.

"How is it that you were able to fight Ardis so effortlessly? You did things in that cave you'd never done before and haven't done since."

"I don't know. It's all just a blur. The concussion, the chapel, the fighting—I hardly even remember Ardis."

"You were brilliant."

"It's gone now."

"'Haps we can get it back."

Ryan stopped. "Peter, why don't you hate me?"

"I did briefly," Peter admitted, "but not over what happened to Don."

"It was 'cause I killed Pippa."

"I wasn't rational that day. You wouldn't have hurt Don for all the world, little brother. I won't lie to you and say I don't see you at some fault, but to hate you for it wouldn't help anybody. I'd rather use Don's death for good, and helping you make sure nothing like that ever happens again is the best thing I can think of."

"I'm sorry. I haven't told you that."

"There was no need."

"Aye, there was." He started walking again. "I was afraid of the dark when I was little."

"I remember."

"Well, Don tried to help me. He said the best way to get over being scared of the dark is to be the scariest thing in it."

"He said the same thing to Mary once."

"I'm not very scary," said Ryan.

Peter chuckled. "You're the garou who killed Ardis. I bet there are scores of vampires who would think you're *very* scary. But I understand what you mean."

"I *want* to be the scariest thing in the dark. I've been lax in my training. The next time I come up against a vampire, I don't want it to be a blur. I want to know what I'm doing. Will you help me?"

"Of course, I will."

"Good. We'll start tomorrow."

"You really should have Mary look at your chest."

"Nae, it's already scabbed over. It's sore, but it's fine." He went into his room and shut the door.

Peter stopped at Mary's room, which they now shared, and hung his sword up. Mary was working in the infirmary and he wasn't ready to go to bed, so he went to the common room and drew a tankard of ale. They were running low; the monks weren't there to brew it anymore, and new monks hadn't yet been assigned to the House of Blevins.

The chessboard sat in the middle of the table, untouched since his last game with Don. They had sat there for so many hours, mulling over thousands of games. Don had been the better player, but Peter hadn't made it easy on him. If he couldn't win, he did his best to force a draw or at least make Don work for the mate. He had never once conceded a victory to Don.

He stood there for a long time, looking at the chessboard and toying with Don's silver cross, knowing he would never play another game. He tipped his king.

"Farewell, brother," he said before leaving the common room.

* * *

Aidan had known how angry Mary was and tried to be understanding about her relationship with Peter, but Will hadn't taken it well. He had even gone so far as to accuse her of asking Peter to move into her room to make them jealous. She had responded by telling him that if she had been trying to make them jealous, she would have moved into Peter's room, which was near theirs, and made as much noise as she could while they were in bed together.

Mary didn't care what either of them thought. They thought she had turned to Peter out of her animosity toward them, but they couldn't possibly comprehend what she felt for Peter. They didn't know how he had watched over her as a child or when she was Omega. They didn't know about Adam or Connor, and she wasn't going to tell them.

Even if she had been alone, Mary wouldn't have stayed with the soul brothers. She could barely stand to be in the same room with them anymore. She didn't know why all of her ire was directed at them, but that was just the way it was.

It wasn't Aidan's fault Ian thought he had lost his soul, and it wasn't Ryan's fault Don was dead. Don had been responsible for his own actions, as had Ryan and Ian, who would undoubtedly suffer for them for years. Mary felt nothing toward Ian and Ryan but fondness and compassion. Aidan, however—and Will by extension—she wanted to choke.

How could Aidan ask someone to do something he didn't have the stones to do himself? If Ian had refused to torture that vampire, would he have done it? No. He would have turned to Peter, and in Peter's mind at least, it would have destroyed everything he had become. And then rebuking and demoting Ryan while he suffered in the infirmary opened more old wounds than Aidan could know. She could smell Aidan's remorse now and see his sadness and insecurity, and part of her wanted to comfort him, but he had brought his regret on himself and she had little interest in making it easier on him.

Mary also thought about leaving, but like Peter, there were those she didn't want to live without. Maybe they should all leave. Let Will and Aidan and whoever still had any interest in following them stay and fight Ireland's vampires, and the rest of them could go away and form their own pack.

Ryan and Peter passed the infirmary where she sat, rolling some freshly boiled bandages. They were involved in some weighty discussion about fencing, and Peter was still trying to get Ryan to see her about an injury he had inflicted earlier in the day. Ryan didn't care about the injury; he was only interested in training and improving his skills. Mary sighed sadly. She missed the way Ryan had been before. He had been so sweet and innocent, and she had known he wasn't prepared to kill. Don had known, too, and together they had done everything they could to delay the inevitable. The greatest tragedy was not Don's death. If he were around to ask, he'd be the first to say that saving Ryan was the best thing he had ever done. The greatest tragedy was that the light would never return to Ryan's eyes. The sweetness and gentleness was all gone now.

Gone, too, was the way he went all starry-eyed when she walked past. His crush had reminded her of how she had felt for Peter when she was growing up. She had always treated Ryan with respect and kindness but never more than a little brother, and though she didn't encourage him, she had to admit that his affection for her was flattering. He had more serious things to occupy his time now. He had been distressed over her relationship with Aidan and Will, but he barely noticed her and Peter. She knew it wasn't right, but she missed the attention.

Feelings about her packmates aside, Mary felt guilty being the only garou in the house who was actually happier since the monastery was attacked, but she couldn't help it. Sometimes when Peter touched her or smiled at her, her heart swelled with such utter joy that it almost brought tears to her eyes. She missed Don dreadfully, but she had never been so happy in her life.

Mary expected Peter to realize his feelings for her were just his way of holding onto the only thing left to remind him of Don, but if anything, they seemed to strengthen every day. When the others were around, he didn't really treat her any differently than he always had. They had been the best of friends before, and that aspect of their relationship was still the same. Only his scent gave any sign that his feelings had changed. The nights and private moments were another matter entirely.

She finished rolling bandages and went up the spiral staircase. Peter was at his desk, writing in his journal. She sat on the desk, and he put his arm around her and drew her closer.

"What are you writing about?"

"Chess."

"Chess? You're pouring your heart out about chess?"

"Sounds crazy, no?"

Although she usually didn't read his journal, something on the page caught her eye and she looked down to see a picture of Don. Peter didn't draw often, but he was very good at it, and the sketch looked just like Don. It captured his smile and the devilish look he would get in his eye when he was up to mischief.

"This is wonderful," she said.

"I got to thinking. I don't remember what my father looked like. I don't want that to happen with Don."

Mary bent and kissed him, and he pulled her onto his lap. He smelled of sorrow. He had gone back to being the rock, strong and practical with an iron will and infinite control, but even Peter O'Neill couldn't be strong all the time. "You're hurting," she said.

"Times I think it would be better to just go to bed and not get up again."

"Don wouldn't want you to hide from the world. He was strong and brave, and it would dishonor him to let his death break your spirit."

"I know," he said. "I do all right most of the time, but sometimes I falter."

"Well, when that happens, you can lean on me. I'm strong and brave, too."

He caressed her cheek. "How could I not have loved you all this time?"

"You did, just not in the same way. Or maybe you did and just didn't know it. I know you were jealous when I went to bed with Don."

"I was never jealous of you and Don!"

Mary raised an eyebrow.

"All right, maybe a bit. Nae, I think you're right. It's always been there; I just didn't realize what I was feeling."

"It doesn't matter now anyway. You were worth waiting for, Peter O'Neill."

"Marry me," he said.

"Oh, in an instant."

"You won't like to hear this, but it'll be longer than that. You're Alpha."

"I would rather concede my rank than send word to Rome and wait for Franco Bianco to get here!"

Peter laughed. "Well, 'haps Aidan will make an exception. We should still probably wait till tomorrow. I think Aidan's asleep."

"I don't have a dress."

"You can borrow one of mine."

"Hey," she said brightly, "this will make me a princess!"

"Oh, my God, what have I done?"

Mary laughed and kissed him. "I love you, Peter O'Neill."

"I love you too, Princess."

* * *

Logan lay on his back in the yard, staring up at the waxing Moon. Funny. The Moon was always changing, but she was the only constant in their lives. The house was in a state of upheaval. Grief and anger filled the atmosphere and there was little comfort for anyone, except perhaps Peter and Mary. He could hear Gwendolyn crying for Michael even now.

None of them had thought to just come outside and look at the Moon. Maybe they should *all* be out here. Logan spent a lot of time out here these days. No matter what was going on inside the monastery, out here with Diana, things made sense and there was peace.

Logan's biggest concern was that there would be a split. He may have considered leaving in the past, but now it was important for them to stay together. They were in for some rough years, and though there was animosity, they needed some consistency. And they desperately needed some hope.

There was always hope. Garou's lives were long, and one catastrophe, however significant, would someday just be a distant memory. He missed Don and Michael, but they were dead and he wasn't. He would mourn like the others, but he would heal faster because he had hope where none of the rest of them did. It would come, sooner for some than others.

In the meantime, there was Diana. She smiled down on him now, gleaming, compelling him to come out and play. He stripped off his clothes, shifted, and ran through the gate into the night to commune with his lady.

About the Authors

Wendy Schardein is an online transcriptionist who has been writing for more than twenty years. This is her first published work. Bryan Schardein is a software engineer who coaches chess and teaches martial arts in his rare moments of free time. While he has published several white papers and technical articles, this is his first work of fiction.

They have been married since 2005 and live in Louisville, Kentucky, in a big, loud, crowded, messy, happy house with Wendy's mother, three teenagers, two dogs, a ghost, two part-time ducks, and a partridge in a pear tree.

Excerpt from

The Clan of the Blood

Available 2013

RAGE! Don dead...no home...alone...pain...RAGE!
Though unable to comprehend, much less frame the thoughts, still he knows he is more than this. His entire world has been condensed to savage, cathartic violence—a storm of blood and death with him as its center. He does not care because, at this moment, the horror his existence has become is better than what came before, whatever that was.

He screams. *Howls?* Claws at the ground...a tree...himself. He bleeds. Pain fuels his anger.

Scent...movement...kill! The badger tries to run, but it is not fast enough. *Grab...tear...bite...feed.*

Caught, it bleeds and dies. The brief struggle over, hate and madness rush in to fill the void left in its wake. He throws the pieces of the badger's body. Slams his fists against a tree. The trunk cracks and shatters, bark and shards of wood flying out in all directions. Somewhere, deep in his core, the realization that this is different touches him briefly, but it is swept away before the bloodlust that still consumes him.

He does not tire; he does not slow. Nothing within his reach, animate or inanimate, escapes unscathed. Scents of wildlife, warm-blooded creatures of the forest, guide his chaotic route through the trees. Everything around him must scream and bleed and die and be destroyed until his agony is abated.

Ardis. Pippa. Ryan. Meaningless names paired with unrecognized faces intrude. Hate flares! He wants to kill them. Rip them apart. Tear their flesh. Make them scream. He screams—*howls?*—as mindlessness returns in a seemingly endless cycle that erodes his fury as the water of the river smooths the surface of the stones in its bed.

Suddenly he is again a man, lying in a soft bed in a darkened room. He opens his eyes and gazes about in disorientation, his mind and vision still blurry from sleep. He inhales deeply, his lungs struck with the sting of the blistering air, and he remembers who and where he is..

Peter O'Neill, a garou of the House of Blevins, elite pack of the Order of the White Guard, sat up in bed and ran a hand through sweat-soaked hair, looking out the bedroom window at a landscape he wondered if he would ever grow accustomed to. Alexandria—*Egypt*—was a jarring change from the cool forests of Ireland. He found it strange that he would still have that dream after all these years...after all that had happened.

Faol mòr. "Great wolf" in Gaelic. The monstrous transformation so different from the normal, sentient, wolves they became under the full moon. He had always wondered what it was like. Now he knew—had known for nearly fifty years— and wished he did not.

Turning slightly and looking down at the beautiful woman lying naked beside him, he thought, *She's the one thing I don't regret from that night. If I hadn't been on the tail of my shift to* faol mòr, *we might never have known how much we loved each other.*

He caressed Mary's cheek, and she mumbled in her sleep. This was why he still had the dream and others like it. It was a reminder that no matter how many years had passed or how many miles they had traveled, he was only a breath away from devastation; and maybe next time, he wouldn't manage to get away from the others before his rage overwhelmed him. Perhaps next time it wouldn't be a badger that got ripped apart. It would be his wife. It was for her and for his family that he could never lose control like that again.

Remnants of Life: Legends of Darkness

by Georgia L. Jones

Samantha Garrett lives and dies a good life in the human world. She awakens a new creature, Samoda, a vampire-like warrior in the army of Nuem. She is forced to realize that she has become a part of a world that humans believe to be only "Legends of Darkness." Samoda finds her new life is entwined with the age old story of greed, love, betrayal, and vengeance.
[Urban Fantasy, ages 14+]

The Eyes of Sandala

by Cathy Benedetto

Over seven feet tall and as strong as three men, the dark-skinned Shala share a life-long bond with wild felines. The fierce fighters are blessed with telepathic powers and eyes that radiate a kaleidoscope of colors.

The Shala dwell inside the crater of an extinct volcano. But when invaders appear, they must obey the prophecy and rise to defend the land.
[Epic Fantasy, ages 14+]

Dream Stone

by Valerie Drake

Vashti Chamberlin's mind is haunted by visions of a past life. If she can't take full control of her power by her 21st birthday, it will kill her, and more importantly the evil demons tracking her will win.

Vashti is fighting not only for her life, but for a curious new love she has found on her journey; a love so pure it has spanned centuries.

[Urban Fantasy, ages 14+]

Albrim's Curse

by Trevis Powell

All young Albrim wanted to be was a master bowman like his father. Then a savage attack on his home cost him his family, his arm, and his humanity – all at once! Crippled and contaminated by the Curse, his beloved Gran leaves him in the care of Mute, a giant warrior. Albrim does what he can to assist his master and redeem himself. But can a werewolf ever really recapture his humanity?

[Werewolf Fantasy, ages 14+]